Donna Bak[...]he
youngest of [...]ga-
zine and ne[...] to
short stories and has [...]ntic
novels under a pseudonym. She is married and has
two children and now lives in the Lake District. The
first two titles in The Glassmakers Saga, *Crystal* and
Black Cameo, are also available from Headline.

Reviews for *Crystal*:
'. . . the novel is well conceived and the characters
have charm' *Books Magazine*
'. . . captures the imagination' *Best*
'It's an enthralling tale, obviously well researched
. . . I look forward to the next two sections of this
highly absorbing tale' *Shropshire Star*

Reviews for *Black Cameo*:
'A good family storyline, lots of atmosphere and
strong love all add up to make a book of substance'
Woman's World
'Those who liked the first book will like the second'
Books Magazine
'[Donna Baker] has certainly done her research into
the industrial history of the Black Country . . . [and]
her characters are strongly coloured' *Bristol Evening
Post*

Chalice

The Glassmakers Saga

Donna Baker

HEADLINE

First published in 1989
by HEADLINE BOOK PUBLISHING PLC

First published in paperback in 1990
by HEADLINE BOOK PUBLISHING PLC

10 9 8 7 6 5 4 3 2

ISBN 0 7472 3320 9

Typeset in 10/12½ pt Times by
Colset Private Limited, Singapore

Printed and bound in Great Britain by
Collins, Glasgow

HEADLINE BOOK PUBLISHING PLC
Headline House
79 Great Titchfield Street
London W1P 7FN

To Tom and Peetie Dimitroff

Acknowledgements

For help in the preparation of this book, I would like to thank the Corning Glass Museum, who gave me the freedom of their libraries while I was in Corning, together with Thomas Dimitroff who gave me much friendly help and whose book *200 Years in Painted Post Country*, written with Lois Janes, was invaluable. I also remember with affection the three houses where we enjoyed such comfortable beds and sumptuous breakfasts – especially Rosewood, where we actually slept in the Frederick Carder Room, surrounded by memorabilia of the great glassmaker who came from Stourbridge to Corning. Acknowledgement should also be made to Jane Shadel Spillman's and Estelle Sinclaire Farrar's book *The Cut and Engraved Glass of Corning, 1868–1940*, to *HP Sinclaire, Jr, Glassmaker* by Paul V Gardener, and to *The Flood and The Community*, based on an account of the disastrous flood of 1872 written by R Nicholas Hoye and published by the Corning Glass Works.

Although I may have made some minor changes to the topography of Corning, I have done my best to convey the atmosphere of what I perceived to be a friendly community. Any errors appearing in the text are my own.

Chapter One

So this was Crystal City.

Cordelia, stiff and weary after the long, tedious and sometimes frightening journey, first across the Atlantic in a cramped and uncomfortable steamship and now halfway across New York State in a clanking railcar, walked slowly out of the station and looked around her. And her heart sank.

Was it for this that they had come all this way, she and Timothy? Was it here that they were to find a new life? Would this small and smoky town, crowded with shabby people, its tall chimney stacks pouring forth billowing clouds of darkness, really prove any different from the home they had left?

The air was filled with the same acrid soot, the same grittiness that she had breathed at home. The all too familiar clatter and screech of machinery filled her ears. And already, glancing down at her travelling dress, she could see the stains and grime of industry – the same, it seemed, whether you were in England or America.

Corning – the Crystal City. Well, there was little crystalline about this scene, she thought, and turned to where her twin brother Timothy was carrying out their luggage.

'It's just like Stourbridge,' she said, and there was a world of bitter disappointment in her tone.

The crisis that had faced Timothy Henzel on the death of his father Paul in early 1898 was not immediately apparent.

'It came too soon,' Emily said over and over again.

'Why? Why should I have to lose him so soon? Why, after all we had been through?' Her widow's veil was heavy and she pushed it back with a weary, hopeless gesture. 'I thought we would go into old age together, and now I must spend it alone. Why is God so cruel?'

'Cruel?' Christina Compson, Paul's mother and Emily's stepmother, looked at her with gravity. 'Was it really so cruel? His father had even less time, and his death was a much harsher one. I know; I saw it.'

'But Paul was your *son*!' Emily cried, her eyes bewildered, accusing. 'Do you feel nothing? He was alive in the morning, cheerful, happy and well, looking forward to a new engraving – and then, by teatime, he was dead. What is the purpose of it? It's – it's senseless. Senseless and cruel – yes, cruel to me, if not to him. But can you really believe that he would have *wanted* to die so untimely?'

'None of us wants to die, my love.' Her father, Joe, spoke as gravely as his wife. He looked with sorrow at the woman whose grief made a white mask of her face, distorted her trembling mouth and reddened her eyes. 'But it can't be avoided and to some it comes early. Aye, it seems cruel, but we have to live with it. And you and Paul had a good life, after all – over twenty years married. It's more than some can say.'

Cordelia, sitting quietly beside her mother, suffering her own grief, could not help looking at her grandmother when he spoke those words. She knew, as did all the family, the story of Christina and the young Frenchman, Jean-Paul Thietry, who loved her so briefly, leaving her when he died the seed of the child who had been born Paul Henzel. She knew that Emily, her mother, had been brought into the family at two years old, the daughter of Joe Compson and Maggie Haden, treated always as Christina's daughter; and she knew of the efforts that had been made to part Emily

2

and Paul when, grown up, they had begun to show signs of a deeper attachment than that of brother and sister. There was no blood relationship between them but Christina and Joe had feared for their happiness and sent Paul to France. He had almost been lost there, in the terrible Siege of Paris, but had returned at last – only to find Emily married and desperately unhappy.

The story had been told gradually over the years, explaining many of the things that seemed unusual about the Compson and Henzel families. And Cordelia, living with the examples of both her mother and her grandmother in this age when women's rights were becoming more and more of an issue, had grown up with the idea that women could be something more than men's chattels. They could take over and run a factory, as Christina had done when no more than a girl; they could fight and campaign for women's rights and for better conditions for the poor, as Emily had been doing ever since Cordelia could remember. What they did not do, if their name were Henzel or Compson, was to sit at home idly waiting for calls or doing nothing more arduous than arrange a vase of flowers.

But Emily, who had always been so strong, now seemed unable to take control of her own life. For years her strength had shielded her artistic husband from the realities of the world so that he could concentrate solely on the glass that was his life. As well as continuing her strenuous efforts to improve conditions in the eternally poverty-stricken Lye Waste, where she taught in the little school, ran the soup kitchen in winter and bullied the men to hand their wages over to their wives rather than drink it away in the public houses, she had taken over the running of the house which Christina, still engrossed in the glasshouse, found so tedious – and still found time to campaign vigorously whenever she saw a need. She had been particularly vociferous

3

about marriage: the fact that women had almost no rights; that once married they were considered no more than an extension of their husbands; and that there was very little chance of escape from an unhappy marriage. This disturbed her more than any other wrong.

With Paul struck down so suddenly, Emily seemed to shrink in upon herself. Sitting in the parlour after the funeral, she stared round at them all, her eyes great hollows of pain in the paleness of her face. She seemed smaller than before, her clothes hanging loosely around her. The tears ran constantly down her cheeks and Cordelia, accustomed to seeing that mouth set firm and implacable, those eyes dark with a robust determination that had been handed down directly from Joe Compson himself, felt as disturbed as if the whole of the Black Country had suddenly moved and tilted to one side.

Timothy got up and went to his mother. He sat down beside her on the sofa and slipped his arm around her shoulders, holding her close against him.

'Mother, don't torture yourself in this way,' he said softly. 'Of course Father would not have asked for death so soon. But think – he was luckier than many. He never suffered, never even knew. His heart just stopped beating – no more than that. It was like closing his eyes – as gentle as falling asleep. Wouldn't you have *wished* it to be like that? If it had to come – wouldn't you rather he died so quietly, so happily, than in pain and fear like –' he glanced briefly at his grandmother before going on – 'like Grandfather Thietry?'

Emily turned blank eyes upon him. For a long moment, she stared at his face, though no one could tell whether she saw him or not. Then, slowly, she put up one hand, touched his cheek with her fingers and moved them over the contours, as if she were blind and learning his expression, the cool, regular planes of his face, the nut-brown curls that covered his head, even the long, narrow shape of his silver-grey eyes.

'You are so much like him,' she said in a voice that was no more than a thread of sound in the quiet room. 'So much like he was then . . . before he went to Paris. He was never quite the same after that, you know. He suffered too much, from the women he met, from the things that happened . . . I always knew he hadn't the strength to live. I always knew his genius would kill him in the end.'

With a movement so sharp that it startled everyone, she turned completely into her son's arms, gripping him with hands that shook and looking up into his face with eyes that were now burning fiercely. 'You won't go away, Timothy. You won't leave me.' Her voice strengthened and throbbed in the quiet room. 'You'll stay here, safe in Stourbridge and work as your father did, engraving beautiful glass. You've inherited his talent, his genius – you'll bring it to fruition here. You'll continue the work he was doing, the work that has made Henzel's famous. You'll never go away.'

Cordelia lifted her hand to her mouth. Her eyes, green as a cat's, were shadowed and disturbed. She felt a coldness around her heart.

There was something frightening in the extremity of her mother's reaction. She held Timothy as if she would never let him go. As if she meant each word – that he must never, never leave her.

But wasn't it natural that, with her husband newly in his grave, she should turn to her eldest son? When the worst of her grief had abated, wouldn't she relinquish that fright-ening grip?

Cordelia tried to drive away her sudden dismay. Watch-ing her mother, she knew that Emily was suffering from deep shock. She barely knew what she was doing.

5

But already she could see the dawning fear in her brother's eyes.

In the months following Paul's death, her old autocratic nature reasserting itself, Emily turned more and more to her eldest son. Her campaigns were forgotten; women's rights, the conditions of the poor, even her own family were neglected. Cordelia, the daughter who might have given her comfort, was dismissed to her studies; her younger son Mark, still at school, was discounted. She concentrated wholly on the engraving shops attached to the Henzel glasshouse, and in those shops all her attention was focused on Timothy.

'Yes, it's good,' she would say critically when he showed her a new piece of glass engraved with a fresh pattern. 'But you still have a long way to go. The depth of the cut here – don't you think it's a little too much? Could it not be even finer? And this curve, it's not quite as your father would have done it – see this piece, how graceful it is.' She sighed. 'It's a great pity that the vogue for cameo glass is already beginning to fade. Purely because it can't be made easily, of course – only a true artist can achieve the skill needed for cameo carving, and naturally it is expensive.' She looked again at the decanter in her hand, engraved with the flowing lines and intricate whorls of Timothy's latest design. 'Yes, it's a very nice piece. You've done well.' But her tone implied, *not well enough*, and Timothy bit his lip as he took the decanter back and set it on his bench.

'She isn't satisfied with anything I do,' he told Cordelia later. 'Nothing will ever match Father's work. But I don't *want* to match it. I want to try my own ideas. Things are changing in the glass world, Cordelia, and I want to change with them. *Henzel's* ought to change with them. We have to keep up to date. We did it before – why not now?'

6

'Mother doesn't want anything to change. She wants it all to stay just as it was when Father was alive.'

'But that's ridiculous!' Tim burst out, and his grey eyes darkened with passion. 'Father wouldn't have let things stand still – he was always looking for something new. Look at black cameo, for instance. That was his idea, something different from the cameo other glasshouses had begun to make, and because it was different and because it was beautiful, it succeeded. And going back even further, the crystal that Grandfather and Grandmamma made fifty years ago – why, if Grandmamma hadn't seen what was needed, if she hadn't built the engraving shops and brought Grandfather Thietry over from France, we would never be where we are today.' He paced the room, his slim body taut with impatience and frustration. 'Henzel's can't be just a memorial,' he declared. 'We have to move with the times. In a few years we'll be in the twentieth century – we can't stay mouldering in the nineteenth.'

But Emily refused to listen. 'You have a duty to continue your father's work,' she stated uncompromisingly, and no one could persuade her that Paul Henzel himself would have been amongst the first to embrace new ways.

As the weeks turned to months, Emily was more and more at Timothy's heels. Her disapproval of his new designs increased until he found himself permitted to work only on designs his father had created. Cordelia, watching him with anxiety, saw a smouldering frustration growing in his eyes, a frustration that only his love for his mother kept him from expressing with all the volatile temper he possessed. And she feared its eventual, inevitable explosion.

Her studies forgotten, she would gaze out of the window, thinking of her brother. Until now, while still learning his skills, he had naturally been overshadowed by Paul's reputation in the engraving shop. But Cordelia believed that, of the two, Timothy would finally prove to be the greater genius. Designing, engraving, even calculating the chemical composition of different glasses – all seemed to come with equal ease to his brilliant but restless mind. Experimenting was his great love – he would spend hours, days, months, trying out new formulae, different methods, and she knew that he dreamed of making glass of a kind that had never been seen before. But with Emily curtailing his freedom and even Christina determined to keep Henzel's name prominent for table glass rather than anything more adventurous, it seemed unlikely that he would ever be able to do so.

And it was his restlessness that worried Cordelia most. For Timothy, so talented where glass was concerned, seemed in other ways so young for his age. And, if driven too far, was all too likely to do something foolish . . .

Gradually, the dispute took on greater proportions and began to upset the entire household at Henzel Court. Joe Compson, now over eighty, tended to dismiss its significance; he had been through too many family upsets to worry about this one, he declared. The boy was a fine workman, no doubt about it, though Joe had never really taken to engraving and never would now. And Emily, well, she was stubborn enough like the rest of the family, but she'd see sense in the end. She'd been through a bad time, when all was said and done; you couldn't expect too much of her yet awhile.

Christina, however, took the matter more seriously. And one day, when the dispute between Timothy and his mother had been particularly bitter, she came to the old schoolroom where Cordelia was trying unhappily to forget her worries in study, and settled herself by the window, looking down at the cluttered roofs of the village below.

'I've always loved this view,' she said. 'My father built this house specially so that we could see our own cones and no one else's. I used to sit here for hours while our poor governess tried to teach us the three Rs – Miss Crossley, her name was; I used to call her Crosspatch. Poor soul, she did her best. I'm afraid I was something of a trial to her.'

Cordelia looked at her grandmother and smiled. It was easy enough to imagine her being a trial; even now, at seventy-four, Christina still retained the sprightliness and air of mischievous gaiety that had enslaved Joe so many years ago. As a girl, she had been almost shockingly independent; entirely so when she had found herself pregnant and without any possibility of marriage to the father. Yet she had never taken the easy way out. Flying directly in the face of convention, she had raised her son, run the business her father had left her, and had overcome all the difficulties that life had sent her way. And she still bore her small, slender body as lightly as a girl, her hair bright with the tawny colours of autumn, her eyes flashing a dangerous, tigerish green when she was angry.

'You know,' Christina said, turning from the window and looking directly at Cordelia, 'you're very like me. Not just to look at – though your grandfather often says you're the image of me when I was your age. But in your character, too. You're strong, Cordelia.'

'Strong? I?' Startled, Cordelia looked down at her books. 'How can you know? I've never had to –'

'I know. I recognise the same determination in you. You've never been forced to use it – your mother was only too pleased for you to be educated, so you didn't have to fight for that. Like me, she's always been anxious for women to have their rights. In that way, it's been easy for you. You've never had to test your strength.' Christina leaned forward a little. 'But those times are past, Cordelia. The time is coming when you are going to need it all. And not only you.'

9

Cordelia looked at her and said in a quiet voice: 'Tim . . .'

'Exactly. Your brother is going to need your strength. He's going to need it very badly.'

Cordelia put her hand up to her brow. She had left her hair loose today, hanging in a heavy veil of copper around her face. She pushed it back and looked at her grandmother.

'I don't feel at all strong,' she confessed. 'I don't know what to do to help him. He's so unhappy, but until Mother leaves him alone –'

'Which she'll never do,' Christina interrupted. 'Cordelia, your mother is a very intense person. She loves with all her heart and when she loves she is totally engrossed. She loved your father more deeply than anyone else; when he went to Paris and she thought she had lost him, it almost broke her. It drove her into a marriage that could have killed her. And now she can't accept the fact that he is dead. For all her own strength, she relied on him entirely. He was *essential* to her. In a strange way, she drew her strength from his need of her. Do you understand me?'

'I think so,' Cordelia said, with some doubt.

'It isn't easy to understand. You are so young . . . but we often have to take on responsibilities when we are young.' Christina's eyes dimmed for a moment, then she lifted her chin. 'I did it, your mother did it, and now it's your turn. You have to use that strength of yours, Cordelia, and I can't tell you it will be easy.'

'But how? Do you want me to talk to Mother? I can't believe she'll take any notice –'

'At present, no. She's beyond taking notice of anyone at the moment. But later, when she begins to look around her again and discover that there's still life to be lived, she's going to need you, Cordelia. Just now, her son is everything to her. But you're her daughter, and that matters too.'

Cordelia looked down at the books on her desk. In them lay her only escape from the unhappy atmosphere that filled Henzel Court these days. She held on to them, and to the place she had already been offered at the women's college of Girton at Cambridge University, as if to a lifeline. The thought of the following October, when she would leave home and go to live amongst other young women and study for a degree, had been her only comfort in the weeks that had followed her father's sudden death.

'But I shan't be here,' she said, and knew already what her grandmother was going to ask of her. 'Grandmamma, I shan't be here.'

Christina looked at her steadily. 'Cordelia . . .'

'Please!' Cordelia broke in desperately. 'Please, Grandmamma, don't say it – don't ask it – don't ask me to give up all that I've worked for. Cambridge – Girton – I've dreamed about it for so long. You approved. *Mother* approved. You can't ask me to give it all up now.'

'It's not for ever,' Christina urged. 'For this year only, perhaps. You could go next year, or the year after –'

'Or the year after that, or the year after that. No.' Cordelia shook her head, bronze hair flying. 'If I don't go this year, I never will. *Now* is the time. I must.'

There was a short silence. Christina watched her, her eyes thoughtful, and Cordelia met her calm gaze for as long as she could, then glanced away. Christina gave a little sigh, the kind she often gave when she was preparing to go into battle, to argue, to deny and cajole until she got her own way. And Cordelia sighed, too, for she knew that when Christina was determined, she usually did get her own way.

But not this time. Not, please God, this time . . .

'I am going to Girton,' she said firmly, and met her grandmother's gaze again. This time she did not look away.

'And you won't concern yourself with what happens

here? You'll be able to push your mother and her troubles right out of your mind? You'll be able to forget your brother Timothy? Your twin?'

Cordelia began to feel angry. She knew quite well that her grandmother was playing on Cordelia's loyalty, on the power of her attachment to Timothy, an attachment which had been fostered and encouraged by all the family ever since the twins had lain together in their cot, their tiny hands linked.

'Of course I won't forget,' she said abruptly. 'Of course I'll be concerned. But Grandmamma, you've always told me that women have their own lives to live as well. That *I* had my own life. What would I do if I stayed at home? What use would I be? Do you really want me to sit in the drawing room and receive callers? Arrange flowers?' Her eyes flashed, as Christina's had when she was a girl and forced to fight against her family. 'You've always lived your life the way you wanted to, Grandmamma. Why do you want to stop me from doing the same?'

Christina was silent for a moment, then rose from her chair and stared down through the window at the cones, the crowded roofs, the heavy pall of smoke. She spoke with her back to Cordelia.

'I wonder if you're right,' she said. 'Have I always lived my life as I wanted to? Would I have lived differently if I had had the choice?' She turned sharply. 'You see, there is a difference between us. *You* have the choice – you've always had choices, choices I never had. I was handed a business to run when I was no older than you are now. My whole life was dedicated to that business. The glasshouse always had to come first, always. It does still. I believe it always must, if your name is Henzel.' She came swiftly to Cordelia's desk and leaned on it, her small fists white around the knuckles. 'The glasshouse is in danger,

12

Cordelia, and I believe you are the one who could save it. It isn't just a question of your mother or your brother, you see. It's that out there –' She waved a hand towards the window. 'It's those buildings, those great cones almost a hundred years old, built by a Henzel. It's the people who depend on us for a living. It's *our* living. Our name. Henzel Crystal. And if something isn't done, we shall lose it all.'

She stood for a moment, taut and urgent, looking down into Cordelia's shocked face. Then she sagged suddenly, the fire draining from her, and as Cordelia watched she seemed to turn all at once into an old woman, bent and defeated. She sank back into her chair and looked once again out of the window.

Cordelia's own anger evaporated. She stared at the shrunken figure which had only moments ago been so full of energy and determination, and felt stricken.

'But why?' she asked at last. 'Why do you think things are so bad? We have orders coming in still. Timothy was only saying yesterday –'

'Orders! Oh yes, we've plenty of orders.' Christina spoke the word dismissively, as if orders were the last things the glasshouses wanted. 'But what are they for? Old lines, lines we've been making for five, ten, twenty years. Where are the orders for new glass? New shapes and styles? Glass that will keep us ahead of our competitors? Where are they?'

'But we're not making any –' Cordelia began and Christina snapped in at once, her body straight again, her eyes firing up.

'Exactly! We're not making any. Because Emily won't allow it. Emily! Who has never taken any part in the running of the glasshouse.' Her voice was angry, bitter. 'After all the work I've done, all the work your grandfather has done, after we've both given our whole lives to Henzel Crystal, what happens? *Emily* forbids anything new. And

13

because she's his mother and because he loves her and is sorry for her grief, Timothy accepts her ruling. And do you know what will happen if it goes on?' Christina turned a blazing look on her granddaughter. 'Henzel Crystal will become nothing. Nothing! Oh, we shall go on making glass, good glass, *fine* glass. But we shall never lead the market again. We shall never outstrip our competitors as we have for so many years.'

Quietly, Cordelia said, 'Timothy is just as unhappy about this as you are, Grandmamma. But I still don't see –'

'You don't see what's to be done about it?' Christina bit out the words. 'Isn't that because you don't *want* to see, Cordelia? Because you know what it will mean to you?' She waited, her eyes fixed on Cordelia's face. 'Let me tell you then. Timothy must fight. He must fight his mother, go against her wishes, make the glass he wants to make, make the glass Henzel's *need* him to make. It won't be easy for him to do that, Cordelia. And that is why he will need you at his side. To help him fight her. To fight with him.'

Cordelia stared at her. She thought of her mother, pale, wan, deeply unhappy, her dark eyes following Timothy everywhere, seeing in her son the husband she had lost. She thought of Timothy, concerned only with his work, driven by the art within him, harassed by the disputes, the criticism, the pressure that surrounded him.

'It would kill her,' she said. 'It would destroy them both. Grandmamma, you can't ask it –'

'I can. I do.' Christina stared out of the window again. 'Cordelia, we can overcome these troubles. *You* can overcome them. Give up Girton. Stay at home and help your brother. Help *me*. For the sake of the glasshouse.'

'Leave Stourbridge?'

Cordelia stared at her brother. He returned her look

14

steadily, though she suspected his air of confidence was only assumed.

'You're making fun of me,' she said at last. 'How can you possibly leave Stourbridge?' She looked involuntarily out of the window at the view her grandmother loved, at the factory, the cones, the streets. It was impossible to imagine those streets without Timothy somewhere amongst them, those long buildings without Timothy working in them.

'I've got to,' he said intensely. 'Cordelia, it's the only way. Mother's stifling me. And Grandmamma's no help. She believes I should fight – fight my own mother! When she's in the state she's in now . . . It would kill her.'

'I know,' Cordelia said soberly. 'I told her that too.'

'You? You mean she's asked you to – to –'

'She wants me to give up Girton and stay here. She thinks you'll need me to stand against Mother and make the kind of glass you want to make. The kind of glass Henzel's needs.'

'Henzel's!' he said. 'Always Henzel's . . . The glass-house comes before any of us with Grandmamma, Cordelia. It always has.' He came to stand beside her, look-ing down. 'I feel I'm being pulled apart,' he said. 'Between the two of them: one thinking I'm a second Paul Henzel, making the glass he created, over and over again; the other wanting me to make new glass, yes – but even that won't be the glass *I* want to make, Cordelia. It'll be the glass Grand-mamma wants – the kind of glass Henzel's has always pro-duced. Table glass. Crystal. Cameo.' He turned to her and his eyes glittered, silver in the grey light of early spring. 'That isn't the kind of glass I want to make,' he said and there was an intensity in his voice that Cordelia had never heard before. 'I want to experiment – to try something like the Art Nouveau – oh, I don't even know what it is I want to do! I only know that we could go forward in glass now as we've never done before. And I know that I'll never be able to do it in Stourbridge.' He turned away and flung himself into the battered old armchair, staring restlessly around the room which had seen so much of their childhood and growing up. 'I've got to get away, Cordelia. I've got to.'

She stared at him with doubt in her eyes, fear at her heart.

'But Mother . . . how will you explain to her?'

'I don't believe I can,' he said gloomily. 'She wouldn't listen to explanations anyway. I don't believe she even sees me any more. I'm just a – a ghost to her. A substitute for Father.' He looked up at her and his eyes blazed. 'And that's why I must get away! Don't you see that the longer I stay here, the worse Mother is going to get? She thinks of nothing but me now, nothing but making me even more like Father. It's unhealthy – it's frightening.'

'But she made you promise never to leave,' Cordelia said uncertainly. 'On the day of Father's funeral.'

Timothy shook his head, a new determination about his mouth. 'I never gave my word. She did all the talking – told me I must never leave her. I didn't say a word. How could I, when she was so unhappy? But no one in their right mind would hold me to a promise like that –' He stopped suddenly.

'No one in their right mind,' Cordelia repeated slowly. 'Timothy, what are you saying?'

'Mother isn't in her right mind,' he said simply. 'She hasn't been since Father died. And who could blame her for it? And . . . as long as I'm here, looking so much like him, doing the work that he did, I'm afraid she'll never regain her reason.'

'Regain her reason? You talk as if Mother's going mad!' Cordelia was on her feet, white-faced. 'And you mean to leave her, when she needs you most –'

'That's just it. She *doesn't* need me most – not just now.' His voice was almost cold now, and Cordelia stared at him,

16

seeing a Timothy she had never known before. 'Oh, I know it seems as if she needs me more than ever, but it's an unhealthy need. It's doing her no good. Don't you see that?' He paused for a moment and then added, 'And it's doing me harm too. I can't work like this, Cordelia. I can't think any more. *I can't make my glass.*' There was real anguish in his voice. 'I've got to be able to make my glass, Cordelia.'

He stared at the floor and Cordelia watched him anxiously. Ever since babyhood, they had been close; it had been accepted within the family that they would be, that twins always shared a bond tighter than that between normal brothers and sisters. And even though their lives had necessarily taken different paths as they grew up, with Timothy going with his father into the glasshouse and Cordelia working at her studies, the bond had never loosened.

She knew that for Timothy, his glass was his life. The driving need within him was as great as that of any other artist – painter, sculptor, musician, writer. Each one had a star to follow, an ambition that overrode all other factors. Timothy needed to experiment with glass, to make new kinds, to engrave and decorate, to find methods that had perhaps never been discovered. And nothing could stand in his way, nothing ease that consuming passion to create.

Christina had seen that Timothy was the future for Henzel's, for glassmaking. But even she might not be able to accept the changes he would want to make. Even she would try to hold him back.

'But if you leave Stourbridge . . .' Cordelia began, doubt still in her voice.

'There are other engravers here,' he said. 'And Mother won't interfere with them. It's only me – because she sees Father in me. And I'm not leaving Henzel's with nobody to look after the business. Uncle Roger cares for the ledgers as though they were his children – I believe they are the only things he loves. Cousin Rupert manages the glasshouse, and you know that Grandfather and Grandmother will never truly retire. And Mother will still have you, and Mark – he won't leave school for another two years. She can turn to him without doing any of the damage she's doing to me.' He moved across to her, touching her copper curls with sensitive fingers. 'I don't suppose it'll be for ever, anyway. I'll be able to come back.'

Cordelia turned away and looked once more out of the window. Outside, a March storm was whipping the trees that Joshua Henzel had planted in the garden nearly seventy years ago. Rain beat against the window that the young Christina had liked to look from when she should have been attending to her lessons. The tall red-brick cones of the glasshouse loomed high into the sulphurous sky, and smoke coughed up from their open tops and was torn away by the hungry wind. She leaned her forehead against the cold pane, thinking of Girton, of all she had planned.

'You talk as if you were going alone,' she said, and her voice came from a throat that ached. 'But you won't be. I shall come with you, Tim – wherever you choose to go.'

The idea, once discussed, began to take root. Until then, Cordelia suspected, it had been little more than a frantic dream in Tim's mind, a desperate hankering for something he had thought out of the question. He had told her about it almost in the expectation that she would dissuade him, angry and passionate because he had believed it would all come to nothing. But now, with her support, he began to see it as a possibility, a reality.

'Where will you go?' she asked. 'To Lorraine – to the château?'

Timothy shook his head. 'I thought of that. But it's still too close to home, in a way. The old Thietry glasshouses, they're all part of Henzel's now – they were Father's, and Mother is sure to feel that they're hers too. She'll want to command me as much there as here – she might even make the journey after us. No, if we're to go away, it must be somewhere completely new.' He paused for a moment, and then said quietly, 'I think I should go to America.'

'*America?* But we know nobody there.'

'We know Uncle Harry and Aunt Ruth. They've lived there for – oh, forty years or more, ever since Uncle Harry went to help build railways and bridges and things. And where do they live now that he's retired?' He paused and looked at her before going on triumphantly, 'Corning! One of the most important glassmaking centres in the United States! What could be better? Look,' he went on seriously, 'if I really mean to make a fresh start, it has to be somewhere *really* fresh, don't you see that? A place where Mother won't follow because she'll have no influence. Where I can begin again on my terms, making the kind of glass I want to make. England and France are too traditional – America is new, it's a country that's looking ahead into a new age.' He spoke quickly, eagerly. 'In less than three years we'll be beginning a new century. The twentieth century! Everything will be changing – things are changing now, so quickly. Trains, bicycles, even motor-cars – and glass. Glass will change too, Cordelia, it's beginning to already, and I must be where the changes are taking place.' He strode about the room, waving his hands. 'Art Nouveau – the work that Gallé and others have been doing – Tiffany, it's all the kind of thing *I* should be doing . . .' His voice died away as he stared at his sister. 'Yes,' he said slowly. 'I must go away – and America is the place where I should be. But to start again, alone,' he shivered, 'it won't be easy.'

'But you won't be alone.' Cordelia came close and laid her hand on his arm. 'I shall be with you.'

Timothy shook his head. 'No. You have your own life to live. Girton – the school you hope to run one day – you can't give all that up. Cordelia, I've been thinking – I can't ask that of you. You must stay, go on with your studies . . .'

She looked at him with sudden hope, but his eyes were shadowed, not meeting hers, and she saw that although he believed he meant what he said, he really wanted her to go with him – needed her to go with him. And she knew that in any case she could not have borne to see him go without her.

She sighed, renouncing again the dreams she had had and smiling as brightly as if they had never mattered at all, were only a passing fancy.

'And who says so?' She lifted her head, looking directly at him. 'I shall survive without a university education. Millions of women have done so already. And as for teaching in a school, don't they have schools in America?' She stopped for a moment, afraid that her voice would betray her, and then gathered strength and went on. 'In any case, as you said yourself, it's not going to be for ever – only until Mother is quite recovered.'

Timothy turned away, his shoulders suddenly bowed. 'And that's another thing,' he said. 'How are we going to tell her? She'll never agree –' He looked almost ready to give up, to concede defeat before the battle was even begun, and Cordelia felt a sudden surge of determination. He was *right* – he mustn't give in. And she knew that this was when he needed her strength.

'She won't know!' She caught at his sleeve, forcing him to turn back and face her. 'Tim, you don't think we dare even hint at this to Mother? Of *course* she won't agree. We shall have to do it secretly – write to Uncle Harry, make all our arrangements and then just slip away. Say we're going on a visit somewhere – to Aunt Adele in Warwickshire, perhaps, or Aunt Alice, or *anywhere*.' She shook his arm desperately. 'I know what you're going to say – that it's cruel and underhand, that she'll never forgive us. But the only alternative is to stay here – where she'll get worse and worse, and end up destroying you both! And me with you,' she added softly.

He stared at her. 'And if Mother does lose her mind – even when we've gone? Would we ever forgive ourselves?'

'I don't know,' Cordelia said honestly. 'I've lain awake night after night, worrying about that very possibility. But I can only say that I've watched her, and I think she will become much worse if we stay. Tim, I don't see what else we can do.'

'No,' he said, and his voice was heavy. 'No, I don't think we have any choice.' He looked down at her and his eyes were sombre, as dark as winter clouds. 'But I'll go alone, Cordelia. I can't be responsible for ruining your life as well.'

'You won't be responsible for ruining anyone's life,' she said steadily. 'And I am coming with you.'

Now several weeks later, they were here. The subterfuge was over. Carrying only the luggage they would have needed for a week in Warwickshire, they had made their escape, travelling to Liverpool where they had found berths on a ship bound for New York. With the ship almost ready to sail, they had written to both their mother and grandmother. From New York they had journeyed across the State to the little glassmaking town of Corning – Crystal City. They had secretly written to Harry and Ruth before leaving home, and had telegraphed from New York; whether their journey was approved or not, they would at least be expected.

And as Cordelia stared at the chimneys and the dirt, she was beset by doubt. If it had been possible to call back the past months, to return to the day when Christina had come to sit in the old schoolroom and sown those first seeds in her mind, she would have done so.

'It's just like Stourbridge,' she said again, and the tall man who was helping Timothy with their luggage stopped and came to stand beside her.

'Is it?' His voice was deep and slow, with just a touch of that twang she had become accustomed to since arriving in America. 'Look up, Miss Henzel, look through the smoke and the soot at the hills all around. Do you see anything like that in England's Black Country? Do you see forests like that, green and thick? And look at the river, the lovely Chemung, winding its way through the valleys. Can the canal you know compare with that?' he said, pointing, then shook his head. 'I've never been to England but I've heard a good deal about it, and your brother has told me more as we've travelled along. You grew up in an industrial town, Miss Henzel, you must have known that there would be smoke and dirt and noise. But here, at least, it can be escaped. There's peace enough for those who look for it.'

Peace! The word sounded oddly in Cordelia's ears. Perhaps one day she would seek it, but she was not ready for peace – not yet. There was something else she must experience first.

But there was no time to think of that now, and Cordelia dared not compare the life she had longed for with this weary journey half-way across the world to a town that, whatever anyone might say, seemed no less cramped and dirty than Stourbridge. She looked around once again, seeing the dusty buildings, the unpaved roads, the hurrying people in their shabby working clothes. These were men no different from the glassmakers of her own village of

Wordsley, leaving their poor homes to toil in the hot glass-house, making tableware of a luxurious fineness that they could never hope to afford themselves. Their faces were the same, worn with work and care, thin with anxiety over families that they could barely support. Any pride they might have in their work was restricted to those like the gaffers who blew the fine shapes, the cutters and engravers like her own father and brother, whose work reached the realms of artistry. For the footmakers and servitors, the takers-in and gatherers, there was little except a hope that one day they too might rise to these heights; a faint hope indeed, for with only one gaffer to a chair, few apprentices could expect to progress far unless they were the sons of gaffers to start with.

She was startled from her thoughts by a tug at her arm, and turned to find her brother beside her.

'Come on, Cordelia – you're standing there in a dream. How many boxes should there be? I can't remember.' Timothy ran long fingers through his brown, curly hair. 'Do give me a hand.' He tugged her arm again and his grey eyes searched hers. 'Are you all right?' he asked more quietly, and she felt a quick surge of love for the brother she had come so far to support.

'Yes, of course I am. And surely you must know by now that we have five boxes altogether.' A pitifully small number for travelling halfway across the world, but it would have been impossible to pack more without arousing her mother's suspicions. She ran a calculating eye over the pile of luggage that had been handed down from the high door of the train. Why didn't American railroads have platforms? she wondered briefly, and shrugged. Everything was different in this strange country. Almost the same – but never quite. And that was more disconcerting than a country where everything was totally strange, for here as soon as you began to relax and feel at home another small difference would declare itself and remind you once again that you were a stranger.

As she looked at the luggage, her eye caught that of the man standing beside it, the man they had met on the train and who had helped them with their luggage and given them a good deal of information about the town they were visiting. Tall, with hair that glinted gold in the sunshine filtering now through the smoke, he was watching her with a faint smile on his sunburnt face. Immediately, her skin prickled. Several times during their journey, she had caught his dark blue eyes fixed on her in that way that was both bold and thoughtful. It had made her feel uncomfortable and, kind and helpful though he had undoubtedly been, she had felt relieved that they would be parting as soon as they reached Corning. But here he still was, and Cordelia could not help the sharp note in her voice when she spoke to him.

'Yes, our boxes are all there. It's kind of you to have helped us, Mr Novak. I'm sure we need detain you no further now.'

'On the contrary. I've already told your brother that my trap is at your disposal. Since your uncle doesn't know the time of your arrival, he's hardly likely to be here to meet you. My driver'll be ready outside.'

'Oh no, we wouldn't dream of putting you to such trouble. We're quite capable of hiring a cab –' Cordelia began, but he lifted a long, narrow hand and shook his head firmly.

'I reckon you are, too. All the same, why not use my trap today? It's here and ready.' His smile deepened with amusement. 'You needn't be scared of me, Miss Henzel. I shan't abduct either you or your luggage. In fact, I shan't even ride with you – you can travel all cosy together with all your luggage, and I'll walk to my lodgings – it's no distance. As you'll soon find out, nothing in Corning is very far from anything else.'

Cordelia looked at him and saw that there was no further argument to be made. And she couldn't help feeling glad, even though she had a definite feeling that she didn't want to be beholden to this man. She was suddenly aware of a great weariness, a desperate longing to reach her uncle's house, to sink into a chair and feel herself at least partly at home. The events of the past weeks crowded in upon her exhausted brain and she lifted a hand to her brow. She craved rest, forgetfulness. It was a sensation completely new to her, and for a moment she felt weak and frightened.

'You're tired out.' Jensen Novak was at her side, his voice low and gentle now so that she felt sudden tears hot in her eyes. 'Please don't worry any more. Go home to your uncle's house and rest. I'll see that everything arrives safely.'

Cordelia looked up at him and inclined her head.

'Thank you, Mr Novak. It's most kind of you.' He slipped his hand under her elbow to help her up into the trap and she felt the strength of his fingers. 'Thank you very much,' she repeated almost inaudibly.

He kept his hand on her arm for a moment, holding her so that she was forced to look down into his eyes. They were smiling, as dark as sapphires yet with a depth that she could not plumb, and for a moment she found herself unable to look away.

'You're welcome, Miss Henzel. I hope we'll meet again, when you've recovered from your journey.'

'Yes . . .' Cordelia said, and was annoyed to hear her voice stuttering. 'Yes, I'm sure we will . . .'

He released her arm and nodded to his driver. 'Take the young lady and gentleman to the house on the corner of Birch and Second Street, Parkin. And then go back to the stable. I'll see you there.'

The trap moved forward and clattered away down the street. And when Cordelia glanced over her shoulder, she saw that Jensen Novak was still standing there, watching, his hair gleaming in the golden sunshine.

Timothy's voice broke in upon her thoughts.

'Well, here we are, sis. What d'you think of Corning?'

She looked at him. Was he regretting their journey? Was he already wishing himself back in Stourbridge, in his own family's glasshouse where he knew everyone and was known and respected by all the men?

It was up to her, she knew, to drive away those regrets, to encourage him in this new life. This was, after all, why she had come. There would be worries enough anyway – they were both anxious for news of their mother. Suppose the shock of their desertion had totally unbalanced her? It was a fear that had haunted Cordelia through many uncomfortable nights at sea and on the train. Would they ever be able to forgive themselves?

But she had never voiced these fears to Timothy. They had come here for his sake as well as their mother's – to give his genius the chance it needed to develop, to blossom as it should. If they failed in that, they might as well have stayed at home.

She looked around her, trying to stave off these unwelcome thoughts. Now that they had left the centre of Corning, with its busy streets, its factories and railroads, they were entering a more pleasant, leafier area. The streets here seemed to be all straight, criss-crossing each other in the grid pattern that was so popular in American towns. The houses were large and of different styles, most of them frame-built with white clapboard facing which gave them a pleasant, airy look. Their gardens were filled with flowers and spacious lawns, and there were no fences between them. It was almost like a park.

'Does Uncle Harry live in one of these houses, do you suppose?' she remarked. 'They look quite grand.'

'Well, he's a wealthy enough man – he worked all his life on the railroads, planning them and building bridges and tunnels.'

'Yes, of course. I wonder if he and Aunt Ruth are expecting us yet? It's a pity we couldn't have arranged our arrival more conveniently – but our telegram should have arrived by now, so I should think they'll know we'd be here soon. So long as we don't arrive first!' She laughed. 'I'm looking forward so much to seeing them again. When was the last time they came to England, Tim?'

'I don't know – five years ago?' The trap was drawing up on the corner of two streets now and the driver indicated the nearest house. 'Anyway, we'll be seeing them any minute now.'

They jumped down from the trap and stood for a moment looking up at the house. It was one of the nicest on the street, Cordelia thought, with its white clapboard walls, its grey slate roof, the porch that ran round the ground floor and the little turret on the corner. Suddenly nervous and excited, she tugged at her brother's arm. 'Come on, Tim! Let's knock.' They ran together up the steps on to the porch that ran the length of the house, and rapped on the big front door.

There was silence.

'Ring the bell,' Cordelia suggested, noticing the pull at the side of the door. 'There must be someone in – a servant, at least.'

But there was still no answer. And they stared at each other, suddenly uncertain.

'They're out,' Tim said.

'Well, there's no reason why they shouldn't be – they didn't know we'd be arriving today.' Trying to control her disappointment, Cordelia went to the edge of the porch and called to the driver. 'You can bring the boxes up here, please. My uncle and aunt won't be long, I'm sure. Try again, Tim, just in case they didn't hear.'

She watched as Parkin carried up the boxes and thanked him. He touched his cap and drove away, leaving them alone. Cordelia turned again to her brother.

'Tim . . .?'

'They're not here,' he said. 'Cordelia, they're not here.'

'They've just gone out for a while. It means nothing, Tim.'

'But nobody's here,' he said, and she heard the dismay in his voice. 'No servants – nobody. And we've come all the way from England . . .'

Cordelia stared at him aghast. Could he be right? Could there really be nobody here? She looked again at the house, noticing now its strange, empty look. Where could they be? What had happened to Uncle Harry and Aunt Ruth?

'He's right, miss,' said a voice from the sidewalk, and they both whirled round to face the man who stood there looking up at them. 'Mr and Mrs Henzel have gone away on a trip. They won't be back for – oh, six, nine months, maybe a year. That's what they told us before they went.'

'Gone away?' Cordelia repeated. 'But where – where have they gone?'

'Why, England, I reckon. Got relatives there. They've gone to England, to visit with their family.'

28

Chapter Two

'America? They've gone to *America*?'

Emily stared at the letter in Christina's hand. She turned her eyes from Christina's stricken face to Joe's bewildered frown, as if demanding to be told that she had misheard. And when she saw that she had not, her expression hardened.

'It's a foolish joke,' she said. 'I see nothing at all funny in it. Please try not to be so childish, the two of you.'

'It's not a joke, Emily,' Christina said flatly. 'This letter makes it quite plain. When we all thought they were spending a week or two in Warwickshire, they were on their way to Liverpool to board a ship for New York. Cordelia probably wrote this from the quay itself, at the very last moment, to make sure that there was no possibility of our stopping them.'

Her voice was bitter. She thought of the conversation she had had with Cordelia in the old schoolroom. Hadn't she persuaded the girl then that her place was here with Timothy and her mother, keeping them together, keeping Henzel's itself together? Hadn't Cordelia understood the importance of Timothy's staying here, where he was so badly needed? She moved impatiently to the window, looking down at the cones. The glasshouse . . .

'But they must be stopped!' Emily exclaimed. 'They must be brought back. They're my children – they're still under twenty-one, they're under my jurisdiction. They can't simply leave – go to another country. The whole thing is ridiculous.' She stood by the table, twisting her hands together, her voice trembling. 'It's all that girl's fault, you know – Cordelia. Jealous and self-willed, as she's always been. She's seen how close Timothy and I have become since Paul died, and she can't bear it. That's why she's planned this – to take my son away from me. Well, she's gone too far this time. She'll regret this.' Her mouth set in a hard line. 'There'll be no Cambridge education for that girl once she's back home, I'll see to that.'

'Now then, Emily –' Joe began, but she turned on him, her dark eyes flashing.

'Well, why *should* she? Look at the chances that girl's had – chances I never had. A good schooling, plenty of opportunity to study, her wishes consulted at every stage, allowed to choose her own way. And the chance of going to a women's college, which didn't even *exist* when I was her age. And she throws it all away! Just because she's jealous.'

'And Timothy?' Christina demanded. 'Why do you suppose *he's* gone? Emily, you must face the truth. This has nothing to do with jealousy. Cordelia wanted very much to go to Cambridge – she wouldn't have taken this step if something else hadn't mattered more to her. And that has to be Timothy.' She sighed. 'Emily, I know this is hard for you, and I'm no more happy about it than you are. But don't you see, you've driven Tim too hard these past months. Always there in the glasshouse, watching him, urging him to make the glass Paul used to make, always talking to him about his father, always –'

'So now it's my fault! My fault because I tried to find comfort in my son.' Emily was white, her mouth working with the bitter self-pity that had overtaken her since Paul's death, a self-pity she had never succumbed to in all the difficulties of her youth. Her bearing stiff, she walked slowly to the fireplace. On the mantelpiece above stood the great Compson Chalice, blown by Joe for Christina fifty years before. Next to it was the first piece of black cameo, carved by Paul when he had set out to produce the most sought-after cameo glass of a new era: a great vase in shining ebony glass, with a delicate classical pattern carved in the white glass that had been fused outside it, its handles fashioned into dragons' heads and covered with shimmering gold leaf.

Emily looked up at it. Silently, she reached up and took down the heavy piece of glass. She examined it with care, as if she had never seen it before. And Joe and Christina watched, half afraid, not daring to move.

'I had hoped a piece of glass of equal stature would stand beside these,' she said at last. 'A piece made by Timothy. Now I know it never will. His glass will stand on an American mantelpiece – never on this one.'

She replaced the vase and Christina looked down at the letter she still held in her lap and said helplessly, 'Emily, don't say that. They'll come back. It's really only a visit.'

'Only a visit,' Emily said bitterly. 'Paul said that when he went to Paris, and it was three years before he came home – and when he did, it was at the risk of his life. It was "only a visit" when his father, Jean-Paul, came here, and he *never* went home. And even further back, when his father Marc Thietry –'

'Emily, that's enough.' Christina rose from her chair. 'There is no need to go back into old history. Every family has its pains and its tragedies, and we all have to learn to live with them. You haven't done so; you've made no attempt to do so. I may say, Emily, that I am ashamed and disappointed in you; I had thought you made of stronger stuff. But since you don't seem able to tolerate Timothy's need to live his own life, you must do without him. Quite clearly, neither he nor Cordelia intends to allow you to ruin his future.'

Emily stared at her. The skin of her face seemed to have shrunk inwards, leaving her features sharp, her eyes no more than smouldering hollows. When she spoke again, her voice was unnaturally calm and as cold as ice. It cut through the air like a knife.

'Ruin his future?' she repeated. 'Ruin it? How can I be ruining the future of the only person I care about – the only person who cares about me?' Her voice was thin with an anger more intense than any Christina had ever seen in her. 'You're saying I drove him away, aren't you. And it wouldn't be anything to do with you, would it – the way you always put your precious glasshouse first.' Her scornful eyes raked her stepmother's small figure. 'If I've driven him hard, Mamma, you've done so too. You're equally to blame for this.'

'Emily –'

'It's true,' Emily insisted. 'The glasshouse, always the glasshouse. Always Henzel's. You don't care about anything else, about me, about Paul, your grandchildren –' She turned away, as if unable to bear the sight of the woman who had brought her up. 'You never have cared.'

'Emily – how can you say that? I've done nothing but care for you all. And why shouldn't I think of the glasshouse? Hasn't it been my life? Your grandfather's life? Your father's?' Her own feelings of betrayal rose once again in her mind as she added quietly, 'Couldn't I have been forgiven for thinking that it was Timothy's life also? And can you have forgotten that I have my own grief – that I have lost my son?'

'Lost your son? And haven't I lost mine? And my daughter? Not to mention a husband who was everything to me, everything!' Emily's calmness deserted her and she began to weep, sinking down into a chair. 'Oh, I know what's in your mind, I know what you're doing. You've never wanted me to have anyone to love, have you?' Her voice was trembling and tears ran unchecked down her face. 'I've always been unwanted here – always the outcast. Why did you ever bring me to this house, if this was the way you meant to treat me? Why didn't you leave me to die there in the mud house where I was born, where at least there was one person who loved me?'

'*Emily!*' Joe's voice was like thunder and Christina reached out quickly to touch his hand. But for once he shook her off. His eyes were fixed on his daughter's face and Christina thought that she had never seen him so angry. She looked at Emily and saw that his sudden roar had shaken her too, so that she stopped crying and stared up at her father, white-faced and wide-eyed. 'Now you listen to me, my girl,' he growled and Emily shrank visibly in her chair. 'I've heard just about enough from you in these past months. Ever since Paul died, you've demanded all the attention in this house, aye, and got it too, and precious little good it's done you or anyone else. What makes you think you've got first refusal on grief? Don't you think we mourn Paul too? Don't you think we miss the youngsters about the house? It's been like a morgue here lately, and you don't make it any better. You don't even try.' Christina touched his hand again, her eyes begging him to stop, but he shook his head. 'No, my love, I've sat by and listened long enough. Emily's my girl, when all's said and done, and if her father can't give her the rough edge of his tongue when she needs it, it's a poor lookout.' He turned his attention back to Emily again. 'Now, I know you've been through a bad time, and there's nobody more sorry for it than I am. But everybody has their cross to bear. We just have to pick ourselves up again and go on as best we can. Not wallow in self-pity like you've been doing.' He raised his voice against Emily's protest. 'Aye, self-pity, for that's all it is. You're making a lifetime's career of it, Emily, and it's got to stop. Don't you see, you're driving everyone away with it. Your friends, the people you used to work with and campaign with, even your own children . . . Does young Mark ever sit willingly in the same room with you now?'

'Mark . . .?' For a moment, it was almost as if Emily had forgotten who Mark was. She stared at her father and Christina was reminded of the many clashes of will between them in the past. They were so alike, these two, with their stubborn chins and their dark, angry eyes. 'Mark has his studies,' Emily said, but she said it weakly, as if acknowledging that her father was right.

'And does he need to study out of this house? Did you even *know* that he spends more time at his friends' houses than he does here?' Joe shook his head. 'You've been so sorry for yourself, Emily, that you've forgotten other people need care too. That boy's lost his father, and he's only fourteen. Does he have to lose his mother too?'

'He hasn't lost me –'

'He has,' Joe said inexorably. 'For you are no mother to him any more.'

There was a long silence. Then Emily said in a trembling voice, 'I'm no use to anyone, am I? Timothy, Cordelia, Mark – I've failed them all. It would have been better if I had died instead of Paul.'

'Don't start again,' Joe said quietly. ' I mean it, Emily. I've had as much of your self-pity as I can stand. Stop thinking you're the only person who's ever been bereaved. Start thinking about other people for a change.' He leaned forward. 'There are women out there who have lost everything – husbands, sons, daughters, even their homes. Why don't you do something to help *them*, since you know so well what they're suffering? Why don't you do something useful, as you did before? When are you going to stop being a parasite?'

Emily stared at him as, her head shaking, her mouth trembling, she rose to her feet. She pushed the chair away from her so violently that it almost fell. And then she turned, groping clumsily for the door, and they heard her stumbling footsteps as she ran blindly up the stairs.

'I'm sorry, my love,' Joe said at last. 'I've been holding that back for a long time and this morning my patience just snapped. I hate to hear her abuse you in that way. It's so unfair, after the way you cared for her and loved her. She's done it before –'

'And been sorry for it. She'll be sorry again – although I almost wish she wouldn't be. The burden of remorse, added to all that she's carrying now, could be just too much.' Then she too walked to the mantelpiece and looked up at the two great glasses.

'My poor Emily,' she said quietly. 'I know what she's suffering at this moment . . . But it does get better, the pain does recede and life does begin again. As it did for us, Joe.' She lifted down the Chalice, the first piece of lead crystal they had made to their own recipe, the piece that had first brought fame to the house of Henzel. She turned it in her hands, looking at the engraving Jean-Paul had made without her knowledge: the representation of the view from Dob Hill, the swirling smoke, the towering cone; and, on the other side, the entwined initials J and C.

'Cordelia has always reminded me of myself as a young girl,' she said sadly. 'And this was to have been my legacy to her. I wonder if she will ever hold it now.'

Life at Henzel Court seemed hollow and empty to Christina now. How could it be otherwise, she asked herself as she stared out over the teeming streets, with three such

35

important members of the family gone? Paul, her beloved son, the firstborn over whom she had refused to compromise, dead; his son and daughter, the twins whose birth had nearly killed Emily, halfway across the world. And Emily herself still lost in her own world of misery and despair, still with bitter accusation in her eyes whenever she looked at her father or stepmother.

'Will she ever be able to forgive them?' she would ask Joe as they sat at night by the fire that was still needed in the big library on English summer evenings. 'Tim and Cordelia, going away like that . . . I know Cordelia wrote that they felt it would be better for Emily as well as for Tim, but how could that be true? They seem to have done more harm than good.'

'It might have made no difference at all – maybe without Paul she'll never be the same again anyway.' Joe lifted the poker and stirred the fire. 'But they weren't thinking only of Emily, were they, my love? Maybe that's what Cordelia tells herself, to help her own conscience – but Tim was thinking mostly about his glass. It's all that really matters to him, you know that.'

'I never thought he was quite so ruthless. Or that Cordelia would encourage him. Joe, he could have experimented here – he didn't have to go rushing to the other side of the world. Emily would have come round –'

'And you?' Joe asked quietly. 'Would you have come round too? You're ruthless too, where the glasshouse is concerned. Oh yes –' he raised a hand to forestall Christina's heated response – 'I know you've had to be. Ever since old Joshua died. But Tim's part of the new generation, Christina. The young are different. Wilful – determined on their own way.' He looked at her, his face grave but with a twinkle somewhere deep in his dark brown eyes. 'Or are they so very different after all?'

Christina stared at him, then relaxed and smiled reluctantly. 'All right, Joe. I know what you mean. And perhaps you're right. In Timothy's place, or Cordelia's, I might well have done the same. Yes, perhaps he did feel he had to go away and Cordelia had to go with him. Perhaps, indeed, they could have done nothing else. But – Emily seems so sad now, so unhappy. And for me – well, it seems that without Tim, everything we've worked for has come to an end.'

'We still have Mark.'

'I know. But Mark's young yet, too young to understand what's happening. And he's at school all day and working at his books in the evening. It will be years before he's ready to take over, and even then . . . he hasn't Timothy's talent.' Christina sighed. 'Besides which, Emily seems barely to notice him. Everything she had was concentrated on Timothy.'

'And that's just why he went,' Joe declared. 'Christina, we can't order everything to our own liking. We can only do our best. Whether what those two did was right or not, all we can do is look after Emily, and bring her back to normal, if it's possible at all.' He shook his head. 'I don't like to see her this way any more than you do, my love. But she's always been a prey to her emotions. Look what she was like over her mother. And then when she thought she'd lost Paul before. She got over it, though, didn't she? Went down the Lye and worked for the folk there. Maybe that's what she should be doing now.'

'Working at the Lye?' Christina said with a smile.

'Why not, if it would help her? That's what she needs, mark my words. Emily was always better when she had someone else to think about – when she could do something to help. Why, even in the nursery, she always had to be in charge, you know that. If she could find something now to take her interest –'

'It's not so easy this time. She has all her old interests, ready to be taken up again – her work for the poor, her campaigns for women's rights. But she seems to have lost heart with all of them.'

'Then we can only wait for her to find it again,' Joe said quietly, and he reached out his great hand and took Christina's in a firm, warm clasp.

Christina looked into the fire. They had spent many hours here, she and Joe, ever since those early days when, as the best gaffer in the Henzel glasshouses, he had come to discuss new designs for the lead crystal they had begun to produce. The library had changed since then: from the old oil lamps that had flickered over their early meetings, they had progressed to the yellow pools of light cast by gas mantles and now her grandson Mark was beginning to talk of electric lighting. But the big table, where she and Joe had pored over his drawings and Harry had worked at his schoolbooks, was the same. And the firelight, casting a companionable warmth over their ageing bodies, was no different from the firelight of all those years ago.

Christina found it difficult to believe that she was growing old. The years seemed to have slipped past unnoticed, and she felt no different inside from the way she had felt as a young girl, teasing her long-suffering Aunt Susan and jaunting off to the glasshouse with the father who had indulged her so. Yet she had been little more than a girl when responsibility had come to her, and she had borne it ever since, through times that were difficult as well as happy. The early struggles with the glasshouse; her confusion before she was able to acknowledge at last her love for the rough glassmaker Joe Compson. And then, even after their marriage, the problems that had still beset them; the arrival of Joe's daughter Emily; the growing attachment between her and Paul; the jealousy of Roger, their younger son, and the terrible accident – as the family always referred to it – which had left him as he was today, scarred in mind as well as body.

Those were just a few of the memories that crowded into Christina's mind. But alongside these were other, happier ones. The early days of their marriage, when she and Joe had discovered all the delights of the love they bore each other; the birth of their own two children, Roger and Sarah – and the continuing pleasure that Sarah had always brought them, from the time she was a fat and chuckling baby to today, when she had matured to a plump and serene woman who seemed genuinely happy to devote her life to her irascible brother.

There had been plenty of days when the family had been happy together, Christina thought, days when she and Joe had taken the children on outings to the countryside and delighted in letting them run free in grassy meadows, paddle in clear-running streams or climb trees. Days when they had sported in the snow before the eternal smoke of the Stourbridge chimneys had fouled it; days when they had sat around the fire, telling stories and singing songs. Yes, there were many good things to remember. However bad the bad times are, she told herself, there are always better ones ahead.

But not, it seemed, for Emily, who had lost the one person she loved and needed most.

'I shall be busy tomorrow morning,' she said after a while. 'Rupert and young Samuel are coming at ten-thirty and Roger will be with them. We have some business to discuss.'

Joe frowned. 'I wish you'd let go a bit, my love. It's time you retired from all that.'

'As you have?' Her eyes laughed at him. 'The day hardly

39

passes when you aren't in that cone on some pretext, Joe Compson, and blowing as well as you ever did when one of the gaffers gives you the chance!'

'That's different,' he growled. 'Blowing keeps me fit – there's naught like glassblowing for keeping a man's muscles in trim. And once it's done, it's over. But running the whole show – that's worry and strain. You ought to be taking a rest from it.'

'Now that I'm an old woman, you mean.' Christina's chin tilted in the familiar way and she knew that to Joe she would never be an old woman. 'Joe, don't worry so much. I won't let the glasshouse become a burden to me. Samuel is very able – well prepared to take over from Rupert, whose retirement is equally overdue since he's nearly the same age as I am. That's what we are to discuss this morning, in fact – the arrangements for the business now that the next generation is to take over. Even though it seems that the future is not going to be as I had expected,' she added with a trace of asperity.

'I see. And you mean to make Samuel managing director, I suppose.'

'Him – or Roger.'

'Roger?'

'Why not? He's our son, our only son now, Joe.' Christina met his eyes. 'Samuel is from the other branch of the family – it still goes hard with me to let him step in over my own son's head, even though we ended the feud years ago. And we must consider Mark as well.'

'Mark?'

'Isn't he the next generation . . . now?'

'You've discounted Timothy altogether, then,' Joe said quietly, and Christina met his eyes.

'Don't you think it's wise?'

'Wise? I've never pretended to be wise. All I know is, it's

a pity. The boy's only been gone a week or two – he could be back by the autumn.'

'And do you really think he will be? Think, Joe! He's gone to America, a new country, full of vitality and life, brimming with new ideas and eager to carry them out. Of course he won't come back! Corning is a flourishing glass-making town – why they even call it Crystal City – he'll settle in with Harry and Ruth, who are certain to make a fuss of them both, he'll find some go-ahead glassmaker who will be ready to let him try his innovations, and he'll never think of Stourbridge again. Henzel Crystal has lost Timothy, Joe, and all because – oh, well, never mind. Perhaps Emily is right – it was my fault as well. But all I ever wanted was the best for us all – the best for Henzel's.' She stirred impatiently. 'Clearly, Timothy didn't believe that it could be the best for him too.' There was a moment's silence and then she went on in a different tone, 'We must make quite sure that we don't lose Mark as well.'

'Well, I don't think there's much danger of that. Mark's a chip off the old block,' Joe said with satisfaction. 'The spitting image of me, young Mark is.'

'Yes, but he won't be able to follow in your footsteps, Joe. He can't become a glassblower and gaffer. If he enters Henzel Crystal at all –'

'At all? Have you got doubts about him, then?'

'If he enters Henzel Crystal at all, it must be on the management side. Yes, of course he must learn the crafts of blowing, cutting and engraving – but he'll never work in those ways, Joe, you know that.'

'Aye, I do. And can't help regretting it a bit, Christina. It's in my blood, after all, and I believe it's in his too. I can feel it in him when we're in the cone together . . . But I know you're right. The boy's got brains as well as brawn, and it's brains Henzel Crystal needs.'

'We've some fine blowers, Joe,' Christina said gently, knowing how much his craft meant to her husband and how he must long to see his grandson follow in his own footsteps. 'Ben Taylor – we did well the day we brought him into the business. He and Paul did some wonderful work together. And young Frank is as good as his father already.' She paused for a moment, thinking. 'I don't want to arrange Mark's life for him, Joe – goodness knows, we should have learned by now that it just won't work. But we must look ahead. And there's the château to consider as well. We still have responsibilities there.'

'The château . . .' Thietry Cristal, buried deep in the Lorraine, had never seemed real to Joe, although he had visited the Paris showroom with Christina, Paul and Emily at the time of the Paris exhibition in 1867. After the Franco-Prussian War the château, along with the rest of the Lorraine, had been annexed by Germany. But Marc Thietry had willed both it and the Paris side of the business to his grandson Paul, and the Henzel family had taken responsibility for it.

'What do you need to discuss there?' Joe asked now. 'Isn't that René fellow in charge?'

'Yes, he is, since nobody knows what happened to Gabriel's and Annette's children.' Christina sighed, thinking of the terrible things that had happened during that tumultuous year. Gabriel, Marc's great-nephew, who had hoped to inherit the business until Paul arrived on the scene, had been left alone to carry on the business under Prussian rule, his victory tasting sour in his mouth for it was all he had. His wife Annette had disappeared, some said as the mistress of one of the Prussian generals, others that she had been executed for spying; his children had vanished too and Gabriel either could not or would not say what had happened to them. Sent to America, away from the fight-

ing, or massacred in those dreadful days? Nobody knew –
but if they had gone abroad, surely Gabriel would have kept
contact with them?

Christina had never met Gabriel or any of the Lorraine
Thietrys. But she had seen the shadows in Paul's eyes when
he spoke of them, and knew that more had happened in the
château than he ever spoke of. And she could not help
wondering at the odd note in his voice when he had told her
that René, Gabriel's nephew by marriage, had returned
from the war. Gabriel, it seemed, was failing fast; and when
he died, René had taken over the management of the château
and the Thietry glasshouse. Paul had decided to leave the
situation as it was. His interest then lay solely in Henzel
Crystal; he did not, it seemed, want to stir up old memories
by visiting France ever again.

Joe had fallen asleep, and Christina gave him a loving
look. Still magnificent at over eighty, he had never lost the
qualities for which she had always loved him – the sturdy,
sometimes raging independence, the straightforward integ-
rity that he had brought from his own class. Joe would
never compromise, and since compromise was equally
lacking from Christina's character, they had experienced
many storms together. But beneath their tempests there had
always been that respect for each other which they never
lost; the respect and deep, abiding love which drew them
together again, always ready to listen and perhaps to be
converted. Or, if not, to concede. Neither would carry a
quarrel to irrevocable lengths.

Christina watched the dark face, surmounted now
by hair that, though thick as ever, was white. She and Joe
had been together for nearly fifty years – a long time.
Inevitably, death must come to part them, perhaps quite
soon. How would she feel if Joe were taken first? Would
she be like Emily, helpless without the man who had

43

stood by her for so long? Would she too want to die?

How would she feel if, having lost Joe, someone took away the person who gave her the most comfort . . .?

Oh, Emily, Emily, she thought, her heart going out in pity to the sad-faced woman who haunted the house like a wraith of unhappiness. What have we done to you?

'All the same, we do have an interest in the Thietry side of the business,' Christina said next morning as she sat in consultation with Roger, Rupert and his son Samuel. 'I feel someone should go to Paris, and perhaps to the Lorraine as well, just to see that all is well. The inheritance goes of course to Paul's children now, but with Timothy in America and Mark still at school, we ought to have someone there to oversee matters.'

'It makes good business sense.' Roger looked at the figures in his ledgers. 'René seems to be making a good job of his management, but there might well be room for improvement . . . Whom do you suggest should go, Mamma?'

Christina looked at him and felt the inevitable sadness at the sight of her son, once so handsome and now so brutally scarred. It was true that it was his own treachery that had brought about his disfigurement, but she could never feel any anger towards him, or wish him any further punishment. And with the weals had come a temper that lost him any friends he might have made. Only with his sister Sarah, tender and loving, who had stayed at his side during the painful months of his slow recovery, did he behave with anything less than irascibility.

Yes, Roger was to be pitied. And if his only interest was – as it always had been – Henzel Crystal, then he surely deserved now to choose his own path?

'Would you like to go, Roger?' she suggested tentatively,

knowing his dislike of being seen by strangers. 'I can think of no one better to undertake the task.'

He looked at her with bitterness, as she had known he would, but beneath it there was a certain pleasure. Although he could never forget his deformities, Roger was also fully aware of his value to the business, and he liked it to be acknowledged – even, she thought wryly, if he never admitted it. He would not go to the Lorraine, but he would have been displeased not to have been asked.

'I think not, Mamma,' he said with a coldness that did not hurt because she understood it. 'I suggest Samuel.'

Samuel was, of course, the obvious choice, the only one who could go. He looked at Christina now, his eyes bright, and she felt another pang. He was so much like Jeremy, the cousin who had done his best to wrest Henzel Crystal from her control. But in Samuel's blue eyes there was no devious glint, and there was no touch in his regular features of the dissipation that had blurred Jeremy's good looks. She was happy for him to share in the management of Henzel Crystal, just as she had been happy to agree to his father Rupert's suggestion that the two family firms should merge, over twenty years ago. With the old feud buried, it had been a good partnership.

'Do you wish to go, Samuel?' she asked. 'It means leaving your responsibilities here.' And with Timothy gone, perhaps never to return, his prospects could have been even better. 'I have been thinking that we ought to have someone there permanently – René is not a Thietry, and with Gabriel dead and little hope of ever tracing his children –'

'I should like it very much,' Samuel said quickly, his face flushing a little. 'You're right, we should have a member of the family there. And I believe I could bring even more success to the business if I had a free rein.'

'And I trust you to do that.' Christina smiled at him. 'I

shall be happy to think of you in Lorraine, Samuel, managing that side of our business at least for the time being. Now . . . this leaves us with some rearrangements to make here.'

She looked slowly round the table at the men: Rupert, of her own generation, ready as Joe had said to retire; his son Samuel, forty years old but clearly excited at the thought of a new life abroad; and her own son, Roger, at fifty a bitter and disappointed man who lived for his ledgers and accounts.

'Will you take over full management of Henzel Crystal from now on, Roger?' she asked gently. 'At least until either Timothy or Mark is ready. You are the most able, and I should like to see you in charge.'

She watched the dull discoloration of his scars and knew that he was as deeply moved as he could ever be. His twisted lips moved slightly; his eyelids, one of which would never fully open, flickered. He looked at her for one of the few times since the accident, and when he spoke his voice was husky; although, being Roger, his words were as brusque as ever.

'Since you offer me the position, I suppose I'd better take it, Mamma – after all, you are in control. And I am, as you say, the only man capable of doing it.'

Christina smiled, knowing that the apparent churlishness was only on the surface. Inside, she sensed a wild jubilation that at last he had achieved what he had longed for all his life – even though it was still not truly his, for both Timothy and Mark had a prior claim. But Roger himself would be ready to retire before either would want to take over, and he was sensible enough now to know it.

'Then that's decided,' she said, rising to her feet. 'And there's only one thing more to say – from today, Roger, I shall wish to be concerned only with the most vital matters. You are in full charge of Henzel Crystal, just as Samuel will be in full charge of Thietry. Rupert and I are retiring.'

She walked to the door, knowing the effect of her words, and turned to smile before going quietly outside. And then stood for a few moments, regaining her composure. For with the relief of having made the announcement there was, as there must be after so many years, a deep and agonising sadness. Henzel's had been her life, her work for over half a century. Like an old monarch, she had thought she would never abdicate her position. And now, with the Crown Prince absent, who knew what would happen to her little kingdom?

She turned her back on the library door and all that it had meant to her, and went back to her husband.

Joe, however, greeted her with an expression of concern.

'What is it?' she asked at once, and then saw the telegram in his hand. Fear gripped her heart at once. 'What's happened? The twins – have they not arrived? Has there been an accident? Or is it Harry – or Ruth? Joe, *tell* me!'

'Hush, my love, hush. It's nothing like that.' But his face was grave all the same, and Christina stared at him with eyes filled with terror. 'Nobody's ill or hurt – nothing like that. And as for the youngsters having arrived or not, it's far too soon for a letter – you know that. No –' he looked down again at the sheet of paper in his hand – 'it's something different. Christina, Harry never received their letter, or your telegram. He never heard that Timothy and Cordelia were going to America. He knew nothing about it.'

'Knew nothing about it? Then what? Joe, I don't understand.'

'He left Corning before your letter got there,' Joe said. 'This letter's to tell us he and Ruth were about to close up the house and go on that long trip they've been promising themselves. Seems to have been a pretty sudden decision, but

47

they're coming to England first, Christina, before jaunting off all over the Continent. I'd have thought my sister'd have more sense at her age! But anyway, they'll be here in less than a fortnight.'

'But they can't be,' Christina said stupidly. 'Cordelia and Timothy are on their way there. They may even be there already.'

'I know,' Joe said grimly. 'And they'll be there alone.'

Chapter Three

During those first few weeks in Corning, Cordelia felt more lost and lonely than she had ever imagined possible.

The news that their uncle and aunt had left Corning on a trip to England had come as a considerable shock. Standing there on the empty porch, their luggage at their feet, she and Timothy had stared at each other in something very like despair. Cordelia had felt great waves of fatigue wash over her. Surely it could not be true? Fate could not be so malicious.

'They've gone to England?' She stared down at the thin, rangy man who stood below the porch. 'Are you sure?'

'Certain. We live right next door, we've known the Henzels ever since they came here. Nice couple.' He looked curiously at them. 'You come on a visit? You sound like you're English.'

'We are. Mr and Mrs Henzel are our uncle and aunt. Great-uncle and great-aunt, really. We wrote to say we were coming, but they must have left before the letter arrived.' Cordelia brushed back the curls that lay damp with heat on her forehead and looked at her brother. 'Timothy, what are we going to do?'

He looked as helpless as she felt and his face was white and exhausted. She felt a pang of anxiety; he had suffered very much from sea-sickness on the crossing and had looked almost ready to faint once or twice on the train. 'I don't know, sis. Find somewhere to stay, I suppose. There must be hotels in the town.'

'Yes, of course.' She looked again at the neighbour. 'Is it

possible to get a cab? We can't leave our boxes here. Can you recommend anywhere we could stay?'

'Well, there's the Pickwick Hotel, on West Market Street. Or the Dickinson, or the Steuben on East Market . . . Guess there's quite a few, when you come to count 'em.' He stood pulling thoughtfully at his lip for a moment. 'Look, you stay right here and I'll fetch my pony. Can't have Harry Henzel's folk stranded. I'll take you downtown and you can pick where you want to put up.'

He disappeared round the side of the next house, and Cordelia sank down on one of the boxes and put her head into her hands. It was all too much – the long journey here, the weariness, the shattered hopes. She thought of her relief at having finally arrived, the thankfulness with which she'd looked forward to meeting her aunt and uncle again, her longing to rest in a real armchair, to sleep once more in a real bed . . . And now she must begin all over again, face a future that was fraught with problems in a strange and unknown land.

'So here you are, you poor things! Look at them, Bob, just settin' here not knowin' what to do!' The voice broke into her misery, warm and motherly. 'Why, they're nothin' but children. Now you come along with me, both of you, and we'll see what we can do about this.'

Cordelia raised her head. Hurrying up the porch steps was a middle-aged woman, as plump as the man behind her was thin. Her face was creased with concern, and as Cordelia rose to her feet she found herself enfolded in an almost suffocating embrace. Half stifled, she emerged to see the woman turn to Tim and clasp him in the same way. Cordelia smothered a sudden hysterical giggle.

'Men!' the woman said, standing back to survey them both. 'They don't have no idea! I jes' caught my Bob coming to harness up the pony. Wasn't going to say a word to me, mind – all he had in mind was to take you right back downtown to a hotel or some such. As if I'd let him do any such thing! Least we can do is give you somethin' to eat and drink after all the way you've come.' Still talking, she took Cordelia by the hand and led her down the steps. 'Now, you come right in home with me and leave Bob to load up those boxes of yours. You too, young man – you look as bone-tired as your sister here. That's right, ain't it?' she added, turning to Cordelia. 'You are brother and sister? Niece and nephew to the Henzels?'

'That's right.' Too weak to protest, Cordelia allowed herself to be led across a strip of garden and into the house next door. 'Uncle Harry is our grandmother's brother, and Aunt Ruth is our grandfather's sister. We were hoping to stay with them, but they couldn't have received our letter.'

'No, I guess it's on its way back to England at this very moment. I've been lookin' after that – packin' up all the post and sendin' it off to an address they gave me in England. Stourbridge, it was. That where you come from?'

'Yes.' Again, Cordelia had to repress a desire to giggle. To think of Uncle Harry and Aunt Ruth travelling across the Atlantic to England, just when she and Timothy were on their way here! Why, their ships might even have passed at sea . . . Taking a grip on herself, she looked round the room into which they had been led. It was long, with large doors opening into a further room at the far end where she could see a big dining table of dark, polished wood laid with silver cutlery and candelabra. The main room was evidently the sitting-room, with a wide upholstered sofa facing the fireplace and a smaller couch on either side. Other comfortable-looking armchairs stood in the corners, and there were several small tables and a great many plants. The glass-fronted cabinets were filled with gleaming crystal tableware, and the tops were crowded with photographs.

The whole room had a welcoming feel, and Cordelia began to feel its warmth creep into her heart.

'What a lovely home you have. It's so kind of you to bring us here, Mrs –'

'There, and if I haven't forgot to tell you my name!' A plump hand flew to an equally plump cheek. 'My, what manners you'll think I have. I'm Martha Robinson, dear, and my husband there's Bob. And you – is your name Henzel too, like your uncle?'

'Yes. Cordelia and Timothy.' Cordelia held out her hand with a grateful smile. 'And it *is* kind of you to bring us into your home. We didn't know what to do when Mr Robinson told us –'

'Well, of course you didn't! Who would? But now you're here, and I'm goin' to have some fresh coffee made and then we'll all sit down and decide what's to be done.' Martha Robinson bustled out of the door and could be heard giving orders in another part of the house. Cordelia and Timothy looked at each other and Cordelia lifted her shoulders slightly and spread her hands.

'Well, what are we to do?'

'Sit down and drink the coffee when it comes,' Timothy said firmly. 'And then we'll have to find somewhere to stay. It sounds as if there are several hotels here, anyway – we're bound to find something suitable. After that – well, I suppose we'll have to find lodgings of some kind.'

'Lodgings? But we can't afford –' Anything she might have said was drowned by the return of Mrs Robinson, followed by a young servant girl bearing a tray. The enticing smell of coffee rose from a pot and there was a large plate of biscuits to go with it. Cordelia took one look and forgot everything but how hungry she was.

'This is just to fill a hole until we can get you somethin' more substantial,' Martha Robinson said, pouring the coffee. 'I can see you've not had a proper meal since you left New York. Not that the food there's fit to eat, and I daresay it's worse on those awful ships. I told your aunt, when she said she was goin' overseas to Europe, you'd better take plenty of provender with you for you'll starve away to nothin' on that steamer. And there's not much of her there to start with, is there, Bob?' She turned as her husband loped into the room. 'Have you got all those boxes stacked in the trap?'

He nodded. 'I have. Any coffee there?'

'Of course there's coffee here. Isn't there always? Live on coffee, if I let him,' she added to Cordelia. 'But I make sure he's fed better'n that. He's nothing but a bit of wire as it is. Now then – what do you two plan to do? I'd have you here and welcome, but we're expectin' our daughter and her children tomorrow and there just ain't room for any more. I feel real bad about that, but –'

'Oh, please,' Cordelia said quickly. 'We wouldn't dream of putting you out. You've been kind enough already. And if Mr Robinson really wouldn't mind taking us to a hotel –'

'As if he would! But you'll sit there and rest for a bit before you even think of goin' off to a hotel. And I've got my girl makin' somethin' for you to eat too.' She looked, bright-eyed as a robin, from Cordelia to Timothy. 'It's been a long journey for you both, and you're so young to be travellin' like this, too. Let's see, which is the eldest?'

'Cordelia is,' Timothy said, setting down his cup. To her relief, he looked better now, with some colour coming back into his cheeks. 'But only by an hour. We're twins.'

'Twins! Well, ain't that somethin?' The round head with its greying hair shook from side to side in wonderment. 'Do you know, I've never met real twins before. But you ain't a bit alike!'

'Well, not all twins are,' Cordelia said. 'But we're very close.'

'Well, of *course* you are. Now, have another cookie and tell me all about yourselves. Why did you come all this way to see your uncle and aunt without lettin' 'em know first? Oh, I remember, you did write but it was too late . . . Still, it must have been pretty sudden.'

Cordelia took a biscuit – cookie? she thought, storing the word away for future use – and answered cautiously, not sure how much of their business she wanted Mrs Robinson to know. She seemed very kind, but . . . 'It was quite sudden, I suppose,' she said. 'But our father died recently and we needed to get away for a while. And since my brother is interested in glassmaking, and Uncle Harry lived here, we decided to come to Corning.' It was all true enough, although she felt slightly ashamed when she saw the expression of sympathy on Mrs Robinson's face. But how could she possibly explain about her mother and the changes her grief had wrought in her? How could she say that they had virtually run away? She bit into the cookie and looked at Timothy.

'Is that right?' The American woman's plump cheeks trembled a little and her voice deepened with compassion. 'Your father? Why, that must have been Harry's nephew Paul – didn't he tell us about that, Bob? Real upset, he and Ruth were over that – well, that's why they decided to bring their own trip forward. Hadn't meant to go till next year. So that was your Pa. Well, that's just dreadfully sad. And now to find your uncle not here after all. And your dear aunt – such a lovely person, she'd have done you so much good.' She turned her attention to her husband. 'Now, Bob, I don't want these two sweet children trailin' all around the town lookin' for somewhere to stay. You just get right down to Market Street now and find somewhere nice for 'em. Two good rooms, mind. I don't want 'em in any place that's not suitable – you know what I mean? Tell 'em we'll be right down as soon as we've had dinner, and the rooms had better be good and ready.'

Bob gave Cordelia a humorous glance. 'See how she bullies me?' he said. 'Nothin' but orderin' about from mornin' till night. Guess I'd better go, or she'll start in with the rolling-pin . . .' He made a mock ducking movement, as if his wife were about to throw something at him, and departed. Martha watched him go with fond exasperation.

'Don't you take any notice of Bob,' she said. 'He's all talk . . . Now, where were we? Tell me about your family, now. Heard so much about them, it's almost as if we knew 'em. Your grandmother, that would be Harry Henzel's sister, Christina, that he talks about . . .?'

It was much later when Cordelia and Timothy finally found themselves settling into two rooms at the Pickwick Hotel, and they were almost too exhausted to do any more than unpack a few things, wash and fall into bed. Cordelia felt as if she could sleep for a week; she hardly cared what might happen to them next, so long as she wasn't woken up to hear about it. Nevertheless, she found herself wide awake next morning as dawn brought the first grey light into the room, and she lay for a long time staring at the shape of the window, her thoughts whirling in her mind.

'So what do we do?' Timothy asked as they ate breakfast together. It was their first real American breakfast, for they had been travelling ever since disembarking from the ship in New York, and they were slightly startled by the large platter of pancakes which had arrived, accompanied by waffles, fresh fruit, buckwheat biscuits and muffins which were quite different from those at home. It was certainly sustaining though, Cordelia thought, and it was good to see Timothy eating heartily once more.

'What do you want to do?' she countered, taking a sip of

coffee. 'You said something yesterday about finding lodgings. But –'

He shrugged. 'Well, there's not much choice really, is there, with Uncle Harry away? We have to find somewhere to live.' He glanced round the hotel dining-room. 'I suppose this would do – it's quite comfortable. Or would you rather we had somewhere on our own? We'd need a servant or two –'

'Tim, we couldn't possibly stay here. It would be far too expensive. And I don't know what lodgings cost, or servants, but I'm quite sure they're too much for us. We only have a limited amount of money, Tim, until you start earning –'

'Earning?' he said, his dismay almost comical. 'But, Cordelia, I didn't come to *earn* – I want to experiment. Make different kinds of glass. I can't waste my time doing things like cutting, just to earn money.'

'You won't be able to waste time eating then, either,' she said grimly, 'for we are not going to write home for money.'

Tim stared at her and then ran his fingers through his hair. 'Cordelia, I don't think you understand –'

'No, Tim. It's you who doesn't understand.' Cordelia poured more coffee and then set the pot down with a tiny thump. 'It's time you faced up to what life is all about, Tim. We've come a long way for this. A long way, so that you could take the opportunities that America offers to young men like you, men with ideas and skills. But I don't think America is going to welcome you with open arms just because you're Timothy Henzel. I realised that on Ellis Island, when they were turning people back just because they weren't perfect. In this country, you've got to prove yourself – a name counts for nothing, Tim, nothing. You have to give America something before America starts giving back. And that means working. At anything. Cutting, engraving – and if you can't do that, gathering and taking in. Anything to keep us alive while you're waiting for the real opportunity to come along. Because that's what it comes down to, Tim. We're going to have to work, just to stay alive. Nobody else is going to keep us.'

She stopped and looked at her brother, wondering if he really understood what she was saying, if he shared at all in her proud determination to make their own way, now that they were here. In a perverse way, she was almost glad that their uncle and aunt were away. It left them completely free – free to make all their own decisions, free to go where they chose, live how they chose. For the first time, she felt excitement run through her veins.

'I'll work too,' she said. 'I'll find a teaching job in one of the schools. If I can't do that, I'll work as a packer. I don't mind. I'll do anything.' She leaned forward. 'It'll be *fun*, Tim.'

'Fun?' he said. 'Fun? And where do you suggest we live, Cordelia, while we're having all this fun? In a ditch?'

'No, of course not – we'll find lodgings. I'm only telling you that we can't afford anything expensive – not yet. But we need to find somewhere as quickly as possible – in fact, we'll go out this morning and start looking straightaway.' Cordelia finished her coffee and stood up. 'Tim, don't look so sulky! This is an adventure. Here we are in America, all by ourselves –' her voice quivered a little as she said it but she quickly regained control – 'and we can do just as we please. Aren't we *lucky*!'

'Lucky?' Tim said, and looked wonderingly, first at her and then around the high-ceilinged restaurant. 'Lucky . . . Why, yes, I suppose we are.'

Thank goodness for that! Cordelia thought as she watched him lead the way out with a new jauntiness in his step. Thank goodness he's accepted it.

But then, she had always been able to convince Timothy of

her own point of view. All she had to do now was convince herself.

Since then, however, even Cordelia's determined optimism had flagged. Finding lodgings had not been easy; many of the houses which advertised rooms to let were in the poorer parts of town, crowded by large families who seemed to live impossibly cramped lives in only one or two rooms. Eventually they found two rooms in a large house on Second Avenue, not far from their uncle's house. 'At least we'll be able to see when he and Aunt Ruth come back,' Cordelia commented wryly. 'Tim, you realise our money will only pay our rent for about eight weeks, together with the other things we'll need? We really shall have to find work.'

'That's all right, sis.' Timothy had quite recovered his good spirits and seemed convinced now that he only had to introduce himself to some of the town's leading glassmakers for them to fall at his feet, begging for his services. 'Now that we're settled here, I'll start making contacts. There are two main glassmakers here – Thomas Hawkes and the Houghton family. I'll see them first and decide which is the best offer.'

Cordelia nodded. 'And I'll make some enquiries about teaching. There are several schools here – the Roman Catholic church, St Mary's, has its own, though I suppose they require their teachers to be Roman Catholic too. And there's a Free Academy up on the hill, and several junior schools. I'm sure to find a post somewhere.' She looked around her room, which they had decided to use as their sitting-room as well, leaving Timothy's room free for any work that he might want to do there. 'It's not exactly palatial, but we'll soon be able to afford something better.'

Palatial was not the word Martha Robinson used for their accommodation either. When she came to see them a few days later, still full of apologies for not being able to take them in herself, she looked in dismay at the plainly furnished rooms with their shabby curtains and bare wooden floors.

'You can't really mean to stay here,' she exclaimed. 'Why, it's nothin' but a workman's lodgin' house! I don't like to think what your aunt and uncle would say if they came back and found you here.'

'Well, I don't suppose they will, and please don't write and tell them,' Cordelia said firmly. 'We've written to the family ourselves, telling them we're very comfortable – we don't want to worry them, and we don't want to ask for any money.'

Martha looked at her shrewdly. 'There's more to this "holiday" of yours than meets the eye,' she declared. 'Not much money, hardly any luggage, looking for jobs. You can't tell me it's all hunky-dory. Still, if you don't want to tell me, I'm not goin' to pry. I just don't like to see you livin' poor, that's all, when you're obviously not used to it.'

Cordelia felt ashamed of her secretiveness, but knew that she didn't want to become involved in long explanations. 'Well, perhaps it's not just a holiday,' she admitted, 'but I can't really tell you any more than that, I'm afraid, Martha. We just needed to get away – we've done nothing wrong, I promise you.'

'As if you wo-uld!' Martha had a trick of elongating her words in the ringing voice that she always used. 'Why, anyone with half an eye can see that you're just a couple of innocent babes, the pair of you. Now look, you're to accept a few bits of furniture from me and Bob, jes' to make this place a mite more comfortable, all right? No, I won't take no for an answer! I feel bad enough as it is about not takin' you in myself. I'll send him straight round with the trap, and you mind you use 'em – it's what they're for, you understand?'

Cordelia smiled and agreed – she had already learned that it was useless to try to refuse any of Martha's many little kindnesses. When the 'few bits of furniture' arrived, however, she almost sent Bob straight back with them.

'I can't possibly accept these! They're far too good – these lovely chairs, and those rugs – no, Bob, you must take them home, we couldn't take them.'

'More'n my life's worth to take these home now,' Bob said laconically. 'Have to drop 'em off at the dump if you won't take 'em – Martha wouldn't let 'em back in the house. Not until you're settled with Harry and Ruth, anyway.'

'Well, if they're really on loan . . .' Cordelia felt her eyes sting. 'Thank you, Bob. You're both very kind. I don't know what we'd have done if we hadn't met you that first day.'

'Met someone else, I guess,' Bob said, beginning to unload the trap. 'Corning folk are all pretty helpful, you'll find. Reminds me – there was a youngish fella round lookin' for you earlier today. Said he met you on the train.'

'Oh – Mr Novak!' Cordelia felt her cheeks grow warm. 'I'd forgotten about him.' She blushed a little more at the lie; Jensen Novak's face had come into her mind several times and she had thrust it away from her with some difficulty. 'Yes, it was his trap we arrived in that first day. What did he want?'

'Said he wondered how you were settlin' in. Surprised when we told him you weren't stayin' with your uncle, of course.'

'Well, I hope you told him we were quite all right,' Cordelia said a little sharply. Jensen Novak had been helpful enough on the train, and kind to loan them his trap, but there was something disturbing about those dark blue eyes and the half-mocking smile on the sculpted lips.

'Oh, yeah,' Bob said, carrying a small rosewood table

into Timothy's room, 'I told him that. And where's the young master this morning?'

'He's gone to see the glass manufacturers. Mr Houghton, I think he said.' Cordelia spoke casually, but she was aware of a tightening in her breast, an anxiety that Timothy should do well at this morning's interview. He had set out with such high hopes, and it was so important. She prayed that he would not come back disappointed.

Timothy Henzel had left their lodgings in high spirits. Under his arm he carried a package that contained the few samples of his best work he had managed to smuggle out of Stourbridge. Bare-headed, hardly noticing the heat of the morning sun, he hurried along Second Street until he reached the corner of Pine.

Amory Houghton Junior, President of the Corning Glass Works, lived here and Timothy had obtained an appointment to meet Amory and his son Alanson at nine this morning. His heart beat quickly; in a few moments, he would come face to face with the man who was surely the most important figure in town. The next half-hour or so would tell whether he was the most progressive or not.

Timothy glanced at the heavy parcel under his arm. This was his credential, the standard by which he would be judged – but it was also the standard by which he would judge others. The reaction of Amory and Alanson Houghton to the glass he intended to show them was as important to Timothy as the offer they might make him.

'I didn't come all this way to kowtow to glass-cutters,' he had told his sister proudly. 'And that's basically what these Americans are, sis. It's just about all they know over here – look at the stuff they have in their shops. Why, Grandfather would have a seizure if he saw me chopping away like that at good crystal. No, it's new ideas that they need in Corning, and if they'll only stop being dazzled by the prickles and bristles they're turning out at present, I can show 'em some.'

Cordelia had looked at him with caution in her eyes, a caution that irritated Timothy.

'Don't say so to start with,' she advised. 'Americans have a lot of pride. They may welcome new ideas, but I don't imagine they'll take kindly to a young unknown Englishman telling them what to do.'

'The name Henzel isn't exactly unknown, even here,' Timothy said stiffly, annoyed by her words, and walked away to pack up his parcel.

The corner house on Pine Street was a large, imposing building with a wide porch on which its occupants could sit in the shade of tall, leafy trees. Confidently, Timothy ran up the steps and rang the bell.

The house was as grand inside as it was out. Timothy glanced around as he was admitted to the hall, his eyes taking in a confused impression of large pictures, cabinets filled with glass and the heads and horns of gigantic animals fixed to the walls. A maid as neatly attired as any at home showed him into a large, pleasantly furnished drawing-room. After the dimness of the hall, it was almost dazzlingly light, and Timothy blinked a little.

Amory Houghton came forward, holding out his hand. His grip was strong and vigorous.

'So you're Harry Henzel's great-nephew. And this is my son, Alanson. Sit down, why don't you, and let's be comfortable.' He waited while Timothy sat on a low sofa and set his package carefully on a small, highly polished table, then settled himself behind a large desk and stared fixedly at Timothy. He was a large man, with a stern face, spectacles and a short beard. Timothy guessed his age to be about sixty. He held the steady gaze as long as he could, then glanced away at the younger man.

Alanson Houghton looked about thirty-five. He had a smooth, calm face with hair brushed back from the centre of his forehead. He had no beard, and his eyes were friendly behind horn-rimmed spectacles. He gave Timothy a smile.

'Nice to meet you, Mr Henzel. Looks like you've brought some glass to show us.' He glanced at the parcel. 'Why not do that first?'

Timothy felt a wash of relief and, for the first time, realised that he had been tense and nervous in the presence of these two men, so sure of themselves and their position. Immediately he felt irritated – why should he be afraid of them, for goodness' sake? He was willing to wager that neither of them could actually make a piece of glass – certainly not anything to touch what Timothy could achieve. Setting his jaw a little, he unwrapped his box and lifted out the first of his pieces: a vase in amber satin glass with a spiralled air-trap design winding like ripples around its whole body. Inside it was opaque white; it glowed softly on the desk where Timothy placed it.

The two Houghtons examined it closely, saying nothing, and Tim felt his hackles rise a little. Give them a chance, he told himself silently.

'What else have you in there?'

'Some cameo glass – a vase of Henzel Black Cameo and a piece of ruby.' Timothy displayed a second vase, deep black with a white relief carving depicting a classical scene with a Roman god astride a leaping stallion. As the Americans looked at this, he drew out and unwrapped a plaque of glowing ruby, patterned with deep-cut white roses.

'And this.' He took out his last item and saw Amory Houghton's eyebrows rise as he reached out to take it. 'It's an experiment,' he said, and heard the touch of defiance in his tone.

'I believe you.' The older man turned the glass over and over in his hands. 'What do you call this?'

'I don't have a name for it yet.' Timothy watched with an anxiety he would have liked to conceal. Their reaction to this piece was crucial to him. The vase was the piece that had caused most dispute between himself and his father when he had first made it, and his mother had forbidden him ever to make anything like it again. Cordelia had been against his producing it at too early a stage in his dealings with the Americans, but he had insisted. 'This is the kind of glass I want to make,' he had told her passionately, 'and no one who won't allow me my experiments can be of any use to me.'

The glass was different from anything Henzel's had ever produced – different from anything even Timothy had seen before. Next to the classical elegance of the cameo glass, the simplicity of the spiralled vase, it looked strange, almost unearthly, its squat shape like that of an overfed woman, its colour difficult to determine – now orange, now green as the light caught it in Amory Houghton's turning hands.

'This is not unlike the glass made by Tiffany,' Amory Houghton said at last, and his son gave Timothy a quick glance. 'Were you deliberately imitating his work?'

'Not at all.' Timothy stood up. 'I don't imitate any man,' he said proudly. 'The cameo designs are my own, and so is the experimental glass. I am an innovator, not an imitator.'

'And a firebrand, to boot,' Houghton said dryly. 'Sit down, young man, and stop getting hot around the collar. You have to allow us to ask our questions if we're to be of any use to one another. Now, tell us what your aim is. To produce more glass in this style?'

'Perhaps. Perhaps not. I told you, this is just an experiment. You may not like it – but you may like very much what I can produce if I am allowed to try my ideas further.'

Amory Houghton set the vase down. 'And that's what you require? Facilities to conduct your experiments at our expense? Glass mixtures to your own recipes, blowers to make the shapes you demand, cutters and engravers perhaps –'

'I do my own cutting and engraving. I can oversee my own mixing too, and even blow when necessary.'

'A man of every trade, indeed. But you'll not pretend that you mean to do that. You're asking for the fullest facilities a glasshouse can offer, isn't that so?' Amory turned to his son. 'Don't you think that's what the young man's asking for, Alanson?'

'Sounds like it,' Alanson agreed, but his voice was not unfriendly. He looked at Timothy and gestured towards the chair. 'Sit down, Mr Henzel. Let's talk this over. Now,' he continued when Timothy had rather reluctantly settled himself on the sofa again, 'tell us a little about yourself. Why did you come to America? What's wrong with staying in England?'

Timothy hesitated. He didn't like the turn the meeting was taking. If they didn't like his glass, why not say so? Why ask his personal history – a story he didn't much want to relate anyway.

But Amory Houghton was the most influential man in town – not that that mattered to Timothy. All he cared about was that the man ran a glasshouse, and a successful one at that.

It was now several weeks since Timothy had been able to make any glass and his hands and brain itched for the feel of a smooth, untouched blank in his hands, waiting for him to create whatever pattern or design he chose on its gleaming surface. Cameo-carving, cutting, engraving, etching, each different art was a form of nourishment to Timothy; since he had first been allowed into the glasshouse as a small child, he had known that here lay not only his future but his entire life. And until recently, there had never been any doubt but that he would follow his father and bring further acclaim to the already famous Henzel Crystal.

Emily's distress at losing her husband, turning as it had upon herself and distorting her feeling for her son, had made it impossible for Timothy to stay and follow the path he had mapped out for himself. But he had begun to wonder if he could have stayed, even if Paul had lived. His desire to experiment, to try new forms of glass, new colours, new shapes and designs, had already begun to create a rift between him and his father. The vase now standing on Amory Houghton's desk had almost brought matters to a head. Paul had disliked it intensely and, although he hadn't actually forbidden them, had expressed strong disapproval of any further experiments. Christina, still in love with cameo glass, had been inclined to support him. And Emily had carried her own disapproval even further – to its ultimate conclusion.

'Why did you come here?' Alanson Houghton repeated patiently.

Timothy decided that honesty must be his only course. If he planned to stay in Corning he must be accepted for what he was, or not at all.

'I needed more freedom,' he said bluntly. 'I couldn't go ahead with my work in the way that I wanted to. Glass is changing – it's a fluid thing, it changes even while it's being made. That's the whole essence of glass. By holding it back, forcing it to set in the same moulds, the same shapes and styles as we've been using for the past fifty, hundred, two hundred years, we're denying it its true nature.' He reached out and lifted the new vase towards him, looking down at its odd shape, its strange colouring. 'You may dislike this – it may be that nobody will like it. But it's a beginning. From

66

this, I mean to produce something beautiful, that everyone will like and want for themselves. Something new, that no one has ever made before. It's time we produced something new,' he went on eagerly. 'Gallé began it, with his Art Nouveau. Tiffany is doing it too, with his Favrile. But there are still other kinds of glass to be made – I know it. And I can do it – if only someone will give me the chance.'

Timothy stopped speaking. He was leaning forward in his chair, almost on the edge of it, his arms wrapped tightly around the vase, holding it to his chest almost as he might hold a woman. His voice throbbed with passion, his grey eyes burned with it. His whole body was as taut as a statue – the statue of some classical god, frozen in the midst of a feat of strength.

Amory and Alanson Houghton gazed at him. Their faces were grave, their eyes slightly narrowed. They looked at the vase clutched in Timothy's arms, and then they looked at each other.

'I reckon we ought to give this young man a chance, Pa,' Alanson Houghton said at last.

Timothy watched, not daring to relax yet.

'What d'you suggest, Alanson?'

'Why, we can use a new engraver and cutter, can't we? Especially one as talented as this young man seems to be.' Alanson Houghton seemed almost to have forgotten that Timothy was still in the room. 'Take him on, he's a fine artist, anyone can see that. And maybe after a while –'

'You – you mean you'd offer me a job?' Timothy broke in. 'A job as an engraver and cutter? In your glasshouse?'

'That's about the size of it,' Alanson said, and looked at him. 'Not good enough for you?'

'But – I thought I'd explained.' Timothy gestured towards the table, held out the vase in his hand. 'I need to be free. I need to work out my own ideas, I can't –'

'Can't work alongside the rest of the men?' Alanson stood up. 'Then I'm sorry, Mr Henzel, I'm afraid you're not the man for us. You see, we run a business here, not a facility for young Englishmen who're dissatisfied with their lot at home to come in and make free with what we've worked hard to build up. Sure, you'll have your chance to present your ideas, and if we like 'em we'll let you have your head. But you have to prove yourself first. You have to show us that you really can stick to a job, even if it's to someone else's design and it's a design you don't much care for. This is still a pretty new country, Mr Henzel, and we mean to make our mark in the world. And we do it by hard work. Understand?'

'Yes, I understand that,' Tim retorted. 'And I'm as hard a worker as the next man. But I –'

'There it is,' Alanson Houghton said with a note of finality in his voice. 'Take it or leave it, Mr Henzel. Come and work at Corning Glass, by all means – but on our terms. And then we'll consider your ideas for experimentation. If you don't like that arrangement –' He shrugged. 'Well, I doubt if Corning's the right place for you after all. I doubt if America itself is. But that –' he paused and gave Timothy a direct look – 'is for you to decide.'

A few minutes later Timothy found himself outside on the street. It looked just as it had before: a broad, straight road shaded by leafy trees, lined with houses that smiled with prosperity. The smoke and grime of the factories did not penetrate here; the gardens were green and bright with flowers.

But there was a change. The friendly face of the little town, its pleasant streets, the wooded hills that surrounded it, had altered, become almost hostile. He felt rejected, and his heart burned.

How dared they turn him away like that! He, a member

of the greatest glassmaking family in England, descended from one of the first families who had escaped from persecution in France three centuries ago, and still closely allied to one of France's own great glasshouses. He, Timothy Henzel, son of Paul who had first made black cameo, grandson of Joe Compson, the finest blower ever seen.

Trembling with fury, Timothy walked back along Pine Street. The Houghtons were not the only glassmakers in Corning. He had a list of others in his pocket – Thomas Hawkes, Egginton, Sinclaire, and if they failed, there were others, even further afield in Painted Post and Elmira.

And if none of these were interested in Henzel skills . . .? Timothy could scarcely envisage such a possibility. But in that case, he would find Cordelia and tell her to pack at once.

Chapter Four

Cordelia, having seen her brother off and thanked Bob Robinson for the furniture, found herself with nothing more to do. She looked out through the dusty window at the sunshine filtering down through the trees and decided to go for a walk. Since she was here in Corning, she might as well make the best of it. And even though her heart still yearned for university and the dream she had had of earning her own living by teaching – perhaps at the North London Collegiate, made famous by Miss Buss, or even the exclusive Ladies' College at Cheltenham where Miss Beale's name was spoken with such awe – she had no intention of letting anyone know her feelings. Least of all her twin, who would at once feel guilty and probably insist on returning to Stourbridge forthwith.

And that was something she could not allow. Coming to America had been as great a leap into the dark for Timothy as it had been for her. He had come because he was driven, because the genius she so firmly believed him to possess needed an outlet impossible in Stourbridge. Now that they were here, that genius must be given every opportunity to flower. He could not be allowed to return because he thought his sister was unhappy.

She watched Bob's trap clatter off down the street. And then fetched her hat and set off to explore Crystal City.

Most of Corning's buildings were fairly new. Only sixty years ago, Martha had said, there had been nothing but a few farm dwellings; then a townsite was planned and named after Erastus Corning, who had bought most of the land. Flour mills opened to grind the corn grown over the fertile fields; near the river, where regular flooding flattened the valley, tobacco was grown, to be used for the cigar production for which Corning was first known. To build factories, bricks were needed and brickworks appeared to supply the demand. The railroad came; a tavern was built; stores appeared and then a bank; schools were opened and churches erected. By the 1840s there was a thriving community and larger homes began to be built; homes grand enough to house the manufacturers whose prosperity was increasing so rapidly.

Cordelia walked slowly up Birch Street, past her uncle's house. This part of the town was built on the slopes of the hill that enclosed the Chemung valley to the south; it had been cleared of the virgin forest, and the streets laid out in the grid pattern so popular in American towns. Many of the streets running up from the broad, flat river-banks to the hill were named after trees – Chestnut, Walnut, Pine, Cedar and Birch. The streets that crossed them were numbered – First, Second, Third, up to Seventh. Then there were Chemung Street, Pearl, Columbia and Steuben, after the county in which Corning was situated. And that, so far, was the extent of Cordelia's exploration.

After a few moments, she came to the Monkey Run and stopped to look down at it.

The Monkey Run was a twisting stream which came down the hill and joined the river not far from the bridge which crossed to Knoxville, the northern part of Corning. It ran fast and clear, quite unlike any stream there was to be seen in Stourbridge. The only water there was the canal, Cordelia thought as she looked down at the chattering water, and that was always grimy and opaque.

'So here you are,' said a voice softly in her ear.

Cordelia gave a little jump and looked round. 'Mr Novak! I didn't expect to see you.'

'No?' Jensen Novak came to stand beside her, leaning over the low wall to gaze down at the swiftly-running water. 'Perhaps you should always expect to see me. Corning's a small town, after all, people are running into each other all the time.' He looked at her. 'It's really impossible to avoid people. Not even worth trying.'

'Really?' Cordelia said a little faintly. He was standing rather closer than she liked, his sleeve almost brushing hers. She moved away a little. 'It – it's very hot this morning.'

'About average for the time of year.' His dark blue eyes reflected the shimmer of the water, the skin at their corners slightly crinkled as if with amusement. 'I guess it seems hot to you, though, after England. Is it true that it rains there all the time?'

'Not at all – we have some very fine weather.' Cordelia's tone was sharper than she had intended. She tried to soften it. 'Not as hot as this, though, I agree. But surely it's strange for you too – Sweden must be colder than England.'

'In winter, sure.' His voice was just touched with unfamiliar accent, softening his 's's and minutely altering the vowels. He was hatless; the sun caught his hair and gave it a sheen of gold. 'But you need to remember that it's a long time since I lived in Sweden. My parents brought me here when I was only fifteen. I'm accustomed to American weather now.'

'It seems very pleasant at the moment,' Cordelia said politely.

'It is. And later, in the fall, when the frost turns the trees to flame, then you'll see something really spectacular. But it isn't always as peaceful as this.' He nodded out towards the broad plains on either side of the river. 'Get a lot of rain and that river turns nasty. Hasn't anyone told you about the floods hereabouts?'

'The floods? I've heard people mention flooding, but I supposed it was only in the fields.' Why was she talking like this, her voice so brittle?

Jensen Novak shook his head emphatically. 'Don't we wish it were! No, that river can rise up faster than you can hem a handkerchief. Most times it stays in the river flats, but if it takes a notion to come creeping into the town there's not much we can do to stop it.' He glanced down at the stream that rippled under their feet. 'And this Monkey Run – why, you never know what it's going to do. There's times it's just dry dust, and times when it's a torrent. Keep clear of it when the weather's bad,' he said with a quick look at her. 'We don't want a pretty girl like you washed away.'

Cordelia looked doubtfully at the innocent stream rippling beneath their feet. It seemed impossible to imagine it as a raging torrent, sweeping relentlessly down to a river that was swollen and angry rather than lazily peaceful. Perhaps Jensen Novak was given to exaggeration.

He was still watching her. She looked up at him, realising for the first time just how tall he was. When she had first met him in the railway carriage, she had been too exhausted to take much notice, aware only that he was looking at her rather more than good manners allowed. And in the flurry of getting their luggage out she had barely glanced at him. Now she saw that he was glitteringly handsome. And, no doubt, insufferably conceited.

'Why don't we stop beating about the bush?' he asked quietly. 'I called at your uncle's house to see how you were. It's all closed up. The next-door neighbour told me you'd moved into lodgings.'

'Yes, that's right. Uncle Harry and Aunt Ruth have gone on holiday. We won't be in lodgings for long – just until they come back.'

'He said they'd gone to England. They'll be gone for months.' He took her by the shoulders suddenly and turned her to face him. 'Miss Henzel, don't play games with me. I'm concerned about you –'

'You don't have to be!' she flashed, and bit her lip. There really wasn't any need to be so rude. 'We're quite all right,' she added more calmly, and tried to turn away.

But his hands were still on her shoulders, holding her back. She lifted her head, to look up at him, her eyes stormy. 'Mr Novak –'

'Why didn't you let me know at once?' he demanded. 'You had Parkin there with the trap. He'd have brought you straight round to me, we could have had you sorted out in no time –'

'We managed perfectly well! And by the time we realised the house was empty, Parkin had gone and we didn't know your address. Besides, the Robinsons were very kind. They took us in and gave us refreshment, and Mr Robinson took us to the Pickwick Hotel –'

'Why didn't you stay there, then?' he broke in. 'Why did you have to go to some sleazy lodging house?'

'It isn't sleazy!' But she knew that it was far from being the kind of place their family would have liked them to live in. 'It's perfectly clean,' she went on stubbornly, 'and the Robinsons have lent us some extra furniture. We shall be quite comfortable.'

He shook his head. 'Why not tell the truth, Miss Henzel? It's all you can afford, isn't it? Just what are you and your brother doing in Corning? You're obviously pretty well-off – you wear good clothes, you act like you're used to having money. Yet you come all this way with hardly any luggage, your relatives don't know you're coming, you move into cheap lodgings because you can't afford to stay in a hotel – so what's it all about? There's something wrong, and if you need help, I wish you'd tell me.'

Cordelia tried to keep her gaze steady, but could not. She let her eyes drop, and said in a low voice, 'I told you, Mr Novak, we're perfectly all right. There isn't any need at all to be concerned about us. We've got lodgings and enough money, and Timothy's gone to see Mr Houghton this morning to inquire about work in the glass factory. I'm sure he told you on the train that he's a glass engraver. Our family have their own glasshouse in England.'

'I know that. That just makes it seem all the more strange –'

'There's nothing strange about it at all! We simply came here to give Tim a chance to try some new glassmaking. He wants to interest someone in experimental glass. Timothy has a great deal of talent,' she said proudly. 'Whoever agrees to sponsor him will be a very fortunate man.'

'Indeed. That's very interesting. So he's gone to see the Houghtons. Is he planning to visit Tom Hawkes as well? And tell me, does Novak Crystal figure anywhere on his list?'

'Novak Crystal?'

He bowed ironically. 'At your service, ma'am.'

Cordelia stared at him. 'I didn't know you were a glassmaker.'

'That's because you were half asleep while your brother and I were talking on the train.' He frowned. 'You still haven't explained why you're so hard-up. Seems to me there must be some family trouble over this – didn't they want you to come?'

This was so near the truth that Cordelia recoiled. She shook her head at once. 'No – you're quite wrong – it was nothing like that. We just – we just want to be independent, to manage for ourselves. And we shall,' she finished defiantly, and looked him in the eye again. Nothing – *nothing* – would persuade her to tell him or anyone else about her mother.

He studied her for a few moments, then shrugged slightly. 'As you like. I don't wish to pry into your family affairs. But now that you're here, I can't help feeling concerned –'

'I've told you, there's no need.'

'Need or not, I still feel it. Look, let me see these lodgings of yours. I may be able to suggest something better. And I may be able to help your brother, too.'

'I'm sure,' Cordelia said coolly, ' that Mr Houghton will be pleased to give him the opportunity he needs. When he sees Tim's glass –'

'Amory Houghton is a businessman,' Jensen Novak stated. 'And a good one, too. I'm afraid your brother may not find it so easy to persuade him to take on a stranger and give him the run of the glasshouse – which I guess is what he wants.'

'Timothy's prepared to work.'

'He'll have to be. This is America.'

'He's a fine engraver. He takes after our father and grandfather. His reputation in England –'

'Won't help him here, I'm afraid.' The American looked down at her and said seriously, 'Miss Henzel, I don't know if you realise just how hard life can be here. This is the land of opportunity, but you have to be prepared to work for your living. I know – my family had a hard enough time when we first came. It's not easy, making your way in a new land.'

'Is America so new?' Cordelia asked. 'It's already over a hundred years since Independence was declared, and it had been settled for a long time before that.'

'But now we're really getting into our stride.' He waved his hand at the town that lay spread below them. 'Everywhere's growing, prospering. America's becoming more than just a colony, a place to rifle for the wealth that lies under the rocks. It's becoming a world power – before too

77

long, it'll be the greatest power the world has ever known. And there's no room for slackers. Everyone's got to pitch in and do their share.'

'As Timothy and I will,' Cordelia said stiffly, and turned to walk on up the hill.

Jensen Novak was still beside her, as if determined to stay with her until she returned to the lodging house. Cordelia sighed. The American wasn't going to be so easy to get rid of – he seemed to think he'd been appointed their guardian. Well, perhaps once he saw that Timothy was working with the Houghtons, he would forget his so-called concern and leave them alone. Until then, short of causing a scene in the street, there was nothing she could do.

He offered her his arm and, after a moment's hesitation, she took it, wondering how soon she could politely let it go. It felt warm and strong under her fingers. Feeling uneasy in the silence, she decided to ask a few questions of her own.

'Have you lived in Corning for long?'

'Came here as a boy. My father was a glass-cutter and after a year or two we set up our own shop. Expanded a bit – started making our own blanks – then moved out to Ohio. Got places in Findlay, Ohio, and White Mills, Pennsylvania, now, as well as the Corning factory.' He spoke laconically. 'I haven't lived in Corning for a good few years now,' he added. 'But I have a kind of feeling I'd like to settle here. I'm thinking of building a new house, way up on the hill.'

Cordelia followed his glance. The hill that rose to the south of Corning was covered thickly with green forest. Gradually, it was being cleared and new homes built on its slopes. Even from here, she could see that they were grand homes; the kind of homes that would give a man status. To live in one of those, you had to be wealthy and, in America, to be wealthy you had to be successful.

78

So why, she wondered suddenly, was Jensen Novak taking such an interest in herself and Timothy? Why did he have the time to roam around the streets, apparently with nothing to do? What did he want from them?

She shivered, feeling her mistrust return, and made up her mind that they would accept no further help from him. She would make her escape as soon as possible, and have nothing more to do with this tall, too-handsome Swedish-American with the enigmatic smile.

'Have you got over the journey now?' he asked abruptly. 'It must have been pretty exhausting – the long sea voyage and then having to go through Ellis Island. I hear that's a grim place.'

'It is.' Cordelia shivered. 'It's more like a prison. We all had to wear numbers, just like cattle, and we had to go through long corridors to a huge hall. It was like the inside of a great cathedral, but much more hateful. I was so afraid I'd lose Tim. I couldn't see how we'd ever find each other again.'

'Still, you came through all right.'

'Yes, eventually. But not everyone did. The doctors examined us all and if they found anything wrong they marked the person's clothes. Some had "H" for heart disease, some had "F" for a rash on their face. Some children near us had rickets and they were marked with an "L". And the girl next to me had "E" and she was sent straight back to the ship.'

' "E"? What was that for?'

'Some kind of eye disease. They said she would go blind.' Cordelia looked up at him. 'America doesn't welcome those who can't give a lot back,' she said quietly. And then, after a few moments' silence: 'But surely you came through Ellis Island too? You know what it's like.'

He shook his head. 'Ellis wasn't operating when we came

over. They were clearing immigrants through Castle Garden then. But I guess it was just as bad.'

Cordelia stopped. The street was now rising steeply up the hill and she had been forced to quicken her steps to keep up with her long-legged companion. She withdrew her arm and said, 'I really don't think you need accompany me any further, Mr Novak. I'm sure I'm quite safe here and I don't want to keep you from your business.'

Once again he gave her his direct glance, and she saw his lips twitch a little. They seemed to be permanently on the verge of amusement, those lips, she thought, and wondered if he might be laughing at her.

'Nobody keeps me from my business unless I choose to allow them,' he said lightly. 'But I'm sure you're right, Miss Henzel. You're really quite safe in Corning. We have very little crime – so long as you stay this side of the river.'

'This side of the river?' Cordelia asked, and wished he would remove that disconcerting gaze.

'Certainly. Look.' Briefly, he touched her shoulders, turning her so that she looked down the hill, past the big frame houses and across the river to the wide banks where the glasshouses were situated. 'On the far side of the river is where the poorer people live – the people who work in the factories and the mills. You'd be well advised to stay away from those streets.'

'Indeed? And why should I be afraid of honest working people? We have them in Stourbridge, too, you know, and none of them has ever troubled me in any way. Why should they do so here?'

He looked at her, soberly this time. 'In Stourbridge, you're known. You're Miss Henzel, daughter of the master. Of course no one would touch you there. But here . . . things are different. Here, nobody knows you. And those houses aren't occupied by the kind of working people you're accustomed to. We have a whole big immigrant population here. Irish, Germans, Italians, yes, and Scandinavians too. And they don't all shake down well together. We've had fights, stabbings and not long ago some local boys got on the Erie freight train and threw rocks at the Italian houses beside the track. And it didn't stop there; the Italians retaliated with shotguns and one of those boys lost an eye.'

Cordelia was silent for a moment. She was reluctant to allow this rather patronising American to tell her where she might and might not go, but the picture he had conjured up of threatening foreigners, looking on her as an alien, an intruder, was certainly a little daunting. Then she thought of her mother, going as a young girl into the equally inhospitable area of the Lye Waste at home. She lifted her chin and returned Jensen Novak's direct gaze with one of her own.

'You're very kind to warn me,' she said politely. 'I'll remember what you've said.'

'But you won't necessarily take notice of it.'

'Not necessarily,' she agreed in her sweetest tone. 'And now, I'm sure you ought to be going. There must be so many things you need to attend to.'

For a few seconds, their glances met, clashed and drew apart. Then he said coolly, 'But you were going to show me your lodgings, Miss Henzel. And there's no time like the present, wouldn't you agree?'

Cordelia felt her jaw tighten. She had hoped that he might have forgotten his desire to see where she and Timothy were living. She had even hoped that she would be able to dissuade him. But she could see now that her hopes had been false ones. Jensen Novak meant what he said, and he meant to have his way.

She had a strong feeling that Jensen Novak always did get his way.

* * *

'*Leave Corning?* But we've hardly arrived!'

Cordelia stood in the middle of the shabby room, still cluttered with the Robinsons' furniture which she had not yet had time to arrange, and stared at her brother's sulky face. 'Tim, what are you talking about? How can we leave Corning?'

'Quite easily. We simply pack our bags, get on a train and go.' His voice was sullen and defiant, and Cordelia sighed.

'Go where, pray? Back home to Stourbridge, where Mother will forbid your experiments? To France? You know it's too late for that now. Or have you some other destination in mind?' She watched his mutinous face. 'Tim, what did you expect? That the whole of Corning would welcome you with open arms?'

'Well, I expected a bit more than to be offered an ordinary job in the cutting shop!' Tim burst out. 'They just laughed at me, sis! I could see them doing it – not openly, but in their minds. They're laughing even now, I'd lay money on it. And I won't have it! I won't be treated that way.' He began to stamp up and down the room.

'If they're laughing at you at all, it'll be because of your childish behaviour,' Cordelia said sharply, thankful that she had asked Jensen Novak to wait outside while she and Timothy talked. One look at her brother's face when she had seen him pacing up and down the sidewalk waiting for her, had been enough to tell her that there was something seriously wrong. 'Tim, don't you realise that in this country you have to *prove* yourself. You have to make them believe that you're good – telling them just isn't enough. There are so many coming here with talent and ideas – why should yours be any better than the next man's? Why *should* they give you a better chance?' She realised that she was repeating Jensen's words and stopped. But they made sense.

'I showed them my glass.'

'And they have only your word for it that it *is* your glass,' Cordelia said calmly, ignoring the furious expostulation that followed. 'Yes, Tim, I know you're not a liar or a rogue. But they don't – how could they? They must wonder why you left England. With a flourishing family business there, a reputation already for fine work, why should you come to America and start again? You must admit it could seem odd to them.'

'So why did you let me come here?' Timothy demanded, wheeling in his restless pacing. 'Why didn't you say all this before? Why didn't you stop me?' He glared at her accusingly. 'If you knew this would happen, why did you just let me go ahead – are you trying deliberately to ruin my life?'

'*Tim!*' Cordelia felt a stab of pain at his accusation. She clenched her fists in the folds of her skirt, fighting down the angry words that surged into her mind. She, ruin his life! How could Tim even suggest such a thing – when in reality it had been her hopes, her dreams, which had been sacrificed. She took a deep breath, reminding herself that his pride in his work had been hurt and that this, for Tim, was the sharpest humiliation he could experience.

'I didn't make you come here, Tim,' she said quietly. 'You made up your own mind. And I believe it was the right decision. Tim –' she went to him, laying her hands on his shoulders, looking up into his face –' Tim, can't you see that the offer the Houghtons made you was a good one – a sensible one. Why don't you reconsider it? Work with them for a while –'

'*For* them,' Tim broke in bitterly, looking away from her face.

'For them, then. Let them see just how good you are, how much you deserve to be allowed a chance. It won't take long, Tim. They'll soon see what you're worth and then you'll be given every facility they have, I'm sure of it. Why not try it, at least?'

He stood quite still. She could feel the tension in him, and she kept her fingers pressed lightly but firmly against the shoulders that were so slender, yet so strong. To do the kind of work Tim did, holding large, heavy pieces of glass against a spinning copper wheel and use it to engrave patterns of intricate delicacy, called for immense strength, a tough, sinewy power that was quite different from the broad-chested muscularity of glassblowers like her grandfather, Joe Compson. He was a giant of a man, but Tim had inherited neither his size nor his disposition – that had been left for their younger brother, Mark. Tim took after the French side of the family – the Thietrys, slender, silver-eyed and volatile.

'Try it,' Cordelia said softly, and felt him relax slightly under her touch. But almost before she had time to feel relieved, he had tensed again and jerked himself away from her.

'Try it, you say? Take their job, that they've been so charitable as to offer me – work as an ordinary engraver, at patterns someone else has designed, patterns I don't even like – having to *cut* glass even when you know how barbaric I think such stuff, and hope all the time that someone may notice my work and think it better than the next man's? How long do you think I might have to wait for recognition, Cordelia? A month, two months – a year? *Ten* years?' He shook his head. 'No, I won't do it. I must find someone who will take me on *my* terms – someone who has the wit and the foresight to see that I have something more to offer than the ordinary engraver. I could have done that at home, Cordelia. I came here for freedom. I need to be able to evolve new colours, new mixtures, new shapes and styles. But it seems to me there's no one in this supposedly go-ahead country that's bold enough to let me try.'

'Now there,' said a voice from the doorway, making them both jump, 'I think you may be wrong.'

Cordelia whipped round, her heart kicking suddenly against her ribs, and felt her face burn.

'Mr Novak!' she took herself in hand sternly. 'I'm sorry – I'm afraid I forgot you were outside.'

'I decided I'd waited long enough. The front door was open so I marched straight in.' His dark blue eyes went from one to the other. 'Sorry if I interrupted a private discussion, only you weren't exactly whispering.'

'There was no reason why we should,' Cordelia said coldly, 'since we aren't in a public place. Well, you wanted to see our lodgings and here you are. Have a good look round. And then I expect you'll want to be on your way.'

'Not particularly,' he said amiably. 'I'm quite happy to visit with you two and carry on this interesting conversation.' He turned to Tim, who was standing in the middle of the room looking bemused. 'I understand you're hoping to revolutionise the glass industry here in Corning, Mr Henzel?'

'I didn't say that,' Tim muttered. He looked truculent and embarrassed. He shot Cordelia a glance under his brows but she lifted one shoulder slightly and moved away. Suddenly, she was tired of helping Tim and she wished that Jensen Novak would go. She sat down.

'But I've heard you're a fine engraver and that you have a great many new ideas.' The tall American looked reflectively at the younger man. Tim's brown curly hair was dishevelled from his having constantly run his fingers through it, his tie was half undone and his jacket loose. He looked like a schoolboy, just home from a game in the street. Not in the least, Cordelia thought, a figure to command respect from an elegant American businessman.

And Jensen Novak was elegant, there was no doubt about that. A good three inches taller than Tim, he wore a dove-grey suit with a waistcoat that fitted like a second skin over his fine cambric shirt. Across his flat waist hung a gold watch chain, his trousers were pressed with razor sharpness and his shoes shone like the ebony glass that Paul Henzel had used for his black cameo.

'Isn't it true?' Jensen persisted.

Tim shrugged. 'You'd better ask the people I've been to see. Thomas Hawkes – he's not interested at the moment in making glass, only cutting it. The Houghtons – they offered me a *job*, if you please!' The bitterness cut through his words. 'Turned me out into the street feeling like a beggar! Ask *them* if they think I'm a "fine engraver with new ideas" – they're more likely to tell you I'm a hoaxer and a charlatan. And my own sister thinks they're right!'

'Tim, I never said that!' Cordelia jumped to her feet. 'I merely said that from their point of view, it seemed a reasonable offer –'

'But you're not here to look at things from their point of view,' Tim broke in. 'You're supposed to be seeing *mine*. Otherwise, why did you come?'

Why indeed, Cordelia thought. Aloud, she said coldly, 'I came to look after you, Tim, and if you go on in this fashion I shall begin to wish we'd brought a nursemaid as well. You're behaving extremely childishly, and in front of a visitor too.' She turned and gave Jensen Novak her sweetest smile. 'Please forgive us, Mr Novak. You can't really be interested in our little problems.'

'Very nicely put,' the American said, 'but do you know, I think I am, rather. Your brother interests me, Miss Henzel. I'd like to hear some more.' He turned away from the indignant Cordelia and addressed himself once more to

Timothy. 'Do I understand, then, that you don't intend to go and work with Amory Houghton?'

'For,' Timothy corrected him. 'Work *for*. No, I damned well don't.'

'He's offered you a place but you don't wish to take it?'

'That's right. And wouldn't take a *partnership* if he offered it now, not if he went on his bended knees.' Tim's voice was rising again. 'I'd rather go back to England and I've already told Cordelia to pack. She doesn't like it here, anyway, she's miserable away from her friends.'

'Tim, that's not really true –'

'Isn't it?' He faced her. 'Tell me why you're looking like a lost kitten then ever since we left home. You've put a brave face on it all, even in these horrid rooms, but you don't fool me – I've been your twin for too long.'

Cordelia stared at him and turned away. How could she tell Timothy that it wasn't her friends she missed, but her studies? Her ambitions had been no secret before their father had died, but Tim had forgotten them. She could not remind him now.

'Not long enough, it seems,' she said as lightly as she could manage. 'I've simply been rather tired, Tim, no more than that. I like Corning and I don't want to leave. I don't want to go back to England and tell everyone we've failed.'

'Failed?' Timothy said sharply.

'Why, of course. How else would they see it if you had to confess that no one would take you into their glasshouse? And how do you think Mother would feel? She'd never trust you again – you'd be an ordinary engraver in your own family business then, and never again be given a chance to progress.'

She saw his expression change. The truculence faded, to be replaced by a thoughtfulness that disposed of the schoolboy look. He frowned and Cordelia dared to hope that she had at last found the right approach.

'I don't intend to go home as a failure,' he began, and she gave a sigh of relief. 'But that doesn't mean I have to stay in Corning. There are other places making glass.'

'All the same, I think your sister's right,' Jensen Novak said suddenly, and Cordelia jumped slightly at the sound of his voice. Absorbed once again in her brother, she had almost forgotten the presence of the other man. 'Leaving here at all is going to look like failure, wherever you go. I'd advise you to stick it out. Find someone else – some other glassmaker, willing to take a few risks. You were saying when I came in that there wasn't anyone here ready to do that – but I tell you again, you're wrong.'

Timothy looked at him, dawning hope warring with uncertainty. 'Wrong? You know of someone? Someone who'd let me try my ideas, who wouldn't want me to waste my time with cut glass and old-fashioned ideas?'

'I might,' Jensen Novak said, keeping his eyes on Timothy's face.

'Well, tell me who he is!' An eager boy again, Timothy snatched up his parcel. 'I'll go to see him straightaway.'

The American laughed and put out a hand. 'Not so fast, friend! You don't need to go anywhere. He's standing right here in front of you.'

'You?' Timothy laid the box down and stared. 'But –'

'Why so astounded? You knew I owned a glassmaking business.'

'When we talked together on the train, you said . . .' Timothy stammered, 'you said you'd been away from Corning, I thought perhaps –'

'You thought my businesses in Pennsylvania and Ohio had run into trouble, is that right? Or maybe you just didn't think about it at all – why should you, after all? No, I can assure you that all my glasshouses are doing very well indeed and I mean to expand here in Corning. And not just in traditional glass – I agree with you, it's time to try new ideas. Understand, if we're to work together it's got to be on my terms – your experiments could cost me a lot of money before they start to make any, that's if they ever do, and I'll want some return in the meantime. But I guess we can come to a satisfactory arrangement about that. Now – are you going to show me your glass? And then maybe we can begin to talk business.'

Cordelia, watching as the two men turned to the box of glass, felt as if a strong wind had suddenly blown through the room, sweeping everything before it. She looked at Timothy's flushed, excited face, clear of all the anger and humiliation that had marred it earlier.

She supposed she should be glad if this were to prove the chance Tim had been looking for. But something held her back from sharing the pleasure on her twin's face. Somehow, it was all happening far too easily.

Timothy, of course, had no doubts at all. He went off immediately to see Jensen's glasshouse, returning late in the afternoon full of enthusiasm. For almost an hour he strode exultantly about the two rooms, extolling the virtues of his new mentor, discoursing on his plans for the future – a future that had all at once, Cordelia thought cynically, become as glittering as the cut glass he so despised. At last, pausing for breath, he noticed her expression and frowned.

'What's on your mind, Cordelia? Don't you trust Mr Novak? Seems a pretty genuine sort of chap to me.'

Cordelia hesitated. She could hardly say that she distrusted Jensen Novak with every fibre of her body. Timothy would demand evidence, and she had none to offer. Nothing but a feeling, deep inside, that he hadn't told them everything about himself – that there was something he was concealing.

'It's just that he seems so keen to take you into his glass-house,' she said feebly, and her brother gave a snort of laughter.

'And that's enough to tell you he's a crackpot! Thank you for the compliment, sister dear – I suppose the Houghtons and all those others who refused my services rate high in your estimation as sane, sensible businessmen, likely to go far. Well, perhaps they will – but not as far as Novak Crystal, once I'm established there. They'll be sorry then that they didn't snatch at the opportunity when it was offered them.'

Cordelia gave him a cold look. 'Well, nobody will blow your bugle for you if you don't do it yourself,' she said. 'Let's trust that your self-confidence is not misplaced. And if things go wrong between you and Mr Novak, don't say I didn't warn you. Very well, I admit I know nothing against the man, I just don't think I like him much, that's all. He's too – too eager to push himself in.'

'He simply knows a good thing when he sees it,' Tim said complacently. 'All right, so I'm crowing – but why not? He's offered me the facilities of his glasshouse to do whatever I will, provided I spend some time cutting and engraving for him too. What could be better? And you'll see what I can do with the freedom he's offered me – I know what an opportunity it is, and I shan't waste it.'

Cordelia looked at her brother. His face was shining with delight and she thought of how he had looked that morning, sulky and disappointed, ready to throw away everything and return to England. And she reached out her hand and laid it on his.

'I know you won't waste your chances, Tim,' she said quietly. 'And I know you're not really boasting either. You know your worth and you don't see any reason to hide it – why should you? You're a fine glassmaker and you're going to astound everyone. You're doing the right thing, and I'll stand by you whatever happens.'

Timothy looked slightly surprised, as if he had never doubted that she would, and Cordelia felt a little ashamed. She should not have scolded him as she had done earlier; she should have offered support, sympathy, comfort; she should have remembered that Timothy was an artist, possibly a genius. He lived on a different plane from other men and allowances must be made.

But she would have been happier if his excitement had not been brought about by an alliance with Jensen Novak.

Chapter Five

Jensen Novak walked slowly beside the Chemung river, lost in thought.

He was still not certain that returning to Corning, as a permanent arrangement, was a good idea. He'd been back often enough on quick visits, of course – to see to things at the glasshouse, to look up one or two old friends, even to recruit workers for the business in Findlay, or Pennsylvania. But to live here – was it really wise? Wouldn't it just be stirring up old memories?

He shook himself impatiently. There were memories everywhere, and most of them painful. Staying in White Mills, with all the reminders there, could be no worse than returning here where Freya's fragile ghost still haunted the streets. And he'd stuck that for long enough, hadn't he? Could this be any worse?

Those two Henzels had brought it all back, he knew that. Coming here all wide-eyed and innocent, the boy expecting to land a prime position in one of the best glasshouses, the girl tossing that gleaming coppery head of hers and flashing independence with her green eyes at anyone who dared offer help. My God, but she was a proud little devil! And if young Timothy had the talent, she certainly had enough personality and determination for the two of them. If that was what she was like as a sister, Jensen hardly dared consider what she might be like as a wife.

Not that he was thinking of her in those terms, even if he'd been able to. But some man would, some day. And Jensen hoped that whoever it was, he'd appreciate just what he was taking on – that he'd be man enough to cope with her. A girl like that could present a challenge to the most masterful of husbands.

Jensen shook himself impatiently. What was he doing, thinking this way? Cordelia Henzel and her future were nothing to him – only in as much as her brother was concerned. And in Timothy Henzel's future, he *was* interested.

Jensen, back in Corning with his own memories and his own decisions to be made, had been mildly amused at first by the two youngsters he had met on the train and had been glad enough to be diverted by Timothy's eager questions; although, even while answering them, he had found his eyes constantly straying to the pale face of the girl who sat with her eyes half closed in the corner, clearly tired almost to death yet fighting not to give in. His own curiosity aroused, he had found himself wondering about them. He had offered the use of his trap as much from a desire to further the acquaintance as from helpfulness. And when he had set out to call at Harry Henzel's house a few days later he had found himself looking forward to meeting them again.

He could barely explain to himself why he had been so ready at first to take Timothy Henzel into his glasshouse and give him the facilities he asked for. But when he saw the glass the young man produced, and heard him talk of his ideas, he knew that he was not making a mistake. Timothy Henzel had something that only a few glassmakers just then could display – vision. And he also had the courage to follow that vision through, and make glass of it.

He reminded Jensen of himself as a young boy, urging his father to go into business alone, to set up his own glasshouse, to expand. And perhaps that was the attraction – perhaps, through Timothy Henzel, Jensen was trying to recover his own youth, live it once more but without the pain. At the thought, he snorted contemptuously. What

94

utter nonsense! He had enough to do with living his own life, never mind trying to live someone else's.

All the same, he wasn't displeased at the idea of seeing more of the young Henzels and watching how they made out in their new endeavours. Particularly the girl. Jensen had a feeling she was going to cause quite a storm in the place before she was through. He just hoped she didn't allow that independent spirit of hers to make life too hard. It was difficult enough, making your way in a new country.

Jensen Novak's own life had not been easy. He recalled only too clearly the hardships of his childhood, the need that had finally driven his father to abandon his homeland and take ship for America. The New World, it had been called, the land of the free, where men of all countries came together to forge the bonds of a new nation. There, all men were equal and the only requirement made of you was a willingness to work hard. Well, his father had had that and so had he . . . but that hadn't put an end to hardship. At least, not for a long time.

Jensen remembered the boarding house where they had first lived, he and his parents and his little sister Freya. The overcrowding, the damp, the sheer squalor of living several families to a room with no space to dry wet clothes, no possibility of keeping things clean. There was always noise, he thought with a shudder, always a baby crying or a woman weeping, a man bawling drunkenly or children squabbling. The only escape had been to the glasshouse where he and his father had obtained work, and they were glad enough to get away from the crowded room to the factory, glad enough to work all the hours their employer would give them and to save their hard-earned dollars for a room of their own.

Perhaps it hadn't taken too long, though it seemed an eternity at the time. But at last they were out of the boarding

95

house and had not one but two rooms of their own, in a large house near the factory. From there, Jensen had been able to walk down to the river when his work was over and look across at the wooded hills, at the grand homes that were being built there, higher and higher as the forest was cleared. The more prosperous a man was, the higher he lived up the hill; and the fifteen-year-old Jensen had stared hungrily across the river and made up his mind that one day he would own the highest house of all. A house with so many rooms that he would never be able to count them; a house fit for a queen, in which he would install his mother and his little sister.

But already it was too late for Freya. Never strong, she had begun to show signs of the consumption that attacked so many who lived in overcrowded conditions. Her bright eyes and flushed cheeks gave her at first a spurious appearance of health, soon belied by the body that grew thinner daily in spite of her ravenous but quickly satisfied appetite. The cough that had merely irritated the other occupants of their shared room became a serious worry to the little family. When they found blood spattering her pillow one morning, they looked at each other with fear in their eyes.

From then on, they took every possible care of Freya. Every spare cent went towards nourishing foods – eggs, milk from their neighbour's cow, wine – and medicines. But for little Freya it had always been too late. She died on the day before their first Christmas in America, and Jensen, hearing his parents' bitter laments at having left the country they had loved and brought their frail daughter to an even harder life, held her cooling body in his arms and vowed again that he would one day build the highest house in Corning and make the name Novak respected throughout the State.

'Just so that it'll have been worthwhile,' he muttered,

kissing the unresponsive lips. 'Just so that your life won't have been wasted.'

After that, it had seemed that there was nothing to do but work. Jensen and his father continued to go each day to the glass factory which had been moved here from Brooklyn when industrial unrest had begun to threaten production – for America was not such a new country that it could escape the growing trend towards trade unions and strikes. They worked hard and earned good wages. Jensen became a fine glass-cutter and one day proposed to his father that they should set up their own cutting shop.

'We could do well,' he urged, his mind set on that high house overlooking the town. 'We've enough money saved to start up. We can buy in blanks and take on a boy. We could make enough to live on and save some more – start our own glasshouse next, with one pot at first, then a second pot, then a third. If we don't do it, we'll be working for Amory Houghton for the rest of our lives and making him rich. Wouldn't we rather be rich ourselves?'

'Rich?' Lars Novak repeated, as if it were a word new to his vocabulary. 'Son, I've never thought of being rich, only of having enough to live comfortably.'

'Well, I have.' Jensen's young face was set with determination, his fine brows and firm, sculpted mouth echoing the same straight line. 'Ever since Freya died, I've thought of being rich. I never mean to let a member of my family die like that again, Pappa – of not having enough. If we could have afforded the right food, the right medicine, a decent home to live in –'

'It was all my fault,' Lars said, his shoulders sinking in his habitual depression. 'I should never have brought her here. We were better off at home –'

'We were *not* better off at home,' Jensen said firmly. 'If we had stayed at home, Freya would have died all the sooner. I'm sorry, Pappa, but that's the truth. We were just beginning to get our heads above water in this country, but for Freya it was too late before we even came. You know she was always troubled by that cough . . . But it's never going to happen again. We're going to be rich, like the Houghtons. We're going to live in a fine house, wear good clothes, and have servants to do the work that Momma does now. I promise you.'

Lars, too weary to argue, had given in and they had set up their own small glassworks. Again, it had been hard, but eventually their fortunes had worked out as Jensen had predicted. Looking for expansion, they had gone to Pennsylvania and then to Ohio. And then, with the business truly established at last, with the comfortable home and servants Jensen had promised, Lars Novak had finally given up. The depression that had haunted him for years had beaten him at last and one day he had simply turned his face to the wall and died.

Of the years that had followed his father's death, Jensen did not allow himself to think. There had been happiness in them; but remembering that happiness forced him also to think of the pain. And even now he found the memories almost impossible to tolerate.

Instead, he turned and paced slowly back along the river bank and thought of Timothy Henzel. And, reluctantly, of his sister, Cordelia.

Timothy strode down towards the town, his arms swinging, step jaunty. He had already forgotten what he had considered his humiliation at the hands of Amory and Alanson Houghton. All his attention now was focused on the new and shining future which was opening before him with Jensen Novak.

What a fine man the American was! The kind of man you

knew must exist in this exciting country, a man who had come seeking the gold that they said paved the streets, and had found it. And was now willing to share some of that gold in the seeking of beauty, of art; beauty and art that would themselves bring even greater riches.

It took a man of vision to see that. And Timothy, arriving at Tioga Street where the railroad had brought him and Cordelia on that first day, thought contemptuously that the other manufacturers he had visited, big and important though they were in Corning, lacked that vision. They'd had everything their own way; with no one else making glass on any large scale, they had been able to make any kind of glass they chose and be confident of a market. They had grown complacent.

Well, he and Jensen would soon change that. The glass manufacturers of Corning were going to be surprised when Novak Crystal began to capture the market with the new, exciting styles he meant to produce. Already, his head was buzzing with ideas and he could hardly wait to begin to put them into practice.

The railroad station was crowded and busy, but Timothy spared it barely a glance. No doubt his Uncle Harry, when at home, spent a good deal of time here, watching the locomotives that had been his life, talking with the men who designed and drove them. Harry had been a respected railroad engineer and Bob Robinson had told Timothy that his advice was still sought by his successors who frequently came this way. Over twelve thousand trains passed through Corning each year and the station here on Tioga, built just over fifteen years ago, was an imposing red-brick building of three storeys which impressed visitors to the town.

Timothy was on his way to the glasshouse and had not intended to linger at the station. But its bustle had caught his attention and he stopped for a moment, watching the new arrivals. Most of them, he guessed, were businessmen or commercial travellers, coming to discuss their work with the local manufacturers or to show their wares in the local stores. Some were clearly on family visits, and these were being welcomed joyfully by little knots of people waiting on the sidewalk. A few, he thought, were probably immigrants, for they looked weary and bewildered as they climbed down from the carriages, and if there was no one there to welcome them they stood helplessly surrounded by pitiful heaps of luggage before slowly making their way towards the town.

As the arrivals moved away, other people took their places – those who were about to depart. Mostly, it was easy to recognise them and even to guess the results of their visits: businessmen were serious or satisfied; commercial travellers jaunty or downcast. Families stood about in little groups either making polite conversation or lost, at the end of what had been perhaps an overlong visit, for further words. One cluster of people was dressed in black and each wore a solemn expression; another, laughing and chattering, surrounded a radiant young couple dressed in wedding finery.

But it was the small tableau nearest to Timothy that caught and held his attention. A young man, no more than two or three years older than Timothy himself, and a girl a little younger, with the dark hair and olive complexion of the Italian immigrants Timothy had seen around the town. They were standing close together, their hands entwined, with a look on their faces so despairing that Timothy told himself he ought not to be staring, and turned away.

But as he turned, he saw that there was a third person, also part of the tableau – a second black-haired girl, who stood a little apart and watched – and he could not prevent himself from looking again. There was something about the second girl's face that caught at his heart; something in the dark blue eyes, brilliant with the tears that stood in them, that seemed to pluck at a string somewhere inside him and set up a resonance that trembled through his whole body. He moved slightly, deeper into the shadow of the wall, and watched, fascinated.

The boy and girl, standing so still and so engrossed in each other, were clearly lovers about to be parted. It was a scene that must have been enacted here and on other railway stations a thousand times. But did they all gaze at each other with such entreaty, such anguish? And the second girl – who was she? The distress in her face was painful to see, yet she held no man in her arms. And Timothy was surprised by a sudden desire to take her in his own arms and comfort her, soothe away the pain and wipe the vivid eyes dry.

The lovers were talking to each other, but he could not hear the words; the station was filled with noise, of voices chattering and calling to each other, of boxes being unloaded and flung to the ground, of carts being wheeled to and fro and, above all, of the locomotive, sighing and spluttering as it made ready to move off again. A messenger boy strolled past whistling, and somewhere nearby a woman laughed raucously. The voices of the boy and the girl were lost.

But Timothy needed no words. He watched the girl lift her wet face and push back the thick black hair that streamed down her back, and he felt suddenly embarrassed. What was he doing, watching them? But he could not turn away.

The young man was saying something now, words of reassurance perhaps, telling his sweetheart that he would soon be back, that their separation wouldn't last long. Perhaps he was going away to work. All three were dressed shabbily. Perhaps they were too poor even to marry; he had to help support his own family, and she –

101

The air was split by a shrill whistle and the two caught each other in their arms and hugged. At the second impatient screech from the engine they held apart, staring into each other's eyes for a moment. The second girl stepped forward, holding up her arms and as a porter called out, the boy bent his head to give each girl a quick, final kiss, and climbed on to the train.

The locomotive steamed slowly out of the station. Timothy watched as the two girls, arms around each other now, stood quite still until it was completely out sight. They turned and said something to each other, and then the first girl walked rapidly away, out of the station. The second, her eyes still filled with tears, stumbled towards the track.

She didn't see the second train already entering the station. But Timothy, still watching her, heard its warning sound. He heard, too, the shouts of other bystanders, was conscious of their movements as the girl walked straight into the path of the oncoming engine. He was not even aware of moving himself. But he was first to fling himself at her, first to catch her arm and drag her back from danger, first to hold her against him as if afraid that she would tear herself out of his arms.

'What are you doing, for God's sake? Don't you realise you could have been killed?'

She stared up at him. He saw that her vivid eyes were surrounded by thick, dark lashes, that even her eyelids had a smoky blueness about them. The pupils were wide with shock, the smooth skin of her cheeks white.

'Mother of Christ,' she whispered, 'I wasn't even thinking about another train. Are ye telling me ye saved my life?'

'He surely did,' a voice said, and Timothy saw that they were surrounded by people, the businessmen, commercial travellers and family groups. 'You've got a deal to thank this young man for, miss. If it hadn't been for him, you'd be talking your way in past St Peter now, and that's a fact.'

The girl shivered. She felt light and slender in Timothy's arms, as fragile as a bird and quivering with the fear a bird shows when held in a boy's hand. He loosened his clasp slightly, but kept one arm around her, fearing that she would fall if he let her go and reluctant to release the trembling body.

'You need something to drink, to take away the shock,' he said gently. 'Come with me.'

'Take her to the waiting room and get her some good hot coffee,' someone advised, and Timothy, still accompanied by a small group of people all offering advice, led the girl to the door of the refreshment room. Here, their advisers left them, and he took her in and settled her at a table while he fetched two coffees.

'Drink that. It'll make you feel better.'

She looked at him, still dazed, her full lips slightly parted, still quivering a little. Gently, Timothy reached across and held one arm behind her shoulders, steadying her head while he lifted the steaming cup to her mouth. She sipped obediently and then took a deep breath.

'Thank ye, sir,' she said, and he recognised her accent as Irish. 'I can manage it myself now.'

'Are you sure?' He removed his arm and watched as she lifted the cup, drinking deeply as if she were genuinely thirsty as well as shaken. He looked at her clothes and noticed again how shabby they were. 'Would you like something to eat as well?'

Instantly, she shook her head. 'Oh no, sir, thank ye, I've been enough trouble as it is.' But Timothy, his senses sharpened, caught the involuntary flicker of her eyes and got up. He went to the counter and came back with a plate of bread and cheese which he placed in front of her.

'Please have this. I'm sure you haven't eaten this morning,

you look so pale. Probably it was the excitement of having to come to the station.' he added delicately.

'Yes, I expect it was.' She looked at the food, then at his face. 'Ye really shouldn't, though, sir. I don't need –'

'Please eat it,' Timothy said gently, and met her eyes. For a moment, their gaze held; he felt the hairs on the back of his neck begin to rise. And then she lowered her eyes and said quietly, 'Thank ye, sir.'

Timothy watched her as she ate. The colour was already coming back into her cheeks, a colour that reminded him of the wild hedgerow roses at home. Her teeth were small but strong and white, like gleaming pearls, sheltered by the red lips. Her face was thin under the mass of curling black hair; it ought to be round, he thought, and knew that he had been right about her; she was poor and didn't get enough to eat.

'Where do you live?' he asked, and she looked up as if startled to find him still there.

'On the other side of the river, sir, in Knoxville. There's a good few Irish around there.'

'You live with your family?'

'Aye, me mother and father and six brothers and sisters.' She finished the cheese and drank the last of the coffee. 'Thank ye sir, that was real good.'

'Don't go yet. Have another cup of coffee.' She looked at him uncertainly and he fetched the second cup, half afraid that she would disappear while he was at the counter. The refreshment room was full of bustle and noise, but no one else was sitting at their table when he got back. He set the cup before her and sat opposite.

'So you're a family of seven. That's quite a lot.'

She shook her head. 'It's not all of us, sir. I've two more sisters away at service and a brother –' Her eyes filled with tears and she looked down quickly at her coffee –' well, me brother, he's just gone away, sir. I was seeing him off just now. That's why I wasn't looking where I was going, I guess.'

Her brother! Timothy stared at her. 'Where is he going?'

The thin shoulders shrugged. 'I don't know. Somewhere – anywhere. Wherever the train takes him. He's gone off to find his fortune somewhere else. I don't know when I'll see him again.'

So the young man had been her brother and the other girl, as Timothy had surmised, his sweetheart. Timothy tried to imagine having to leave Cordelia, perhaps to come to America alone.

She brushed away the tears and got up. 'I'll have to go now, sir. I've been away long enough as it is. Thank ye for the coffee and the cheese – they've done me real good. And thank ye for saving me from the train.'

She gave him a brief smile, no less enchanting for the tears that were still shining on her cheeks, and turned. Timothy scrambled to his feet.

'Wait! Don't go yet –'

But she was already at the door. And as he followed her, he tripped over a large bag that someone had just set down beside the next table. Catching at the table to save himself, he all but pulled it over, spilling two cups of coffee in the process. And by the time order had been restored and he had made his apologies and escaped, the girl had vanished.

Damn! he thought, standing in the now empty station. And I don't even know her name.

He couldn't even remember where she had told him she lived.

Grainne hurried home across the bridge, passing the big glass-works with barely a glance. Her father was in there, and several other members of her family. Her mother was in the packing shed, where Grainne herself ought to be at this very moment. But she couldn't have let Declan and Carina go to the station alone, and she couldn't go back to work without giving an eye to little Bridget and making sure she was all right.

She thought again of the events of the previous night, and shivered. It had been nothing unusual, her father coming home drunk on a Friday – most of his cronies went straight to the saloon when they received their pay. It wasn't unusual for him to be in a bad temper either, blaming everybody but himself for the shortcomings which a day later would fill him with remorse. But he had never come home in quite such a furious rage, so that little Bridget shrank back on the old sofa against the wall and even young Danny retreated, wide-eyed and wary.

It wasn't his youngest children who had angered Kevin O'Donnell, though. It was his eldest son's name that he roared out when he came thundering through the door as his wife Mary peeled potatoes at the sink and Grainne mixed flour for a pudding to fill the family's bellies.

'Declan! Where is he? Where's the boy who's going to bring shame on this house? Don't try to hide him, for I'll find him in the end.'

Mary turned and stared at him, astonished. 'Hide Declan? Why would I be wanting to do that? And what sort of shame is he likely to bring on us – *he* doesn't come home drunk every Friday pay-day!'

Kevin stood in the middle of the room, swaying a little, glaring at her. 'Mind your tongue, woman! It's Declan I'm wanting. And when I find him, by God, I'll give him a thrashing he'll not forget for the rest of his life – now where is he?'

Mary dropped the potato she was peeling back into the water and came quickly across the kitchen to her husband. She laid both hands on his arms and looked up into his face. 'You're not well, Kevin. Ye need to lie down for a bit. Go along in and rest, and I'll call ye when supper's ready –'

'Supper!' He shook her off. 'I'll not let a bite past my lips until I've settled things with that boy.' He was unbuckling his heavy belt as he spoke, and Grainne lifted her hand to her mouth. Kevin had been known to swing with a large, heavy hand at any of his children who annoyed him, but even when drunk he had never taken his belt to them. What could Declan have done? And how could her father expect to thrash a son who was himself a grown man and as big as he?

'Kevin, please! Ye must tell me what's wrong. Declan's done nothing to be ashamed of, I know it – isn't he my own son and as fine a boy as ever crossed the sea? It's a mistake, Kevin, it has to be.'

'Mistake is it?' He glowered down at her. 'So I'm making a mistake, am I, when I see my son, my own boy, consorting with one of those Italian harlots? I suppose ye think I should smile and shake her by the hand, give her dirty face a kiss even and bring her home for supper? Why, I'd rather ask the Devil himself in for a cup of tea, and that's the truth of it.'

'Then perhaps you'd better do that, since he's more fit company for ye than a decent girl,' exclaimed a voice from the door, and they all swung round. Grainne saw her father's face darken and his hands went again to his belt while Mary thrust herself forward, standing between her husband and her son, her hands already in the air as if to ward off the blows she expected to fall.

'Kevin, you're not to touch him!' She turned to Declan, whose bulk now filled the doorway. 'Your father's not himself, Declan – he doesn't know what he's saying. I'll just get him to rest for a while and then we'll have our supper –'

'He knows full well what he's saying,' Declan growled, and Grainne thought how much like his father he looked in that moment – big and solid, his face dark with anger, eyes flashing dangerously. 'And I heard every word. So she's a harlot, is she?' he went on, addressing his father now. 'Ye'll take back that word. Or *I'll* give ye a thrashing ye'll remember all your life.'

'Ye'll not lift a finger towards your father! And he'll not touch ye either. I won't have fighting in this house, I'm warning the both of ye –'

Kevin thrust his wife aside. 'Keep out of this, Mary. I'll deal with the young jackanapes.' He came close to his son, pushing his red face forward. 'So I'll take the word back, will I? And just give me one good reason why I should.'

'Because it's not true! Carina's a decent girl and she comes from a decent family. She –'

'*Decent*, is it?' Kevin gave a hoot of sneering laughter. 'D'ye hear that, Mary? A *decent* Italian girl! Well, Satan must have been looking the other way when she was born, for she's the only one on God's earth. Scum, the Italians are, and well ye know it,' he went on, turning swiftly back to Declan. 'And I'll not have any son of mine seen with one, and so I'm telling ye.'

'Kevin, they're not that bad – they're good Catholics, and they work hard –'

'Aye, and take all our jobs! Isn't that just what they came over here for, to take the bread out of honest, hard-working Irishmen's mouths? They should have been turned back at Ellis, the whole damn' lot of them, and never allowed into a decent country. Anyone around here'll tell ye that.' Once again, he turned back to Declan. 'Ye'll not be seeing any more of that girl,' he stated. 'Understand?'

'I understand you,' Declan said quietly. 'But I'll see Carina as much as I like. And nothing ye say or do is going to stop me.' He raised his voice above his father's roar of rage. 'And ye'll take back that word ye used about her, or I swear I'll murder ye!'

Grainne cried out then, but her voice was lost in the noise and confusion as the two men launched themselves at each other. She heard her mother's scream, little Bridget's wail of fright and young Danny's shout of fear and anger; she heard Kevin's agonised fury as his great fists punched at Declan and met the wall instead. They came together in a violent hug of rage and staggered out into the yard; and Grainne, clutching at her mother, followed them and saw them raining blows on each other, pushing, punching, kicking and gouging. They fell to the ground and rolled together; one was on top, banging the other's head, one was stretching stiff and lethal fingers towards the other's eyes. It was a fight such as she had never seen before, in all the brawls that were so regular a part of life in this area of Corning; and there was nothing anyone could do to stop them.

Mary rushed inside and came out with the bowl of water and potato peelings. She threw it over them, but they didn't even notice it. The neighbours had begun to collect and she entreated them to stop it somehow, but the men shook their heads. It was a private fight, they said, and they wouldn't be thanked for interfering – besides, who could get near enough? The two bodies were kicking and rolling in the dust; there was nothing to be done but wait until they tired, or one was dead.

'But it's Kevin and Declan!' Mary implored them. 'I can't stand by and let them kill each other. Please help me – please, put a stop to it.'

'They'll stop when they've had enough, missus,' one of the men said. 'You don't have to worry, they won't really hurt each other.'

'They've hurt each other already,' Mary said sadly. 'Nothing will ever be the same again now.'

The two men were tiring; Grainne could see that her father, older and the worse for drink already, was almost at the end of his strength. She ran forward and caught at her brother's shoulders, tugging him away. 'Leave it now, Declan. Can't ye see he's had enough? Let him up, now.'

Declan turned and stared up at her. His eyes were dazed. Blood ran down his face from a cut above his eyebrow, and his face was grimy from dirty water, potato peelings and dust from the ground.

'Leave it,' Grainne repeated quietly, and drew him unresisting to his feet.

Mary knelt beside her husband and lifted his head against her breast. His nose was pouring with blood and one eye was already swelling and blackened. He was groaning; he lifted one hand and Grainne saw that two of the fingers were dislocated and stood out at an angle that sickened her.

'Oh, Declan, Declan, what have ye done?' she murmured and looked him over. 'Are ye hurt yourself, now?'

He felt himself gingerly all over. 'Not bad, I don't think.' His dark eyes, so like her own, were bewildered. 'Grainne, I had to do it. He called Carina a – a –'

'I heard him. Come inside and get washed. You've blood coming from somewhere . . . And we'll need someone to set me Dad's fingers, it looks as if you've broken them, and God knows what other damage you've done.'

'He did that himself, hitting the wall when I ducked. Grainne, I never meant – but when he said that –'

'I know, I know.' She took him inside and took the kettle from the fire. 'Sit down and I'll fetch the bowl and a cloth.' She became aware of Bridget, still crouched against the wall, her eyes wide with terror. 'It's all right, Bridget, it's all over now. Nothing else is going to happen. Everything's going to be all right.'

But she knew that nothing was going to be all right, ever again.

It was clear from that moment that the two men would

never be able to live in the same house after that; Kevin would never accept his son's relationship with one of the hated Italians. And although it had clearly broken her heart to do so, it was Declan whom Mary O'Donnell had sent away.

'Ye know it's the only way,' she said, tears running down her cheeks. 'He's me husband and that's all there is to be said about it.' She looked at her eldest son and touched his bruised cheek with her fingers. 'You're young, ye'll make a good life somewhere,' she said softly. 'Go and find a fortune, and maybe one day ye'll be able to come back to us. But it has to be this way now, ye know that.'

'I'll come back to Corning to fetch Carina when I'm settled. But I'll not come back here – not while he's here,' Declan said warningly, and she shook her head.

'I know that, son.'

Declan had gone out then and they all knew that he had gone to the Italian community by the railroad tracks, to tell Carina what had happened. Would she go with him? Grainne wondered. But when he came back, her brother told her that Carina must stay here in Corning. 'They're even poorer than we are,' he said miserably. 'They can't manage without the money she earns. And I can't ask her to come away with me, when I don't know where I'll need to go or what I'll have to do . . . But I'll come back for her one day,' he said with fierce determination. 'And, until then, will ye be a friend to her, Grainne?'

They had barely slept that night. Declan had little enough to pack, but somehow they'd found a good many little things to make his new life more comfortable. And neither Grainne nor her brother had gone to bed; they'd simply stayed there in the kitchen, wanting to be close until the last moment, knowing that it might be years before they could be together again. As the grey dawn crept into the rooms

111

that they rented in the big lodging house, they had woken from an uneasy sleep on kitchen chairs and stretched their limbs uncomfortably.

'It's almost time to go,' Grainne said softly, and Declan nodded.

She packed up the last of the bread in the house with a bit of cheese, and slipped it into his pocket. And then, without waking any of the rest of the family, they left the house and walked through Knoxville and across the bridge to the Tioga Street station, where Carina stood waiting, her eyes swollen with tears and her face heavy with grief.

Well, it was over now. Declan had gone and was on his way to Buffalo. She wondered when she would see him again, and knew that it might not be for years.

The young man who had saved her from the train was forgotten.

Chapter Six

The trees hung weary branches over the sidewalks, giving a shade barely cooler than the dusty road that lay exposed to the full blaze of the sun. In front of each house, the grass was brown and dry, the few flowers still surviving seemed to gasp for water. Cordelia, setting out to do the morning shopping, paused as she came out of the house and looked at them pityingly. Since coming to the lodging-house, she had made it her task to look after the scrap of garden in front of her window, and she had intended to water the flowers last night but had forgotten. Now they would have to wait until evening, for to water them in this direct heat would do more harm than good.

As the summer had progressed, the weather had grown hotter than she had believed possible. She had known it would be warmer than in England of course – but knowing and experiencing seemed to be two different matters. It was almost impossible to keep cool. Opening the windows seemed to make matters worse indoors, letting in the sultry air, though the wire screens at each door and window did at least keep the flies out.

Cordelia raised her parasol. It was far too elegant for morning shopping, but her other one had been torn and she had not had time to mend it. Housekeeping, even in two rooms, was taking up more time than she had anticipated. There always seemed to be something to do – washing, sweeping the dust from the floor, shopping for and cooking their supper on the small stove that made the room even hotter – there was no end to it. During the past few weeks, she thought wryly, she had learned a great deal of respect for the servants at Henzel Court.

Slowly, she walked down to the town, stopping at the railroad-crossing gates to wait for a train to pass. The flagman, recognising her, gave her a cheerful greeting and she smiled at him. It was comforting to be known, even if only by a few people; accustomed to being acknowledged by almost everyone in Wordsley, she still felt something of an alien in this little town. Would she ever feel completely at home here, or would she always be a stranger?

Market Street was quiet this morning. Unlike the main streets of many small American towns and villages, its buildings were all of brick and stone – a disastrous fire had swept along its length forty years ago and destroyed the wooden structures, forcing upon Corning a modernisation that might otherwise have only taken place piecemeal. Now, it was wide and gracious, with four- or five-storey buildings on either side; the road itself was paved with red Corning bricks, and a sidewalk on either side made it possible to walk along and browse in shop windows without danger from the new trolley cars which rattled along the tracks laid down the middle of the street.

Cordelia loved Market Street. She enjoyed its feeling of spaciousness, so different from the narrow streets of Stourbridge, and she liked the tall red buildings with their flat faces and wide windows. She walked slowly, thinking of the gaiety it had presented soon after she and Timothy had arrived, when the country had been celebrating the Fourth of July. The buildings had been draped with flags and banners, bunting had been stretched across the road from one rooftop to another and the shop windows had been filled with colour. The whole town had been alive with celebration on that day, and she and Tim, guided by the Robinsons, had joined in, feeling themselves welcomed by this warm-hearted community.

But since then, the jubilation fading as people returned to their normal lives, Cordelia had felt once again that she was a stranger. And she knew that it was because she had nothing to do with her life – no work of her own to make her feel needed and useful. The cooking, washing and sweeping she discounted. These were just aspects of living. They were not real work, not as her mother and her grandmother knew it.

For once there were no trolleys clattering along the street; just a few carts and traps waiting beside the sidewalk. The heat beat up from the red brick paving. Cordelia crossed over to be in the shade and hesitated for a moment, wondering which way to go next.

'Good morning, Miss Henzel. Nice to see you. Hot enough for you?'

Cordelia turned quickly and saw Jensen Novak emerging from a nearby shop, bare-headed as usual, his face tanned so that his teeth gleamed whiter than ever when he smiled. For a moment, she felt breathless, but her voice was steady enough as she answered.

'Good morning, Mr Novak. Yes, it is warm, isn't it – warmer than I'm accustomed to, I admit.' Heavens, she sounded like some prim miss from a romantic novel! Cordelia shook herself angrily. Why did this man always make her react so unnaturally – as if she were a doll? She took a breath and started again, smiling with a little more ease.

'To tell you the truth,' she said, 'we never have it so warm in England and I don't know quite how to cope with it.'

'With an ice-cold lemonade for a start,' he said and touched her elbow with his fingertips. 'Come and share one with me and tell me all your news.'

Cordelia hesitated, but what harm could there be in it after all? She followed him into the Pickwick Hotel, where they sat in a small, discreet parlour. Jensen Novak ordered a lemonade for Cordelia and a beer for himself and then sat back in his chair, studying her with a frankness that made her blush.

'I don't know what you find so interesting about me,' she remarked tartly, and he laughed.

'All kinds of things, Miss Henzel – you've no idea!' The drinks arrived and he lifted his beer to her as if proposing a toast. 'To your very good health and a long life in Corning. Or isn't that what you would wish for?'

'Very good health, yes; a long life in Corning – I don't know.' Cordelia sipped the lemonade. It was freshly made and deliciously sharp and cold. 'I haven't really been here long enough to decide.'

'But didn't you say you loved Corning already, and didn't want to leave it? You remember – the day when I came to talk to your brother.' He watched her face and said quietly, 'That was simply for his benefit, wasn't it? To make him stay and try again when he felt that Crystal City was rejecting him.'

'Well, and suppose it was?'

'Heavens above, don't look so truculent – I admire you for it. And I think your brother is a very lucky man.'

'I think so too,' Cordelia said. 'It was very good of you to take him on. He's a wonderful glassmaker, but he can be difficult.'

'Oh, I know that!' Novak replied, laughing again. 'When your brother has an idea in his head, he's as stubborn as a Missouri mule. But we're shaking down pretty well together, taking all things into consideration.'

Cordelia looked at him with anxiety. 'You sound as if you have reservations. You're not sorry you gave Tim his chance?'

'Not sorry at all. He's going to make a fine glassmaker – provided he keeps his feet on the ground. He's a little liable to fly off at a tangent, you know, and he's very much aware of his own worth.'

'You mean he's conceited,' Cordelia said bluntly.

'Not yet. Not entirely. But – yes, there's a risk. He's young, of course, and still has some maturing to do.' The blue eyes darkened suddenly under their firm brows. He looked down at his glass for a moment, as if debating what to say, then added quietly, 'He needs you more than he thinks. I guess you're the one who has the most influence with him.'

Cordelia looked at him questioningly. Then she said, 'You're trying to tell me something, aren't you, Mr Novak? You're not happy about Tim. Why?'

He gave her a long, steady look. 'There's nothing to tell you – not at present. Timothy's not giving me any worries at all, and I hope it'll carry on that way. But he needs watching. He came to America for freedom and by heck he's got it. No doting mamma at his elbow at home, no watchful father at work. He can come and go as he pleases and nobody to wonder where or when – except for you.'

'I don't understand what you're saying,' Cordelia said. 'Are you expecting Tim to get into some kind of scrape?'

'He could get into all kinds of scrapes.' Jensen Novak hitched his chair forward a little and looked seriously into her face. 'Miss Henzel, your brother could very well be the genius he already half believes himself to be. I hope he is. He could give the world some beautiful glass. But he's also a very normal young man. He's in a new country and he feels himself to be without restrictions. That could go to his head. He's making friends and not all of them are the kind you or I would choose for him. That's normal too – any young man is going to make friends his family don't alto-gether like. But in his home town, he'd be restrained by the conventions and expectations of the people he lives amongst. Here it's different. And without anyone to guide him –'

'You seem to know all about these new friends,' Cordelia said. 'Can't you guide him?'

'I would. But I shan't be here much longer. That's why I wanted to speak to you.'

'You're going away?' Cordelia stared at him.

'Shortly, yes. I have to attend to my other businesses, and I have some personal affairs to sort out.'

'Oh.' Cordelia felt oddly blank. 'But you – you will be coming back?'

'Oh yes.' He smiled at her. 'I'll be coming back.'

There was a short silence. Cordelia lifted her glass and sipped the cool liquid. She could think of nothing to say. At last she said, 'You don't really think Tim is in any kind of . . . danger, do you?'

'Danger? Of what?'

'Of getting into trouble,' she said impatiently. 'Mr Novak, you brought the subject up –'

'Indeed I did, and I'm sorry, my thoughts had wandered elsewhere.' He twisted his mouth in apology. 'Miss Henzel –'

'Oh, please,' Cordelia broke in, 'can't we dispense with all that? Can't you call me Cordelia? We meet enough, it seems, and all this *Mr Novak, Miss Henzel* wastes so much time.'

She saw his eyebrows go up and looked down into her glass, feeling her cheeks grow hot. She was surprised herself by her sudden outburst; she had certainly not intended it. Indeed, she felt she hardly knew him at all; then she heard him say in a tone that was far from displeased, 'I'd be delighted. And you, of course, will call me Jensen.' And it was done. Not, perhaps, in the way her school etiquette books had decreed it should happen, but things did seem different in America.

118

After a slight pause, Jensen Novak began to speak again. 'Don't let my words worry you too much, Cordelia. I don't really think Tim will get into any serious scrapes. He's far too intelligent for that. I just don't like some of the company he's beginning to keep –'

'But surely they must be your own employees – people he's met in your company.'

'That's not entirely true, though I admit that some of these friends he's making are amongst my own men – young clerks, a salesman, no harm in them bar a little wildness, perhaps. But there's nothing I can do about that. I don't employ men because of their morals but because of their skills.' He glanced at her and she nodded reluctantly. 'And the others – well, there's young Hyde, from the bank, Davis the undertaker's son – they're all of them of what you English would call "good family".'

'So what is your objection?'

'Miss Henzel – Cordelia – it isn't my place to object. Only to warn you that without the normal restraints of home and family, a young man like your brother – shall we say impressionable? – might get into company that's a little wilder than you might like. I simply think he still needs a little guidance . . . Anyway, I don't imagine they'll lead your brother far astray – not with a sister like you to keep him on the straight and narrow.' He smiled suddenly, with a warmth and humour to which she couldn't help responding. 'And what about yourself, Cordelia? We seem to do nothing but discuss your brother – how are *you* finding your new life? Do you think you really will grow to like Corning – even to love it? Will it give you what you want?'

'What I want?' Cordelia repeated, and made a small, rueful grimace. 'I don't know, Mr – Jensen. I'm not even sure what it is that I want.'

He studied her for a moment. 'You know, I don't think

that's true. I think you're a young lady with very definite ideas about what she wants. Maybe you think it can't be got here, is that it? Maybe what you want is still back in England, and that's why you look so sad and wistful at times.'

Cordelia's head snapped up and she stared at him. Her cheeks were hot again. She opened her mouth to deny it, but no words came.

'A man?' he asked gently. 'Were you in love in England, Cordelia? Is that what you're hankering after?'

'No, indeed it isn't! I've never been in love in my life, nor do I wish to be.' Her voice rose indignantly and she saw one or two people glance towards her. Lowering her tone, she said intensely, 'I don't ever intend to marry. I believe in having a career.'

'A career! Say, that's very forward-thinking. So you're a campaigner for women's rights? A follower of Elizabeth Cady Stanton and Susan Anthony?'

Cordelia gave him a sharp look. Was he mocking her, as so many men did when a woman dared to voice such an ambition? But his face was perfectly serious and she felt suddenly anxious to go on – to tell this man about her hopes and dreams, all shattered now. But since arriving in Corning, she had had no one to talk to, no one to confide in. Even her brother was too absorbed in his own new ventures to pay her much attention, and in any case she had vowed never to let him think that she regretted coming to America. Would it really do any harm to talk to Jensen Novak?

'Well, I've never done any campaigning, though my mother has in England. I simply wanted to live the kind of life they've always believed women should live.' She hesitated, then added quietly, 'I was going to go to university before we decided to come here.'

'You were?' Again, she gave him a quick look, but there was nothing but interest in his eyes. 'And you gave it up to come and take care of your brother?'

'I suppose most women would accept that it was the proper thing to do,' she said. 'I do too – I love Tim, and I believe he's a genius. I'm nothing like that. I have a brain but I can't give the world what Tim can. All the same –'

'All the same, it's hard to give up your own dreams,' he said and Cordelia's glance this time was wondering; she had never expected to find such understanding, particularly in this tall American with the dark blue eyes and the smile that seemed so often to mock.

'What did you mean to do after university?' he asked.

'Teach. I wanted to obtain a post in a really good school – the North London Collegiate, perhaps, or one of the new schools for young ladies. And one day, I would have liked to become a headmistress myself – perhaps even open my own school.' She leaned forward. 'I had such ideas for a school of my own! I would have taught the girls all the subjects the boys learn – I'd have fitted them for real careers. Medicine, the law – anything they chose to take up. Women *should* be able to do these things – we have brains just as good as men's and we can bring something else to the world too, a different perspective, a different dimension.'

'And do you believe that women should also be given the vote?'

'Of course I do! And go into Parliament too. And one day, they will – wait and see.'

Jensen smiled. 'Cordelia, you've come to the right place – the first speech for Women's Rights was made at Seneca Falls, not far from here, way back in 1848. If you want to campaign –'

'I don't,' Cordelia said honestly. 'All I want to do is teach.'

'Well, and can't you do that here? All right, you haven't

121

been to your smart university, but you could find a job in one of our schools.'

'I've tried. They won't have me.'

Jensen stared at her. 'Won't have you?'

'No. The schools are on holiday just now, but even when they start again in the autumn – the fall – they say they'll be full. They don't need any more teachers. And if they did, they'd rather they were American. I'd teach them wrong, apparently.' She lifted her shoulders and let them drop again. 'If I want a job in Corning, I'll have to do something in one of the factories. Or learn to use a typewriter and find myself a job in a business office.' She did not add that attending the Elmira Business College would in itself cost money, money that she and Tim did not have. 'So it looks as if my career will have to wait until we return to England.'

'You do intend to return then?' he asked quickly. 'I rather gathered that Tim was happy enough here. He likes the freedom to develop his glass without someone at his elbow. I don't think he'll be ready to go back for a long while yet – or perhaps you mean to go back without him.'

Cordelia looked at him and remembered his words about Timothy when they had first come in. *He needs you more than he thinks . . . you are the one who has most influence with him . . .*

'No,' she said, looking down at her lemonade again. ' I don't think I'll be going back without him.'

Waiting at the crossing gates by the Tioga Street station, Cordelia felt homesickness wash over her in a tide of longing. She wanted desperately to see her mother again, to assure herself that Emily was well, that she wasn't still suffering from the pain of their departure and that her grief over Paul's death might at last be abating. She wanted to talk again with her grandmother Christina, to look into the

122

green eyes so like her own, feel the contact of a mind and heart that matched hers. She wanted to rest against the bulk of her grandfather, still, at eighty-two, willing to take off his coat in the glasshouse and blow as fine a bowl or wineglass as ever. She even, Cordelia thought with a half-smile, wanted to see Mark again – the younger brother who had arrived on the scene when she and Tim were six years old and everyone had thought Paul and Emily's tiny family complete.

How were they all at home? she wondered. And had she and Tim truly been forgiven for running away? She had written as soon as they had arrived in Corning, giving Martha Robinson's address and saying only that they were in comfortable lodgings; she had tried hard to explain their reasons for leaving in the way that they had, reiterating the love and respect she and her brother both still felt for their family, hinting again that their absence was to be only temporary. But as time went on, she doubted more and more the truth of that – even if she and Timothy were to go back, would they be welcome? Would their mother ever recover from the bitter anger that had prevented her so far from even sending a brief note? Would Christina ever write with more warmth than had been displayed in the short, cool letters she had sent them so far?

No, they had betrayed their family, betrayed Henzel's and forgiveness would not come easily. And Cordelia's feelings of loneliness grew as she thought sadly of all they had left behind and lost.

The train clanked by and the flagman opened the gates. Cordelia gave him the smile he was waiting for and passed through, heading for the bridge that crossed the river into Knoxville. So far, she had not ventured into this part of Corning but this morning, restless after her meeting with Jensen Novak, disturbed about Timothy and unhappy about the family in England, she felt the need to explore further afield.

The Chemung River, meandering through the broad, wooded valleys, cut the town of Corning in two. In fact, the two places had only recently become one town – Knoxville had been dismissed by the more superior Corningites until the arrival of the Lackawanna railroad had increased the smaller village's prestige. Now it was incorporated as the 'Fifth Ward' of Corning which, in 1890, had itself been given the status of City. The two were connected by an iron bridge over four hundred feet long.

Cordelia walked briskly across, pausing to look down at the slowly moving waters below. The dry weather meant that the river was low, its bottom clearly visible; she remembered that Jensen had told her it could flood, and found it difficult to believe. Raising her parasol and lifting her face to the sky, she wondered if it would ever rain again.

The streets of Knoxville were laid out in the same grid pattern as that of Corning, a pattern of straight, criss-crossing lines. Bridge Street, Fulton Street, Pulteney Street . . . Cordelia wandered amongst them, noticing the difference in the houses. Here on the north bank of the river there was a distinct air of shabbiness, in some of the streets even neglect. The houses were almost all of frame construction, but their clapboard facings weren't newly painted like those in the 'tree' streets on the south side and up the hill. If they had ever been painted at all, the paint was blistered and peeling, the wood splintered and rotting. Some of them were small one-storey shacks; others were large enough but their gardens were no more than rough patches of earth with only a few blades of grass struggling through, and where curtains did hang at the windows they were grimy and torn.

Jensen had told her that the working people of the town

lived in Knoxville. Some of them were evidently well enough off to keep their homes neat; there were signs that an effort had been made, that curtains had been washed and mended and looked fresh at open windows. Lines of washing and mats being beaten testified to housewifely pride. But in other areas, it was clear there was not enough money. And families were too large for the wages being earned. Small children scrabbled in the dust, their thin, dirty faces raised to stare curiously as Cordelia went by, and she saw how pitifully inadequate their clothes were. Perhaps at this time of year it didn't matter that they were half-naked – but later, when the cold weather came, would they be wrapped in warm coats and scarves, would their grimy feet be shod in sturdy boots? And if they didn't have enough to eat during the summer, when the body required less nourishment anyway, would they be strong enough to withstand disease during a long, bitter winter?

As she walked, she became aware that a small crowd of children was following her, keeping a yard or two behind and whispering amongst themselves. Uneasy, conscious of the clothes that must look so fine to them and of the elaborate parasol, she stopped and looked back at them.

'Good morning, children. Isn't it a beautiful morning?'

They stared back blankly and she scolded herself for her foolishness. What did a beautiful morning mean to them? They were poor, hungry, ill-clad – these were the things that mattered. She saw one or two of the little girls put their hands up to their mouths and break into nervous giggles.

The boys were bolder. One of them stepped forward and said in a strong Irish accent: 'We don't care about the morning, miss. We just want a penny or two for some cookies. Could ye not spare us some?'

'A penny or two . . .?' Cordelia looked at them. The cost of her parasol alone would have fed these poor little scraps

125

for a week. She took out her purse and held out a handful of coins. 'Go and buy yourselves whatever you want.'

With a yell, the children flung themselves on her, knocking the money from her hand and scrabbling eagerly on the ground for it. Cordelia watched helplessly, wanting to restore some kind of order and make sure the money was fairly shared out, but she knew that they would take no further notice of her now. The boy who had spoken to her, however, was made of stronger stuff. Within a few minutes he had organised the little pack of children and commanded them to hand all the money over to him. Without another glance at Cordelia, he then announced that they would go straight to the bakery and, yelling and screaming once more, they set off at a run, leaving Cordelia alone on the sidewalk.

She took a breath. It had happened so quickly, and now the street was deserted. But then she noticed a small girl standing beside a stunted bush, staring at her.

'Hullo – aren't you going with the others? Don't you want some cookies too?'

The child shook her head. She could be no more than four or five years old, Cordelia thought, and although she was as raggedly dressed as the rest of the children, it was clear that someone took care of her. Her dark curls were tousled but clean, her cheeks rosy and the dirt on them superficial, as if she had been allowed out that morning only after a thorough wash. Keeping one thumb firmly in her mouth, she stared at Cordelia with huge eyes, so dark a blue that they were almost black, and edged a little closer to the bush and put out the other hand as if its prickly branches offered reassurance.

'Don't be frightened,' Cordelia said gently. 'I won't hurt you. What's your name?'

The child was silent for a moment. Then she removed her

thumb from her mouth and said, 'I'm called Bridget.' Her voice was soft, almost too soft to hear, and she looked at Cordelia with eyes that seemed about to melt.

'Bridget? That's a pretty name. Is it Irish?'

'I don't know,' the child said doubtfully. And then, in an obvious attempt to be helpful, she added, 'Me brother Garrett's Irish.'

'Is he? Then I expect you are, too.' Cordelia looked down at her and then, rather helplessly, along the street. There was nobody about now. She wondered what to do; she could hardly walk away and leave this mite alone. 'Didn't you want to go with the others?' she asked again.

'They've gone to buy cookies.'

Bridget shook her head. 'They wouldn't give me any, I'm too little. And I wanted to stay here.' The thumb strayed again towards her mouth, but just before she replaced it she said longingly, 'I wanted to look at your pretty clothes. You look like a butterfly's wings.'

Cordelia stared at her and felt an ache in her throat. She had put on her plainest blouse and skirt this morning and only her parasol looked at all 'pretty' to her. But to this child, living her short life amongst the dust and drabness of poverty, she looked like a butterfly.

'Come and see my parasol,' she said, opening it and displaying the pale, ruched chiffon of the lining. 'Isn't it a lovely colour? You'd look nice in that, with your dark hair.'

'I'd like a dress that colour,' the child said, and reached out a tentative and dirty finger to touch it. 'It's soft.'

'It's called chiffon.' Cordelia crouched beside her, showing her the stitching, the gathering that made it billow so delicately. 'Sometimes ladies wear it for party frocks.'

'I've never been to a party. Tell me about them.'

Bridget had moved away from her bush now and laid her

hand on Cordelia's knee, looking into her face with a trusting expression in the dark blue eyes.

'Well, a party is – it's when you ask a lot of people to your house. Friends and relatives. You make everything tidy and you give them something to eat and drink.'

'Is that all? Don't you play games?'

'Oh yes, sometimes. Especially at Christmas.' Cordelia thought of Christmas parties back in England, with Christina glowing in her favourite bronze and green dress, Joe supervising the decorating of the big Christmas tree, her parents laughing together. What would Christmas be like in Henzel Court this year? 'And we sing too,' she went on, thrusting the image away. 'We stand round the piano and my brother plays it, and we sing a lot of songs.'

'How many brothers have you got?' Bridget seemed to have recovered from her shyness and was clearly eager to find out as much as she could about this strange, butterfly-like creature before she flew away again.

'I've got two brothers. One's a lot younger than me and he's still at school. The other is my twin.'

'What's a twi –' But Bridget's question was drowned by the sudden sound of running feet and an excited voice calling her name. She gave Cordelia a quick glance and stepped away. 'Here I am, Grainne.'

'Oh, so there ye are, at last!' A girl a little taller than Cordelia came flying round the corner and skidded to a halt, scooping the child into her arms. 'And just what have ye been doing with yourself? Look at the state of ye! And pawing this lady's skirts an' all. I'm real sorry,' she said, turning to Cordelia. 'She shouldn't have been a nuisance to ye.'

'She wasn't a nuisance at all.' Cordelia straightened up, looking at the girl with interest. 'Is she your little girl? She's very like you.'

The dark blue eyes widened slightly and the black curls tossed. 'Mine? No, she's me little sister and a demon at that.' She hugged Bridget to her, belying her fierce words. 'Plague of me life, so she is. What's she been saying to ye? I thought she was with the others.'

'She was, but they all ran off to the bakery.' Cordelia interpreted the girl's stare. 'I gave them some pennies.'

'Oh, I see. Begging, were they? Well, Bridget knows she's to do none of that so I hope she didn't take anything from ye.'

'No, she didn't. She just wanted to –' Cordelia glanced at the girl's clothes and realised suddenly that they were as shabby as Bridget's. 'She just wanted to ask me some questions,' she said, thinking how absurd the words sounded.

'Oh, I'll believe that. Full of questions, this one is. She wants to know it all, from why the sun rises in the morning to why it sets at night, and then some more besides. She fair plagues the brains out of me head, wanting to know everything.' The girl set her sister down on the ground again. 'Have I not told ye ye're not to pester people with all your why this and why that?' she demanded. 'It's school ye need, and a school all to yourself, but devil a chance there is of that for folk like us. I'm sorry, miss, if she was a bother to ye.'

'But she wasn't a bother.' Cordelia looked at Bridget, who was holding her sister's skirt now, her thumb firmly back in her mouth. 'Do you mean she doesn't go to school? I suppose she's too young at present –'

'Not at all,' the Irish girl declared. 'She's past six years old, though she might not look it. And that quick in her mind, she fair leaves me gasping at times. No, there's no school here for the likes of us, not since Miss Miller took sick. They can't find anyone else to take it on, that's the truth of it. And sure ye can't blame anyone in their right mind for not wanting to deal with the devils they call children around here.'

'So none of the children go to school?' Cordelia asked.

'None of them hereabouts, not until they find some poor wretch who needs the job more than they need their sanity.'

Cordelia laughed. 'Oh, it can't be that bad! They're only children, after all.'

'Ye think so? Just because their horns aren't through yet – wait'll ye see them undressed and ye'll see the tails on them. Why d'ye think poor Miss Miller took sick?'

Cordelia looked at her thoughtfully. 'Is there a school house?'

'Oh aye, over on Hamilton.' The girl indicated with a flick of her black curls. 'It's nothing much, but what would ye expect?'

'And all the children in this area, they'd go there?'

'That's right.' The blue eyes were curious. 'And a good thing too, they're running wild as it is. Are ye from the education people then?'

'No, I'm just out walking.' Cordelia caught the scepticism in the other girl's eyes; who would choose to walk in the poorer streets of Knoxville, after all? 'I haven't been in Corning long,' she explained. 'I don't know it at all well, so I'm – well, exploring.'

'Exploring, is it?' The musical voice was still incredulous. 'Well, there's not much to see around here. I guess you're living over the river. English, are ye?'

'Yes, I am. I'm here with my brother – he works in one of the glasshouses. My name's Cordelia Henzel.' She sensed that the other girl was fidgeting to go – perhaps she had work waiting to be done at home. She sought for a way of keeping her there. 'What's your name?'

'Grainne O'Donnell. I came here from Ireland, if ye hadn't guessed already. And now, if ye'll excuse me, I'll have to be getting back. Me dad needs his dinner cooked for twelve o'clock and if it isn't there'll be hell's own debts to pay, begging your pardon.' She reached down and took Bridget's hand in a firm grip. 'Say goodbye to the lady now, sweetheart.'

'Oh – no – please don't go.' Cordelia searched wildly for a further excuse. 'Look, could I come with you? It's so hot – I'm terribly thirsty, I wonder if you could spare me a cup of water? I won't be in your way while you get your father's dinner ready.'

'Water? Well, I guess that's no trouble. Come along then.' She strode off along the street, her skirts swinging freely, while Cordelia hurried beside her. 'I hope ye won't mind it out of the bucket,' Grainne said over her shoulder. 'The council's bringing us tap water soon, but they're a devil of a time getting it connected up and I don't reckon our places down by Post Creek will ever get it. They'll have run out of pipes before they get to us. But the carrier brings it round most days, so we don't go short, though young Bridget here uses more than her fair share just getting the dirt off at nights.' She turned a corner into another street and stopped in front of a large, sprawling frame house. 'Well, this is our humble abode – the ground floor of it, anyway. Step inside if ye like, there's no one else at home.'

She led the way through the open door into a small, dark hallway. Cordelia followed cautiously. There was an odd smell, which seemed to be composed partly of beer and partly of strong disinfectant, with the powerful addition of boiled green vegetables. Leading from the hallway were several doors, and Grainne flung one of these open and displayed a large room which seemed to function as both kitchen and parlour. Cordelia's first impression was of stifling heat, and she saw that there was a stove burning – ready, she supposed, to cook Mr O'Donnell's dinner.

The walls were covered with dark wallpaper, but the sun streaming through the windows showed a room that was scrupulously clean. No dust dulled the surface of the bare kitchen table, nor the dresser that stood against one wall with a motley collection of crockery placed neatly on its shelves. The wooden chairs ranged around the table showed signs of careful mending; by the window stood a bench with two pottery bowls and a couple of pans; there was a jug with cooking utensils bunched inside it and a small pile of vegetables. Against the other wall was an old sofa with a cat stretched out at one end feeding a litter of kittens.

Bridget immediately threw herself on the cat with cries of gladness, and Grainne went to a bucket that stood at one end of the bench and dipped some water into a cup.

'There ye are, miss. Sit down for a bit, ye look real weary.' Her eyes were concerned. 'How far did ye come this morning, then?'

'I walked from Second Street. Not far – but it's so hot.' Cordelia drank gratefully and smiled. 'I hadn't realised quite how thirsty I was. Thank you very much.'

'Oh, 'tis no trouble.' Grainne went to the bench and began to pare the vegetables. 'Ye just sit there till you're ready to walk back. That's quite a step over from Second. Have ye relatives there?'

'Yes, but they're away at present – we rent two rooms there.' She caught the girl's look of surprise and added quickly, 'It's enough for my brother and me – we don't need much room.'

'Do ye not, now?' The nimble fingers worked on. 'And d'ye think ye'll like living in Corning?'

'Well, it's not supposed to be for ever – just for a while, to give my brother more experience. Our family are glassmakers in England, you see. I expect we'll go back before very long.'

'Well, it's not such a bad place – depending who ye are, of course. Life's pretty hard for some of us, but it's no worse than it was back in the old country. And at least the weather's better. Always raining back home, it was.'

'I would quite welcome some rain now,' Cordelia said. 'A light English shower – how lovely it would be.'

'Aye, it would, but we don't go in for light showers here – it's more likely to be a thunderstorm fit to take your ears off, and then floods all through the house. Mind, if you're high up the hill over in Corning you're probably safe enough. I reckon they knew what they were doing when they started to build up there.' The vegetables were dropped into a pan of water which was placed over the fire. 'Now I'll just make a bit of pudding – we've some meat today.'

'How many of your family come home to dinner?' Cordelia asked, watching the preparations.

'Only me father and three of me brothers. The rest have their dinner at work, they take a bite with them or maybe go into one of the diners. And young Danny, of course, he'll be in. And me and Bridget.'

'That's dinner for seven people! Who's Danny?'

'He's the youngest brother, he'll have been out in the streets – off to the bakery with your pennies, I'd guess. Another one who ought to be at school. I tell ye, they're just turning the whole place into a jungle and they're the monkeys – heaven only knows what they'll grow up to. Fighting maniacs like me dad I wouldn't be sur –' She stopped suddenly and turned back to her work, colour flooding into her cheeks. 'I tell ye, miss,' she said after a moment, 'we need that school.'

'You do,' Cordelia said thoughtfully. 'You do indeed.' She watched in silence for a while, wondering why it was that she felt so comfortable with this girl, so at ease. Their backgrounds were so different, their lives in such contrast,

133

yet it was almost as though they were sisters. As though Grainne O'Donnell had come all the way from Ireland and Cordelia had taken that long, tedious journey from England, simply to meet as sisters.

'Does your mother work?' she asked, and Grainne sighed.

'We all work, miss. Me Mam's away at the mill now. I'm only home because the glasshouse is closed for the hot weather. Me Dad and the boys are out working in the fields until it opens again. Most times we're all out all day and then young Danny and Bridget have to fend for themselves if there's no school. He's supposed to look out for his sister, but ye know what spalpeens boys can be.'

'And how many of you are there altogether? You have other brothers?'

'Aye, four of 'em.' A shadow crossed the girl's face. 'They're not all at home now, though. Patrick and Michael board at the farm where they work, and me brother Declan –' her voice faltered a little – 'he's gone away.'

'To work?'

'It's to be hoped so, if he's not to starve.' Grainne stopped, biting her lip and staring down at the pudding mixture. Then, as if she must talk to someone, she burst out: 'We don't know where he is, miss, and that's the truth of it! He left here a good three weeks ago after a fight with me Dad, and we've never heard a word since. And me Mam in a way to breaking her heart, so she is – I don't know how she'll bear it if we don't hear something soon.'

Cordelia stared at her helplessly. Tears had sprung to the Irish girl's eyes, and she brushed them away with an impatient hand, only to make room for more. Impulsively, Cordelia went to her and slipped an arm around her shoulders, drawing the slender body close.

'Please don't cry. I'm sure he'll be all right. He probably

doesn't want to write until he can give you good news –
you'll hear soon, I'm sure. Please, Grainne.'

Grainne sniffed and shook her head so that the tears flew
glittering from her lashes. 'It's easy to say that, miss, but ye
don't know – ye can't.'

'No, I can't,' Cordelia said honestly. 'But I can tell you
this – my own father was thought lost once. He was caught
up in a terrible war, in a siege, and the family gave him up
for dead. But he came back, eventually. And I'm sure your
brother will too.'

'Well, I hope so, for me Mam's getting thinner and paler
every day just waiting.' Grainne began to mix the pudding
again. 'And it's good of ye to bother about it all, miss.' She
chopped a few pieces of meat with considerable vigour and
dropped them into the mixture. 'There, that'll stick their
feet to the ground this afternoon. Me Dad'll ask if I threw
the meat in from the top of the hill, but I can't help that – I
can't be making meat out of thin air.' She wrapped the
pudding in a cloth and dropped it into a pan of boiling
water.

Cordelia felt that it was time for her to go. She picked up
her parcels and then put them down again.

'Thank you again for the water. And it's been nice to talk
to you and Bridget.' She stooped and tickled the kittens,
taking the opportunity to give the little girl a quick kiss.
'Perhaps you wouldn't mind if I came again, when I'm
passing this way?' The words sounded foolish in her ears –
why would she be passing this way? She could see the
thought going through Grainne's mind and added firmly:
'I'd like to see you again.'

Grainne looked at her in surprise, 'Aye, you're welcome
to come if you've a mind. It's not what you're used to,
though, a lady like ye. We're just common working folk
here and we're a bit rough.'

'I don't mind that,' Cordelia said. 'My grandfather was a common working man. There's nothing special about us.'

'Well, 'tis up to ye.' Clearly, the Irish girl didn't expect to see her again. 'The neighbours'll think we're going up in the world, I know that.'

Cordelia laughed and left the house, feeling lighter at heart than she had done since leaving England. She knew that she would come again, and that Grainne would be pleased to see her; she knew that they would become friends, and the knowledge warmed her lonely heart.

But as she walked slowly back across the bridge to Corning, she knew that she would go to Knoxville for more than simply to visit Grainne. There was a school there – a school that was empty and unused because no teacher could be found for it. And Cordelia had already made up her mind that the school on Hamilton would be hers.

Timothy came out of the glasshouse, looked up at the thick green of the trees that covered the hills, and smiled. He put his fists up to his chin, flexed his muscles and then stretched his arms wide, encompassing the entire town and its verdant surroundings. He felt relaxed and at peace.

Since starting to work at Jensen's glasshouse, on the Knoxville side of the river, Timothy had settled in as if he had been born in Corning. He suffered none of the homesickness that plagued his sister, neither did the heat bother him as it did her. Now that he could work again, he asked little else, and he was slightly impatient of the closing of all the glasshouses for a few weeks' vacation in the summer. Still, no doubt it was too hot for working around the furnaces, and he had arranged that his room was available for him to use whenever he felt inclined, with plenty of blanks at his disposal, so there was no reason why his own work in carving and engraving should be delayed.

All the same, he thought, a fellow ought to have a little fun occasionally. And this evening, once he had been back to their rooms and changed his clothes, he intended to meet a few of the friends he had made here and have an evening out.

There was plenty to do around Corning – the Americans might know how to work, but they also knew how to enjoy themselves. Already the cinder cycling tracks throughout the town were alive with boys and young men, even girls and women, pedalling rapidly beneath the trees. Some of the more mischievous were 'scorching' along the sidewalks, to the terror of old ladies and nursemaids with children, but they were quickly called to order by the more sober riders. But this didn't make the sidewalks as safe as many walkers would have liked – as he turned the corner, Timothy himself was almost knocked down by two girls hurtling along on roller skates. They veered wildly as they saw him and shot away down Second Street, giggling hysterically.

Timothy wondered idly what he and the others would do this evening. A game of tennis, perhaps, or maybe it was too hot. They might swim or fish along the river, or perhaps go pigeon-shooting in the woods. Perhaps there might be some fun over at Vischer's, the driving park and fairground just west of Knoxville; you could often see someone practising for the trotting races there, or watch some boxing or wrestling. These last two were sports that Timothy had no desire to take part in, although he enjoyed watching them. His grandfather, Joe Compson, had been a respected prizefighter in his youth, but Timothy had not inherited Joe's physique, nor his temper, and he was too much aware of the value of his slender hands and long, sensitive fingers and knew he could not afford to damage them.

'Going out?' Cordelia said watching him change into a fresh shirt and clean jacket. 'Oh, Tim, I was hoping we might spend this evening together. It's so lovely when it gets cooler – couldn't we take a walk up the hill, or down by the river?'

'Sorry – arranged to meet some of the fellows,' Timothy said, stopping by the washstand to fix his tie. 'Maybe tomorrow evening.'

'Which fellows? Where are you going?' Cordelia's voice sounded sharp and querulous even to herself and she wasn't surprised when her brother shrugged impatiently, an irritated expression crossing his face.

'Just fellows – you don't know them. And I don't know where we'll go, we'll decide that when we meet. Look, you're not my keeper, Cordelia. I suppose I am allowed to go out alone once in a while?'

Cordelia bit her lip. 'Of course. But it's not just once in a while, Tim – it's almost every night. Don't you think you could stay home now and then, to keep me company?'

'Look, I'm working pretty hard down there at the glass-works. I need a little fun and relaxation. I deserve it. All you have to do all day is sit about and go for little strolls. Your whole life is relaxation. Why do you begrudge me the few hours I can snatch in the evenings?'

He spoke in an injured tone and Cordelia knew that there was no use in arguing with him. In this mood, he would twist anything she said to make her seem even more unreasonable. Her own sense of injustice rose. So her whole life was relaxation, was it? Did he have any idea how hard it was to keep even these two rooms clean and tidy, to supply him with the fresh shirts he demanded, to shop and cook every day in this exhausting heat? Did he really suppose she enjoyed it? 'Of course I don't grudge you your fun,' she said quietly. 'I'd just like us to share it a little sometimes, that's all.' She turned and went into the sitting-room, leaving Timothy feeling half triumphant and half ashamed.

That was telling her, he thought; but the memory of her face, disappointed but resigned, stayed with him throughout the evening and marred the fun he told himself he was having.

The rest of the young men whose circle he had joined were waiting down at the bridge and it was soon decided that they would begin the evening by watching the baseball game in Riverside Park. There were games here almost every evening, as well as at weekends; every school, every factory, every neighbourhood had a team and each game was thoroughly reported in the local newspaper. Tim, although still vague about the rules, enjoyed the matches as much as anyone else and shouted as loudly as the rest for the team they were supporting tonight. They left the ground still arguing over the result, and then stopped, wondering what to do next.

'Why not billiards?' suggested Frank Cady, Timothy's closest crony. 'There are plenty on Market Street. Let's go to Hall's – you can get good ice cream there, and cigars too.'

The little group turned as one and made for the long street which was the centre of Corning life, the place where all the best shops were, all the restaurants and saloons. The tall red-brick buildings were mostly quiet now, as darkness fell; there were just a few lights left burning in the shop windows for anyone who might care to browse. Only from a few open windows could be heard music and voices, and it was towards one of these that Timothy and his friends strode.

'Ice cream!' Andrew Hyde said as they moved along, taking up all the sidewalk so that other people had to step into the road to avoid them. 'What I could use is a long, cool beer.'

'Well, you can have that, too. And maybe a bet or two with old Dan. He'd bet on a raindrop race down a window-pane, Dan would. You lucky with the dice, Tim?'

'I don't know – I've never played much,' Timothy stammered, and his companions laughed.

'Now's the time to learn, then! And maybe we'll have a game of cards if the pool tables are full. Teach the English a trick or two,hey?' Frank laughed at his pun and the others joined in. Timothy grinned. This was living, he thought. There was nothing like this in Wordsley or Stourbridge. Nothing he had ever found, anyway.

Jensen Novak would have warned him against going out with his new-found friends. But Jensen was in Ohio, attending to business and 'personal affairs' of which he chose not to speak. And Cordelia, fretting over the books she had brought home from the lending library, could do nothing.

Tim, pushing the thought of his sister irritably to the back of his mind again, followed his companions into the smoky atmosphere of the billiard saloon. What did it matter what a lot of women thought, anyway? He was a man, wasn't he – and if this was how men spent their time, that was highly acceptable to him. He worked hard enough for his fun, after all.

Pulling some dollar bills from his pocket, Timothy called for beer and cigars. He would show these Americans that the English knew how to enjoy themselves.

Chapter Seven

Timothy was alone in the glasshouse. During the summer closure, he was the only one still coming in. He spent his time working on the blanks that had been made, making new engravings or designing patterns for the rich cut glass that was so popular, and which he disliked but had agreed to work on in exchange for the facilities Jensen had offered him.

His small workroom was as neat and tidy as a glass-maker's office could ever be. On the shelves that lined the walls stood an array of glass – wineglasses, tumblers, decanters and jugs. They were all experimental, some whose shapes had been well received and which were now a part of regular production, some which had never been produced in quantity. There were patterns that could be found now in homes all over the State as Novak Crystal grew in popularity, and patterns which had failed from the outset. That was what experimenting meant, Tim thought as he sat down at his bench and stared at the vase he intended to work on today. Trying new things, knowing that they wouldn't all be acceptable to the capricious taste of the public. That was why he could work with Jensen Novak, who had dragged himself out of poverty by vision and hard work, who had inherited nothing but his skills.

For Tim, that was the most refreshing, stimulating aspect of his new life. Until he had left Stourbridge and come to America he had never quite realised how oppressed he had been by his family traditions. Behind him stretched generations of Henzels, going right back to the original Lorrainer families who had come from France three centuries and more ago. He couldn't move in his home town without being reminded of them all – the Tyzacks, the Titterys, all the proud descendants of the first noble glassmakers. And of his own family in particular – old Joshua Henzel, who had died of a stroke and left Christina with a glasshouse to defend; Joe Compson, the glassmaker she had married; his own father Paul, the engraver and carver of cameo who had been without compare. And his other grandfather, Jean-Paul Thietry, who had come from France and whose talent was flowering now in his own work.

Timothy had been taught to revere the traditions of his family. Only when he had begun to breathe the air of Corning did he realise that as well as a source of pride they had also begun to raise a barrier around him, a wall of glass as difficult to surmount as a cliff of smooth, towering ice. He had been a prisoner there, a captive of tradition, and only now was he able to move freely, to let his mind range over all the possibilities that glass held for him, to unleash the passion that had been held in check.

The vase he held now was one that had been specially blown and shaped with Timothy in attendance, telling the blower exactly the effect he had in mind, showing him the drawings he had made beforehand. It was wide-mouthed, of middle height, with a lip that turned out and a heavy foot. Its proportions had been important, for the engraving Timothy intended to make – a pool at the base of the vase, with kingfishers resting on boughs above and smaller birds flying amongst leafy branches that reached to the rim of the vase – needed precisely the correct proportions. It was an intricate pattern and there was little room for error; whereas in many complex engravings mistakes could be incorporated into the general scheme, Timothy intended that this one should be exact, with each minute particle of engraving distinctly separated from the rest even as it formed an integral part of the whole.

The silent building was peaceful. Timothy lifted the heavy vase and weighed it thoughtfully in his hands. He turned it slowly, examining the shimmering surface, noting the texture of the glass, testing its thickness. This was always a moment of tension for him; soon he would take up his engraving tools and make the first, irrevocable mark in the shining smoothness. He felt a reluctance to begin, to commit himself, yet he knew that once the first mark had been made his nervousness would vanish and he would forget time as he bent, engrossed and oblivious of the outside world, to the task he had set himself.

That was the key! *The task he had set himself.* Nobody now told him what to do, what he must make. Timothy felt the surge of excitement that all creative artists must experience in the work that only they can do, and the vase trembled in his hands. Without allowing himself further delay, he set his elbows on the pads that he used to steady his arms, rested the foot of the vase on a third pad and reached for his tools. He held the slender engraving chisel delicately between his fingers, touched it against the glass and began.

Jensen Novak, coming quietly into the empty glasshouse, heard the minute sounds of Timothy's labours. He came to the open doorway of the workroom and stood quite still, watching.

Timothy was quite unconscious of Jensen's presence. Concentrating, absorbed, his eyes were fixed on his work. The engraving was coming to life under his sensitive fingers, the beauty of the image he was creating superimposed on the beauty of the shape that received it. Jensen watched, appreciating the skill that lay in those long, slender fingers. His own talent lay in cutting rather than engraving, but

Timothy could do either with equal ease, and Jensen made no secret of his admiration.

He admired too the restless creativity that drove Timothy to experiment with other forms of glass. It was as though the younger man – still little more than a boy, in Jensen's eyes – could not set eyes on any kind of glass, old or new, without feeling a desire to make it, too. Art Nouveau, cameo, sulphide, filigree – he had tried them all. And could have become a master in any field, Jensen thought, had that been good enough for him. But for Timothy Henzel, it seemed, nothing was good enough but that he should develop his own glass – glass that would be associated with his name and no other. Glass that would be venerated through future years, handed down from generation to generation, kept in private collections and admired in museums.

Jensen knew that there were those in Corning who had already dismissed Timothy Henzel as nothing more than a common engraver – finer than most, it must be admitted, but still nothing more. 'A creator? An innovator? Have you seen that monstrosity of a vase he carries around as a sample of his "innovations"?' they would exclaim, and roar with laughter. Why, it was nothing but a frigger, and not even a good one.

Jensen knew better. In Timothy's work, youthful and unformed as it was, he recognised something that had never been done before. Something that was akin to the work of Gallé and Tiffany, yet different from either. And he reminded himself that those same people had laughed at the bicycle which now thronged the streets in great numbers, had laughed again at its newer cousin, the motorcycle which had recently appeared in Corning, and presumably would laugh equally heartily at the automobile which Jensen believed would change the face of transport just as the railroads had already done. And doubtless also at the flying machines that would surely come.

These were the men who would scorn any change, any new development. Because it frightened them.

Jensen was not afraid of change. He enjoyed all the new developments of the age. And he understood that with so many changes taking place, it was inevitable that public taste would change with them. They would demand new, modern homes, modern furniture to put in them – modern glassware for their tables.

That was what he and Timothy Henzel, working together, would produce.

Timothy stopped his work. He laid his engraving tools down, stood the vase carefully upright, leaned back in his chair and stretched widely.

'You're doing some fine work there,' Jensen said quietly from the doorway, and grinned as Timothy jerked round in his chair. 'Sorry to surprise you. I didn't want to disturb the great man at work.'

Tim relaxed. 'How long have you been there?'

'Around half an hour, I guess.' He nodded at the vase. 'It's coming along well. Looks good.'

Timothy looked at his work with a critical eye. That was another thing Jensen admired about him – whatever he did, he put his whole mind and heart into it as he worked. He might dislike cut glass, but he made it to the best of his considerable ability. He might think an engraving pattern over-simple, but it would be executed with all the meticulous care he gave to his most complex work. Even so, like all the finest artists, he was never quite satisfied. It was as if he strove all the time for a degree of perfection that could never be attained.

'It isn't bad,' Timothy said at last, tipping his chair back. 'Be better when it's finished. I'm not sure I've got the tree proportions right . . . I didn't know you were coming back from Pennsylvania today.'

'Nobody did. I wired Nat and had him bring the trap to meet me. I'd finished my business – didn't seem much to hang about for. I guess I wanted to come back home.' Jensen grinned wryly. 'Sign of old age!'

Tim nodded absently and Jensen knew that his mind was already back with his work. He could almost see the itch in Timothy's fingers as he let his chair come back to the ground again and leaned forward to study the effect of his engraving. One finger came out and slowly traced the pattern and then, without taking his eyes from the vase, he reached out for the chisels.

Jensen watched for a few more minutes and then slipped quietly out. Timothy would not look up again until his hands and arms were too tired to work, his eyes too weary to see. He certainly would not notice Jensen's presence; nor yet his absence.

Outside, Jensen hesitated for a moment, looking up and down the street. With the factory closed, there was little for him to do, and equally little point in going back to his lodgings. Perhaps he should go and take a look at the new house now being built for him up on the hill – see how it was progressing. The architect he'd employed had told him it should be finished by Christmas. If so, Jensen had made up his mind to move in the following Easter and there'd be plenty to do before that.

He wondered briefly just why he had been so eager to return to this little town. There had been enough calls on his time in Pennsylvania, after all, and he had enough friends there – more than he had here. He'd intended to stay longer, if he hadn't had this sudden urge to come back. And his sudden departure had upset Karin.

Jensen walked up the steep hill, thinking of the last eve-

146

ning he had spent in the house in White Mills. Karin's face, small and tragic, framed in curls as golden as his own, haunted his memory. Why had he been so anxious to leave her? What was there in Corning that could compensate for being without her?

'I don't know why you have to go,' she had said, and his silent heart had echoed the words even as he knew that he must. 'You never stay more than a few days now. Don't you love me anymore?'

'Honey . . .' He had caught her in his arms, feeling the small, fragile body against his, sensing the beating of the heart against his ribs. 'Of course I love you. It's nothing to do with you – I've got business there, a glasshouse, you know I have to go back.' But it wasn't true; the glasshouse was closed for the summer heat, there was little to be done. 'I'll see you again soon,' he said helplessly.

'And then I'll come to Corning with you, and we'll be together always in the new house.' She sat up in the bed. 'You promised me.'

'Sweetheart, I'm not going to break that promise. I want you with me – you know that. And I'll come back for you as soon as I possibly can.' He kissed the flushed face tenderly and pressed her back against the pillows. 'Now go to sleep. It's late.'

Still clinging to his hand, she had done so. And Jensen, despite the lateness of the hour, had stayed beside her through the night, watching the face he loved so dearly and thinking back over the long painful years.

'What'll we do tonight, then?' The group of young men, anxious for entertainment after a day's work in the stifling heat of workshops and offices, were reluctant to go indoors again, even to play billiards or cards in the saloon. They wandered beside the river, watching the small boys who were bathing naked in the shallow water. 'Swim?'

'Swam this afternoon,' Jeff Davis said laconically.

'Go down to Riverside? There might be a ball game on.'

'Sick of ball games.'

'Well then, what?' The half-dozen looked at each other. They were restless, aware of a charge in the atmosphere. There would be a storm later, and the gathering electricity in the sultry air had seeped into their bodies, making nerves and muscles twitch. Each one was aware that it needed only a subtle alteration in their attitude for a quarrel to break out.

'Tell you what,' Andrew Hyde said suddenly, 'there's a cockfight down at the pit. We could go to that.'

'A cockfight!' There was an immediate brightening in the atmosphere. 'That's good sport.' Frank Cady glanced at Timothy. 'Don't suppose you have cockfights in England, do you?'

'We used to. They're illegal now.' Timothy felt himself hang back a little. He had heard his parents and grandparents discuss cockfighting. His grandfather, Joe, had seen a good many as a boy in the back streets of Wordsley. He had described their bloodiness, the excitement they had produced in the onlookers. 'I saw no harm in them then,' he would say thoughtfully, 'but we never gave much account to the feelings of birds. I'd not like to watch it again, and that's a fact. They fight to the death, you know; tear each other to shreds. Aye they're brave birds, fighting cocks, they'll never give up. I admire 'em for that, but I don't want to see 'em do it anymore.'

'It's barbaric,' Emily had declared, her face flushed with anger. 'The most barbaric sport man could devise, setting two animals against each other in the knowledge that one must die. I'm glad it's been outlawed.'

'It still goes on, though. They still hold mains in secret.'

148

'Then I hope the law finds out and deals with them as harshly as they deal with their unfortunate birds,' Emily said. 'I hope you'll never attend such a thing, Tim.' And with her dark eyes fixed on his face, Timothy had shaken his head. It was an easy enough promise to make back in Wordsley where he was confident of his position and there was always something more attractive to engage his attention. But now, looking at his companions' faces, he found it a promise less easy to keep.

'I'm not sure –' he began, but Frank and Andrew stared at him and his words faltered into silence.

'Look, there's nothing against 'em here. No one sees anything wrong with 'em, bar a few old ladies who don't understand and haven't ever seen one. You ain't squeamish, I hope?'

The tinge of scorn in Frank's voice was enough. Timothy shook his head at once. 'Of course I'm not. I'll come – I'm game.'

This made the others laugh. 'Game as a rooster, hey? Let's go then – we'll be late for the start if we don't move fast.'

Laughing and chattering, their tension dispersed now that they had a purpose, the group swung away down the road. The main, Tim discovered, was being held at East Corning and it was decided to hire a couple of cabs to take them there quickly. As they scrambled in, Tim saw that they were not the only ones who were going to attend the cockfight, for the road was full of men, young and old, all on their way to watch the sport.

Once again, he thought of his mother's face, distressed and angry as it always was when she spoke of cruelty of any kind, and the promise she had extracted from him. But it wasn't really a promise, was it? he argued silently. She'd only said she *hoped* he would never attend a fight. He'd never actually promised he wouldn't.

Comforted by this thought, yet still slightly uneasy, Timothy pushed the thought of his mother out of his mind, only to find her face immediately replaced by that of his sister. Cordelia, he knew, would disapprove just as strongly as Emily, and have no hesitation in saying so. But Cordelia wasn't his keeper – they might be twins, but he was a man now and didn't need a sister to keep him in order. In any case, there was no reason why she should know – he didn't have to tell her what he did with his spare time.

But unable to drive these uncomfortable thoughts away, Tim bounced along the road in the cab, hardly listening to the joking and laughter of his companions. He came out of his reverie with a start when Jeff poked him in the ribs, saying, 'There's the pit, look. There's a crowd here already – we'll have to push to get a good view.'

The cab came to a halt and Timothy followed Jeff's pointing finger. On a large patch of unused ground he saw a gathering of people and as he stood up in the trap he could see that they were standing round a circular space formed by a low wall, about a foot or so high. On the outskirts of the crowd were several men who stood talking together, each holding large white bags.

'The roosters are in there,' Frank observed as they passed the men. 'See how they're already struggling to get out! They know they're in for a fight, I reckon, and they can't wait.'

'Perhaps they want to escape,' Timothy observed, and Frank gave a hoot of laughter.

'Escape! Why would they want to do that? These game-birds love fighting – they live for it. It's what they're bred for, and it comes natural to 'em.' Already, his face was flushed with excitement, his eyes bright, and Timothy caught his anticipation. Perhaps Frank was right, after all – the birds were natural fighters, it was their instinct.

What was cruel about watching them do what they would do in the wild anyway?

The rest of the group had already reached the gathering crowd of onlookers, and were beginning to lay their bets. Of the cockers here tonight, only two were considered good breeders and most of the bets were laid in their favour. This didn't seem to worry the third, who stood a little apart with a slight smile on his face, as if he knew something the others did not.

Timothy watched as the first setters entered the pit, carrying one bag each, and the noise of the betting increased to a roar.

'Two to one on Moran!'

'A dollar on Palmer!'

'Two dollars on Palmer!'

'Moran, a dollar!'

His ears caught another sound; a low, crooning chuckle which came from one of the bags. The crowd looked towards it and laughed; the chuckle increased and became a threat, the anger of a trapped, frustrated bird which had been carefully fed and brought to peak fighting condition and was ready to fly at his opponent the moment he was let out of the bag. The ring of men was silent now. Tim saw their eyes narrow as they leaned slightly forward expectantly. With the timing of an expert showman the man called Palmer began to untie the neck of his bag.

The crowd was completely still. All eyes were fixed on the bird that the setter drew out, and as they beheld its full glory there was a collective sigh, no more than a brushing of air across the pit.

'Looks a good 'un,' Frank murmured in Timothy's ear. 'See those spurs!'

Timothy stared at the bird which was being held up for examination. At first glance, it was just like an ordinary farmyard cockerel, but as he looked further, he could see that this was no common dunghill fowl. This bird had been fed on the best and richest of corn, groomed until he looked as if he'd been polished. He trembled in the setter's hand like a racehorse waiting for the starter's gun, and his red eyes darted this way and that, as if searching for his enemy. He was almost entirely red, with an orange neck that stretched immediately towards the sky, his beak already questing a foe. His back and shoulders were a brilliant, gleaming rich chestnut, and his wings were dark, almost burgundy in shade with a bar of rich, dark blue. His tail, breast and thighs were blue also, the colour of wet slate, and his sinewy legs were yellow, with long, vicious claws and spurs that shone as if made of steel.

'Well, they are, aren't they,' Andrew said when Timothy pointed this out. 'See, they take off the cock's real spurs and put those on instead. Makes a better fight.'

A better fight! Timothy looked again at those wicked swords and thought of them ripping through an opponent's flesh . . . But there was no time for such thoughts now. The second bird was already being taken from its bag by the setter, and again the crowd leaned forward a little, eager to see what kind of cock was expected to match the first.

This bird was red and black, with angry eyes and clipped wings. In fact, Tim noticed, he had been clipped all over, with his tail docked, his wings shaped to a point and his combs and wattles removed, giving him an advantage over his rival, for injury to the comb could sometimes cause enough loss of blood to kill a gamecock. His spurs were at least an inch and a half long and his beak too had been sharpened so that it was a weapon as deadly as a dagger.

'My money's on that one,' Frank muttered. 'Moran's birds are devils. They never refuse.'

The birds having been agreed to match the descriptions

152

already given, the two setters retreated to opposite sides of the pit and began to prepare them for the battle. They smoothed the feathers, talking to them in soft, encouraging voices; then they moistened the bindings of their spurs. Finally, when the tension in the birds had been raised to its pitch, they held them up opposite each other, holding them tightly as they struggled to be free.

The betting had begun again, and the feverish excitement now caught at Timothy so that he shouted as loudly as anyone else and fished all his money from his pockets in his desire to lay his wager and, taking Frank's advice, decided to put his cash on Moran's bird. Frank laughed and advised him to put some back. 'You'll want it for the next battle – it's no fun if you haven't any money on a bird.' Meanwhile, in the pit, the two setters were still taunting their birds, letting them see each other, come almost within striking distance, then drawing them back out of reach again. The birds were trembling and squawking now, their necks stretched out, feet thrust threateningly before them. In a moment, if they were not loosed, the setters themselves would feel the brunt of their anger.

There was a sudden murmur. The betting ceased and all faces turned to the ring. The teller, the only other man in the ring, gave the signal and the birds were released.

Immediately, they flew at each other, leaping forward on their strong, scaly legs. But they did not attack at once; instead, beak to beak, they paused, sparring a little, watching each other for the first lunge. Which bird made it, was impossible to tell; it was as if they both reacted to some invisible signal. In less than a blink, they were no more than a squawking, whirling furious mass of feathers, their wings flapping like powerful sails to keep them upright, beaks and feet lunging in a flash of red and orange and silver. The brilliance of their colours was a fiery explosion against the dusty ground. Which bird was winning nobody could tell, but the spectators, crouching and leaning forward in their eagerness, kept up a constant yelling of encouragement and excitement which seemed to drive the fighters to further fury.

They came apart with a sudden rushing, wrenching gasp, as if they had been so firmly clamped together that their parting produced its own thunderclap. For a moment, Moran's bird stood triumphant; then Moran picked him up and began to examine him.

The other bird, which Tim had thought the finer, had suffered more. His comb was already torn and bleeding, his legs unsteady as he staggered to the side of the pit. Several of his feathers had been ripped out and hung broken from his wings and breast. Blood spattered his neck and his head was drooping.

His setter took him up and looked him over. Then, with a glance at Moran, he took him to the centre of the pit. The two birds faced each other once more.

This time the strike was even more furious. Injured though he was, Palmer's bird refused to give in. He fought desperately, striking out with claws and spurs, ripping a line of blood down the red breast, and then, as Moran's bird struck at his wattles, caught him in a blow in the eye. Blood poured from it and the cock shook his head, spattering some of the onlookers. The damage was now serious on both sides, but neither of the setters attempted to catch their bird. Instead, their hands on their knees, they yelled encouragement with the rest of the crowd, shouting with triumph when more blood was drawn, cursing when it looked as if their bird might withdraw and refuse to fight any more.

'Kill him!' Frank screamed, beside himself with excitement, and the cry was taken up by both sides as the two birds came together again and red, orange and black feathers flew from the enraged protagonists. 'Kill! Kill! Kill!'

Moran's bird had lost both eyes now, but he still fought on, striking out wildly in the direction he expected to find his enemy. But Palmer's bird was in no better condition; a long slicing attack from the other cock's spurs had left his chest open to the bone. When they fell apart for the last time, it was clear that he was dying fast. He staggered, half-fell and lunged forward again. Moran's bird, blind as he now was, could not avoid the blow; it caught him on the head and sent him reeling. Covered in blood, he fell to the ground and lay twitching for a moment.

'Palmer! Palmer!' the crowd yelled, but the teller shook his head. The fight was not over yet. The two setters picked up their birds, handling the broken bodies as gently as if they were their own newborn babies, and set them once again facing each other.

'They can't! They're almost dead!' Tim exclaimed, and Frank grinned and shook his head.

'That's the beauty of the fighting cock. He never gives in. Look!' His face was flushed and his eyes burned with a feverish excitement as he turned back again to the pit. Timothy looked with horrified fascination, sickened by what he saw yet unable to glance away. He felt bile rise into his mouth and swallowed it. The excitement of the crowd surged around him; he felt its effect in his own body, felt his heart race and, to his astonishment, heard his own voice join that of the rest.

The cocks were making one last effort. Weakened by injury and loss of blood, they were nevertheless still striking at one another, lunging with helpless, flailing feet, uttering little gurgling croaks of dying rage. Their dance was over, there was no more sparring or lunging, they simply lay together, scratching, pecking as if that was all that was left to them. And at last, when their movements had all but stopped, the eyes of Palmer's bird glazed over and he ceased to move.

The teller began to count. One. Two. Three. Four. All around the ring there was now a breathless hush. Moran's bird continued to peck, feebly but steadily. Nine. Ten. Eleven. The crowd leaned forward and Palmer stared at his bird as if willing it to show signs of life. Nineteen. Twenty. Twenty-one.

'How long does he count for?' Timothy whispered, and Frank answered without taking his eyes from the pit.

'Forty. Then if Moran's bird is still alive, he'll be the winner. He's going, though; going fast.'

Thirty. Thirty-one. The tension grew. Nobody stirred. Moran's bird was growing feebler with every count. Blind, his chest ripped open, his head battered and bloody, he sought his opponent with the beak that had been honed to such a deadly sharpness. Thirty-five. Thirty-six. His head drooped. Thirty-seven. Thirty-eight. He was dead. He could not have lived, with his blood pooling around him from the many wounds he had been dealt. Thirty-nine – he moved! He lifted his beak in one last great attempt to gain the revenge he had already taken. Forty . . .

'He's won!' Frank exulted. 'Did you see that? Right at the end – what a bird, *what* a bird! I told you, they never give in. They're marvellous, wonderful! How much will we have won? What did you lay?'

'I can't remember.' Tim watched as the setters moved forward to pick up the pathetic blood-soaked bundles of feathers which were all that was left of the birds that had been so carefully reared, so richly fed and so lovingly handled. Talking to each other now as if they had never been rivals, comparing notes on the performances their birds had put up, they carried the bodies away, and the pit was prepared for the next battle.

'Come on, we'll collect our winnings.' Frank pushed through the crowd and they waited in the line for the money to be paid out. Everyone was chattering excitedly; the fever of the battle still burned in their eyes. They talked of the fight they had just seen, of other fights in the past and more to come. Moran was generally adjudged to be the best cocker in the district, his birds kept in the finest condition. 'He's got a grand walk at his place,' Frank confided. 'I've been to see it. And he knows all about breeding and trimming, too.'

'How many fights will there be tonight?' Timothy wasn't sure he wanted to stay any longer. The battle he had just witnessed had left him feeling odd – sickened but excited. He had responded, as had every other man, to the undeniable courage shown by the two birds, but he knew dimly that his response wasn't simply due to their courage. Somewhere inside, he felt a fascination that had more to do with the sheer brutality of the whole affair – the furious killing instinct that had driven the two cocks, the blind desire to tear each other to shreds even if it meant death in the process . . . He felt uncomfortable, as if he too were being driven by something dark and sinister, something that made him feel afraid yet curious to experience again.

'Battles,' Andrew corrected him. 'Oh, two more, I think. You can't do more than three or five in an evening. It's always got to be an odd number, you see, so that there's a clear winner.' He collected the money due to him and counted it, looking pleased with the result. 'What I like is a Welsh main, when you have cocks all of the same weight and fight them like a tournament. The last two to survive fight the last battle, and the one that wins that is the winner overall. And then of course there's the battle royal – now, that *is* fun.'

'Battle royal?'

157

'When you put any number of cocks – ten or twelve, maybe even more – in together and let 'em fight it out between 'em. You should see the feathers fly then!' Frank grinned. 'We don't have 'em much, though. It comes expensive in birds and it don't last long enough. Hey, they're getting the next pair in.'

The two birds did not kill each other in the next battle. Moran's bird won, leaving the ring looking as fit and keen to fight as he had when he entered it. Timothy and Frank stood at the side of the pit, waiting for the last battle of the evening.

'It's Lowell this time,' one of the others said. 'I've never seen one of his birds before. Anyone know anything about them?'

Nobody did. Lowell was a cocker who was new to the area, having come from Brooklyn a few months ago. This was his first fight and his birds were therefore an unknown quantity. Betting went slowly until the two setters went into the pit and produced their birds.

'Now look at that!' Frank murmured admiringly, and raised his voice to offer a bet.

The bird drawn out of the bag was large but slim, all bone and muscle. Its eye were red and angry, darting this way and that as it took in its surroundings. Its plumage gleamed. It was completely black.

There was something sinister about the bird, Timothy thought, staring at it in fascination. Almost evil, as if it were one of Satan's chickens. The red eyes seemed to meet his then and a thrill ran through him; it was as if the bird had divined his thoughts and agreed with them. You are right, it seemed to say. I am evil. But you won't be able to ignore me.

Tim felt his heart thump. Something told him that he should leave now, that to stay longer would do him irrevocable harm. He wanted to move, but his feet refused to obey him. He tried to turn his head, but the red eyes of the cock were still fixed on his and he could not look away.

'Now that,' Frank said in an awed tone, 'is a bird *and* a half.'

Now the second bird was produced, and it too drew murmurs of appreciation, but there was nothing like the shiver that had run through the crowd when Lowell's bird had been displayed. As they watched the two men fondling their birds, the onlookers shifted slightly, moving imperceptibly closer. A taut silence hung between them.

For Timothy, the suspense was almost unbearable. He found himself crouching forward with the rest, his eyes fixed on the two straining bundles of muscle and feather. The glossy necks were stretched out, the beaks already snapping. The bodies struggled, the tightly-held legs jerked in the shackling hands. The setters looked at each other, than at the teller; and he nodded.

Immediately, the battle began, more furiously than either of the previous two and from the first second Lowell's black bird had the upper hand. With legs that seemed to work with the unassailable power of the pistons of a great engine, it struck over and over again at the cock which dodged and sparred opposite and tried so frantically to find a way past the terrible guard of claws and spurs. The breast was already laid open, an eye knocked away, a long cut sliced in the head and neck. The other cock, fighting back bravely, managed to tear at his enemy's wings, but with little result; a few feathers dropped to the ground but the black cock seemed barely to notice the retaliation. He moved in quickly with his beak and speared the other eye. One more blow, and it was over; and the teller's voice, counting to forty, was almost lost in the triumphant crowing that rent the air.

The teller's voice ceased. The setters moved in to pick up their birds, Lowell with a triumphant grin that stretched from one ear to the other. He thrust the victorious bird back into its bag and was immediately surrounded by congratulators, who slapped him on the back and declared that his gamecock was the finest they'd ever seen in Corning, and that they'd always back him from now on. The winners made for the men who had taken their wagers, already planning how they would spend the money. The losers, marking Lowell's name for future occasions, slouched off into the dusk.

'Well, that was a good evening,' Frank declared as he and Timothy and the rest went off in search of a cab to carry them home. 'Fine sport. Now what do we do?'

The others laughed and thumped him on the back. 'What do you think, Frank? What do we usually do after a cockfight?' Their suggestions were obscene, shocking. They grinned and guffawed and nudged each other and Timothy. 'What about you, Tim Henzel? Coming with us?'

Timothy looked at them. He felt sick and vaguely ashamed, as if he had taken part in some debauchery. Yet his heart was still thumping with the thrill of the last battle, the excitement surging through his veins like a drug. His body was restless, urging him on to something else – to cast himself into some new adventure, some way of releasing this pent-up excitement, this craving for more. The evenings spent at the billiard saloons, smoking and drinking, evenings which he had thought daring, seemed suddenly tame and lifeless. He thought of the birds with their brilliant plumage, hurling themselves into battle, and he felt his blood race.

'Nothing like a woman after a cockfight,' Frank said slyly, and dug him hard in the ribs. 'Come on, young Tim.'

Timothy stared at Frank as he swung himself up into the hack and grinned down, his dark face lit like a satyr's by the flickering lamps. He saw the challenge there. Prove yourself, Frank seemed to be saying. Prove yourself a man, like the rest of us.

Yes. He was a man now and entitled to a man's pleasures. It had nothing to do with his family. Cockfighting, women – whatever he cared to enjoy. So long as it didn't affect his ability to make fine glass.

Chapter Eight

With September, came the first golden touch of autumn. The fall, they called it here, but the meaning of that word would not become apparent until well into October, when the leaves dropped a bronze and scarlet carpet on the ground. Now the leaves were only tinged with the blaze that would come, with just a few early flames of gold amongst the ripening green.

To Cordelia's relief the air had cooled, bringing a hint of sharpness to the misty mornings. The glasshouses had reopened and all the factories were busy. The centre of the town was once more smoky from the tall, billowing chimney stacks, but most of their gritty outpourings went straight up into the still air and gradually dispersed, so that the sunlight could still filter through.

Today, as she stepped outside, she looked up at a sky that was pale, drifted with high, feathery clouds, and felt her heart lift with excitement. This was the moment she had longed for, planned for – even back in England she had looked forward to this moment, although it had come in an unexpected way. She had not thought it would be in a one-room schoolhouse in the poor part of a small American town.

But what did it matter? She would be teaching – in charge of her own destiny and guiding that of the children in her care. And as Cordelia set off down the road, she gave a little skip of delight.

It hadn't been easy obtaining permission to reopen the school. The local school board, although anxious to find someone to teach, was still doubtful about the abilities of the young English girl. What would she know about American ways? Would she be able to handle the rougher element amongst the local children – which could be very rough indeed? they warned her. But Cordelia smiled and remained insistent. Teaching was all she had ever wanted to do, she told them, and she was quite well qualified enough to impart the three Rs to these children. Hadn't she passed the Senior Oxford Local examinations at a particularly young age? Hadn't she been virtually guaranteed a place at the women's college at Girton, in the world-famous university of Cambridge? As for controlling the wilder boys, she was quite sure that they would present no problem. The secret, she said with a confident smile, was simply to get them interested in their lessons.

The members of the school board had cast each other significant glances at this, but eventually agreed that it could do no harm to let the young woman try. No doubt she would fail, but in the meantime the school would have been open and at least some of the children attending it. That, until they found someone really capable of taking on the job, was all they could do.

Cordelia was well aware of their scepticism and determined to prove them wrong. Her mind unsullied by any formal training or stale ideas, she had spent a good deal of time in preparing her lessons. She would, she learned, have approximately forty pupils, ranging in age from five to eleven. This prospect in itself could have been daunting enough, but to add to her difficulties the children would all be immigrants, some of them recent ones who might not even be able to speak English. And even between those who did, there might be friction inherited from their parents.

'Well, we shall all have to help each other,' she had declared when this was pointed out to her. 'I intend my school to be a happy one and I won't have my children squabbling because their fathers come from different countries, whatever they may do outside. Why, surely this is supposed to be a land of the free, for all nations to build together as one – how can we do that without teaching the children to tolerate each other?'

'Listen to the fine words!' Timothy jeered. '*My* school! *My* children! Anyone would imagine you were running the most exclusive school in America, and all it is –'

'Is a rather cramped schoolhouse with pupils who don't even have shoes for their feet,' Cordelia said quietly. 'You don't need to point that out to me, thank you, Tim. Just remember that our own mother taught in a school for children just as poor as these once. And our grandfather probably *attended* one – if he went to school at all. I see no shame in what I'm doing.'

'Neither do I,' said Jensen, who had called in to discuss patterns with Tim and stayed to drink a cup of coffee. 'You're quite right, Cordelia – these youngsters need desperately to be taught, and taught more than how to read and write. If America's to prosper, every man jack must learn to respect his neighbours, whether they're Italian, German or Irish. They've all come here to be *Americans*, that's what they have to remember. And it'd be a good thing for you to remember it too, Tim.'

'Well, I never meant to sneer,' Tim said, taken aback. 'I was only funning. I think it's a grand thing, Cordelia, and I'm glad you're doing it. Honestly.'

Cordelia smiled, never able to remain angry with her brother for long. In any case, it was too pleasant to have him home for once to spoil the occasion by quarrelling. She realised suddenly how little time Tim spent at home these days – wrapped up in her preparations for the school, she had hardly noticed how often he was absent in the evenings, or how late he returned. Now, looking at him more carefully, she saw his face had an unhealthy pallor and he looked tired, as though his life was not suiting him. She waited until Jensen had taken his leave, then came to kneel by his chair, her hand on his arm.

'Are you well, Tim? You look pale.'

'I'm all right.' He shook her hand away and she drew it back, feeling hurt by his abrupt rejection. 'Don't fuss, Cordelia.'

'I'm sorry, I didn't mean to fuss. But I seem to have seen so little of you lately, and –'

'Look, I've told you before,' Tim said roughly, 'I'm working hard at that glasshouse. I've got a lot of ideas and while Jensen's agreeable to my experimenting –'

'But you're not there all the time. Not in the evenings.'

'Sometimes I am,' he said defensively.

'But not always. Not when you go out dressed for entertainment and come in past midnight. Tim, where do you go? It worries me –'

'And I've told you it's none of your business!' Tim jumped to his feet. 'Can't you ever stop prying, Cordelia? Can't you leave me alone for a moment?' He glared down at her, his face flushed with anger now. 'You complain that I don't stay at home, but when I am here you do nothing but pry and nag – is it any wonder that I choose to go out instead? I've friends who appreciate me out there, if you want to know, and since there's no peace here I think I'll go and join them now.' He made for the door. 'I *was* going to stay here and wind wool, or whatever you wanted me to do this evening, but not if you're going to make my life a misery!' And he flung out and slammed the door behind him.

Cordelia stayed quite still, kneeling on the floor by the empty chair. After a few minutes, she leant forward and let her head rest against the cushions. The happy tone of the evening had been shattered – why?

It was as if Timothy had drawn completely away from her – as if they no longer shared any point of contact. The slightest comment on her part, the most casual query, was likely to produce this angry response, the accusations that she was nagging him, prying into his affairs, making him miserable. Yet in the past he'd been only too happy to tell her about his life outside the home. Together, they'd laughed over stories of what happened at his school, fulminated against the unfairness of some of the masters, worked and worried over the subjects that Timothy disliked most. And after he'd left school, when he'd begun to make friends and lead a life outside the home, he'd still confided in her. He had never in all their lives kept secrets from her.

And now, when they were alone together in a strange country, when they surely needed each other most for support and comfort, for the sharing of pleasures and disappointments alike, he had begun to treat her as a stranger.

Cordelia could remember Timothy behaving like this only once before. It was a long time ago, back in their childhood, when he had committed some misdemeanour he'd known she would disapprove of. Cordelia couldn't even remember now what it was, but she remembered Tim's mutinous, sulky face, the way he'd flung himself away from her and rushed from the room when she had begun to question him.

Were his new friends and his new pleasures a source of discomfort to him? Maybe he thought she would disapprove. Perhaps he was angry because he felt guilty and ashamed. She pushed these worrying ideas away as she reached her destination.

The schoolhouse stood by itself in a grassy playground,

surrounded by a white fence that matched the clapboard. It looked neat and clean; the school board had agreed that if it were to be opened again, it should be painted and refurnished. Cordelia looked at it with pride.

Already there was a small knot of children waiting, and she recognised Danny, Grainne's brother, the boy who had already proved himself a leader when she had given them the pennies. Cordelia had grown to know him better since that day, through frequent visits to the O'Donnell house, and had made up her mind that she must get Danny on her side and keep him there, if she were to make any success of this job. But Danny was not going to be easy to win over, she thought now, meeting his wary eyes. He enjoyed his freedom and his position amongst the other children too much to want to hand over authority to a mere schoolmarm.

'All right, children, you can wait outside until I'm ready to let you in,' she announced firmly. 'I shall ring the bell in five minutes' time, and I expect you all to form yourselves into two lines at once. One for the girls and one for the boys. Do you understand that?'

The children nodded, wide-eyed. Little Bridget was there, she saw, her thumb firmly in her mouth. Grainne must have sent her with Danny. Now that the glasshouses were working again, everyone would have left the house at least an hour ago, the younger children trusted to see themselves to school. Cordelia was surprised to find Danny there at all, and guessed that only curiosity would have brought him.

She went into the schoolhouse and looked around.

The building consisted of one room, filled with small desks and benches which all faced the low platform on which stood the teacher's desk. In the middle of the room there was a black, pot-bellied stove with a woodbox beside it. Down both sides ran long benches and shelves where the few books were ranged, behind the teacher's desk was a large blackboard and, at one side, the flag of the United States.

It was plain enough, not to say shabby, but in her imagination she saw the desks filled with bright-eyed children, eager to learn the lessons she had prepared. Closing her eyes, she heard their young voices chanting the multiplication tables and singing the songs she longed to teach them. She visualised the room gaily decorated with paper-chains and fir branches at Christmas, imagined it bright with spring flowers at Easter. She thought of the plays they would perform for appreciative parents, the concerts they would give and the picnics and rambles they would enjoy.

Well, there was no time to stand here dreaming. It was nine o'clock, and time to begin. Cordelia went to the door and began to ring the bell.

She looked outside, expecting to see the two neat lines she had ordered. The children, however, were standing in little groups, half uncertain, half unwilling. Cordelia called out to them.

'Come along, children, didn't you hear the bell? When you hear that, it means you must stop whatever you are doing and line up for school. Two lines, please. The girls here, by this door, and the boys there.' She wondered briefly what was the purpose of having separate doors for the sexes when both led into the same room, but as she saw them struggling to be first through decided that it must be so that the girls did not get trampled underfoot! Hastily following them inside, she attempted to call the seething mass of children to order.

'Sit at your desks, please! Boys on that side, girls on this.' Heavens, how long was it since these children had been at school? Had some of them *ever* been into a classroom? 'Silence!' she shouted, unheard amongst the noise. 'Be *quiet*!'

Most of the girls, she was thankful to see, did sit down at desks and half of them turned their faces towards her. But a few older ones, determined not to be outdone by the boys, were already climbing on the desks and there were at least three fights beginning in different parts of the classroom. Cordelia gazed helplessly at them. How could one begin to control the children when they couldn't even hear her and had no intention of listening anyway? How could she ever teach them anything?

Suddenly angry, she picked up the school bell and rang it vigorously. Its tones resounded through the room and the fighting boys stopped scrapping and turned astonished faces in her direction. There was a moment's silence, and Cordelia took immediate advantage of it.

'If you don't all stop that noise *at once*,' she declared in a tone as ringing as the bell, 'you'll be sent outside and not allowed back in. Do you understand me? You will never be allowed to come to school again!'

She uttered it as if it were the most awful threat she could imagine. The children gaped at her in astonishment and then Danny, speaking boldly because she had been to his house and he felt a proprietary interest in her, said in a bewildered tone, 'We never wanted to come anyway, miss. Me da' made us.'

The others joined in with their own agreement. 'Aye, 'twas me da' said we had to come.'

'Mammy told us we'd got to.'

'Me big brother said he'd flay me if I didn't go to school when I had the chance.'

Cordelia tried not to smile. Monkeys, making their own jungle, Grainne had said, but she saw them all as innocents who had never been given a chance. It would never do to let them see her smile, though – innocents they might be, but they would be quick enough to spot any sign of possible weakness, and not too innocent to exploit it. She rapped sharply on the desk to quieten the noise that was already beginning to break out again.

'So you've all been told you must come to school. And that means you must be quiet and well-behaved while you're here, and do your best to learn. If you do this, we shall get along very well and have good times together. If not – well, I've told you what will happen to anyone who doesn't behave.' She paused. 'I'm your teacher, Miss Henzel. Can you all say that? Miss *Henzel*.' She waited while a few voices stumbled over the unfamiliar name. 'Good. Now, I want you to say that to me every morning. I shall say "Good morning, children" and you must say "Good morning, Miss Henzel". Let's try it now, shall we? Good morning, children.'

'Good morning, Miss Henzel,' the children responded raggedly, and Cordelia smiled.

'That was very good. How many of you have been to school before? No – don't shout out your answers. Raise your hands – one will do – and wait until I ask for your answer. And tell me your name.' She waited as a few hands straggled into the air, and counted quickly. 'Nine of you. I see. Then I shall rely on you nine to help me with the others until they get used to it. 'She saw that Danny was one of the nine. 'Danny, you will be my monitor for today. Do you know what a monitor is?'

'It's someone that does all the work, miss,' he said sulkily, and the others laughed.

'That's partly true, Danny, but really a monitor is someone who can be trusted to be sensible and helpful. Do you think you can do that? I shall need quite a lot of help today.'

'What sort of help?' he asked, clearly reluctant to commit himself.

'Well, in giving out slates and pencils, that sort of thing. Until we begin to work I don't really know what sort of help

171

I'll need – I expect I shall need quite a lot of monitors to do different jobs, but today we'll do them together. Does that sound fair?'

'Suppose so.' His tone was grudging but at least his hostility seemed to have diminished slightly. Cordelia wondered if she might congratulate herself, but decided that it was much too early. But counting Danny's agreement, however grudging, as a small victory, she knew that it would be best to consolidate it and give him something to do immediately, thus confirming his status in both his and the other children's eyes. Once he had been seen to declare himself on her side, his own pride would compel him to stay there – and compel him also to win the others over.

'Give out the slates and pencils then, Danny. And when you've done that I want you to come and stand here beside me while everyone tells me their name. Sit down, please, the rest of you.'

The children sat down, some with a show of reluctance, as if wanting her to know that they were only here because there was at present nothing better to do outside. She wondered just what the previous schoolmistress, Miss Miller, had been like. No disciplinarian, if the nine who had attended her classes were anything to go by. The rest, apart from those like Bridget who would have been too young, seemed to have simply run wild.

Danny finished handing out the slates and pencils, and came to the platform.

'Now, I want you all to stand up, one at a time as I point to you, and tell me your names. For the first few days, you will all sit just where you are now – once I know you all, we'll sort you into groups. Danny, as the children say their names and how old they are, please write them down on this sheet of paper.' A thought struck her and she added quietly, 'You can write, can't you?'

'Yes, miss.'

'Good. Then let's begin.' She pointed at the child in the front row, a big, aggressive-looking boy of eight or so. 'Stand up, please, and tell me your name.'

'Stand up,' Danny added threateningly, and the boy scrambled hastily to his feet.

'Jacky Harris, miss. I'll be nine come October.'

'Very good, Jacky. That was well answered. Next?'

'Paddy O'Hara, miss.'

'Maria Putti.' An Italian accent there, amongst the Irish.

'Henry Pfeiffer, miss.'

'Jimmy Rooney.'

'Emmy Fike.'

Steadily, she went through the whole school, with Danny laboriously writing down the names beside her. Some of the smallest children, often with their thumbs firmly in their mouths like Bridget, were too shy to answer, and Cordelia did not insist. Danny invariably knew the names of each child present, and there was as often as not a bigger brother or sister to speak up for the dumbstruck 'babies'. By the end of the session, Cordelia was able to see that the entire school represented less than twenty-five families, with two or more children from some.

'Thank you, everybody. Danny, you may go back to your seat. Now, it will take me a little while to remember all your names, so when I ask you to speak, please say who you are again.' She looked at them. They were beginning to shift restlessly in their seats, their faces growing hostile. It was time to engage their interest.

'How many of you have heard of Paul Revere?' she asked suddenly.

They stared blankly. 'He don't live down this way, miss,' one girl volunteered.

'Does he come from Elmira?' a boy suggested. 'There's

a boy called Paul lives next door to my grandmother there.'

The rest shook their heads.

'Is he supposed to be here, then?'

'No,' Cordelia said, taking out one of the books she had brought with her, 'he isn't here and he doesn't live in Elmira. Paul Revere was the man who warned the American revolutionaries that the British redcoats were coming, over a hundred years ago. He rode through the night on his horse and he roused everyone along the way – people in villages and farms, who got up out of their beds and surprised the soldiers and sent them running. It's an exciting story. Do you want me to tell it to you?'

The children stared at her. Danny glanced round pugnaciously, and announced that they did. 'It's got to be better than doing sums,' he added in justification and the others made grimaces of agreement.

'Well, we'll see,' Cordelia said. 'You might even find you enjoy doing sums, when we do them my way.' She was beginning to enjoy herself. The children were a challenge; she sensed that they were wild enough to walk out at any moment, if they chose to do so. It was up to her to keep them there by holding their interest. She spared a brief thought for the girls she might have taught, meek and submissive in their neat uniforms, and then looked again at the thin, wary faces before her. A challenge, yes. And a worthwhile one.

She began softly:

> 'Listen, my children, and you shall hear
> Of the midnight ride of Paul Revere . . .'

Slowly, giving emphasis to each phrase and making certain that the children understood the story, she read

Longfellow's poem which told the dramatic story of that brave gallop through the night. The children listened: first with barely concealed impatience; then with reluctantly dawning interest; finally with bright-eyed excitement. The last few verses were punctuated by exclamation.

> '. . . the farmers gave them ball for ball,
> From behind each fence and farmyard wall,
> Chasing the redcoats down the lane . . .'

They cheered loudly. Cordelia stopped to let the shouting die down, and then continued:

> 'And only pausing to fire and load,'

But she was forced to stop again and lift both hands for silence. 'Just one more verse, children. Listen quietly now.' And she read the last few lines:

> 'So through the night rode Paul Revere,
> And so through the night went his cry of alarm
> To every Middlesex village and farm –
> A cry of defiance and not of fear,
> A voice in the darkness, a knock at the door,
> And a word that shall echo for evermore!
> For, borne on the night-wind of the past,
> Through all our history to the last,
> In the hour of darkness and peril and need,
> The people will waken and listen to hear
> The hurrying hoof-beats of that steed,
> And the midnight message of Paul Revere.'

She stopped and closed the book. And now the children were silent.

Cordelia looked at them and felt a tiny glow of triumph in her heart. She had caught them. And she knew that she would keep them.

It was only when she had seen off the last of the children that afternoon, waving to them as they ran away down the street, that Cordelia realised how utterly exhausted she was.

She stood for a moment in the warm sunshine, leaning against the door. The schoolroom needed tidying, but it must wait a few moments while she regained her strength. She needed to rest, to recover from the noise made by forty children and the strain of keeping their attention for nearly six hours, with only short breaks for playtimes and dinner.

Reading 'Paul Revere' to them had been an inspiration, she thought, remembering their eager questions, and she had promised to read it again. 'But not yet. We'll save it for a special treat.' There were other poems that would appeal to them, as well as teach them the history of their new country – poems such as the exciting tale of the Bunker Hill Battle at Boston, of the courage of Molly Pitcher during the battle of Monmouth, and the story of the Kentucky Belle. And once she had them fascinated by the rhymes and rhythms of poetry, she would lead them gently on to other great sagas, perhaps even encourage them to write their own verses . . .

Cordelia went into the schoolroom, tired but content. It was quiet in there now, but tomorrow it would be filled once again with the voices of children. She had no doubt that they would all return; she had worked hard to make every moment of the day interesting to all of them, big and small. Soon she would have to split them into groups, start them on work that was fitted to their ages and abilities; but there was plenty of time for that. Just at the beginning, it was more important to gain their confidence – to make them *want* to come to school.

'You're looking well pleased.'

Cordelia looked round startled, and then smiled. Jensen Novak stood in the doorway, his tall, lean body blocking out the sunshine. It gleamed gold on his hair, but his face was in shadow.

'The school's over for today – I'm just packing up to go home. You're too late to enrol now.'

He grinned. 'Well, I wasn't actually hoping to.' His voice was lazy and amused. He shifted from the doorway and came in, looking round the big room with interest. 'So this is your new enterprise. How did the first day go?'

'Quite well, I think. I read them some poetry.' She laughed at the way his eyebrows rose.

'Poetry? To those little street-arabs? You're kidding!'

'Indeed I'm not. I read them *Paul Revere's Ride* – you know it?'

'I know it.' He pursed his lips in a silent whistle. 'And they liked it?'

'Loved it. They want it again, but I'm not giving it to them yet.'

He laughed. 'I see you know how to handle kids!'

'I don't know,' Cordelia said soberly. 'I don't know if I can handle them, really. Today might just have been chance – they're curious to see what I'm like, what school's like. Tomorrow will be the test – and the next day. I just wonder if they'll all come back, and if they'll listen to me when they do.'

'They'll come back,' he said 'and if they don't want to listen to you, they'll surely want to look at you.'

Cordelia gave him a quick, startled glance and then turned away to stack a pile of books more tidily. She was suddenly acutely aware of the fact that they were alone in the schoolhouse. Outside, she could hear birds singing, the clip-clop of hooves along the road, the rattle of a cart. In the schoolroom, it was very quiet.

'You don't have a lot of books here,' Jensen said casually, and she answered quickly, relief in her voice.

'No, that's one thing I want to put right. We need a lot more books, books for every age I have here. And exercise books, too, as well as slates. I want them to be able to look back at their work, see what they've done. I'm going to start a scheme of rewards too – little tokens of some kind that they can be given for good work and keep. Maybe at the end of each term we could have prizes for those who have done best.' She was chattering and she knew it, but she would say anything to take that disturbingly intent look from Jensen Novak's eyes. 'By the way, why did you call in?' she asked desperately. 'Was there something you wanted?'

'Not particularly. I just wanted to see how you were getting along.' He perched himself on the front desk and grinned at her, his teeth very white. 'You've taken on quite a task here, Cordelia. Wouldn't a teaching post in one of the bigger schools over the river – the Free Academy, or St Mary's, for instance – have been more to your taste?'

Cordelia shrugged. 'It wasn't a matter of taste. I told you, they wouldn't take me there. This school was needed and I thought I could do the job. It's as simple as that.'

'Not that simple,' he said quietly. 'I know what the kids are like around here. You looked tired now, after only one day. D'you really think you're going to be able to handle them, day in, day out? When the novelty's worn off and they don't want to come? When they're out of sorts with themselves and with you, and the boys are fighting and pulling the girls' hair, and the girls are crying? Poetry won't be the answer all the time, you know. Don't you think you'll wish then that you'd waited till there was a chance at one of the bigger schools, where at least there are other teachers to help you keep control?'

'And what makes you think the children will behave like that?' she asked scornfully. 'What makes you such an expert on them?'

He looked at her gravely. There was no half-mocking smile on his face now; his lips were sober, his eyes filled with shadows.

'I know about these kids because I was one of them once. I never went to school – I had to work from the day we arrived. But I know what these streets are like, what hardship, poverty and hard living do to youngsters. They weren't brought up soft like you and your brother, Cordelia. They come here in the morning with empty bellies and they'll go to bed with not much more. Learning don't mean much when there's not enough bread on the table and not enough blankets on the bed.'

Cordelia was silent for a moment. Then she said, 'It might help them to earn the money to buy the bread and the blankets, though.'

'True. If you can keep 'em long enough.'

'I will,' Cordelia said, and she looked into his eyes as if she were making a promise. 'I kept them today. I'll keep them in the future. My boys and girls will leave this school ready to face the world, Jensen. And they'll understand the value of education – they'll know that there's more there for them if they want it. I hope they'll want it.'

'I hope so too.' He met her gaze, his eyes intent. 'And I have a feeling that they will, Cordelia. I believe you'll succeed. Now –' he swung his feet to the ground and stood up, tall and lithe – ' why don't you come down to the glasshouse with me. There's something I want to show you.'

Cordelia looked at him questioningly, but he grinned,

shook his head and laid a finger on her lips. The touch, so fleeting and so intimate, scorched like a brief kiss of fire on her soft skin. And then he had turned away, leaving her with one hand raised half-way to her mouth, staring at his back as he walked slowly out of the door.

Novak Crystal had expanded since the days when Jensen and his father had begun their cutting-shop in an old barn. From a one-pot furnace in a hastily erected shanty they had progressed to a large building of local brick with a furnace that held ten pots. Here, they had produced enough glass and made enough profit to be able to set up their later factories in Pennsylvania and Ohio.

The newer glasshouses were larger and more productive. But Jensen had never forgotten his vow, made over his sister's dead body, that he would make this one the finest of them all and build his house on the hill, high above the city. For a long time, it had seemed a dream that must be shelved. Now he had returned to make it come true.

'You have to make your own dreams come true,' he observed as he helped Cordelia up into his trap. 'Did you know that?'

She looked at him, startled, then gave his statement some thought. 'I suppose you do. My grandmother did. But they don't always come true, no matter what you do.'

'You know that already? Yes, I reckon you're right. Maybe we shouldn't even try too hard – maybe some dreams should remain just that. Dreams.'

Cordelia looked at him again, wondering at the sorrow in his voice. What had happened in his life that caused him to speak so sadly, that brought such shadows to his eyes? How little she knew of this man, she thought suddenly, yet how familiar he sometimes seemed to her, as if they had known each other long ago and half-forgotten the meeting. As if each was groping for recognition . . . She shook herself and turned away. Jensen Novak always made her feel unsettled, and it was a sensation she disliked.

'Here we are,' Jensen said, and as he brought the pony to a halt Cordelia wondered what he intended to show her. It was the first time she had been to his glasshouse; the first time, indeed, that she had been into any glasshouse since leaving England. After arriving in Corning to find her aunt and uncle's house closed and empty, her time had been almost wholly taken up with domestic concerns – finding a home for herself and Timothy, putting it into order, learning the household skills that had hitherto been mysteries known only to maids and servants. Even when she had mastered these, there had been the school and her new duties there. And always, that feeling that she should not become too involved with Jensen Novak . . . She looked about her with interest.

'I guess you'll find it a bit different from what you're used to,' Jensen remarked as he led her through the door.

Cordelia stood still, her eyes moving quickly over the scene before her. It was, indeed, different from her own family's glassworks. Here there was no great cone towering into the sky with tapering, smoke-blackened sides, its base almost filled by the great domed furnace and the chairs of men working at each glowing pot of molten glass. Instead, the furnace stood at one end of an echoing hall, its chimney rearing straight and solid through the beamed roof to soar a hundred feet into the sky. Only a few small, barred windows brought a dusty daylight into the hall, which was lit mostly by the lamps which hung from the ceiling. And, as all glasshouses must be, by the fiery blaze of the pots themselves and their simmering contents.

Cordelia watched as the men, working in their teams at each chair, swung the red-hot metal on the end of the irons.

To her surprise, she found it an odd, poignant comfort –
the way they worked was so familiar, so like the way of the
glassmakers at home, that it brought an ache to her throat.
That old man there, so big and broad, could have been her
grandfather, joining in as gaffer as he so often did at
Henzel's. The middle-aged man blowing a wineglass with
such ease could be Ben Taylor, who had worked since he
was a boy with her own father, blowing the blanks for Paul
to engrave; and the younger man beside him was, in the dim,
flickering light, the image of Ben's son, Frank.

It was a ballet that was performed wherever glass was
made, and always in the same sultry darkness, always in this
reddening glow that made the watcher think of Hell, with
the glassmakers as demons toiling with harpoon and trident
at the mouth of an eternal fire.

'It's not so very different,' she said to Jensen, and was
unaware of the longing in her voice.

He looked at her with an understanding she did not see,
and touched her arm gently to lead her round to the far side
of the great red brick furnace where a young gatherer,
stripped to the waist, had just handed an iron, tipped with
deep, burnished gold, to the gaffer.

'Tim!' Cordelia said in surprise.

Her brother turned and grinned. 'Hullo, sis. Come to
watch some work being done?'

'But what are you doing here?'

'An experiment. Look.'

Wondering, Cordelia stood beside him and watched as
the glassblower put the iron to his lips and began to blow.
He was a big man and his cheeks puffed out as if he were
blowing with the full capacity of his enormous lungs; but
Cordelia, a glassmaker's daughter, knew that the breath
travelling down that long pipe would be carefully controlled, that if it were not the swelling glass would be

distorted and deformed. Instead, the shape that formed and grew before her eyes was perfect – a graceful vase with gently curving sides.

The gaffer sat down at his rough wooden chair and began to marver the vase further, shaping and stroking it with the pucellas and battledore which were so familiar to Cordelia. He drew out the neck, elongating it to a slenderness that would barely take the stem of one rose. And that, Cordelia thought, was all that it needed to make it perfect. Just as books needed readers to make them complete, so vases needed flowers. In this case, a single, perfect rose.

But there was something strange about this vase. Something different. She stared at it.

'What colour is it going to be?'

Tim laughed, a high, excited sound. 'She's seen it, Jensen! I told you my sister was no fool.'

'I never thought she was,' the American said quietly. 'Show her, Timothy.'

Timothy took Cordelia by the arm to lead her away. The gaffer had almost finished his work now; he had taken the vase to the glory-hole several times to reheat it as he caressed it into shape. Now he snapped away the short punty-iron that held its base, and the taker-in, holding it carefully with wooden tongs, carried it to the *lehr* and set it on a shelf where it would move slowly through the long tunnel, its temperature decreasing as it went. There were already several other pieces of the same glass there, Cordelia saw, some like the vase she had just watched being made, others of different shapes and sizes. But all of the same strange colour.

'Tim –' she began, but her brother shook his head and tugged once again at her arm. Mystified, she followed him.

He led her to the other side of the great hall. Here, more

processes of glassmaking were going on; women were unloading the cooled glass from the end of the *lehr* and standing the pieces carefully on trays, others were lifting them and examining them carefully under a bright light, discarding any that were flawed. Further still, Cordelia saw the cutters and engravers at work, holding glasses and decanters against a spinning copper wheel, while a steady stream of fine sand poured constantly down from above. She wanted to cover her ears against the noise, which set her teeth on edge. But Timothy was talking again, that same note of excitement quivering in his voice.

'It's our new glass, Cordelia. See – this is the colour you've just watched being blown at the pot. What do you think of it?'

He lifted a vase exactly like the one Cordelia had seen, and she stared at it.

'Tim, how beautiful. It's – it's iridescent. It seems to shimmer like – like silk, or taffeta. I can't tell whether it's green or blue. And then in another light, it's gold or bronze.' Awed, she reached out for the vase and took it, turning it slowly in her own hands, letting her fingers trail softly across the sheen of its gleaming surface. 'How do you do it?'

'Ah – trade secret.' Timothy grinned triumphantly. 'But you like it? You think it'll sell?'

'I should think everyone who sees it will want to own it.'

'That's what we're hoping,' Jensen said, and she started slightly. She had almost forgotten he was there with them. She handed the vase back to her brother and turned to look up at the American. 'All it needs now is a name.'

'A name?'

'Sure. Every design needs a name, and this is something quite new.' He gave her a challenging glance. 'We thought you might be able to come up with something.'

'Me? You want me to think of a name for your new glass?' Cordelia felt her cheeks blush with pleasure. 'May I have time to think?'

'Of course. We didn't expect you to produce a name from the air.' Jensen's voice was warm and Cordelia found herself responding to it, her lips parting in a smile that lit her whole face. She caught the slight darkening of his eyes as he looked at her, and gave a tiny, involuntary gasp; then turned quickly away.

'I'll tell you as soon as I've thought of something,' she said, speaking directly to her brother. 'What will you do with this – engrave it? Have you any other ideas for new glass?'

'More than I can cope with, and no, I won't engrave it. Nor cut it,' Tim added with a sideways glance at Jensen. 'I agree with Grandfather there, sis – don't like cutting, and I think even engraving can ruin a good shape. And when you've got both shape and colour – well, why gild the lily? The whole point of an iridescent glass is that it's smooth, so that the shape can work its own magic on the colour – see what happens as you turn it?' The vase glimmered in the harsh light, now green, now gold. 'Cut that and you'd lose the whole effect.'

'Tim's quite right,' Jensen said. 'And I think he's started to think that way at just the right moment. Cut glass will never completely lose its popularity, and there'll always be a place for engraving, too – but right now, we need something new. Something to surprise people with – because people love surprises. They like to give 'em to others, too. And that's what this new glass will do. Folk will buy it, put it in their homes and wait for the comments.' He touched the vase with one long finger. 'All it needs now is the right name to sell it.'

'I'll think of something,' Cordelia promised, and she

looked with eyes as glowing and iridescent as the glass from one man to the other. 'I'll think of a name for your new glass. And for any other new glass you make, too.' She lifted her head and her tawny curls shone as if the blaze of the furnace had reached fingers of light to touch her hair. 'A new school and a new glass. What a day this is for the Henzels, Tim.'

Jensen Novak watched her. His dark blue eyes were hooded, his expression unreadable. And as brother and sister caught at each other's hand in their excitement and joy, he turned abruptly and moved away across the clattering glasshouse.

Chapter Nine

Jensen strode along the tree-lined street to the house he had rented. Barely noticing the soft dusky twilight that came earlier each evening as the year drew in, his mind was filled with thoughts of Cordelia Henzel.

He wished that it were not so. He had told himself five years ago that all that was finished for him. It could bring nothing but pain, a pain he had suffered too deeply ever to endure again. And he had known, from the moment of their first meeting on the train, that this young English girl had the power to cause him that pain, if he allowed her. She might not know it, sitting there so innocent with her kitten's eyes, her pale, creamy complexion and her tawny hair tumbling in a soft riot of copper curls over her wide, smooth forehead, but she possessed a weapon that threatened to be lethal to his lonely heart. And although he had determined to avoid her, it seemed that his treacherous body took him out of his way to engineer meetings. Why else should he be found so often sauntering casually along Second Street?

Impatiently, he turned on his heel and marched back along the road. He could not tolerate the idea of going inside his stuffy, too-silent house, not while he was in this restless mood. He came to the corner and wheeled sharply to climb the hill. Good, hard physical exercise was what he needed to drive these thoughts from his mind.

But Cordelia would not be driven out. As the evening grew darker, her face was even clearer before his eyes. As the roosting birds fell silent, her voice rang clear in his ears.

And, as he came to the edge of the stream that twisted down the hill and looked down into the glittering waters, it was her laughter that chimed softly in his ear.

It could not go on. He wanted to talk to her, to tell her the truth about himself – about himself and about Karin. Yet that would presuppose an intimacy which he felt she didn't want. What *did* she want, anyway?

Jensen felt that he would never be able fully to plumb the mystery of Cordelia's mind. And told himself, hopelessly, that he would never have the right.

One day soon, he would have to go back to White Mills and carry out his promise to bring Karin here. And Cordelia Henzel would move even further out of his reach.

Over the river, in Knoxville, Grainne was washing her sister Bridget and making her ready for bed.

'And don't forget to say your prayers,' she commanded, giving the black curls a thorough brushing. 'Ye and Danny both. Now, say goodnight to your Mammy.'

Bridget, wearing the old shirt of Danny's which she slept in, trotted over to where her mother lay on the sofa and lifted her face for a kiss. Mary O'Donnell hugged her close for a moment and then lay back against her pillow. Her face was thin and pale, and to Grainne's anxious eye she looked more weary than ever.

'I wish you'd give up that auld job in the mill,' Grainne said when she had tucked Bridget into the bed they shared in the other room. 'We could manage fine if I did some cleaning jobs after work. Mrs Hungerford's looking for someone to do the rough, so they were telling me today.'

Her mother shook her head. 'It'd be too much for ye, Grainne, with all ye do here. Who'd look after the little ones? Danny runs wild enough as it is, and Bridget looks to ye more than she does me now. And it's not hard work I do in the mill. I can manage that as long as I know you're here of an evening.'

'If it isn't hard work, why do ye come home so bone-weary every night?' Grainne demanded. 'Mother, I'm young and strong, it'd be nothing to me to do another job. Just looking at glass to see it's not flawed isn't hard labour, now is it? Look, I could go earlier in the mornings – it's bound to be a morning job at the Hungerfords, and the earlier the better for that sort of work. Just a bit of scrubbing and cleaning, and you'd not know I was doing it. And Danny sees himself and Bridget to school.' She sighed. 'If only our Declan was here. With his wage, we could manage easily and you'd never have to work again. Ye could just lie there and be a lady.'

'It's his cheery face and his joking I miss most,' Mary said sadly. 'I miss him every hour of the day, Grainne, and that's the truth.'

'We all do, Mother.' Grainne thought of the day when she had gone with Declan to the railroad station to see him off, after he had had that terrible fight with their father. That was the day when she had almost walked under a train and that good-looking young Englishman had saved her and given her coffee and bread. She had never seen him again; perhaps he'd just been visiting and was now miles away, having forgotten the Irish girl he'd held so briefly in his arms . . . 'Still, at least we know where he is now,' she went on brightly, bringing her thoughts back to her brother. 'And we know he's all right – got himself a good job and writes regular.'

'Read me his last letter again. I like to hear his words – it's almost as good as having him here in the room.'

Grainne went to the dresser and took down the small pile of letters that had come from Declan. Since those first few weeks, when they had received only scraps of information to tell them he was still alive, her brother had found himself a job in one of the Pennsylvanian glasshouses and settled into lodgings. He seemed happy enough, writing to tell them of his work as a cutter and making humorous little sketches of the people who shared his lodgings. He had always been good with a pencil, Grainne thought as she read his latest note aloud, and ought to be designing the patterns he cut. But you needed training for that, at an art college or such, and there had never been money for that kind of thing in the O'Donnell household.

There was never money for anything, she thought, going to the fire to heat some milk for her mother. No matter how hard they worked, the family never did any more than scrape along, with just enough wage coming in to feed them all, to pay the rent on the rooms here and to keep themselves decently, if not adequately, clothed.

If their father didn't spend so much on drink, it would be different. But he'd been that way ever since Grainne could remember – ever since they'd left Killarney to come here. And there'd be no changing him this late in the day. Not even with his wife lying there night after night on the sofa, barely strong enough to drag herself to work each morning, needing good, strong medicine more than he needed his drink, but never getting it.

Grainne sighed and poured the milk into a cup. Tomorrow, when she was paid, she'd get some eggs and beat one into the milk her mother drank each evening. It was little enough, but it might help to give her a good night's rest and some strength.

'Declan says he'll send some money soon,' she said cheerfully. 'That'll be a help, won't it, now?'

'It will that.' Mary drank some of the milk and leaned her head back. 'But I'd a sight rather he was here than away in

Pennsylvania. Whose glasshouse does he say he's working in there?'

'He doesn't mention the name. But he seems to be doing fine. He'll come back soon, Mother. Me Dad'll soon forget the fight and we'll have Declan home again before ye can say Paddy Murphy's potato. See if I'm right.'

'I hope ye are,' Mary said softly, 'for if he doesn't come soon I don't think I'll see him again.'

Grainne came swiftly across the kitchen and dropped on her knees beside the sofa, taking her mother's shoulders in her hands. Their thinness frightened her, but she spoke strongly, almost angrily.

'Now, you're not to be talking like that, Mother! Not see our Declan again, indeed – that's just foolish talk and you know it. Why, there's years left in ye yet, haven't ye to wait to see our Bridget marry some fine, rich man and bring comfort to us all? This is just a passing sickness – you've been working too hard all these years and now ye need a rest, there's no more to it than that.' She pressed her lips to the wasted cheek. 'Drink your milk, there's a dear, now, and go to sleep. I'll be here and as quiet as a mouse, and I'll not let me Dad wake ye up when he comes home from the saloon.'

Mary smiled faintly and did as she was told. Gently, Grainne laid her back on the pillow and tucked the thin blanket more comfortably around her. Already, her mother's eyes were closing. She drew a stool close to the bed and sat there, holding the thin, cold hand and watching with anxious love.

Declan should come home. Her father must be made to see that the quarrel was over and should be forgotten. They needed him. Her mother, especially, needed him. And for all her brave words, Grainne was terribly afraid that Mary might be right – if he didn't come soon, she would never see her eldest son again.

September slipped into October and the air sharpened. The trees had begun to flame now, as if fire had touched their boughs. The valley was surrounded by a blaze of colour as the burnished tints of gold, orange and scarlet swept away the green of summer and threw a mantle of shimmering silk over the thickly wooded hills. Children went out to gather nuts and berries and, in the orchards, trees were hung with crimson apples and golden plums as if with lanterns for some outdoor celebration.

In Jensen's glasshouse, the work went on as steadily as before. At Cordelia's suggestion, they called the new glass Opalene and it was now in production. Its glossy sheen had attracted immediate attention and orders were pouring in for the wineglasses, decanters, jugs and vases which Timothy had designed. There was also considerable interest in the stranger shapes he was making – the free-flowing designs he had based on natural objects such as stones, leaves and running water – and in the way he was blending the new Opalene with clear crystal, and even carving it in sculptures such as had never before been seen in glass.

'This is what I came to Corning for,' he told Cordelia jubilantly. 'I would never have been allowed to do this at home. Mother would have had a fit! And as for Grandfather, he would have disowned me on the spot.'

'Grandmother wouldn't,' Cordelia observed, and Timothy laughed.

'No, Grandmother wouldn't. She's different – still young in her mind and her heart. You know, I think I'll make her something special, something to mark the new era in glassmaking. Something she could stand up on that mantelpiece alongside the Compson Chalice and Father's first piece of black cameo. What do you think it should be?'

'A new piece of glass for Grandmother,' Cordelia said

thoughtfully. 'Yes – it might be just the thing to convince her that we were right to come.' A peace-offering to take home with them when they finally left Corning, to show that their hearts still belonged in the Black Country. 'Why not a new chalice, to stand beside the old one?' she suggested. 'With the cameo vase in the middle, it would make a fine set. Three generations of glass . . . It's a wonderful thought, Tim.'

'A new chalice? I wanted to do something different – something that would show just how far I've advanced since we came here. That shape I showed you the other day – the bowl with the jagged edge. I thought I might do something like that.'

'It wouldn't look so imposing. No, Tim, if you want it to stand in Henzel Court and be admired, you'd be best to stick with a traditional object. Make it of the most modern glass you can – but don't shock them yet with these new shapes. You know how they think – glass must be functional as well as ornamental. A lovely chalice, in Opalene or the new glass you're experimenting on now, with the gold inlay – that could look truly magnificent.'

'It would. You're right. And the new glass is going to be even better than Opalene, Cordelia.' Tim rose to his feet, vibrant with an energy that would not let him sit still. 'Gold and silver, inlaid in the glass itself – that's what I'm working on now. Can you imagine it, Cordelia, a huge vase shimmering with precious metals – a gift fit for kings and queens! That's the kind of thing Jensen and I aim to make. And smaller pieces, too – pieces that the families who care about their homes, who want to fill them with beauty, will want to buy. Something they can buy from nobody else – that's what we're going to produce. Glass that nobody else has ever dreamed of.'

Cordelia listened to the excitement in his voice and

watched the light in his eyes. Seldom before had she seen him like this – alive with every fibre, as incandescent as his own molten glass as he described his vision of what that glass could be. His face glowed with an enthusiasm that came directly from being permitted at last to carry his vision through from dream to reality. Only a true genius, she thought, could do that; only a genius would have the vision in the first place.

And that Timothy was a genius seemed now to be in no doubt. Jensen had given him an entirely free hand in the glasshouse, and he was like a child in Aladdin's cave, surrounded by treasures; only in Tim's case, the treasures were in his own mind and the true delight lay in their creation.

Why, then, did he seem to have these other needs – needs that took him out of the house, night after night, to return late with a face shining with a less healthy colour, eyes that were feverish and burning and refused to meet her own? Cordelia had waited up for him at first, terrified that he had met with an accident, running out to the door as soon as she heard his step. She had seen the guilty shame in his face quickly replaced by self-righteous anger, as if he found relief from his guilt in accusing her of nagging and interfering. Interfering! The reproach hurt her more deeply than anything else; as if she, Timothy's twin, could ever *interfere* in his life.

Where did he go? He had never told her directly, and his secretiveness brought her fresh pain. She watched him, listened to the remarks he let fall, read the newspapers and heard comments made by Martha or Bob about the activities of the young men of Corning.

'They get a bit wild, this time of year,' Martha remarked tolerantly. 'And there's plenty for them to do – the races, cockfights, a bit of dog-baitin'. Mind, I don't like it myself – never been happy seein' animals set against each

194

other. And I'm glad my Bob don't go. But there's plenty who do, and nothin' against it in law.'

Nothing against it in law, but Cordelia knew that Tim must remember their family's disapproval of such sports. Was that why he was ashamed? Had he been watching two birds tear each other to shreds?

Or was there more than that? Cordelia had the impression that whatever Tim did with his evenings, he didn't really enjoy them. It was as if he felt he must go, for other reasons – to prove himself amongst his fellows, perhaps.

But Cordelia had too much to occupy her these days to worry overmuch about Timothy. Her work at the school was proving more exciting, more of a challenge, than she had ever dared hope. She now had a class of forty-five children and had managed to sort them into groups – readers and non-readers, those who could write and those who were still learning clumsily to hold a pencil. Keeping them all in order and busy all day was a task that stretched her ingenuity to its limits, yet she rarely closed the schoolhouse door at the end of the day without a feeling of having made some achievement, however tiny. And the children had woven themselves tightly around her heart; she loved them for their pugnacious refusal to allow poverty to defeat them, for their cheeky determination not to be beaten. And she believed they had begun to love her too.

'Our Bridget never stops talkin' about ye these days,' Grainne remarked one day when Cordelia called in to see how Mary was. 'It's Miss Henzel this and Miss Henzel that till we're fair bemused by it. And even Danny thinks the sun shines out of ye. Didn't he bring ye some leaves the other day, for the Nature table, he said?'

'That's right.' Danny had come in bearing a huge sheaf of leaves, blazing with colour – maple in red and gold, beech as coppery as Cordelia's hair, tawny-fingered chestnut. He had stalked through the crowd of boys gathered at the school gate, ignoring their jibes, and deposited the bouquet firmly on Cordelia's desk. Since then they had decorated the whole schoolroom, bringing a shaft of warm colour to every corner, and the rest of the boys had vied with one another to bring her a gift that would outshine Danny's – a scarlet apple from one, a basket of hickory nuts from another, a huge squash from a third.

Cordelia had brought some of these offerings to the O'Donnells and was gratified to see Mary eat some of the apple. The Irishwoman's appetite had grown even poorer now, and she was thin and pale enough to be almost translucent. She had at last agreed to give up working and lay for most of the time on the old sofa in the kitchen. Cordelia shared Grainne's fear that she might not live to see Declan again, but there seemed to be little they could do. Declan had lost the first job he had acquired in Pennsylvania and was now looking for work again. The possibility of his earning the fare home seemed remote, and the O'Donnells could not afford to send him the money.

'Why don't you let me help?' Cordelia asked once again when she and Grainne were alone together. 'I'm sure Tim and I could manage –'

'No. It's good of ye to offer, but we couldn't take it. You've little enough yourselves, I can see that, and we've always prided ourselves on never going on the borrow. What we don't earn, we don't have, and it's as simple as that.'

'But when it's your mother's life –'

But Grainne shook her head firmly and Cordelia burst out, 'Well, it's a pity your father doesn't take the same attitude about his drinking, then! He spends enough money at the saloon to bring Declan back tomorrow. Can't you stop him – can't you make him see what's happening to your mother?'

'He knows well enough,' Grainne said quietly. 'That's why he drinks. Ye see, Cordelia, ye don't know much about the sort of people we are. The sort of man me Dad is. He's a very sensitive sort of man –'

'So sensitive he'll let your mother die without seeing her son again, just for the price of a few beers!'

'It's not that easy, Cordelia. Me Dad tries hard. He works hard. He spends his life doing a job he hates, just to bring some money into the house. Look, he's never had a chance. Fifteen children they had, the pair of them, and twelve surviving. It takes a lot of work and a lot of money to bring up that number.'

'I know, but –'

'He's had to give his whole life to his family. He's never lived the way he wanted to. If he wants a few drinks of a Friday, just to make it bearable, who am I to grudge him? And if it gives him a bit of comfort now – no, Cordelia, he's only come home fighting drunk that once, over Declan and the Italian girl. And even though it meant we lost Declan, I still can't find it in me heart to blame the auld man.'

Cordelia was silent for a few moments. Then she said, 'What about the Italian girl, Grainne? Is she still waiting for Declan?'

Grainne shook her head sadly. 'Her family didn't like it any more than me Dad did. They made her marry some Italian boy – she lives down in Painted Post now.'

'So it was all wasted,' Cordelia said sadly, and Grainne nodded.

'Seems like it. But that's the way of the world, Cordelia. We can't have the things we want. We just have to try to want the things we have.'

Cordelia went home, thinking about Grainne's words. Did she 'want the things she had'? The school, her life with Tim, their lodgings – all so different from the life she had envisaged at home. There, as members of the Henzel family, successful glassmakers and known throughout the Black Country, she had enjoyed a position she had not even realised she had. She had grown up in a comfortable home, with plenty of good food, good clothes and transport to wherever she might want to go. She had been surrounded by a family and friends who loved her, had never wanted for company, and she had been able to acquire the education that was so important to her.

Here in Corning, all that had disappeared. Their lodgings, though made more comfortable because of the furniture lent to them by the Robinsons, were mediocre and shabby. Because they didn't know how much Timothy would be able to earn, the money they had brought with them had had to be saved and eked out gradually. And Cordelia had been forced to learn the skills of cooking and housekeeping that she had always considered the task of other people and barely even noticed at home.

Alone, too proud to ask for help or advice, she had struggled with unfamiliar jobs; washing and ironing clothes, cleaning, shopping, preparing and cooking their food. There had been days when she had been almost ready to sit down and weep, to tell Tim that she would give up, they would return home – but always, as he came in through the door with his face bright with excitement over some new piece of glass, some fresh idea, she would remind herself of their reason for travelling all this way, and bite back the words.

Yet when Harry's letter had arrived from England yesterday, telling them that they must move into the house on Birch Street and stay there until he and Ruth returned, there had been no doubt in her mind as to what the answer should be.

'No. We'll stay where we are. I'd rather be independent.'

They were at the Robinsons' house, where they had gone to spend the evening, and Jensen had been invited too. The others looked at her with surprise.

'But, Cordelia, you'd be so much more comfortable there,' Martha said. 'Harry and Ruth's house is so nice. And those lodgings of yours – well, they're just plain shabby.'

'All the same, I'd rather stay there,' Cordelia said firmly. 'We're quite happy, aren't we, Tim? We can manage very well by ourselves. I know Uncle Harry and Aunt Ruth mean well, but the fact remains that if we move into their house we'll be dependent on them. And when they come back, we'll just be their nephew and niece – here under their care. And since we've been on our own –'

'But of course you'd be under their care,' Martha said, looking bewildered. 'They're your uncle and aunt. It's only right. You know, I still wish you'd come and stayed right here with us once our daughter went back home. I told you there was room, you'd have been real welcome. But with Harry's house gettin' opened up again –'

'We aren't going there,' Cordelia repeated, and looked at her brother. 'You don't want to, do you, Tim?'

Timothy looked uncomfortable, and she knew he was thinking of his own independence – his freedom to come and go as he pleased, without questions that might be either kindly or disapproving. 'Well, not really. But I'd like a bit more room. I want somewhere to work – you must agree we're pretty cramped in the lodgings.'

'Harry's place is the answer then,' Bob Robinson remarked, taking his pipe from his mouth. 'Plenty of room there.'

'Not the only answer, though.' Jensen, who had been listening to the discussion, spoke suddenly. 'There's another option you might like to consider.'

They turned and looked at him.

'And what's that?' Cordelia asked.

'My lodgings. The house I've been renting. You know my own place'll be finished pretty soon – I reckon to be moving up the hill soon after Christmas. Why not take over that? It's no palace, but it's a darned sight better'n where you are now.'

'That's a good idea!' Tim said at once. 'There's plenty of room there and we could easily afford it now. What do you say, Cordelia?'

'I don't know.' She hesitated. Jensen had already done so much for them . . . 'It would mean waiting until after Christmas,' she hedged. 'There must be other houses we could rent.'

'A minute ago you were happy to stay where we are!' Tim exclaimed, but Jensen smiled – as if, Cordelia thought, he could see straight into her mind and knew exactly what was going on there.

'That's no problem. I'm going back to White Mills pretty soon and don't see myself coming back to Corning for any length of time until I'm ready to move in. I can easily put up in the Pickwick whenever I do drop by. You could move in – let's see, in a couple of weeks' time, how would that suit you?'

'That's marvellous,' Tim said eagerly, and they all looked at Cordelia.

'Sounds a good enough plan,' Bob remarked, and Martha nodded.

'That's a good house Jensen's been renting. Should suit you and Tim fine, and it won't worry your uncle and aunt any to know you're in decent lodgings. Though I guess they'll still wonder why you don't want to go into their place . . . You're sure you won't change your mind about that, Cordelia?'

'Quite sure,' she said firmly. But her eyes were on Jensen. Since he'd said he was going away, he hadn't looked at her. She wished suddenly that they were alone – and then was thankful that they were not. 'Very well, we'll take the house when you leave, Jensen. In a fortnight's time, you say?'

'About then, I guess.' He looked at her now and she felt a quiver within her as she saw the darkness of his eyes. 'I reckon to be away about six weeks, all told,' he added quietly. 'Though I'll be back odd times, just to see everything's going right . . . I guess I'll call in and say hello.'

'Of course,' Cordelia said, but her mind was on the house – the house Jensen had lived in. Her and Timothy living there. Being in the rooms he had inhabited, using the things he had used. The thought gave her a strange sensation; one she wasn't sure she liked but wanted to explore again.

They were still waiting to move into their new lodgings when Tim came home with the news that a circus was coming to Corning. 'The posters are all over town,' he said excitedly. 'And see this big advertisement in the *Journal* – it takes up a whole page.' Together, they bent over the newspaper that Tim spread over the table and scanned it eagerly. 'Twenty-two elephants, Cordelia – can you imagine! Four big rings – how shall we ever be able to watch them all? Trained horses and ponies, acrobats and gymnasts, clowns, wild beasts, Cleopatra, Queen of Egypt, musical bands – Cordelia, we must go to it. I'll take some time off . . . It says here they need four railway trains to bring it all – it must be magnificent.'

'I'll give the children the day off school,' Cordelia said.

'They won't be able to concentrate on their lessons anyway. How long will it stay?'

'Oh, several days I imagine. There's so much to see, everyone will need to go more than once. There will be sideshows as well, and exhibitions. The best performance will be on Saturday night, so we'll go then – you and I.' He gave her a slightly shamefaced glance. 'You're right – you don't have enough fun, and I mean to make it up to you.'

Cordelia looked at him, standing there with the newspaper in his hand, his hair tousled, his eyes as bright as a child's. And you are still a child in so many ways, she thought affectionately. But, here in America, growing to be a man. A man she would be proud to call her brother.

A man her mother and grandparents would be proud of too when he eventually returned to England.

Timothy was still reading the advertisement. 'It says here that there will be a Wild West Show as well, with real cowboys and Indians – that'll be exciting. And they have a trapeze artist who has performed before all the crowned heads of Europe, what do you think of that?'

'Including Queen Victoria?' Cordelia asked sceptically. 'He must be a very old trapeze artist, then, for I don't believe she has been to a circus since she was a young woman – if she ever went to one at all.'

'Well, all except Queen Victoria, perhaps.' Tim said doubtfully. 'Anyway, I'm sure he must be very good. And there's bound to be a minstrel group and boxing and cheapjacks – it'll be fun, whatever there is.'

The circus was every bit as exciting as Tim had promised. Together they sat in the front row and watched with wide eyes as the elephants marched in – only twelve of the twenty-two promised, but as Tim pointed out, there wasn't really room for them all in the ring at once and no doubt the others would be performing later. They each wore an embroidered cap which stretched down over the thick part of their trunks, and matching garters around their wrinkled knees, with bells sewn on them. They paraded round the ring, solemn as judges but with tiny, twinkling eyes, each one holding the tail of the elephant in front firmly in his trunk. The leading elephant bore a large howdah, like a tent of scarlet silk, on his broad back, and on his neck sat a small Indian boy with a turban and a long pointed stick.

The elephants were followed by ponies, two dozen perfect little dapple greys who cantered round the ring to the crack of the ringmaster's whip, their riders brilliantly dressed in silks and satins of rainbow hues, and covered with glittering sequins and jewels that made Cordelia gasp. Tim grinned at her incredulity and whispered, 'They're not real, they're just paste,' and she laughed but continued to stare as if she were looking at the Crown Jewels.

The evening passed rapidly, a dazzling kaleidoscope of music and colour and movement. The trapeze artist was certainly too young to have performed before Queen Victoria, but he was impressive none the less and Cordelia felt her heart leap to her throat as she stared up at his daring flight through the highest recesses of the great tent. The acrobats displayed an almost impossible agility as they tumbled in the sawdust, and the conjuror had everyone believing implicitly in his magic. The lion-tamer controlled his beasts with nothing more than a chair and a whip, and whenever the entertainment threatened to flag, on came the ponies once more, with their riders accomplishing the most impressive feats on their bare backs, or a tumble of clowns burst in and had everyone holding their sides with their antics.

At last the whole company entered in a glittering parade to take their final bow. With the rest of the audience,

Cordelia and Timothy stood up, cheering and clapping until hands and voices were sore. And then, chattering excitedly, they made their way to the doors and out into the cool night air.

Most of the sideshows had stopped now, but there were still a few calling the people to come and sample their candies, to take a look at America's Handsomest Woman or to gaze on the priceless beauty of a Princess of India. Timothy, reluctant to leave, wandered slowly over to a little cluster of lights.

'Hullo!' he said. 'Here's a glassmaker.'

Cordelia followed his glance. In a corner of the field, sandwiched between a boxing booth and an apparatus for young men to test the strength of their muscles, stood a little bench. On it were the lamps and glass tubes, the selection of birds and animals and flowers, that were the paraphernalia of a lamp blower. Cordelia and Timothy had seen such things a hundred times at fairs and glassmakers' picnics in England, but it was the first time they had come across one in Corning, and they drew nearer, curious to see if there were any difference.

The man behind the bench was dark and stocky, with broad, muscular shoulders and a deep chest. His hands looked too large, the fingers too thick, to be handling the slender glass tubes with which he worked. But they moved nimbly, holding the flame steady against the slender tube, shaping and fashioning it with a rapidity that was impressive even to Timothy. Within a few moments, he had produced a bird on a twig, a long-stemmed flower and a small sailing ship. He set them beside the other pieces he had made – the tinkling bells, the tiny glass slipper, the prancing pony – and glanced up.

His dark eyes met Cordelia's in a bold, insolent stare. She smiled in spite of herself, ready as most women to forgive an impertinent look from a fairground gipsy, here today and gone tomorrow and undeniably attractive. His teeth flashed white as he grinned back, and she felt an unexpected tremor inside. And then his eyes moved to Tim.

Cordelia saw the shock in them. She saw him blink, saw his eyes widen and turn almost black before narrowing to slits. She saw his full lips part a little, almost as if he were speaking a name. Then he laid down his lamp and glass and, with his eyes still on Timothy, began to pack away the assortment of birds and animals he had made.

There was no one else near them. The glassblower's bench was badly placed, between the two more interesting booths. And the ground was emptying now that the circus was over.

'Don't go yet,' Timothy said to the glassblower. 'I was hoping to see some more of your work.'

'I'll be here again tomorrow.' He had a deep voice, with a trace of an accent which Cordelia could not quite place. He was still staring at Timothy, as if he dared not take his eyes off him. Cordelia saw his eyes move slowly over her brother's face, taking in his nut-brown hair, his silver-grey eyes, his easy smile. It was almost as if he knew Timothy already – yet Tim made no sign of recognition and was now examining the glass pieces with interest and asking questions.

'You know about glass?' the dark man said. 'You are a glassmaker too?'

'Yes, but not this sort. I work in one of the glasshouses here.'

'But you are not American?'

'No, my sister and I are English. We're over here on a visit and I'm doing experiments in new kinds of glass.' Timothy held up a tiny hummingbird, hovering over a wide-petalled flower, and turned it so that the light caught and gleamed on its surface. 'You're good at this. Have you never thought of working in a glasshouse?'

'I once believed that I would. My family owned a glass-house, before we came to this country.' The eyes were dark and brooding. 'I thought that I would grow up there, happy in the little community that we had built over the years. But it was not to be. The plans one makes as a child never are, it seems to me.'

Cordelia saw Timothy glance up as the bitter note in the deep voice registered with him. Suddenly, she felt afraid. She looked at the man's olive skin, his black hair and deep brown eyes, and wanted to be away from him, out of his sight. She felt a threat emanating from that brooding expression, a menace she could not define.

'Tim – let's go. It's getting late.' She laid her hand on his arm.

'In a minute.' He moved impatiently. 'This is interesting . . . What happened?' he asked the glassblower. 'Why did you come to America? If your family had their own glass-house in – where did you come from?'

'From France. From the part of France that Germany snatched from us during the cruel war of 1871.' The man raised his eyes and looked steadily at Timothy's face. 'Let me ask you something. Have you ever heard of the name Henzel?'

Cordelia gasped. Fear licked through her and she tugged at her brother's arm. But he didn't move. He stood quite still, staring at the glassblower in astonishment.

'Henzel? Why, that's *our* name! How in the world did you –?'

'Timothy, come away! He's nothing but a charlatan, you can see – these places are full of them. He's seen us before, he's found out about us and now he wants – I don't know what he wants, but he means no good, I know it! Come away, Tim, please.'

The man flicked a glance at her and she shivered into

silence. Tim turned and looked down, his eyes bright with surprise and interest.

'Cordelia, what on earth is the matter with you? Whatever harm could he possibly do us?' He turned back to the Frenchman. 'We're Henzels,we come from Stourbridge in England where our family has one of the best glasshouses in the country. But how did you know? Have you been there?'

'No, I have never been to England.' Slowly, deliberately, he wrapped a glass ship and put it into his bag. 'But I believe our families are connected. I suspected it the moment I saw you.' His eyes moved again over Tim's face. 'You are very like an English glassmaker I once knew. He came to visit us and stayed perhaps longer than he should. His name was Paul – Paul Henzel, or Paul Thietry as he was sometimes known.'

There was a brief stillness, a moment of complete silence. It seemed to Cordelia that the world had hesitated in its turning. She turned her head slowly and looked up at her brother. His eyes were silver in the flaring lights, his head thrust slightly forward.

'Paul Henzel was our father,' he said at last. 'And I am like him. He died last year. And you – ?'

'My name is Thietry. Pierre Thietry. My father was called Gabriel and my mother was Annette.' He paused. 'I was only a child when your father came to visit us, but I remember him well. Very well indeed.'

Chapter Ten

There was a long silence. Even the sounds of the fairground seemed to recede as Cordelia stared first at her brother, then at this stranger who declared himself to be no stranger. Pierre Thietry? Could it be possible? She searched her mind for memories, for stories told to them as children. Her father, visiting the Thietry showrooms in Paris, the château in Lorraine where Thietry Cristal was made. Gabriel and Annette. The children, lost at the outbreak of the Franco-Prussian War . . . Was Pierre really one of those children, wandering America as a fairground glassblower? Could he really have remembered Paul and recognised him in her brother Timothy?

No wonder he had stared at them! No wonder he had questioned Timothy. Why, he must have experienced a considerable shock when he first looked up and saw what must have seemed like a ghost from the past watching him at work.

She looked at the Frenchman again. He was watching them through narrowed eyes, his expression withdrawn, brooding, almost hostile. As if he regretted having spoken. His eyes met hers, dark and secretive, and he turned away abruptly and began to pack away the glass tubes he used for blowing his tiny ornaments.

She felt a tiny chill; a feeling almost of menace.

Timothy had noticed nothing. After his first moment of surprise, he welcomed Pierre Thietry almost like a long-lost brother. His face lit up with excitement, he reached across the bench and grasped the Frenchman by the shoulder, slapping his other hand across his back. He laughed aloud and turned to Cordelia, exclaiming in delight at this unexpected meeting. And nothing would do but that Pierre should pack all his things away safely and come at once to eat dinner with them.

'You're part of our family,' he declared. 'Why, I don't know what relation you are to Cordelia and me – second or third cousins half a dozen times removed, I daresay – but it must be something. We can't let you go without hearing all about you, Mother would never forgive us.'

'Your mother?'

'She went to Paris, didn't she, sis? When Father first went, to see the Exhibition in – in –'

'1867,' Cordelia supplied. 'Grandfather and Grandmother went too, and then they came home and Father stayed in France. He was caught in the Siege of Paris and only just escaped. Mother thought he was lost and she'd never see him again.'

'But what happened to you? And your brothers and sisters – how many were there?' asked Tim. 'And your mother – is she in America too?'

Pierre's face darkened. 'We weren't so lucky as your father,' he said briefly. 'Our family was broken up. There are only two of us left now, myself and my sister. But you don't wish to hear all that.'

'Of course we do!' Timothy cried, but Cordelia touched his arm.

'Your sister?' she said, moving a little closer to the broad, sturdy figure. 'Is she with the circus too?'

Pierre's dark brown eyes rested on her. He was not as tall as Timothy, but his breadth made him look the bigger man and he had a tougher look about him, as if he had been forced to fight his way through life. She wondered again how he came to be here – what had happened to him during those lost years, between the war that had been fought nearly thirty years ago, and tonight on an American fairground.

'My sister is here, yes,' he said at last. 'Not with the circus, however – just with me.' There was something odd in the way he chose and spoke his words, but Cordelia had no time to wonder about that. Again, Timothy was leaping in, eyes bright, and she wondered now if he had missed their family in Stourbridge more than she had thought, to be so excited at finding these very distant relatives now.

'Well, you must both come to supper with us,' he declared. 'Let's go and fetch her at once. It's late, I know, but you people keep different hours, and this is an occasion – we must celebrate! Where d'you think she'll be?'

'Oh, I know where she'll be,' Pierre said. He hesitated and again Cordelia was aware of a sense of hostility, as if he were wishing he had never spoken to them. And, at the same time, a second undercurrent – as if Pierre were weighing something up, considering . . . As the thought entered her mind, he seemed to come to a conclusion and closed the box into which he had been packing his equipment, snapping the lock shut with a decisive movement. 'Yes,' he said. 'You must come and see her. She'll be interested, I know.'

Tim gave Cordelia a bright glance and they followed Pierre through the fairground, thronged now with people making their way home. Most of the sideshows were closing down and lamps were being doused. Pierre's steps were slow and when Cordelia glanced up at his face she saw that it was dark and brooding, as if it concealed old, unhappy secrets. She wondered just what lay in his past. Of his childhood in Lorraine, she knew a little. Her father had gone several times to stay at the château, where the Thietry glasshouse was, and he had talked about it to her and Timothy.

A forest glasshouse, he had called it, in the old French tradition, with the houses of the workmen and their families clustered around the foundry with its furnace and pots, and the tolling of the bell to call them to work when the molten glass had reached a workable temperature. 'You never knew with a wood furnace when that might be,' he had said. 'That's why the houses were built so near. And with the château at the other end, it was a community in itself – a big family. Of course, they had gone over to a gas furnace just before I arrived there, but the sense of community was still very strong. Everyone knew everyone else.'

Had it all been split up? Cordelia wondered. When the Prussians began their offensive and took the weak, ill-prepared French Army and shook it like a rat, had the 'big family' been scattered to the four winds? Some must have survived, for Thietry Cristal still continued even though the Lorraine was now annexed by Germany. But it was not the flourishing business it had been. And what had happened to the Thietry children, Pierre and his brothers and sisters, nobody had known until now.

Impulsively, she thrust away her doubts and turned to him. 'I'm so glad we found you. Or you found us – after all, it was you who recognised Timothy. You can't go away again – not yet. Why don't you stay for a while? Do you have to go on with the circus?'

He shrugged. 'My life is my own. I can go with them or leave as I wish. But I have to feed myself and my sister –'

'Oh, but I'm sure Tim could get you a job!' Now that she had accepted him, she was as eager as Timothy to keep contact with this rediscovered part of their family. 'He works with Jensen Novak, one of the best glassmakers in Corning. And you – you can blow as well as do lampwork, can't you? You must have worked in a glasshouse, you grew up in one, you know all the processes.'

'I grew up in one until I was eleven years old,' Pierre said briefly. 'After that . . . Yes, I knew all the processes when I arrived in this country, but that was of little use to an immigrant boy in New York. And life was not easy. We were alone in the world, my brothers and sisters and I. One could not pick and choose one's own way.'

Cordelia stopped and looked at him, trying to see past the broad, muscular figure to a small boy, wide-eyed and afraid, stepping from a ship teeming with refugees from war and hardship in Europe and facing life on a new and strange continent. A continent where everything was different: language, customs, even the buildings they saw around them. To come from a forest château deep in the heart of France, to the towering buildings of New York . . . how must it have been?

'Pierre, you will tell us what happened to you?' she said gently. 'We are your family now, even if we are many times removed. We want to know everything that happened to you – and to your brothers and sisters, too,' she added, suddenly seeing around the small boy a cluster of younger children, all looking to him, trusting him to guide them through the frightening jungle that life had become. Where were they now? 'Please stay,' she repeated.

Pierre looked at her. His eyes were dark, almost opaque in the light from the street lamps. His olive skin was pale and shadowed. He looked alien, a stranger. She had a vision of the boy he must have been, a sense of the man he was now. Her heart beat a little faster and for a moment she was afraid. She took a small step backwards, as if afraid of falling into unknown depths.

If Pierre decided to go on with the circus and forget that he and the Henzels had ever met, then everything would go on very nearly as before. If he decided to stay . . .

Cordelia was not sure. But she had a feeling that this man could somehow change their lives.

The wagon stood a little apart from the others, in a corner of the field. It was built almost like a small house on wheels and Cordelia stopped, charmed by the tiny windows, the little door. Pierre gave her a brief glance and led the way up the steps. He looked too big, too broad to live in such a tiny vehicle. Perhaps he slept outside – underneath, or in a tent. Once again, she felt sharp pity for the boy who had started with so much and had lost almost everything.

Pierre was speaking to someone inside the wagon. After a moment, he withdrew his head and indicated that they should come up. Cordelia followed him eagerly.

'Oh – but you're in bed!' She looked in dismay at the woman who lay on a narrow couch against one wall, and started to back out. 'I'm sorry, we didn't know. We can't intrude. Perhaps we could come tomorrow –'

'Come in, please.' Pierre's voice was abrupt. 'My sister is in bed, yes, but it would be no different tomorrow. She is always in bed.' His eyes were inscrutable. 'She has an injured spine. She never leaves her couch.'

'When the war came,' Pierre said, 'we were all at the château together. We children, our father and mother, René, our grandparents and Véronique, and your father.' He glanced at Timothy, at the nut-brown, curly hair, the silver eyes. 'Our Aunt Geneviève was there too, but somehow one always forgets poor Aunt Geneviève. Everyone always did. She was like a shadow about the place, a dried-up ghost, yet it could barely function without her. I think many families have such a person.'

He paused. They were sitting on the couch along the opposite wall from Ginette. Between them was a low bench on which Pierre had set glasses and a bottle of red wine. Cordelia tasted hers. It was rough and raw, and she set the glass down again. She listened to Pierre, glancing from time to time at his sister.

Ginette was beautiful. Her injuries had evidently not touched her face, which was as smooth and and ivory-pale as a young girl's, framed by long black hair which fell in thick waves to her shoulders. Her eyes were even darker than Pierre's – almost a true black. They watched as her brother talked, and Cordelia was conscious of the same enigmatic secrecy hidden deep inside them. As if underneath the brilliance of her smile, the vivacity that made her disablement all the more cruel, there was a mind that ran on purposeful lines, that planned and assessed. She was reminded of the moment of the fairground, when she had caught the same impression from Pierre – as if he were weighing up something in his mind, coming to a decision . . . Again, she pushed the uncertainties away. After the life they had been forced to leave, it was only natural that these two should be wary.

Cordelia looked again at Pierre. She still had a sense of the unknown when she looked into those dark brown eyes, still had a feeling that there were dark secrets hidden under the thick black hair that fell across the broad forehead. It was as if she knew about Pierre, but only in patches. She could picture his childhood home from stories told her by her father. She knew of her great-grandparents, Marc and Cécile Thietry, who lived in Paris but visited the château every summer. She knew of Gabriel, Pierre's father who had run the château with the help of his wife's nephew René; of Pierre's mother Annette who had borne three sons and twin daughters – one of them Ginette – and was still beautiful; of the fairy child Véronique, the orphan of Marc's brother and his young wife.

But after that – after the day when news of the war had reached the family and the Thietrys, with Paul and

Véronique, had returned to Paris and been besieged there, she knew nothing. Her grandfather had tried afterwards to find out what had happened, but the stories that came back to England were garbled and disturbing. Annette had become the mistress of a Prussian general and gone to Germany with him . . . Gabriel was alone at the château, the children disappeared – dead or sent abroad, he would never say. René was dead, killed in the fighting. Annette had been accused of collaborating with the enemy and executed by her own people . . . There was no way of knowing the truth. And even afterwards, when the chaos was slowly subsiding, when René had crept back to the château and tried to restore some kind of order, there was little to be told. Gabriel had died without ever revealing what had happened to his family, and Paul, the inheritor of a foundry that was now under German rule, had been happy to allow René full control.

'How soon did your father send you to America?' she asked Pierre, and the dark eyes came back to hers as if they too had been looking deep into the past.

'Oh, quite soon. There was a family near us who were sending their children – they foresaw the bloodbath that the war would become, even though the French were still boasting of their own prowess and laughing at the Prussians' folly in thinking to defeat the Emperor Napoleon. They offered to let us travel with their nursemaid and my father agreed. It was as if he knew already that even if we survived the bloodshed, life at the château would never be the same again. As if he had some kind of extra knowledge . . .' He looked at Timothy, his eyes moving again over the brown, curly hair, the grey eyes that were so like Paul's. 'As if he knew that we would have no mother,' he said simply, and Cordelia felt a tiny shudder pull at her skin.

'You don't – you never found out what really happened to her?' she asked tentatively, and the brown eyes turned to her.

'Never.'

The word fell like a stone into the tiny cabin. Outside, men called to each other as they counted their takings and closed down their sideshows for the night. She heard the unfamiliar sounds of exotic animals – a tiger's grunt, the trumpeting of an elephant, the snort of a performing bear. One of the ponies whinnied.

Pierre had withdrawn again into silence. Ginette lay motionless on her bed, her black eyes watching them.

'What was the journey like?' Tim asked. 'I mean, we thought it was bad enough when we came over, but it must have been much worse for you. Those immigrant ships were pretty crowded, weren't they?'

'We were packed in like cattle. We had all left our homes in a hurry and many people had very little luggage – a wicker basket with a few pathetic belongings, a bundle tied up in a blanket or a sheet. We took some food too, for the food provided on the ship was notoriously poor, and often crawling with weevils and other pests. Most families had a cooking pot and a few vegetables and some sausage. Some had brought family keepsakes – a silver cup, a locket with a mother's photograph in, an old watch or a snuffbox. And we passed the time by playing cards or singing. A great many people were seasick.' He smiled without humour. 'It was three weeks only, but to us children it seemed to be months. On the other hand, I suppose we didn't suffer as the adults did – we swarmed all over the ship, finding amusement where we could: catching rats, tormenting the crew, finding our way to the galleys and begging extra scraps of food. I was expected to behave responsibly, of course – I was eleven years old and had two younger brothers and two sisters only two years old. But what would you?' In spite of his years in America, he still spoke like a Frenchman uneasy with the English language, a curious blend of old and new. 'I was a boy, and free of the shackles of home discipline. And I had already seen much horror on my journey across France. It was not so surprising that I should run wild a little.'

'And when you reached America? Where did you go?'

He shrugged. 'We should have gone with the family who brought us here. That was the intention. They were heading for a farm somewhere on the Canadian border, where one of their relatives had settled and prospered. In fact, we should have taken ship for Montreal but in the turmoil of leaving . . . Anyway, there we were in New York. The harbour was filled with ships, all tossing in the choppy waters. We had to wait our turn, for there were thousands of people arriving every day. We could see the decks lined with white faces, and the shore thick with people coming and going, horses and carts transporting cargo and luggage, families losing each other, searching amongst the crowds. It seemed that we would never leave the ship. But finally the inspectors came aboard, checking for infectious and contagious diseases. We had several cases of leprosy and a suspected yellow fever, all kept in isolation – they were removed at once. Once the rest of the passengers were declared clear, we were allowed to go ashore.'

'Oh, Ellis Island!' Timothy said with a grimace. 'Yes, we went through there too, and mighty glad I was to get away from the place, I can tell you.'

Cordelia's brow creased. She was trying to remember what Jensen had told her about his own arrival in America. 'It wasn't Ellis Island then?' she asked. 'Didn't you have to go somewhere down at the Battery for further clearance? A castle – Castle Garden, was that it?'

'That's right. Castle Garden. And it's easy to understand why the authorities later chose to use an island – the arrangements there were so chaotic, so impossible to keep in any order, that many of the immigrants simply disappeared into the crowd and were never seen again. Manhattan was conveniently close, you see, and the buildings were tall. It was truly a jungle – a jungle of brick and stone and concrete. And for those who didn't find it terrifying, it was easy to lose oneself in it without having to wait for the formalities.'

He paused, looking back once again into the past of almost thirty years ago. Again, Cordelia wondered what he saw. A bewildered boy, torn from his home and sent among strangers – or a sturdy little Frenchman, already belligerent at the treatment life had meted out to him, making up his mind to live his own life and not let fate play so large a part in the future?

'Our nursemaid, a woman sent to look after all us children – and there were nine of us, so you can imagine the task she had – was turned back,' Pierre said. 'She failed the eyesight test – she had a condition which they knew would send her blind, and no one with that disease was permitted to enter the country. The children with her were allowed to proceed – their papers proved that they had relatives in America, relatives who were already in New York ready to receive them. But we – the Thietrys – were told that we too must return to France.'

'Return to France!' Cordelia exclaimed. 'But what happened?'

'I would not go,' he said simply. 'I was excited by this new country. I didn't want to go back to France. The others were pleased enough – they hated America from the first moment, and I believed they would be happier returning home. So when they took my brothers and sisters back to the ship, Ginette and I managed to slip away from them – she was like my shadow and refused to leave me. We joined those who made their own way into Manhattan, and we melted away into their new, strange jungle. We were alone, and forced to find our own way of living, and I felt for the first time in my life that I was truly alive.'

'But your brothers and Ginette's twin?' Cordelia asked with a quick, painful glance at the woman in the bed. 'They never returned to the château. What happened to them?'

'We found out much, much later,' Ginette said quietly in the soft, husky voice that was still so strongly French. 'The ship that carried them sank on the journey home. The boilers blew up, and the ship was holed. Only a few people survived.'

There was a long silence. Cordelia, her eyes filled with tears, put out her hand and laid it on Ginette's. Tim cleared his throat and patted Pierre's shoulder. Again, they were all aware of the sounds outside.

'That's a terrible thing to happen,' Cordelia said huskily. 'And so you really were alone. But – why did you never communicate with home – with your father? Or even with the Henzels in England?'

Pierre shrugged. 'There were many reasons, Cordelia, reasons I find difficult to speak of now. Perhaps one day . . . I suppose I was afraid at first that if I wrote to him he would demand that I came home. And I didn't want to see France ever again. Too many things had happened there . . . And then I made my own life, you see. Ginette and I scraped a living on the streets of New York, earning the odd pennies, a dollar occasionally, begging food. And then I found myself wandering in Brooklyn one day. I came across a glasshouse there and drifted inside. It was natural, I suppose, that I should ask for work, and I stayed there for some time.' He grinned ruefully. 'But I was restless. I sometimes think that even if we had not been sent to America when we were, I would have gone eventually. Always, I needed something new – something to blur the memories, perhaps, who knows? And I left the glasshouse and began to wander. I had always enjoyed lampwork as a hobby, and I used to stop at street corners and amuse people and sell my glass birds and animals. Eventually, I found the circus and joined them. And there you have the story of our life!'

He glanced at his sister and she returned his look. It was as if some message had passed between them – as if they had no need of words. It was something Cordelia understood, something that happened sometimes between herself and Timothy. And these two, having only each other, must have developed a closeness as deep as any that existed between twins.

'A little of it, anyway,' she said. 'I have a feeling that there is a great deal you haven't told us . . . But it's late – we must go home. We'll talk again tomorrow.' She looked from one to the other, her eyes soft. 'You *are* going to stay, aren't you? We have room for you in our lodgings, if you would like to come. For a few days, at least.'

Pierre's dark eyes were on her and an unaccustomed heat warmed her skin. She felt the colour come to her cheeks, felt her lips part slightly, and tried unsuccessfully to remove her glance from his. When at last she did, it was to find Ginette watching her as well, with an expression that changed in the moment before a slow smile curved the full red lips.

'Come again tomorrow,' she said huskily. 'We'll talk again then.' And her eyes moved back slowly, inscrutably, to her brother.

Tim and Cordelia walked slowly back to their rooms. The streets were almost empty; nearly everyone had gone home and only a few young men, still over-excited by the circus, roamed about reluctant to go to their beds.

221

'I still can't get over it,' Tim said. 'Meeting Pierre Thietry here, in Corning. Won't they be surprised at home when we write and tell them!'

'Life really is very strange,' Cordelia agreed. 'And yet, I suppose it's not so unusual really, once you know that he's been working with the circus. We knew Gabriel's children were probably in America. And we'd surely have heard if he'd been working in a glasshouse – he would have contacted the château. It's only because he's had such a hard time that he never did – and because he believed that Father might own it now and have no place for him. Did it strike you that he was at all odd about Father, Tim?'

'Odd? How?'

'I don't really know,' Cordelia said thoughtfully. 'There was just a look in his eye when he spoke of him – and the way he looked at you when he first saw you and realised how like him you are. For a moment, it was almost as if he hated you . . . But that's silly. It was just that it was such a shock for him – and for Ginette too. Like a ghost from the past . . . All the same, there was a kind of shadow – I can't explain it any more than that.'

'Imagination,' Tim declared. 'You're always suspicious of people when you first meet them – look how you were with Jensen. Wouldn't have anything to do with him. Anyway, Pierre and Ginette are almost cousins. And they were just children when they knew Father – Ginette couldn't have been much more than a baby.'

'Yes, of course. Oh, wasn't it sad about the rest of the children, Tim! Imagine, all drowning on that ship, when they'd already reached America. And what a good thing that Pierre and Ginette had stayed behind.' She was silent, thinking of the two children, alone in the teeming jungle of New York. 'I'm glad we've found them, aren't you?'

Tim nodded. 'Part of our own family. It feels good.

They're older than us, though, aren't they – what would they be now, do you know?'

'Father was in France in 1868 and Pierre was about eight years old then, so he must be thirty-eight now,' Cordelia said thoughtfully. 'And I remember Father saying that the twins had just been born when he first went to Lorraine – they were just a few months old. So Ginette must be about thirty. And Pierre has taken care of her all those years. He must be very fond of her. I suppose he feels she's all he has left.' Cordelia's face was sad as she thought of what Pierre had told them about his sister. 'And she's lost her twin, Tim – I wonder why she stayed when her twin went on the ship.'

'I daresay we'll find out soon enough,' Timothy observed. 'There's a lot Pierre hasn't told us yet – we've hardly had time, after all. But if he stays in Corning –'

'Oh yes! If they stay in Corning, we'll be able to talk and talk. Oh, I do hope they stay here, don't you, Tim!' Excitedly, she grasped her brother's arm. 'It's all I've wanted – some family of our own. Almost as good as –' She stopped.

'Almost as good as going back to Stourbridge?' Tim asked, and looked down at her gravely. 'Is that what you were going to say, sis? You still don't like it here, do you? You still want to go back.'

They stopped under one of the electric street lamps and Cordelia looked up into her brother's face. She thought suddenly how he had changed since they came here – how he had matured. He still had the boyish face, the immaturity of youth about the curve of his cheek, but his mouth was firmer now, his eyes steady. Leaving his family, travelling across the world, making his own way in his work – all this had brought about a subtle alteration in him. But she sensed that Timothy still needed time to reach his full strength of mind, body and purpose as a man. He had clearly needed the space of America and their new life, to come this far. Would he continue to grow if they went home now?

And she thought about herself. *Did* she want to go back to Stourbridge? Did she want to give up her own life, the one she had carved out for herself? Modest though it might seem to others, it meant a lot to her – the little school where she had sole charge, the house she ran herself. And Jensen . . .

'No, Tim,' she said seriously, 'I don't want to go back. We can't – not to what we had before. And not just because of Father dying and what happened to Mother but because I don't think you can ever go back in life. Perhaps one day we'll go, but it won't be the same. Stourbridge will have changed, and so will we. We're a different Tim and Cordelia from the ones who went away. And we belong in a different place – a different life.'

'That's frightening,' he said, and she nodded.

'It is. But it's life. And life is frightening, Tim. Think of Pierre and Ginette. Think of Father and Mother. Our grandparents. If any of them knew what life was to be, they'd have been frightened. It's better, perhaps, not to think about it.'

'But you have to think about it. *I* have to think about it. I have to think about the future – the glass I'm going to make. I'm going to be a great glassmaker, Cordelia – I have to be.' The light shone in Timothy's eyes and he gripped her hands. 'It's inside me, driving me on all the time – I can't think of anything else. It's the most important thing of all – it's life itself – and I have to think of it, frightening or not. Though to be honest,' he added, 'the only thing that really scares me is not being able to make glass any more. I shouldn't want to live if that were to happen, Cordelia.'

'It won't. I know it won't.' She smiled at him and squeezed

his hands, though in her heart she found Tim's consuming passion alarming. Her father had been absorbed by his art, but never to quite the extent that Timothy was. And when, occasionally and for no apparent reason, he turned momentarily away from glass, as if it had drained him of everything he had to give, he seemed to swing like a pendulum to the other extreme. That was when he sought the company of the wild young men he had made friends with – when he spent his evenings who knew where, his nights playing cards or billiards, and came home late, waking reluctantly next morning and complaining of his head . . .

'Do you think Pierre felt like that?' she asked as they walked on. 'About making glass? He must have found it difficult to work in another man's glasshouse, after having expected to grow up to work in his own. Yet he still went back to it, even though he was doing no more than lampwork.'

'Very fine lampwork. I don't think I've ever seen better.'

'No, neither have I. But – in a good glassworks, he could do so much more, Tim.' She looked up at him again. 'Do you think he will stay here, now he's found us? Do you think Jensen might take him into the glasshouse?'

'I've already decided he will!' Timothy said with a grin. 'Don't forget, I'm not without influence there, Cordelia! It's lucky he hasn't gone away yet. I'll speak to him the first chance I get – and if Pierre wants a job, he shall have one. We'll have a Thietry and a Henzel working together again by the end of the week, or I'm a Dutchman!'

The new house was on the highest street of all, so new that it had yet to be named, though Jensen said most people favoured simply using the next in the numbered sequence – Ninth. As Cordelia reached the rough, levelled track which was all that yet existed of the road, she paused and turned to look down at the view.

The city of Corning – no more than a small town in English terms – lay spread out in the valley beneath, a geometric pattern of streets on either side of the shining river which wound lazily between broad, flat tobacco fields. From here, she could see the house where Martha and Bob Robinson lived, next door to her uncle's still shuttered home. She could see the roof of the house she and Timothy were to rent, where Pierre and Ginette had agreed to live with them. She could see the railroad tracks, the station and the tall, smoking chimneys of Jensen's glasshouse, close to the bank of the river.

Timothy had told her that he had broached the subject of Pierre, confident that their French cousin would receive as warm a welcome from Jensen as they had given him themselves. But to his dismay, Jensen had been unenthusiastic and even a visit to the fairground to see Pierre's work had not changed his mind. For hours Timothy had tried to persuade him, without success; and now, baffled and angry, Cordelia had made up her mind to approach Jensen herself. But he had not been at the glasshouse this afternoon and so she had decided to go up to the new house, where he was still planning his furnishings, and find out just why he was refusing Pierre his chance.

As she came to the front garden, already laid out with grass and shrubs, Jensen came to the door and stood watching her. She felt her heart bump with sudden unevenness – perhaps she had climbed the hill too quickly. He came down the path to meet her, his eyes unsmiling.

'Well? What d'you think of it?'

'It's beautiful,' Cordelia said sincerely, and he nodded.

'Suits me pretty well. I guess I'm going to enjoy living here. Remind you of something in England, does it?'

'Yes, it does. It's very similar to the country south of us – the Malvern Hills and Herefordshire. There's a river there –

the Wye – and it winds just like the Chemung, through valleys surrounded by forested hills. And the trees would be just this colour now . . . We used to go there for holidays sometimes.' Her voice was wistful and she felt his eyes on her. 'You could look out from the hills, right into Wales, and see the mountains in the distance.'

'Mountains like we have here?'

'No. More rugged. Not really high mountains, but very rough and rocky. Very dramatic, especially in bad weather.'

'There were rough, rocky hills where I came from too,' he said reminiscently. 'It seemed pretty tame here at first, but I guess the first winter soon put me right about that.'

Cordelia looked at him. She found it difficult to remember that Jensen, too, was an exile from his own land, with memories of a childhood spent in a very different place. Did he also long to go back? Had leaving his homeland meant leaving his own dreams?

'Is it hard here in winter?'

'It can be. Quite a lot of snow – but it's fun too. Sledging's pretty popular – you'll enjoy that. And skating on the river and canal – do you like skating?'

'I've never tried. We don't often have enough ice, and there's nowhere really to skate.'

'Maybe you'll let me teach you,' he said, and looked down into her face.

She turned away, searching quickly for words. 'I came to talk to you about Pierre.'

'No,' Jensen said and, quiet as his voice was, it was more emphatic than Cordelia had ever heard it. 'No. I'm sorry, Cordelia, but I've already told Tim that it's my final word. I won't have Pierre Thietry working in my glasshouse.'

Cordelia stared at him. She could hear birds singing in the trees that flanked Jensen's garden. The sky was already beginning to darken.

'But why on earth not? He's a good enough workman – you've seen the lampwork he produces –'

'Glasshouse work is entirely different. Lampwork is nothing but a hobby, a fairground amusement –'

'Well, I know that! I'm not suggesting you set up a friggering department, though when I see how popular the stuff is I sometimes wonder if it wouldn't be a good idea. But Pierre isn't just the ordinary lampworker, he's grown up with glass, he has a feeling for it. And his family –'

Jensen flicked his fingers impatiently. 'Family! Don't tell me you're going to give me that old story of glassmaking being in the blood, Cordelia! It's in the family, I agree, just as any other trade is that's passed down from father to son. It's just a way of keeping employment – a question of survival. Bakers, wheelwrights, farmers, smiths, they all do the same thing. It's nothing to do with *blood*.'

'Artistry is,' Cordelia said quickly. 'Our father was an artist and so is Tim. And our father was a Thietry.' She lifted her hands, palms up, and said pleadingly, 'Don't you see, Jensen, Pierre is our *family*. We can't turn him away – '

Feeling suddenly cold, she drew the collar of her velvet jacket higher about her neck. It was deep, glowing amber – Christina's colour, and hers too. Her coppery hair was swept up high, a few untamed curls falling about her face, and the last of her summertime freckles sparkled like gold dust across her cheeks. Her green eyes glinted as she lifted her chin to look at Jensen, and she saw the change in his expression. Oh, why do you have to be so stubborn? she thought with a wave of longing. Why do you have to be so *stupid*?

'But I can,' Jensen said grimly. 'He's not *my* family, Cordelia. And I can turn him away.' He gave her a straight look. 'You may think your brother is so indispensable to me that I won't refuse any request either he or you care to make. Well, in the ordinary way I'd be pleased to take on any man he recommended. But not this one. You'll have to find him a job somewhere else. Maybe Tom Hawkes will take him, or the Houghtons.'

Cordelia's jaw tightened. 'I don't want to ask Tom Hawkes, or the Houghtons. I'm asking you.'

'And wasting your time and mine by doing so.'

Cordelia clasped her hands together to hide her shaking and moved away. The tension that she always felt when they were together made her body feel taut, almost rigid. She twined her fingers tightly and forced her voice to be calm.

'Jensen, why are you so adamant? You don't even know Pierre –'

'I saw him last night. Timothy told me to go and look at the lampworker and I did. I watched him for a good hour.'

'That's not knowing him.'

'And do you know him any better? You met him only three days ago – you know nothing of the man, nothing but what he chose to tell you.'

'Well, you don't even know that,' Cordelia retorted. 'Jensen, he isn't an imposter, if that's what you're thinking. He *recognised* Tim – he asked us if we knew the name Henzel. He *is* Pierre Thietry.'

'I don't doubt it. It makes no difference.' Jensen looked at her, his face shadowed, frowning. He hesitated and Cordelia spoke quickly.

'There's something else, isn't there? Something you're not telling me.'

Jensen made a sound of exasperation. He compressed his lips, looked at her again and then seemed to make up his mind.

'It's nothing I can put my finger on. I just didn't like him.

He has the look of a troublemaker. I've seen it before, and I'm sorry if he's your cousin or whatever, but I just don't want him in my factory.'

Cordelia felt a brief chill shiver across her skin. Momentarily, she recalled her own first impression of Pierre – of his brooding darkness and, yes, an air of indefinable menace.

'Nonsense!' she said sharply. 'You're imagining things, Jensen. If you want my opinion, you're just jealous.'

'*Jealous?*'

'Yes, jealous. Jealous because Tim and I have found someone who belongs to us, and you've been thinking of us as your property –'

'That's just plain stupid!'

'I absolutely agree,' she said angrily. 'As stupid as you refusing to employ Pierre in your factory. Well, there's no more to be said, I suppose. I'm wasting my time and yours, just as you said. I'd better go.' She turned towards the road. 'I suppose it isn't the slightest bit of use telling you about Ginette either. It wouldn't make any difference.' She gave Jensen a swift, upward glance and saw the irritation in his face.

'Ginette?' he said warily.

'Pierre's sister.' She hadn't really wanted to manipulate him in this way, but he'd left her no choice. And, remembering the story he had told her about his own sister Freya, she'd known Ginette was her own trump card.

'Oh, yes, Timothy mentioned he had a sister.'

Cordelia nodded. She might have known that Tim wouldn't have talked about Ginette's condition, still less seen it as a possible lever. 'Younger than Pierre. They were the only ones of the family to stay in America – she was hardly more than a baby then, only three or four years old. Somehow, she got left behind when the others went back on the ship and Pierre had to take care of her. Imagine, a boy of eleven destitute in Manhattan, with a baby sister to look after as well! They just lived on the streets, scraping by on what Pierre could beg or earn. I can hardly bear to think of what they must have suffered.' The tears in her eyes were genuine enough as she thought of the two children, lost and bewildered in the strange city so far from their peaceful country home, surrounded by hurrying people who spoke a language they scarcely understood. She looked up at Jensen and saw the unwilling sympathy dawn in his own eyes. Then his expression hardened and he spoke tersely.

'Yes, I can understand you feeling the way you do, Cordelia. But that was a long time ago – before you were even born. Your cousin's had time to find his feet now, he's as American as I am and he ought to be able to shift for himself. And his sister too. She still lives with him, does she?'

'Yes. Ginette still lives with him,' Cordelia said quietly. 'She has to. You see, she's crippled.'

She looked at him. She had played her trump card, and she believed she had played it well.

'Crippled?' Jensen said without expression, and she knew he must be thinking of his own sister, Freya.

'That's right,' she said coolly. 'Not that it's of any interest to you, of course . . . But she fell from a pony when she was twenty years old, and she hasn't walked since. I suppose she never will now – that's ten years ago, Pierre told us. He looks after her himself, of course, but it's a dreadful life, cooped up in that tiny caravan, being jolted along rough roads from one place to another . . .' She stopped and shrugged. 'But you don't want to hear all this. I'll go and see Mr Houghton. I've always thought he looks such a kind-hearted man . . .'

'All right,' Jensen said as she turned away again. 'All

right, you minx, you can stop play-acting. I know very well what you've been up to.' His eyes glittered dangerously and she felt a brief quiver of fear. 'I'll employ your cousin, or whatever he is. But only on trial, you understand! If he doesn't give satisfaction –'

Cordelia's smile broke out like a flash of sunshine on a stormy day. She moved quickly back to him and laid her hands on his arms, lifting a radiant face to his. 'Oh, Jensen, that's wonderful. Thank you so much. You won't regret it, I know – he's a fine glassmaker. And Tim will be responsible for him.'

'For a man of almost forty?' Jensen smiled sceptically. 'Well, we'll see. I dare say I'm wrong about him, after all. But these fairground johnnies – you can't be too careful. But he probably won't stay long, anyway. Too used to travelling by this time.' He looked down at her, the blue of his eyes darkening to sapphire as they travelled slowly over her excited face. 'Satisfied?'

Cordelia nodded. Not for the world would she have let Jensen see the slight tremor of – what? apprehension? fear? – that twitched at her nerves when she thought of Pierre living and working in Corning. Living in the house that she and Timothy were going to rent once Jensen had left – being in daily contact with her, meeting her eyes across the breakfast table, sharing her evenings. The thought brought a shiver to her spine.

'Now tell me about this sister of his,' Jensen said. 'You say she fell from a horse?'

'One of the circus ponies,' Cordelia said. 'She was one of the riders – a very good one too, Pierre says. You know – in the spangled dress and the jewels, you've seen them cantering around the ring. Ginette used to perform all kinds of tricks, standing up on the horse's back, holding a ballet position on one foot, that kind of thing. One day, something went wrong and she fell – damaged her spine. She's never walked since and has to lie in bed all day, or on a long chair outside on fine days.' She paused, her eyes filling with tears. 'Jensen, it's so sad! She's beautiful – dark, like Pierre, but with such wonderful black hair and eyes. She must have looked like a queen, dressed in those gorgeous clothes. And to be confined to bed like that for the rest of her life! It seems so cruel.'

'And is there nothing to be done for her?'

Cordelia shook her head. 'Pierre said there might be specialists who could help her, but they've never been able to afford to see them. And with moving about so much . . . That's why he wants to settle down and make a home for her. He said he hoped that one day they'll be able to afford good medical help.' She brushed back her curls. 'But I don't mean to wait that long! I shall write to Mother. We ought to help. The glasshouse Pierre's father ran belongs to us now. Pierre must have some rights in it, even if our French grandfather did leave it all to Father. Not legal rights, perhaps – but morally, we owe it to Pierre and Ginette to do whatever we can for them.' She looked at Jensen. 'Don't you agree?'

He inclined his head ironically. 'Perhaps, except that it seems to be me giving the help rather more than you . . . Yes, I think you should write to your mother, Cordelia. This is a family matter. And maybe there can be something done to help your cousins.' He glanced around them at the trees, their tawny leaves a shawl of silky colour against the lowering sky. 'And if that's all – now you're here, I'd like to show you the house. It's not finished inside, of course – I just came to try to decide on some furnishings. Maybe you can help me make up my mind.'

He turned away and Cordelia followed him slowly, staring up at the house. It was a large building with plenty of windows. The roof was gabled at both ends, with small gables along the front where windows denoted the top storey; the windows on each of the other two storeys were large and several of them possessed their own balconies. Running all the way across the front of the house was a wide porch, and below that was the basement, looking into a broad area.

Jensen led her up the porch steps and through the large front door. She stood in the hallway and gazed about her.

'All this is going to be panelled. We're using cherry wood, I like its pleasant, warm glow. And maple. This'll be the dining-room – plenty of room for a good-sized table, you see, for entertaining – and this the parlour. I want a grand piano here – I'm fond of musical evenings. Do you play the piano, Cordelia?'

'Not very well, I'm afraid. I didn't practise enough.'

'No matter. I'm sure you have a sweet singing voice. Come upstairs – you can give me your advice on the master bedroom.'

Cordelia followed him again, still silent. This talk of furnishings and decorations, of musical evenings, of parlours and bedrooms, found her tongue-tied, not certain of her own responses. Why was he asking her advice?

'This is it,' Jensen said softly, drawing her through a door at the top of the stairs. 'This is where I shall be sleeping.'

Cordelia stood just inside. Her cheeks were hot again and she was glad of the dimness in the room. The early dusk of autumn was beginning to gather, creeping in through the windows. She looked around and realised that the room ran along the whole of one end of the house, with windows on three of its sides. At the front, it looked out over the entire valley, down the hill at the chimneys and the streets of the city that lay below, at the gleam of the winding Chemung and the broad green fields that lay on either side. At the side, it looked along the unmade track that would one day be Ninth Street and probably the most exclusive place to live in the whole of Corning. And at the back, it looked straight into the flaming colours of the virgin forest, wild and untamed.

'It's a lovely room,' she said at last. 'But – won't it be cold in winter? All those windows . . .'

'Thick curtains. I thought velvet, what would you say? And a good fire burning here, where you can see it from the bed. There's plenty of room for both. Don't you think it'll be cosy?'

'I'm sure it will.' Cordelia's imagination brought the room to life as he spoke. She saw the firelight playing on the drawn curtains, their rich colours glowing like jewels . . . 'But you don't really need my advice, do you? You have it all very well planned.' Her voice trembled a little and she turned away towards the window.

'I told you, I'd like to hear your ideas. About colours, for instance – now, what would you advise for curtains? Something pretty deep and rich, I'd say myself.'

'Yes, I should think that would do very well.' She was still staring out of the window, hardly seeing the brilliance of the trees. Her heart was thumping. 'Ruby velvet – or perhaps a good strong golden brown.'

'Fall colours,' he said, and she felt him move, coming to stand beside her. 'Yes, I guess you're right.' He put one hand on her shoulder and turned her gently to face him. 'Your colours, Cordelia. You look like the fall yourself in that jacket – it's the colour of those leaves, the dark ones that look like a sunset afire. It matches your hair . . . And with your green eyes and soft, creamy skin, you look like a tree nymph. You are beautiful. Did anyone ever tell you that before, Cordelia?'

She wanted to move, but could not. Her gaze was transfixed by his, by the sapphire depths of his eyes so dark and intent. She whispered: 'No. Nobody's ever told me that.'

'They're fools in England,' he muttered, and her gaze moved to his mouth. His lips were parted and she felt her own begin to open, as if in response. What was happening to her? But still she could not move. 'Fools . . .' he said again, huskily, and bent his head to hers.

The touch of his lips was as soft as the brush of a moth's wing, yet it burned her like a brand. A tremor ran through her body. She felt his hands on her arms, drawing her gently against him; felt her breasts touch the hardness of his chest. His lips were possessing hers now, moving over them, parting them, shaping them to his. Cordelia trembled against him. She had never dreamed that a kiss could be like this; never suspected that it could rouse these sensations, so wild, so sweet, so unfamiliar . . .

'Cordelia . . .' he murmured against her mouth, and the kiss deepened.

It seemed an eternity before he brought the kiss to an end at last, gathering her against him so that her head rested against his shoulder. Beneath her cheek, she could hear the heavy beating of his heart. Her shaking body was enfolded in his arms; she could feel the strength that held her close. All her fears had disappeared. She lifted her face again.

It was very nearly too dark to see now. But she could just make out his features. And to her horror, he was staring down at her now with no expression at all. His eyes were blank. It was almost as if he had forgotten who she was – forgotten even that she was there.

'Jensen?' she whispered, and stepped back a little.

Instantly, he let her go. His arms dropped away from her body and he turned away as if in sudden revulsion. He swept both hands through his thick fair hair and took a swift pace towards the door.

'It's time we went.' His voice was harsh, louder than normal. 'Your brother will be wondering where you are.'

'Jensen – ' She moved quickly across the room, catching at his sleeve. 'Jensen, what's the matter? What have I done? Have – have I been immodest?' She faltered, knowing she was blushing again, and he stopped and looked down at her, unsmiling.

'No, Cordelia – you've done nothing. It isn't your fault. It is mine – entirely mine, for bringing you here at all. I ought to have known better . . .' His hands were running through his hair again. 'Look, forget it, will you? Forget it ever happened. And next time I ask you to come up here with me, make sure there's someone else along. That's if you ever come at all, now you know –' He stopped abruptly.

'Now I know what? That you might kiss me?' Cordelia was miserably conscious of an acute pain deep in her heart. Her whole body was burning now, with shame and humiliation, a humiliation she sought to defeat with anger. 'There's no need to worry about that,' she went on caustically. 'The possibility will never arise again. I shall make quite sure of that.'

He bowed his head. 'I can only say again – I'm sorry. But when I saw you in this room, standing here, with all those brilliant colours behind you, looking as if you were made for the place – ' He shook his head. 'There's something I should tell you, Cordelia, something you ought to know. But – ' He stopped abruptly.

'Yes?' she said coldly, but he turned away and beat his fist lightly on the windowsill.

'No. Not now. I can't even begin. And it's all my own fault.'

'Well,' she said briskly, 'so long as you realise that. And now, perhaps you'll take me home? Tim will be wondering what's happened to me.' She turned and walked past him and through the door. Half-way down the wide stairway, she paused and turned, looking back at the shadowy figure above her. 'Furnish your rooms exactly how you like them,' she said clearly. 'After all, you are the one who will be living here.'

She went on down the stairs, her head held very high. But inside, she was already aware of a deep, gnawing misery. She had achieved what she had come for – but she had a deep sense that important things had been said that afternoon – and others left unsaid. That questions had been asked.

And answered wrongly.

Chapter Eleven

The first snow came softly, a white shroud that fell from clouds bruised grey and yellow which had hung over the valley for three days before giving up their burden. The ground was iron hard with a series of frosts more bitter than any Cordelia and Timothy had ever experienced, and the canal that ran alongside the Chemung to the east of Corning froze hard.

'It's ready for skating now,' Jensen told them as he helped them move their belongings into the rented house he had just vacated. 'I'll take you along and give you a lesson tomorrow, if you like.'

Cordelia looked at her brother. She had already seen some of the more adventurous boys testing the ice, and longed to try it for herself. But the thought of going alone with Jensen, of trusting her body to him on the ice, made her shiver. He had never repeated the kiss they had shared in the new house, but she was always aware of him now; of his tall, lean body, his hair the burning red-gold of molten glass, of the smile that pulled at the corners of his mouth and of the question that always seemed to be hidden in his dark blue eyes. Since then, Cordelia and Jensen had been alone together for only brief periods and she was conscious of the restraint between them. Perhaps, as a modest young woman, she ought to have refused to have anything more to do with him – but then, she wasn't modest, was she? Her shameless response to him and the tingling sensations she felt inside her whenever she thought of the kiss, proved that. And it would have been difficult, anyway, to avoid

Jensen. Corning was a small town, where everyone knew everyone else. And his close connection with Tim made it quite impossible.

Reminded of that visit to his new home, she wondered again why he would want such a large house, for only himself to live in. And what of Martha's speculation that perhaps he might be thinking of marriage?

'A man like that ought to be settled down and raisin' a family by now,' the older woman had said. 'What is he, thirty-four, thirty-five? That's a good age for a man to be married. A woman wants to settle a lot earlier than that, of course,' she had added, and her eyes had fixed themselves thoughtfully on Cordelia's face.

'Not all women want that sort of life,' she had said quickly. 'I don't expect I shall ever get married.' And she'd blushed hotly at Martha's raised eyebrows and knowing smile. 'And you needn't look at me like that, either,' she added crossly, and Martha had laughed.

Soon, however, Jensen would be going away, at least for a while – although he seemed almost reluctant to go, finding reason after reason for postponing his trip. And Cordelia told herself she would be glad when he went. She felt she needed a respite from the constant tension and the daily possibility of meeting him.

'Well?' he asked with a touch of impatience, 'how about it? Shall we have a skating lesson in the morning?'

'Suits me,' Timothy declared. 'And I reckon Cordelia will come along too – she was only saying this morning how she longs to try. But what do we do about skates?'

'Oh, Martha will lend you some – they still have the ones their family used before they left home. I checked it with her before I called in.' He looked at Cordelia. 'There's something else I wanted to ask you. There's a minstrel show at the Opera House in the evening and I've got tickets.

Would you both like to come with me?'

'A minstrel show!' Tim said eagerly. 'Of course we would, wouldn't we, Cordelia? We've never been to one of those.'

'I'm not sure –' Cordelia began, and Tim stared at her in surprise.

'Not sure! When you were saying how sorry you were to miss the last one! Come on, don't be a wet blanket – you know you'll enjoy it. And if Jensen's been to the trouble of getting tickets –'

'But I –' Cordelia looked appealingly at Jensen. Surely he could see how impossible this was? An evening in the Opera House, pleasant though it might be, would bring them into a closer proximity than either of them wanted. She was quite well aware that he had been avoiding any hint of physical contact as scrupulously as she. So how could he think of sitting in the next seat to her all evening in the darkness of a theatre?

'Please come, Cordelia,' he said quietly, and she looked into his eyes and knew she could not refuse.

'I'll tell you what we'll do,' Timothy said. 'We'll make a day of it. Skating in the afternoon instead of the morning, and then we'll come home to change and I'll stand you both dinner in a restaurant before the show. How does that sound?'

'A brainwave, no less,' Jensen declared. 'Cordelia, I suspected your brother had some intelligence lurking somewhere in that tousled head of his, and now he's proved it. Why, he might even make a moderately good glassmaker one of these days!'

'If he tries hard,' Cordelia added, thankful for the lightening of an atmosphere which she had found uncomfortably tense. They laughed, and she rose from her chair. 'Come on, we've sat chattering long enough. There are all those boxes

241

to be brought in, and I haven't even thought of making the beds yet . . . Thank you for suggesting we rent this house, Jensen.' She looked up as he too rose and stood looking down at her with that sudden gravity which always twisted her heart. 'I think we shall be very comfortable here. And I'm looking forward so much to having Pierre and Ginette here too. The rooms they have are very cramped – though of course, they're better than the wagon.'

Jensen said nothing. He simply stood there, quite still, his eyes on hers. And once again, she had the feeling that he wanted to say something. To tell her something important; to ask her some vital question.

She turned quickly away. But she knew that the moment could not be postponed for ever.

'It's kind of ye to come and bring us the things,' Grainne said, setting another rough-hewn log on the kitchen fire. 'I don't know what we'd be doing without ye, Cordelia, and that's God's truth. The eggs and the milk, they're about all me mother can take nowadays. They're just keeping her alive and that's all.'

'Grainne, I'm so sorry.' Cordelia set her basket on the table and moved nearer the fire, holding out frozen fingers to its warmth. She had tramped here through the snow against Martha's concerned advice and would have to walk all the way home again. She looked across to the sofa, where Mary lay sleeping, her cheek as pale as the pillow, her body making no more than a ripple under the blanket Cordelia had brought the last time she came. 'Is she no better?'

'She's not going to be better. We all know that, and there's no use pretending it isn't so. Mother of Christ, nobody gets better of the consumption. It's just a matter of waiting, and trying to get a bit of comfort for her the while.'

Grainne bent and hugged Bridget to her. 'And this one's got a cold an' all. And God knows where our Danny's got to, he's never in these days.'

'It's probably as well for him to be outside. It's healthy enough in the snow, provided you keep warm.' Cordelia spoke without thinking, wanting to give comfort, and bit her lip as she realised that Danny was probably outside without really warm clothing, without even adequate shoes on his feet. 'Grainne, I wish you'd let me send money to Declan and bring him home. Why don't you?'

'Because if you've money to spare, we need it more here.' The Irish girl spoke with a hopelessness that Cordelia had never heard in her voice before. 'I'll tell ye the truth, Cordelia – we're plain desperate here. Me father came home yesterday without a job – he's out looking for another now. And Garrett's been put on short time at the lumber yard. It's this weather, ye see. Nothing can be done with the ground frozen and the river iced in. And it's not even Christmas yet – I tell ye, by February we'll all be starving, and that's the top and bottom of it.'

Cordelia stared at her. There was a dreadful, quiet urgency in the girl's voice which told her that her words were no exaggeration. She looked around the room, cluttered with the living of too many people, at the few cooking utensils, the larder door standing slightly open to reveal empty shelves. Half a loaf stood on the table, and a pot of jam which Cordelia herself had brought from a batch Martha had given her. Was that all the food there was in the house?

'Why didn't you say things were getting so bad?' she asked, and Grainne shrugged.

'I told ye, we've never been beholden to anyone before. We've always managed for ourselves. But that was when we could all work . . . I've had to give up me own job too, ye

243

see, to look after things. I couldn't go out all day and leave me mother this way. And there's Bridget and Danny, too – leave 'em alone and they'll likely set fire to the whole place, and themselves with it.'

'Oh, Grainne . . .' Cordelia said helplessly. She sank down on a stool and stared at her friend. This was the kind of misery her own mother had fought to eliminate in the poverty-stricken areas of the Black Country. 'Isn't there any charity that would help you?' she asked at last. 'Your mother needs medical attention – is there no one to see her?'

'Without money?' Grainne gave a short laugh. 'Oh aye, there's one doctor will come out for nothing, but he's that busy we hardly ever see him. And he can't give his medicines away, now can he? He's got to live too. It's all very fine for the rich folk, they can go up to Dr Purdy's Sanitarium – but there's nothing like that for the likes of us. There's not even a hospital in Corning, for all their fine talk of it being a city. Crystal City!' Her lip curled derisively. 'What use is a bit of fine crystal to the O'Donnells? It won't keep me mother alive, nor put shoes on our Bridget's feet.'

Cordelia stood up briskly. 'Grainne, I'm going now, but I'll be back later. I'm going to get some help for you. And I don't want to hear any talk about being beholden – you're to accept whatever I bring, and no arguments.'

'Arguments? Ye'll hear no arguments from me. Things have gone past pride these days.' Grainne set another piece of wood on the fire and drew Bridget on to her knee, holding her hand out to the flame and rubbing warmth into the little toes. 'Let's just hope me Dad finds another job and quick. Or dear knows where we'll all end up.'

Cordelia hurried out. It had begun to snow again and a bitter wind had risen, driving the snow against her. The flakes seemed to have sharpened in the wind; they were like tiny, frozen needles against her face, stabbing at her with the cruelty of a Chinese torturer. The walk back across the bridge to Corning seemed to stretch ahead of her like an expedition into Greenland. She thought of Kevin O'Donnell, his stomach empty as he trudged the streets looking for work; of Garrett, down at the lumber yard, staring hopelessly into the white fog and knowing that his pay packet would be desperately thin. She thought of Mary, fading away on her sofa in the kitchen that Grainne tried so hard to keep warm and cheerful; and she thought of the many others who must be in a similar plight.

'Have ye been to our house, Miss?'

Startled, she glanced round and saw Danny, muffled almost to the point of disappearing in coats and scarves. He must be wearing almost everything the family possessed . . . He was dragging a makeshift sledge piled high with logs and ends of wood from the lumber yard.

'Hullo, Danny. Yes, I've just been in to see how your mother is. Is that wood for the fire? What a good boy you are.'

He glanced at it disparagingly. 'It's not bad. I'm going to get some more to sell when I've got this lot home. Me mam's dying, isn't she?'

The bald question shocked Cordelia but she could not lie to him. 'Yes, I think she is.'

He nodded. 'She'll be better off out of it. That's what me Dad says. But I wish she hadn't gone and got the consumption, all the same. I don't understand why people have to get things like that. Do ye, Miss?'

Cordelia gazed at him. His face was thin but still retained the sturdy belligerence that she had known she must win to her side in the school. Keep it, Danny, she thought suddenly, you're going to need it to get you through this life. And she felt ashamed of her own soft, easy childhood.

'No, I don't understand why people have to get things like that, either,' she said quietly. 'Take your wood home, Danny. Help your sister as much as you can. I'm coming back later on – I'll see you then.'

He nodded and tramped off again through the snow, and Cordelia watched him with an ache in her heart. He looked so small, so vulnerable, wrapped in his sister's coat and his brother's scarf and cap. Yet there was an air of sturdiness about him, a quality of determination, that roused all her admiration. Danny would never be beaten, she thought. He would grow up to be a fine man, all the finer because of the hardship he was enduring now. It had to be so – or there was no point in anything. No point in anything at all.

The tears froze instantly on her cheeks as she turned away and set off once more towards the long, iron bridge.

'We're not going skating,' she told Timothy as soon as she arrived home. 'There are more important things to do. I need your help.'

'Help? What for? And where have you been? I've been waiting for luncheon.'

Cordelia repressed the desire to tell her brother that if he was hungry he could have found himself something to eat. Timothy would have been shocked at the very idea. Would their father or their grandfather have ever dreamed of getting their own meal ready? The fact that there had always been servants at Henzel Court to wait on them would have been dismissed as irrelevant.

But there was no time to think of that now. And within a few days the maidservant who had been taken on with the house would be back from her parents' home, where she had been given leave to visit, and Cordelia's own burdens would be eased.

Quickly, Cordelia bustled about the kitchen, packing

246

bread, cheese, meat and coffee into her basket. There was a
pie in the meatsafe and she wrapped it in a cloth and put it
on top of a bag of vegetables. Timothy watched her,
bewildered.

'Cordelia, what on earth are you doing? We were going
to have that pie –'

'Well, we're not now,' she informed him crisply. 'We're
taking it to Grainne and her family. And anything else that
might be useful, too – go and fetch down as many blankets
as we can spare, and some warm clothes. And while you're
upstairs – oh, who's that?' she added as the bell jangled at
the front door.

'Jensen, I should think. He said he'd be here at two.
Cordelia, what's all this about –'

'Jensen! Oh, that's good, we can use his trap. It'll be so
much quicker. I'll go and let him in. Tim, do go and get
those blankets. We really don't have any time to waste.'

Together, they hurried out into the hall but Timothy still
did not go upstairs. Instead, he waited as Cordelia pulled
open the door, letting in a blast of icy air and a flurry of
driven snow. Jensen stepped quickly in and pushed the door
shut. His head and shoulders were covered by a thick sack,
already white with snow.

'No skating this afternoon, I'm afraid,' he began cheerfully, and then stopped as he saw their faces. 'What's
wrong?'

'Cordelia's lost her senses,' Timothy began, but Cordelia
gave him a quick push towards the stairs.

'Tim, *please*.' She turned back to Jensen. 'We need your
help. There's a family in Knoxville – the children are in my
school, and the sister is a friend of mine. Their mother's
dying of consumption, the father's lost his job and one
brother is on short time at the lumber yard. The other
brother's in Pennsylvania somewhere and they haven't

247

even the money to bring him home. I want to take food and clothing to them, but it's a long way and we need transport. Will you lend us your trap? It would be such a help. We're all ready, we could start at once.' Her hand was on his arm, tugging him towards the door, and Jensen made a half-humorous grimace.

'Are you asking me, or telling me?' he asked. 'Seems like you've got it all planned . . . Of course I'll help, Cordelia. Listen, do they need fuel as well? I've got a load of logs in my woodshed up at the house, ready for when I move in. I could fetch some of those over too. You can't have too much fuel in this weather.'

'Logs! Oh, that would be wonderful – little Danny's collecting wood from the lumber yard, but it's poor stuff and burns away in no time.' Cordelia turned and called up the stairs. 'Tim, haven't you found those blankets yet? Oh, there you are – yes, all of them. We don't need so many. I *know* they belong to the house, but we can buy more later to replace them. Just now, I want to get them over to the O'Donnells. Let's go. Is the weather much worse, Jensen?'

'It sure is. Don't you hear it?' The wind was whistling around the house now and the windows rattled. 'We'll have to do something about those draughts,' he said, frowning, but Cordelia tugged at his hand.

'Never mind those. Let's go, please.' She pulled open the door and let in another rush of freezing air. 'Your poor pony, Jensen.'

'He'll be all right, provided we don't leave him standing too long. Give me that basket, Cordelia. Tim, put the blankets down there, under the seat, where they'll keep dry. Have you both got plenty of clothes on? You can freeze solid in half an hour, sitting up there.' He gave Cordelia a brief look as she threw a heavy cloak around her shoulders.

'Can't you just give us the address, Cordelia, so you can stay here in the warm?'

'Certainly not.' She scrambled up into the trap and made room for Tim beside her. 'Please, Jensen, don't talk any more – poor Mary O'Donnell's dying over there, and Grainne needs all the help she can get.'

'Right!' Jensen sprang up into the driver's seat and cracked his whip over the pony's head and twitched the reins. 'I don't know who these people are, Cordelia, but if they're friends of yours –'

'Grainne is. And her mother, Mary. And the children are dears – Danny's such a tough little boy, and Bridget is sweet. She's just six years old, Jensen, and she's never had anything – can you imagine that?'

'Yes,' he said quietly, 'I can.'

'Declan's the eldest – he had to go away after a fight with Mr O'Donnell. He was in love with an Italian girl, and the O'Donnells are Irish, and you know what it's like between the Irish and the Italians. Mr O'Donnell swore he'd never have Declan in the house again, but I'm sure if he came back now . . . They need him so much. Mary needs to see him again – she's fretting her heart out over him . . .' Cordelia continued to talk as the pony made the best speed possible in the raging weather, and Jensen listened without comment. Even Tim seemed subdued by her story, and when they finally arrived at the house where the O'Donnells rented their rooms, he was first out of the trap and already at the door with his arms full of blankets while Cordelia and Jensen were still unpacking the boxes.

Danny came to the door, his eyes widening as he saw the three laden visitors.

'Miss Henzel?'

'Let us in, Danny. We've brought some things for your mother and the rest of you.' Cordelia led the way into the

249

kitchen. Grainne was there, serving out a meal of thin soup to her sister and brother, who sat at the table looking cold and weary. The wood Danny had brought in that morning had been almost used up; already the kitchen was growing colder. Mary was propped up on her sofa, a bowl and a spoon in her thin hands. She stared as the three came in.

'I've got some soup from home – Martha Robinson made it for us last night,' Cordelia said. 'We don't need it – she always makes far too much. Can we heat it up in your pan?'

'The fire –' Grainne began, but Jensen had already brought in some wood and was building it up on the hearth. 'Cordelia, I don't know what to say.'

'Don't say anything. There isn't time. I want your mother to have some of this, and then the rest of you. Where are your father and Garrett?'

'Still out. Me Dad won't come back until he finds a job, unless he's forced.' Grainne glanced at the window, thickly encrusted now with snow. 'And he'll not find much in this, that's certain, unless it's clearing snow from the yards of people who've got the money to pay for such things. Holy Mary, what's that you've got there, now?'

'Blankets. As much food as we could carry. And Tim's brought – oh, you haven't met my brother, have you? Tim, come and meet Grainne O'Donnell.' It seemed an odd situation in which to be making formal introductions. 'And this is Jensen Novak, who owns Novak Crystal . . .'

Her voice died away. Tim had stepped forward, out of the shadows. He was staring at Grainne as if he had suddenly laid eyes on a ghost. And Grainne was gazing back, a tiny frown on her forehead, as if trying to place an acquaintance she had almost forgotten.

'You haven't met before, have you?' Cordelia said doubtfully.

'We have.' Tim's face had split into an enormous grin. 'I couldn't believe it was you. I thought I was never going to see you again,' he said to Grainne. 'I thought you'd disappeared for good – left Corning, or maybe never even been here. I thought you must have been a dream.'

'The railroad station,' Grainne said in a whisper. 'Ye saved my life.'

'It was the day your brother went away. You told me about it – but when Cordelia told me, I never even thought . . . You've known each other all this time.'

'And I knew she had a brother too.' They were talking to each other as if they were alone, as if the kitchen and its occupants had evaporated around them leaving them in a world of their own. 'Tim,' she said wonderingly. 'So you're Tim.'

'Every time Cordelia's mentioned you,' he said, 'I've thought what a pretty name Grainne is.'

There was a brief silence. Cordelia found that she had drawn nearer to Jensen as they watched the little tableau. He was close to her now, the warmth of his body reaching out to her, and she felt a sudden desire to turn into his arms, to be enfolded once more against that broad, strong chest. She looked up at him and found his eyes on her face, serious, disturbing.

'Come,' he said quietly, 'we'll bring the rest of the things in from the trap.'

They worked together in silence. Cordelia's mind was buzzing with questions – how had Timothy and Grainne met, what did she mean by saying he had saved her life? But there was something in the way they looked at each other that told her this was a vital moment in their lives. Questions would be out of place now; she must wait for her answers. It was clear enough that they *had* met – somewhere, somehow – and that they'd been half consciously searching for each other ever since. Was this why Timothy was so restless, why he needed the distractions of cockfights and billiards when he was not working?

At last they had everything in the house. The fire had settled to a red glow and the soup was hot. Cordelia wrapped some extra blankets around Mary and filled her bowl, sitting beside her to feed the thick, nourishing broth to her, spoonful by spoonful. She looked at the wasted cheeks, the dry, cracked lips, saw the effort it cost the sick woman to swallow, and her heart felt as if it would break.

Tim came to her side, and she looked up at him through tear-filled eyes.

'Cordelia,' he said, 'I'm going to White Mills to find Declan. I'll bring him back with me. They need him here.'

'I know they do. Oh, Tim, it would be the best thing in the world – but can you do it? The weather –'

'The trains will still be running. It isn't that bad. And Grainne has Declan's address. I could be back on Monday.' She saw the purpose in his eyes. 'I've got enough money with me –'

'Take some more – you may need it.' Cordelia felt in her pocket and drew out her purse. She tipped the money into Timothy's hands. 'There's not very much, but it'll help. If you go home, you'll find –'

'I'm not going home. There isn't time.' He gave a brief glance around the room, taking in Bridget's wide eyes, Danny's shoeless feet, Mary's transparent pallor. 'I'm glad you brought me here,' he said.

'Tim –' she began, but he shook his head and she knew that he was right; there was no time for talking now. She lifted her hand and touched his cheek, and he bent to give her a quick kiss. 'Take care of yourself. Come back as quickly as you can.'

'I shall.' He moved towards the doorway, but Jensen put out a hand.

'Wait – I'll come with you. You need to get to the station as quickly as you can – God knows when the trains are running today, but you don't want to miss one. And I'll go and get that wood.' He gave Cordelia a quick look. 'You'll be all right here? I'll be right back.'

Timothy paused for a moment at the door. Grainne had moved across the room and stood close to him looking up into his face. Cordelia saw the entreaty in the Irish girl's vivid blue eyes, the longing in his. But he made no move to touch her. 'I'll be back soon,' he said gently, 'and I'll bring Declan with me.'

'Let's hope he's in time,' she murmured, and Tim thrust open the door and was gone.

Cordelia turned back to her task of feeding Mary. The kitchen seemed suddenly empty without the two men. She spooned the soup up patiently, thinking about her brother.

In the short time they had spent here, he seemed to have changed – grown. He had entered the shabby kitchen as a boy; he had left it, a man.

How would he be when he returned from Pennsylvania? When he had survived a railroad journey in the most bitterly cold weather he had ever experienced; when he had persuaded a man he had seen only once to come back to the house from which he had been driven away; when he stood once more in this small, poorly-furnished room and looked death in the eye?

Cordelia knew quite well that death was coming very close to Mary O'Donnell now. And, like Grainne, she could only pray that Tim could bring Declan home in time to say good-bye.

'I can't leave you here by yourself tonight,' Jensen said abruptly. 'You've not even a maid to keep you company. I knew it was a bad idea, letting her go home just now.'

'I'll be perfectly all right.' Wearily, Cordelia dropped her cloak on a chair and turned her hands towards the stove which had miraculously stayed alight for the whole day. 'Thank goodness it's warm in here! Jensen, please don't worry. I'll simply go to bed and sleep. I'm tired enough to sleep in a chair – perhaps that's what I'll do,' she said, trying to smile. 'Or I could go to Pierre and Ginette – though where they'd put me, heaven knows,' she added, thinking of the tiny rooms her cousins were sharing until Cordelia and Timothy were ready to welcome them to the rented house.

'You'll do no such thing. You'll come back to the Pickwick with me, they're sure to have a room –'

'No! Really, Jensen, I couldn't bear it – I'm too exhausted. And first thing in the morning I'll be going back to the O'Donnells – you know I only came home tonight because there simply isn't room for me there, with all the family there.' All except Declan, she thought, wondering how far Tim had got on his journey. The trains had been running still from Tioga Street, but the timetable had been abandoned and no one knew just how long any journey might take. The wind had risen to give blizzard conditions, with snow driving ferociously through the air, whirling and gusting in the gale. Coming home had taken the pony over twice as long as the journey to Knoxville this afternoon, and there had been several frightening moments when its hooves had slipped on the treacherous surface and Cordelia had clung to Jensen, convinced that the trap was about to capsize.

Jensen stood looking at her, as if undecided. Then he made up his mind and spoke briskly.

'All right, if you won't come with me, I'll stay here.' He raised his hand against her immediate protest. 'Cordelia, I'm not leaving you here by yourself, and that's flat. And

254

I'm afraid I don't give a damn about propriety – not on a night like this. Besides, who's going to know?'

'Propriety?' Cordelia stared at him. 'I hadn't even thought of that.' But she could not help remembering what had happened on the last occasion when they had been alone together in a house, and her face burned at the recollection. She sought for further dissuasion, knowing that it was useless. Jensen had made up his mind and Cordelia knew him well enough not to realise that there would be no moving him. 'But what about your pony?' she asked at last. 'He can't stand out in the snow all night – he needs his stable and a warm feed.'

'He'll get those. I'll take him back to the Pickwick now. The groom will attend to him. And then I'll collect a few things and walk back here – it's no more than a step.' He frowned. 'I don't like leaving you even to do that –'

'Jensen, for heaven's sake! I'm perfectly all right. And I'll prove it by having a meal ready for you when you return – there's still some of Martha's soup and I'm sure I can find something to go with it.' Cordelia stood up briskly. 'Go then, if you mean to. But I really don't mind if you don't come back. I don't need to be taken care of.'

Jensen looked down at her. 'Don't you, Cordelia? I have a feeling you're wrong there – you need a great deal of taking care of. And I hope that one day you meet the right person to do it.' She looked up at him, silenced, and he hesitated as if about to say something more. And then he turned and left the room; and, seconds later, Cordelia heard the slam of the front door.

She stood quite still for several minutes. The house was empty now, hollow, quiet and, in spite of the stove, oddly cold. Slowly, she wrapped her arms around her body, and shivered.

After a long while, she moved stiffly from the middle of

the room and began to make preparations for Jensen's return.

'That's better,' Jensen leaned back in his chair. 'You're a good cook, Cordelia. Somehow, I didn't expect it of a girl like you.'

'A girl like me? What do you mean by that?'

'Well, you know, English and pretty well-heeled – don't suppose you ever did a day's work in your life before you came here.' He grinned at her. 'That's the kind of picture we get over here, anyway – young ladies sitting at home all day receiving callers, with servants to do all the running around.'

'There are plenty of wealthy people in America who live just like that,' Cordelia pointed out. She began to gather up the soup bowls and fetched a pot of coffee from the top of the stove. 'And although we did have servants, I never sat at home waiting for visitors to arrive – neither did my mother, nor my grandmother. My grandmother had a glasshouse to run when she was no older than I am now, and my mother . . .' She paused suddenly, thinking of Emily. Was she still grieving over Paul's death? Was she still bitter over the way Cordelia and Timothy had left her? Cordelia had written many letters, trying to explain, begging for forgiveness, but so far she had received no answer, although Christina had assured her that Emily was slowly recovering. 'My mother has worked for other people all her life,' she said. 'And in the most squalid of conditions, too. Life has never been easy for her.'

'You sound sad when you speak of her. Is she ill?'

'Not in the ordinary sense.' Cordelia poured coffee and they took it to the big armchairs that stood one on each side of the stove. 'But when my father died – she seemed to lose her way, somehow. She depended on him so much – and yet, while he was alive, we all thought it was the other way about. She always seemed such a strong person – she always took charge, always knew what to do. But afterwards, it was as if all her strength came from him, and she was left without any at all.'

'That can happen,' Jensen said quietly. 'We all draw our strength from each other, Cordelia. That's why it isn't a good thing to be alone.'

She looked at him then, sensing an understanding in him. But he is alone, she thought, alone just as I am alone. And a great hunger crept into her heart and filled it with a yearning she could not define.

'Tell me why you came to America,' he said. 'Didn't you feel that your mother needed you then?'

'Oh yes, she needed us. Especially Tim. But she needed us too much.' Cordelia frowned. 'It's difficult to explain – but she turned to him and *fed* on him. That's the only word I can think of for what happened. It was as if she tried to turn him into our father, as if she forgot he was a different person. She wanted him with her all the time, and she wanted him to make the same kind of glass as our father had. She wouldn't let him experiment, she wouldn't let him develop. And it wasn't just bad for Tim – it was bad for her, too. We could all see that the longer it went on, the worse she would get. We were afraid she would lose her mind.'

'So you had to come away.'

'Yes. And we had to come somewhere where Tim could work on his glass. That's why we chose Corning – and because Uncle Harry lived here. He was a railroad engineer, you know, and he helped bring the Erie railroad to Corning. I suppose he liked it because it was a glassmaking town and reminded him of home – and because the countryside is so like the country south of Stourbridge. So when he retired, he and Aunt Ruth settled here.'

'We've come a long way since I complimented you on your cooking,' Jensen said after a moment. 'You've told me about your grandmother, and about your mother. They were both women who worked – who gave their lives to interests other than their homes and families. What about you? What would you have done, if you hadn't come to Corning?'

'Me?' Cordelia gave a little laugh. 'Oh, I would have done nothing special. I was what they call a bluestocking – I liked to study. In fact, as I told you before, I was going to go to university – to Cambridge. But I would have ended up doing just what I'm doing now, I expect – teaching.'

'And doing it very well,' he observed. 'I've seen those kids in your school when I've come by. You've made a deal of difference to them, Cordelia. They tumble out of there in the afternoons looking happy, as if they've done something worthwhile that day. And they obviously think the world of their teacher.'

Cordelia looked down at her hands, clasped tightly together in her lap. She felt unreasonably pleased by the compliment, and she knew that it wasn't paid lightly. Jensen had taken to calling in at the school occasionally, usually just before they finished for the day when he would, almost reluctantly it seemed, offer Cordelia a ride home in his trap. It was as if he were more interested in the children than in her; had seen the children at their desks, heard them sing the last song and say the last prayer of the school day, and watched them rush out into the fresh air. He had frequently brought wood to eke out their own supply, and had spent some time teaching the bigger boys to handle a saw or an axe.

She had the feeling that he was driven by some inner compulsion, though what it might be she could not guess.

'You're doing something worthwhile, too,' he said. 'Just

as worthwhile as if you were teaching in some fine seminary for young ladies, back in England. I hope you believe that.'

Cordelia looked up at him, meeting his eyes directly, but her fingers involuntarily tightened their grip on each other. She answered steadily, knowing that it was the truth.

'I do believe it, Jensen. I see those children improve every day, and I think of what they would have been like if they'd been allowed to run wild for much longer. I think of what their lives would have been – and what they could be now, with some real education. Children like Danny – he's going to make a fine man one day. He could be a leader – but he could so easily go wrong, with no one to take him in hand. And his sister, Bridget, she's so sweet, so sensitive. I can't bear to think of her growing up into poverty, being worn down with hard work and too many children like her mother. It's education that's the answer, Jensen. Those children are *intelligent* – they can do so much, if only they're given the right chances.'

'I know it,' he said in a low voice. 'I know it from my own experiences.'

He got up and went to the window, drawing back the curtain to look out into the stormy night. Cordelia watched him, her eyes moving slowly over the broad shoulders, the narrow waist and hips. There was a strength in Jensen, a strength that was allied to a sensitivity she had not known in any man before. Even her father, who had been such an artist but was so absorbed by his work; even her grandfather, with his rough, bluff kindness – neither of them had called to something deep inside her as this man did. No man had ever spoken to her heart.

Yet, she still had the feeling that there was something important that Jensen had not told her. He had told her so little of his life. Only that he had come here from Sweden as a boy with his parents and his sister; only that his sister had died and that he had vowed to make a success of his life in her memory. She knew that he and Lars had set up their own cutting shop, then their own pots, that they had expanded and gone to start up new glasshouses in Findlay and in White Mills. His father had died . . . but there, the story stopped. Of what had happened during the years since then, he never spoke.

Perhaps tonight, trapped together in this empty house with the storm raging outside and nothing to do but wait for morning, he would talk to her. Perhaps they would learn all that they wanted to know, about each other.

Cordelia got up and went to the window. She stood beside him, close enough for their arms to touch, and looked out through the thick curtains.

'I wonder where Tim is now,' she said softly. 'I hope the train's getting through and that he's not stranded somewhere in this dreadful weather. And I hope he can bring Declan O'Donnell back in time to see Mary.'

'He'll do his best.' As if without thinking, Jensen laid his arm across Cordelia's shoulders. They watched the snowflakes whirling in their dervish dance, a million wisps of white shavings from the heavy clouds above. Already the footprints Jensen had made as he walked back from the hotel had disappeared. The sidewalks and road were covered with a thick shroud, the trees bowed down with the mass of snow that had fallen on them during the day.

Cordelia shivered and let the curtain drop. The room was warm now and the only sound was a steady hissing from the logs in the stove. The weariness that had beset her when she had first come home had dissipated a little and she realised that it had been brought on as much by hunger as by fatigue. In spite of her worries over Grainne, Mary and Tim, she felt relaxed and at ease. She turned and looked up into Jensen's face, her lips parting in a smile.

His arm tightened around her shoulders. And, as she felt she must have known he would, he bent his head and touched her lips with his.

Cordelia felt her whole body quiver. She reached up with her arms and moved her fingers gently over the back of his neck. She felt his body move, felt his hand at her waist, the fingers strong and firm yet still gentle. His mouth moved over hers and she let her lips respond, finding a delight that she had never expected in this sharing of a kiss. Her whole being was centred on the fusion that was taking place, mouth to mouth; she wanted nothing more than to be here, in the arms of this tall, lean American, giving him her lips with such joyous abandon.

'Cordelia . . .' he muttered at last, and with an easy movement he lifted her right off the ground and carried her across the room. He set her down on her feet, then, before she could move, had settled himself in the large armchair and drawn her down to him.

Cordelia lay on the length of his body, her heart pounding. His arms were round her now, holding her with that same firm gentleness, his long fingers moving slowly over her shoulders and back, caressing her with a tender sensuality that set her skin tingling. She was acutely aware of each tiny nerve ending as his fingers passed over her body, outlining each contoured muscle, each bone, the curling shape of her ears, the curve of her cheek and the hollow of her throat. She lay quiescent in his arms, the rapid pounding of her heart her only movement; and then, as his hand pressed lightly on her cheek, she turned her face to his, her lips already parted for his kiss.

How long they stayed together in the chair, she had no idea. For ever afterwards, she remembered that night as if it had been a dream; a dream of hands that caressed and brought a singing to Cordelia's blood so that she moved restlessly against him, wanting to come even closer, wanting to feel his warmth, his strength, wanting to rid herself of the barriers between them.

Jensen's hand tightened then on her body, began to explore more intimately. He touched her breasts and Cordelia gasped and then whimpered with a shock that was both unexpected and delightful. When he removed his hand, she moved, arching her body a little, seeking to repeat the caress. And when he laid his hand on her breast once more, cupping it firmly in his palm, she lifted her lips to his in a kiss that was now as fierce as it had been gentle, searching and seeking response that she barely understood.

'Ssh . . . ssh, my darling,' he murmured, and lifted his hand away to cup her chin instead. His fingers moved on her throat, holding her mouth against his. And then, gently but firmly, he lifted her from his lap and placed her on her feet before the fire.

'Jensen . . .?' Cordelia said doubtfully, and looked at him as he stood up and laid both hands on her shoulders.

'It has to end there,' he said quietly. 'You know it must, Cordelia. And I know I ought to apologise to you – but I can't. It was delightful, every moment of it.'

'I don't understand,' Cordelia faltered, and he smiled and then looked grave.

'I wish I didn't either. But I do, and I know that what's happened between us tonight must never happen again. There are things you don't know, Cordelia – things it's hard to explain.'

'But you must!' She stared up at him, her eyes heavy with the desire that still held her body in a tormented grip. 'Jensen, you can't behave like this – holding me so, kissing me – and then say – say what you've just said. What do you mean?' A dreadful thought struck her and she remembered her early mistrust of him. 'Are you just playing with me, Jensen? Are you nothing but a philanderer?'

'No!' The word shot from him like the crack of a pistol. 'No, Cordelia, never think that.' He turned away then, his long fingers raking through his hair, his face tortured. 'Maybe I shouldn't have come here tonight,' he muttered. 'Maybe I should have left you to stay alone – but how could I? What choice did I have?' He wheeled abruptly and Cordelia stepped back, almost afraid of the emotion she saw in his blazing eyes. 'The trouble is, I can't stay away from you! I know I must, I know there's no good can come of all this, but every day I find myself driving past that damned school, knowing you're in there, knowing I only have to open the door to see your face. Every day I have to work with your brother, knowing that he shares a house with you, knowing he's seen you and talked with you that morning, that he'll see you and talk with you that night. There are times when I don't know how I'm going to stand it – times when I can't get your face out of my mind, when I hear your voice wherever I go. I know I should keep away – but I damned well can't, and that's the honest truth.'

Cordelia gazed at him. 'But Jensen . . . if you feel that way –' She floundered to a halt, not knowing how to go on. But Jensen smiled grimly and finished her sentence for her.

'If I feel that way, why don't I do the honest thing and tell you? Or tell your brother? Ask for your hand in marriage – is that what you're too modest to say?' He gave a short, bitter laugh. 'If only it were that easy!' He turned away again and paced across the room, then whipped back. 'Cordelia, there's a lot you don't know about me. Things you need to know before we can go any further with this. Things it'd take a deal of time to tell you.' He stopped as the clock on the mantelpiece began to chime and they both turned their eyes towards it. Ten – eleven – twelve. He looked down at her again, his face grave.

'I'll tell you all of it, Cordelia. But not now. We've both been through too much today, and tomorrow's going to be hard too. You need to sleep.'

Cordelia shook her head and began to speak, but he laid his fingertips lightly on her lips, then brushed them across her cheek and down the quivering column of her neck.

'No more now, Cordelia. Believe me, it's better this way.' He hesitated and then added, almost too low for her to hear: 'I wish I could tell you to forget what's happened between us tonight. But I can't forget it myself. I don't want to. If we never have anything else, we'll have had that. Nothing – nobody – can alter the truth that lay between us then.'

He took her by the hand and led her up the stairs to her bedroom door. As she stood inside, still gazing up at him with wide, bewildered green eyes, he gave her a long, grave look. And she had the sudden cold feeling that he was wishing her farewell.

'Goodnight, Cordelia,' he said quietly, and closed the door.

Cordelia stood quite still. She stared at the door, almost willing it to open again. But it did not move. And, after a long time, she heard Jensen's footsteps going slowly, quietly, down the stairs; and then there was nothing but the moaning of the wind and an icy chill that seemed to find its way through her bones and into her very heart.

Chapter Twelve

The storm continued throughout the night, and Cordelia feared that the city would disappear altogether under the weight of the snow that fell. It piled up around the house, reaching above the ground-floor windowsills; when she woke, the room was darkened by snow that had been driven against the glass of her bedroom window, and remained encrusted there like a shutter. Opening the back door, she was met by a furious and bitter gale that blew a million icy spicules into her face, and she saw that the snow had drifted into the corner and was piled high against the door, a solid wall of menacing white.

Hastily, she slammed the door again and turned to find Jensen in the kitchen behind her.

'Not so good,' he said briefly. 'It's a good thing we've plenty of fuel indoors. Look, I'll brisk up the stove while you get some breakfast going, and then we'll have to think about digging ourselves out of here.'

Cordelia did as she was told, thankful that there was plenty to occupy them – with the memory of last night's events still scorching in her mind, she had been almost afraid of meeting Jensen this morning. Quickly, she laid the kitchen table – since living in lodgings, the formality of the dining-room had almost disappeared from her life, and it was certainly out of place in these conditions, particularly as the kitchen was warm and cosy and the dining-room cold and musty. She looked in the cupboards and found coffee, bread and eggs. There was a little milk left from yesterday, but nothing else; she had intended going to the shops yesterday for provisions, and then had taken most of what they did have to the O'Donnells. Well, it would have to do.

'Will we be able to get through to the O'Donnells?' she asked anxiously. 'I promised Grainne I'd go back this morning.'

'God knows. It'll take us all our time just to get out of the house.' Jensen looked at the window, which he had scraped clear of the snow which had clung to it. 'It don't show any signs of letting up. I don't think you ought to go out, Cordelia. I'll try to get over myself later on, to see how they are.'

Cordelia said nothing. So Jensen thought he could tell her what she ought and ought not to do, did he? Well, they would see about that.

He spent the next two hours clearing paths around the house and doing the essential jobs that needed to be done. Cordelia tidied the kitchen and unpacked a few more of her belongings. It was just as well she and Tim hadn't brought much with them, she thought as she hung up her clothes and folded his shirts into a drawer, for they seemed to have accumulated a great deal since they had arrived. Mostly winter clothes – thick jackets and a topcoat for Tim, a cloak and warm gloves and scarves for herself. And good sturdy boots. She took hers down to the kitchen and stood them in front of the stove to warm.

'A cup of good hot coffee now, I think,' Jensen said, appearing like a snowman in the doorway. 'I've cleared it all away round the house, though it's still coming down fast and I guess it'll be all to do again tomorrow. There's not much moving outside – a few folk clearing their yards, and someone trying to make a path along the road for horses, but it's sleighs we need in this weather, not wheels.' He shook the snow from his coat and closed the door. 'That smells good!'

'We've almost nothing else in the house,' Cordelia said,

pouring coffee into a large cup. 'I shall have to go to the store. And to see Pierre and Ginette. And there's school – it's Monday today –'

'Forget it. None of those kids is going to turn up, and they won't expect you to. And Pierre can look after himself, he's done it long enough. As for the stores, well, I guess they'll do their best to open and folks'll be in there buying up all they can see in case this goes on and nothing can get through. Even the railroad has trouble when it's as bad as this.'

'The railroad! But what about Tim? And Declan?'

Jensen shrugged. 'They'll just have to take their chance. There's nothing we can do about it, Cordelia.' He glanced at her worried face. 'Look, they'll be all right. It just means they'll be held up, that's all.'

'I know. And poor Mary O'Donnell –'

'Yes,' he said, 'I know.' He reached out and touched her hand. 'I watched my sister die that way,' he said quietly. 'It's no fun. I know just what they're going through over there.'

Cordelia stared down at his hand, misty and blurred through her tears. She looked up at him and her voice was tremulous as she said, 'You won't try to stop me coming with you, will you, Jensen? You know I must.'

He looked down at her swimming eyes and she saw his face change; a slight, almost imperceptible tightening of the muscles, a darkening of his eyes. He made a tiny movement and she knew that he was on the edge of taking her into his arms. Her heart kicked; not again, she thought, please not again. But she couldn't move; she could only stand and wait, knowing that if he did so she would be lost. She was sharply aware of the slow ticking of the clock, of the pounding of her blood. Her nerves tingled; her body was rigid.

Jensen's eyes moved slowly over her face and she felt his gaze almost as if it were a caress. Her own eyes closed and she lifted her face slightly, as if following the butterfly touch of tender lips. And then, conscious of a subtle change in the room, the lightening of a shadow, she opened her eyes and saw that he had moved away.

'It's bad out there,' he said. 'We'd have to walk all the way. I don't know if you could make it.'

'I walk there every day,' she reminded him tartly. The tension was draining from her body, leaving her momentarily weak. 'Jensen, I'm strong – I'm not some soft Society miss, afraid to get my feet wet or my hands dirty.' She turned to the hearth. 'My boots are here, ready, and so is my cloak. And I'm *coming*. If you don't think I should then I shall simply go alone.'

He stared at her and then grinned suddenly. 'All right, Cordelia, I can see you won't be stopped. We'll go together, and on the way we'll see if the stores are open and get some provisions, for the O'Donnells as well as us.' He stopped and gave her a quizzical look. 'That's if I'm staying here? Maybe you'd rather I went back to the hotel.'

Cordelia felt her cheeks colour. She knew she ought to tell him to return to his hotel. For him to stay here at all was totally against convention and would do her reputation no good if it were known. And after what had happened yesterday evening . . . what could so easily have happened again just a few minutes ago . . .

But the thought of his leaving seemed to tear a great hollow somewhere deep inside her. The house would be empty without him, and it was an emptiness she could not face. Besides, they had some talking to do. Jensen had hinted at things in his life that she didn't know – things he wanted to tell her. And she knew that whatever they were, it was important for her to hear.

She opened her mouth to speak, but before she could do so there was a loud knocking on the door. And a moment later, Bob Robinson was in the room, shaking snow from his shoulders and stamping it from his feet.

'Blame me if it ain't just like the Arctic out there!' he exclaimed. 'Martha and me, we've been worryin' about you and Tim all night. And she sent me over just as soon as I could dig me way out, to tell you you're to come over and stop with us as long as this darned blizzard lasts. So pack your bags, Cordelia, and call that brother of yours out of bed and we'll be off straightaway.' He looked at Jensen and nodded. 'Seems best all round, don't you reckon? I bet that's just what you came to tell her yourself, weren't it?'

Jensen and Cordelia looked at one another. Whether there was relief or disappointment in his glance, she was unable to tell. She wasn't even sure how she felt herself.

She only knew that there was nothing for it but to go to the Robinsons. And that whatever it was Jensen wanted to tell her about himself would have to wait.

Tim had never seen such snow. He sat in the railcar and stared out at a landscape as bleak as a polar ice-cap. The fields and hills stretched away on either side, their whiteness merging with the heavy clouds so that it was impossible to define any horizon. Houses, schools, factories, churches, all were shrouded in a soft, thick blanket of aching white, and the roads were empty.

The journey had already taken twice as long as anyone had expected. It was bitterly cold in the carriages and those who were travelling were as much muffled up in boots, heavy coats, scarves and gloves as if they had been fighting their way through the storm that raged outside. Snow piled up in front of the engine, thrust to one side by the snow-plough fixed to the front, and progress was painfully slow.

Tim sat in his corner, gazing out, but he saw little of what they were passing. His thoughts were back in Knoxville – back in the small, crowded kitchen where a woman lay dying and the girl who tended her had vivid blue eyes set behind thick black lashes, and hair the colour of jet falling heavily around her sad, pale face.

Why had it never occurred to him that his own sister might know the girl he had saved from walking under a train? Why had he never thought that the Grainne O'Donnell about whom Cordelia had so often told him, might be the girl who haunted his dreams? He had been aware that the Irish girl he had held so briefly in his arms lived in Knoxville – wouldn't anyone with any sense have realised that she might well have younger brothers or sisters, children who might attend Cordelia's school? But the thought had never entered his head, and he cursed himself now for a fool. The memory of wasted time hung in his mind like a heavy weight, reproaching him. If only he had known Grainne was so close . . . if only he could have spent the past few months with her, instead of roaming round the town with his friends, killing time in billiard saloons and at cockfights.

It seemed to Timothy now that he had never stopped yearning for the Irish girl with her musical voice and soft, slim body. It seemed that there had never been a moment when she was out of his mind, when her face was not haunting his thoughts. And now that he had found her again, he could not understand why he had not searched, why he had not turned the city upside down in his efforts to find her. What had he been doing all this time? What had be been thinking of?

You know what you've been doing and thinking of, he answered miserably. You've been trying to be a big fellow in Corning – showing off to your friends. Trying to prove that the English could beat the Americans in pleasure-seeking any day, and getting yourself into a lot of situations you didn't find any pleasure in at all.

He thought of the way he had spent his spare time during the past months, and felt sick. What would Grainne say if she knew? He had not even dared to let Cordelia know of the jokes between him and his cronies, the fights between game-cocks that he'd watched, the late-night drinking and the women. The shame and guilt he had felt so often when he saw two fine birds tear each other to shreds in their death battle, and which he had thrust down to the lowest recesses of his heart and tried so hard to ignore, came back to him now in full force. He groaned and buried his head in his hands. He wasn't fit to associate with a girl like Grainne O'Donnell, he told himself miserably.

But he could redeem himself now, perhaps, by bringing her brother home. It was the least – probably the only thing – he could do. And he glanced impatiently out of the window, wondering how far they had come and how long the rest of the journey would take.

'When do you think we'll get to White Mills?' he asked the passenger next to him. The man shrugged.

'Who knows? Maybe we won't get there at all. Snow's gettin' worse – could be stuck here for days.'

'Days?' Tim exclaimed. 'But my business is urgent – I have to fetch a man home to his dying mother.'

'Ain't no use tellin' me – tell him up there.' The man jerked his head towards the sky. 'Ain't none of us can change the weather, son.'

Tim gave an exasperated grunt and then began to deal himself small punches of frustration on his chin. Outside, the white landscape mocked him and he felt infuriatingly helpless. He wanted to get out of the train, use his own strength to drag it along, hurl the snow aside to ease their journey, but instead he was forced to sit here immobile and watch the miles crawl by as slowly as the hours.

'Might's well settle down to it,' his companion remarked. 'Maybe we could hev a game of cards – pass the time a bit.'

Tim shook his head. Cards, when Grainne's mother lay dying and longing for a last glimpse of her son!

'Ain't goin' to do no good gettin' yourself all worked up about it. That's to no one's benefit. Now, a game or two of poker could ease your mind and make the time seem shorter, and who's to be harmed? You ain't religious, I take it?'

'No – no, I've nothing against cards. I enjoy a game at the right time.'

'How you English talk!' the man said, grinning. 'Well, and what righter time is there than bein' stuck in a railroad car in a howlin' blizzard with nothin' else to do but get worked up into a paddy over the weather? Come on – loosen up a bit. Do you good.'

Tim glanced at him and felt the tightness in his face ease a little. His mouth grinned in spite of himself and he gave a reluctant chuckle.

'All right, then. I suppose we might as well. Have you got some cards with you?'

'Always got a pack somewheres.' The man felt in his pockets and brought out a small box. 'Here they are – now, hev you played poker before? Not all you English know it, but I'd be happy to teach you.'

'I've played a bit,' Timothy said cautiously, remembering the games he had played with the others in the saloons, and remembering also their advice about playing with strangers. But this man didn't look like a card-sharper. He hadn't even suggested a game until now, and surely the men who rode the railroads looking for easy pickings started on their victims as soon as the journey had started. No, this was just a friendly way of passing the time.

'We won't play for high stakes,' his new friend said, confirming Timothy's thoughts. 'We'll just take an ante of a dollar or so to start with, for the fun of the thing.' He laid the cards on the table. 'Cut to deal.'

They began to play. With the first bet, Tim doubled the ante and on the second round his opponent doubled that. On

272

the third round, both checked and they revealed their hands. Tim won the pot.

By now, some of the other men in the car had drawn closer and one of them suggested they should form a school. Tim's friend looked at him enquiringly.

'What do you say? Make up five?'

'Suits me,' Tim said. The train was still moving slowly, but it was growing dark outside and there was nothing to look at but the swirling snow as it fell against the window. He shifted in his seat to make room for another man, and the five settled themselves round the table. Tim's friend placed the pack in the centre and they began to cut.

The game went slowly enough at first, with low stakes and a good deal of friendly banter. Tim relaxed and began to enjoy himself. He had won several small sums and no one seemed to be losing heavily. With the ante rising in each game, he felt unworried; he could match any of these players for skill and he had enough money with him to be able to afford to lose a little.

An hour later, his confidence was unbounded and although it was now clear that two of the men were serious gamblers and eager to raise the stakes, he was unconcerned. He grinned when his original partner began to look worried, and shook his head at the suggestion that they might drop out.

'Why? I'm doing fine. I don't mind raising.'

'Well, I do. Reckon I'll just sit back and watch from now on. You can carry on with the cards, though,' he added as if the other players might think he would take them away. 'I'll just be a spectator.'

With his withdrawal, the atmosphere changed. Every man sat forward a little, and Tim saw that their faces had tightened. The burly, red-headed man who sat opposite him glanced around.

'Rest of you okay? Reckon to stay in?' His eyes were on Tim, small, hard eyes of muddy blue. 'You, English?'

'I'm happy,' Tim said, meeting his look. The red-headed man had made several mistakes so far, and Tim was confident of being able to call his bluff. 'Put up the ante.'

The game began.

'Out,' said a small, bullet-headed man on Timothy's right.

'Two,' Tim said.

'Four.'

'Four.'

'I'll raise to four,' Tim said.

The red-headed man looked at him.

'Know what you're doin', English?'

'I think so,' Timothy said blandly. On the next round he bet four again, and on the third he called two.

'I'll see you,' the red-headed man said and then, when Tim's hand was spread on the table, he snorted with disgust. 'A full house! I might've knowed it. All right –' he gave Tim a hard look – 'from now on, we play for real, all right? No holds barred.'

'I already was,' Timothy said, and made a neat pile of his winnings. 'My deal now, I think.'

The owner of the pack leaned forward and breathed in his ear. 'I should watch it, son. These fellas ain't in it just to pass the time.'

Tim laughed confidently. 'It's all right, I know what I'm doing. I won't get in too deep. In any case –' he glanced at the dark window, at the snow still falling outside – 'we'll be in White Mills before too long. I won't have time to lose my shirt!'

'Are we playin' cards, or ain't we?' the red-headed man growled, and Timothy returned his attention to the table.

He won two more games, one with three of a kind and one with a straight. Then he began to lose.

'Pull out now,' his friend advised as Timothy watched yet another high stake disappear into the red-headed man's pile.

'He can't go on like that,' he muttered, and sure enough the next game was won by the bullet-head. Well, that was better than one man having all the luck. It ought to come round to Timothy's turn again soon, provided he could hang on for long enough. On his next bet, he called high. The red-head matched him. Bullet-head won again.

All the money was now in the pot. Tim was suddenly aware that his pockets were almost empty – he had staked very nearly every dollar he had. He felt a cold sweat break out on his forehead. How could such a thing have happened? And what was he to do when he reached White Mills? He didn't even have enough money to buy his own ticket home – and he was supposed to be bringing Declan O'Donnell . . .

A sudden picture of Grainne, bending over the wasted figure of her mother, flashed into his mind and he almost groaned. But just in time he remembered the other men, caught sight of their keen eyes on his face. He dared not let them know how desperate he was. With a tremendous effort, he kept his face blank.

If only he had pulled out while he was winning! Or when he had begun to lose, while he still had money in his pocket. But now he had no choice. He had to continue. There was always the hope that he would win back all his money, and more besides.

He *had* to win . . .

He looked at his cards and his heart leapt.

A straight flush! Nine, ten, jack, queen, king, all in the same suit. Surely nobody would be able to beat that. The possibility of anyone else being dealt an identical hand was too remote even to be considered. And if they did – the winner would be the last to raise the pot in that round. All he had to do was make sure that he was the one, and then call.

'Call,' he said, and his voice trembled a little in spite of himself.

The four players spread their cards face upwards on the table. Everyone leaned forward.

The red-headed man had a royal straight. Ten, jack, queen, king – and ace.

Tim stared at it unbelievingly. He watched the big, raw-looking hands reach out and gather the heap of money towards him. And at that exact moment, the train ran into White Mills station and everyone gave a cheer.

'I did warn you,' the owner of the cards said, collecting them up, and Tim nodded dumbly. The rest of the players had melted away. He watched miserably as people streamed away down the platform. The snow was still falling and the roads were deep with mud and slush.

As he left the station, still dazed by his misfortune, he caught one last glimpse of the men he had been playing cards with. They were all there – the red-headed man, the bullet-headed man, the other two who had said little but played hard. And with them, grinning as if at some huge joke, was the man he had sat next to in the train; the man who had first suggested a game 'to pass the time'; who had provided the cards and then opted out.

'O'Donnell? No one here of that name, son. Don't mean to say he didn't lodge with us for a bit, mind. We get a lot of 'em here, just stay a night or two and then move on.' The man looked over his shoulder and called to someone inside the house. 'D'you remember anyone by the name of O'Donnell, Ma? Glass trade, he'd hev been in.'

A thin woman came out of an inner room, wiping her hands on a dirty apron. She gave Timothy a cursory glance and shook her head. 'If I remembered all the men that stayed here, I'd be on the halls doin' a turn. Try next door, they

276

might know. This here street's full of lodgin' houses – he could've lived in any one of 'em.'

'But it's this address he gave last,' Tim said, producing the last letter Declan had written to his family. 'It was less than a month ago.'

'Month's a long time round here. Try along the street.' She turned away.

'But suppose his family wrote back – surely he'd have come in for any letters that might have arrived for him.'

'Guess he would at that.' The man frowned. 'Hold on, Betty. Wasn't there a young fella in two or three nights back, lookin' for letters?'

She shrugged. 'What if there was? I don't recall his name, and I never asked him where he was lodgin' now. Why should I?'

Her husband looked back at Tim. 'Seems like a dead duck, son. Can't help you nohow.'

Tim looked at him helplessly. He had staked everything – the thought had a bitter humour that he couldn't appreciate – on finding Declan here. Now he didn't know what to do. It was growing late and it was bitterly cold. The thought of trudging up and down the street, over his ankles in icy slush, with nowhere to spend the night if his quest failed, was almost more than he could tolerate.

It would be better to wait until tomorrow, when he could at least try the glasshouses. Declan *must* be in one of those – he would find him easily enough then.

Timothy felt in his pockets. The poker game had left him almost penniless. Almost – but not quite. He still had enough for a night's lodging, provided it was cheap.

He looked around the dimly lit hall. It was bare of furniture, with dirty, broken linoleum on the floor, and the painted walls were scuffed and grubby. There was a curious smell of old cabbage, unwashed clothes and bodies, and sour milk. But it was dry. It was out of the storm.

'Can you give me a bed for the night?' he asked, and then, remembering that even this might be beyond his means, added, 'What do you charge?'

In the O'Donnells' rooms, the family sat silent and tense. Kevin O'Donnell had been out since early morning, tramping the snowy streets looking hopelessly for work. Garrett had been down at the lumber yard but the blizzard had brought work to a standstill; there had been nothing for him to do but gather up off-cuts and unwanted timber and hawk it through the streets for sale, with Danny beside him. Patrick, Michael and Maureen had all been able to go to work, and Bridget and Grainne had remained at home with Mary.

'How is she?' Cordelia asked when she and Jensen finally reached the house and came in, shaking the snow off their coats at the door. Grainne shook her head.

'Failing. She's so weak now, she just lies there and looks at us all, and there's such trouble in her eyes I can't bear to see it. It's our Declan she wants and longs for, and nothing any of us can do about it. How long d'ye think your brother will be, Cordelia?'

'I don't know. The trains are hardly running at all now. If the snow doesn't stop, we'll be cut off from everywhere. We don't even know if he's reached White Mills.' She stood her basket on the table and removed the snow-covered cloth from its contents. 'We've brought you some more bread, and some milk. It's fresh this morning; the Robinsons sent it.'

'Thank God for good friends and neighbours,' Grainne said. 'The people upstairs gave us some buckwheat this morning to make biscuits with, and them nearly as hard pressed as we are – wasn't it good of them? But folk are always kind when there's trouble, I've noticed it before.'

She spoke absently, as if her mind were on other things. 'I hope those two get back all right. I hope Mr Henzel can find Declan. He moves about – keeps giving different addresses. Lord knows whether he's even in White Mills now.'

'I wish I'd gone myself,' Jensen said. 'I know the town, I know the manufacturers. I could have found him and brought him home.' He rubbed his hand over the back of his head. 'Why, he might even be working in my own glasshouse.'

'Tim wanted to go. And he said he knew what Declan looks like.'

'Aye, that's right – he must have seen us all that morning down on Tioga. Oh, he'll find him for sure. We don't need to worry. If only it wasn't for this awful weather!'

Cordelia sat down by the fire and held out her hands. It had seemed, as she and Jensen struggled through the deep snow that morning, as if the sky might be growing lighter at last, as if the snow might be abating. Surely it must do so soon? The storm had been raging for three days and nights now, without respite. Where it had not been cleared, the snow lay seven or eight feet deep; it was piled high against walls and doorways, covering windows and blocking roads. Drifts of twenty feet or more lay across the narrower streets, packed tightly by the wind and already turning to walls of ice. The railroad track was said to be blocked outside the town. While these conditions lasted, she could see no hope of Timothy's return.

For the rest of the day, Cordelia stayed with Grainne while Jensen went back to Corning to bring more fuel down from the hill to the Robinsons. After their insistence that Cordelia should go to stay with them, he had returned to his room in the hotel, but he had told Cordelia that he intended to move into his new house as soon as the weather improved. 'Hotel living's no life at all. I want my own home around me,' he had said, and again his eyes had held that disturbing intentness, as if there were something he wanted her to know. 'But I have to go away again first.'

'Again?' she had asked, and felt a chill at the thought.

'Just once more,' he said, and seemed about to say more. She held her breath, waiting, knowing that the moment was an important one. And then Martha bustled in with coffee and cookies, and the moment was gone. There had not been another such.

By late afternoon, the snow had stopped. The wind died down and the clouds began to roll away. The sky was not clear as darkness fell, but patches of weak, pale blue could be seen between the ripples of sullen grey. People began to emerge from their houses and the scrape of spades on paths could be heard all along the street.

'Thank God!' Grainne said, looking out of the window. 'They'll clear the line now and the trains'll begin to run again. Our Declan could be home the night.'

Cordelia echoed her hope, although in her heart she doubted it. She went to the bed and gave Mary a cup of milk, sip by sip. Could Declan possibly be home by nightfall? Or even by tomorrow? And if he was . . . would he yet be in time to see his mother alive? She looked at the almost transparent face, the burning eyes, and her heart ached.

Jensen would be here soon, to take her home. She felt a tension in the air, a sense of something about to happen. It was almost akin to the feeling she had sometimes had as a child, when she and Tim had been inseparable and seemed able to know each other's thoughts, to be aware when the other was in trouble. It was a tingling of the skin, a nagging at the back of her skull . . . She finished giving Mary the milk and joined Grainne at the window.

Jensen was coming along the snowy street. He was on his

pony, and he was riding the animal as fast as it could go in the deep, soft powder.

'Something's happened,' Cordelia said with certainty, and ran out to meet him.

He brought his pony to a halt and looked down at her, and his face was grave.

'What is it? What's happened? Tim –'

'Tim's all right,' he cut in, and she found that she had been holding her breath. 'As all right as he deserves to be, anyway, the young idiot. I knew I should have gone myself!'

'Why – what's happened?' she asked again, and tugged at his pony's bridle. 'Jensen, *tell* me!'

He dismounted and stood beside her. 'I went round to your place to see that everything was all right and stoke up the stove. While I was there, a telegram arrived –'

'A telegram –'

'– so I took it in and opened it. It was from Tim. The silly young fool lost all his money in a poker game on the train. He spent his last cents in sending the telegram and now I'll have to go myself and fetch him home. Well, I guess I can kill two birds with one stone – I can do my business there and won't have to make the journey again this winter.'

Grainne had come out of the house and stood listening. Now she grasped at Jensen's arm and looked up imploringly into his face.

'But has he found Declan? Has he found me brother yet?'

Jensen looked down at her and his face was a fury of exasperation.

'Will you believe me, he doesn't even say! But if he hasn't found him by the time I get to White Mills, I'll soon track him down. Don't worry, Grainne, I'm off straightaway and you'll soon have your brother back, now that the weather's on the mend. I promise you.'

'Aye, and I believe ye,' she said. 'But will it be in time for me mother? Can ye promise me that?'

'Nobody can promise you that,' Jensen said quietly. 'But if it's humanly possible for it to be done, I'm the man to do it.' He turned back to Cordelia and gave her hand a brief, hard squeeze. 'There's no time to talk now, Cordelia. All I can say is – trust me. Will you do that?'

She looked at him, bewildered. Trust him? Trust him to do what? To bring Timothy and Declan back safely? Surely he already knew that she had placed all her faith in him to do that.

Or was there some other reason for him to ask for her trust? Something to do with the strange way in which he had kissed her and then withdrawn, as if any relationship between them was untenable – as if there were a barrier between them, insurmountable, impossible to destroy.

'Trust me,' he said again. 'Please.' And even as she opened her mouth to ask him why, he was back in the saddle and gone, away down the road towards the bridge, towards the station where a train already stood waiting to leave.

The sky was clear now. A few stars had begun to prick through the apologetic blue. Cordelia stared after Jensen and then turned back to her friend.

'Come in and get warmed up again,' Grainne said, taking her arm. 'And then our Garrett will see you back home. He's coming now, I can see him along the street.' She tugged gently at Cordelia's sleeve. 'Come away in. Ye look as if you'd seen a ghost walking, so ye do.'

Cordelia turned and stared into her eyes. A ghost walking? Perhaps that was what she was seeing. The ghost of her own half-realised dreams.

For Jensen, the journey to White Mills was quicker than it had been for Timothy, and there were no card-players to tempt him. Or perhaps the sternness of his expression and the angry set of his lips were enough to warn off anyone who might have been looking for easy pickings. He spent the journey staring out of the window at the icy waste of winter. Occasionally, he turned his attention to the newspaper he had brought with him; but always, after a few minutes, he would drop it into his lap and return once more to his contemplation of the snow.

He berated himself for not having made an opportunity to speak with Cordelia before leaving Corning. Why had he allowed their friendship to develop at all without having made his own position clear? God knew what she thought now, what she expected – but with every day the need to tell her had become more urgent, and the task more impossible.

He was too damned proud, that was his trouble. Always had been. Too proud to admit that he could have failed. Ever since he had come to this country, he had been determined to prove that he could succeed. And he had done so. He had opened three glass factories, in three different cities – in different States, even – and they had all succeeded.

But that hadn't been enough. He had to succeed in his private life, too. And when the most important part of it had collapsed around him, he hadn't been able to face it. Hadn't been able to talk to a soul about it. He had kept it to himself, hugged his failure to his chest and only those most directly concerned had any real knowledge of it. Only those in White Mills. Nobody in Corning had ever even heard of the disaster that his marriage had brought.

He had never intended to let any woman get close to him again. How could he bring such tragedy into any woman's life, especially one he loved? If it had indeed been all his fault . . . No. It was better never to allow himself to love again. Better not to take the risk.

But somehow that copper-headed English girl, with her steady green eyes and her determination to win her own

283

independence, had got under his skin. And nothing he could do would dislodge her.

He ought to have known from the start, of course. From that very first day, when he had met her and Tim in the railroad car, and had been unable to prevent his eyes from straying to her face. From the moment when he had given in to the urge to call at Harry Henzel's house to enquire after them, and had found them in lodgings instead. Common courtesy, he had called his actions then, but he'd known quite well that there was more to it than that. He wanted to see Cordelia Henzel again – and again. And when Timothy Henzel had been turned down by the Houghtons and had stood there blazing with indignation and fury, it had been like a bright, shining gift dropped in Jensen's lap.

He had thought then that he could control it, that he could meet Cordelia day after day and prevent it from going any further. That he could stop at friendship; that he would never need to touch her, never feel a hunger to kiss her. And he had been wrong.

And now he had gone further than any decent man would without proposing marriage. And she – miraculously, she had not drawn furiously out of his arms, had not delivered the slap that he deserved, but had responded. As if she felt the same need, the same aching hunger.

She would – she must – be expecting a declaration. And instead . . . he would be bringing home Karin.

He could not postpone it any longer. And through fate and his own reluctance, he had left it too late.

He found Timothy at the address he had given, the last address they had had for Declan. It was a poor enough place, cold and shabby and not very clean. But it wouldn't have done young Tim a scrap of harm to have stayed there a bit longer, he thought grimly. Might have taught him a lesson or two about low company and throwing his money away. However, matters were too urgent to think of that now. He paid the woman the money Timothy owed and they went outside. The sky was clear and bright now, the sun shining coldly on snow that had frozen into a hard shell of ice over the roads. They walked together along the street and Tim began to explain what had happened to him.

'Never mind that,' Jensen cut in brusquely. 'What about O'Donnell? Have you found him?'

'Yes, he's been working at your factory for the past fortnight.' Timothy grimaced at the irony of it. 'He was at Dorflinger's at first and then they ran short of work. I went round them all before I got to yours, but when I told him what was wrong at home he said he'd leave straightaway. He just had to finish his shift. I'm meeting him at his lodgings – he was going to try to get together enough for his fare, and I thought I'd have to wait until Cordelia got some money through to me somehow.'

'Well, that won't be necessary now. We'll all go home together.' Jensen hesitated. 'There's someone else, too – someone I have to bring back to Corning. It won't take me long to arrange – it's been fixed for a while now, just waiting for the right time.' He avoided Tim's curious glance – even now, he thought angrily, he couldn't say what was in his mind. 'Look, I'll meet you at the station,' he said hastily. 'And if I'm held up – here's enough money for your fares. Get aboard and look out for me, but don't wait. I'll follow on as soon as I can. The important thing is to get Declan home to his family.'

He peeled some dollar bills from the roll he had in his pocket, and handed them to Tim. The two men paused in the street and looked at each other. Tim took the money and looked down at it.

'You've been a good friend to us, Jensen,' he said. 'I

won't forget this. I just wish there was something I could do for you . . .'

Jensen stared at him for a moment. Then he reached out a hand and laid it on Timothy's shoulder.

'Remember you said that, Tim,' he said soberly. 'I may need a friend one day. And it could be that you'd be the best I could have.'

He lifted his hand, gave Tim's shoulder a light slap, and turned away. Tim watched him out of sight, a puzzled crease between his brows; and then, looking down at the bills curling in his hand, he gave a whoop of relief and turned to run all the way to Declan O'Donnell's lodgings.

The train seemed as impatient to leave as the two young men seated in the first compartment. They could hear it snorting like a bull ready to charge; it almost seemed to be pawing the ground in its anxiety to move.

'D'ye reckon he isn't coming, then?' Declan asked as Tim peered out of the window for the twentieth time.

'I don't know – it's almost time. He was sure he'd be here, but it's this person he was going to fetch – if they weren't ready, I suppose he'd have to wait. They wouldn't even have known he was coming.' Tim frowned. 'I don't really understand it. He's never mentioned bringing anyone back from White Mills before.'

'Someone from the glass factory, I suppose,' Declan said. 'One of his workmen, or an overseer, maybe. Anyway, we've got our fares and we can't go soon enough for me. Tell me the truth, now – d'ye really think me mother's dying?'

Timothy turned back from the window and looked at him with compassion. Until he had met Declan, he had seen this mission as a way of doing something for Grainne – even as a way to her heart. He had known, of course, that her mother was desperately ill, but he had not taken in the full implications; he had not quite faced the fact that she was about to die.

Now he looked into the face of a young man who was about to lose his mother, and the memory of his own grief, for the father who had died so unexpectedly, stirred in him and gave him an insight into the Irishman's mind and heart.

'I think she is,' he said gently. 'But I hope you'll be home in time to say goodbye.'

'I hope so too.' Declan stared out of the window at the hurrying crowds. 'Where do ye suppose all these people are in such a hurry to get to? How did they manage before there were railroads?'

'I don't know,' Tim said helplessly. He wanted to help the other man but he didn't know how. He wanted to reach out and touch him, but he didn't know how Declan would respond. He felt inadequate and wished that Cordelia were with them; women always seemed to know how to cope with situations like these. All he could do was look into the young face and think how like Grainne he was, with his curly dark hair and his blue eyes, their brightness dimmed now with tears he would not shed.

'I don't know why everyone has to be in such a hurry now,' Declan said, speaking as if to himself. 'We're all rushing about, going somewhere, and when we get there it's no different from what we left behind. We left Ireland to look for something better, and what did we find? The same. The same poverty, the same hardships. We might as well have stayed, me mother would have died just the same.'

The train gave a whistle that split the air and they felt the railcar tremble.

'We're about to go,' Tim said. He leapt up and looked out of the window again. 'I still can't see Jensen – oh, there he is! He's just arrived! Jensen – Jensen!' He tore off his hat and waved it frantically out of the window. 'We're up here in the front!' There was a sound of slamming doors, a whistle from the engineer, and the train began to move. Tim shouted again, and waved, then he ducked his head back through the window and dropped into his seat.

'Did he not see ye?' Declan asked, without much interest.

'No – he got in a couple of cars back. Maybe he'll come along the train and look for us. Anyway, we'll see him when we get to Corning.'

'And did ye see whoever it was he was fetching?'

'No.' Tim frowned. 'I'd forgotten that. No, I didn't see anyone else at all. But there must have been someone, Declan – he had an awful lot of luggage.'

Declan shrugged. 'Well, ye'll find out in good time.' He stared out again as the train clanked slowly out of the station. 'I'm glad to be going home, Tim. I've been just miserable away from everybody. And it's a rotten business, leaving your family under shadow.' He hesitated. 'Me Dad – how did he seem to ye?'

'I never saw him. He was out all day, looking for work.'

'For work? D'ye mean to tell me he lost his job an' all?'

'Yes, I'm afraid so. And in this weather –'

'Holy Jesus,' Declan said, 'but they must be near starving. And I've been able to send them hardly any money at all, what with getting meself organised.'

'My sister's been helping out.' Tim felt ashamed that he had done so little himself. Hadn't he heard Cordelia talking about the O'Donnells, worrying about them, saying how hard life was for them? But he had been too engrossed with his work – yes, and with his pleasures too, he admitted with self-castigating honesty. He had listened to the stories Cordelia had told, and had ignored the reality behind them. 'They haven't starved, Declan. She's been taking them things.'

'I don't understand. Why should your sister do that? Who is she?'

'Well, she teaches Danny and Bridget in school. I suppose she met Grainne through that. And I saw you that day at the station – when you left Corning.' Tim paused delicately; Cordelia had told him of Carina's arranged marriage with an Italian but he wasn't sure if Declan knew. 'Your sister nearly walked under the next train,' he said, making light of it. 'I happened to be there and dragged her out of the way, and that's how we met.'

Declan nodded. His thoughts were clearly not on Timothy's conversation, but back again in the crowded rooms where his mother lay waiting for a last sight of him. He rose to his feet and stared out of the window.

The train was making good speed now, in spite of the snow that had drifted back across the line in the flurries of wind that still kept springing up. Outside, in the towns and on the farms, people could be seen moving about, clearing the great white heaps, digging out sheds and houses and livestock. Life was beginning to return to normal.

Declan sat down again and looked at Tim properly for the first time since Timothy had found him and told him why he had come. His eyes, so like Grainne's, were clear. His smile was warm.

'Thanks for coming for me,' he said. 'I'll not forget what ye and your sister have done for the O'Donnells.'

Tim felt himself flush. 'It's little enough,' he muttered, and they lapsed into silence.

During the rest of the journey, they talked a good deal. Declan told Timothy about their life in Ireland, how their father had decided to come to America to escape the grinding poverty there and found life very little better. 'It's fine for some, but if you're at the bottom of the heap in one country I guess you're at the bottom of the heap everywhere.

At least we're all in work here – or we were. But with me Mam taking sick and me Dad losing his job, and me away . . .' He sighed. 'Seems nothing goes right for us, somehow.'

The train thundered on. The track had been mostly cleared now and only the occasional drift slowed them down. It was growing dark as they came down the Chemung valley, and the hills rose like great shadowy guardians on each side. Tim looked at Declan. He could sense the tension in his body, and he felt his own anxiety grow. Would they be in time after all?

'We're almost there,' he said. 'It won't be long now –' And the rest of his words were lost. Lost in a terrible, grinding crash, a thunderous roar of massive sound that shuddered through the length of the train as metal screeched and wood splintered and men and women screamed in fear and sudden agonising, unendurable pain. Tim had a hazy, incredulous view of Declan's body rising in front of him, lifting towards the roof of the railcar and then crashing down again, half disappearing under the wreck of the crumpled steel. The world was collapsing around him, closing in on him, a harsh cacophony of impossible clamour in which he was helpless, tossed about the reeling carriage like a flea in a jamjar. With every second there was a fresh shock, as if some mighty engine were thrusting its way without mercy through the body of the train, determined to shoulder it aside or destroy it in its deadly progress. The noise and the shocks seemed to go on for ever; but at last they stopped. And then there was silence for a few moments before a thin, lonely wailing began and echoed plaintively across the frozen valley.

Chapter Thirteen

News of the railroad crash spread quickly around Corning. It was not an uncommon occurrence – there had been all too many accidents on the Erie Railroad, many of them happening at the crossings where pedestrians, cyclists and larger vehicles were all at risk. Since the installation of crossing gates, things had been better, but there were still places where it was possible, and even necessary, to walk on the line as it passed through the city. And although trains were supposed to slow down to no more than ten miles an hour, there was still the danger of being hit by one that came through too fast, while outside the town more than one crash had occurred; the worst having taken place only a few years before, in Ravenna, Ohio, when a meat freighter ploughed into the back of a wooden coach chartered by forty-four Corning glassmakers, returning from Findlay for their summer holiday.

Seventeen men were killed that day, Bob had told Cordelia as he recalled the horror of the scene. Thirteen of them were so badly burned that they could not be recognised, and all had shared a common burial service and been buried together in St Mary's cemetery. 'Didn't matter whether they was Roman Catholics or not that day,' he said. 'They were Corning men, and that was all that mattered to God, we reckoned.'

The dreadful pictures conjured up by Bob's words flashed before Cordelia's eyes now as Danny came rushing into the O'Donnell house with the news. She started up from her stool, her eyes meeting Grainne's in wild conjecture. She saw Grainne's pale face whiten yet further, her eyes grow black with horror, and she hastened to crush down her own fears and calm the frightened Irish girl.

'We don't know that they were aboard – it could be any train, not theirs at all –'

'It was theirs – I know it,' Grainne whispered. 'All this time, I've known something terrible was going to happen.' She flung a glance at Mary, sleeping on her sofa. 'I thought it was me mother – but now this . . . Oh God, Cordelia, what will we do if it's Declan and Timothy?'

Cordelia stared at her. She could offer no more comfort; her own heart was beating with a sick heaviness. She had been Timothy's twin for too long to ignore the dread that crept grey and chill over her shivering body. Declan and Timothy . . . *and Jensen*, she thought with a fresh thrill of horror. The three of them, together on the train – no, it could not be. It must not be.

'They say there's bodies everywhere,' Danny said with the relish of a nine-year-old. 'And the snow's red with runnin' blood, and –'

'Danny, will ye stop it at once, ye little ghoul!' Grainne turned on him and dealt him a stinging slap across the side of his head that sent him reeling. Cordelia saw a fresh horror darken her eyes and knew that this was probably the first time the gentle girl had ever struck her brother. But there was no time for self-recrimination now. With a swift movement, Grainne snatched up the old cloak that Cordelia had brought and swung it around her shoulders. 'I'm going down there,' she said rapidly. 'Danny, you're to stop here and see after your mother and Bridget, d'ye understand me? I must know if our Declan was on that train –' She turned to Cordelia and held out her hands, her eyes great black hollows of fear. 'Will ye come with me, Cordelia? I don't know if I can face it on me own –'

'Of course I'll come.' Cordelia had her own heavy coat on now and had snatched up the fresh sheets that she had brought for Mary's bed. She had been at the house all day and, intending to stay the night, had only returned to Martha's to fetch bedding and a few items for herself. She picked up her hat and jammed it on her head. 'Do you think your mother –'

'She's sleeping easy now. She'll not wake for hours.' Grainne pulled the door open and they went outside. It was almost fully dark; stars were beginning to prick the sky and the snow gleamed white as bone all around. But here and there in the valley were shreds of mist, drifting aimlessly like a woman's filmy scarf thrown carelessly to the breeze.

'How in the world could a crash have happened?' Cordelia asked as they hurried along. 'Surely, after all this bad weather, the trains would be going slowly – they must have expected snow on the line.'

'Oh, don't ye believe it! Those drivers, they go mad if they think they're going to be late – they drive like bats leaving the fires of hell. Seventy miles an hour they go, and sometimes more. And if there's a drift or a patch of fog and another train happens to have stopped just there – well, what chance do they have? It's crazy.' Grainne stamped along through the snow, throwing her words over her shoulder at Cordelia. She spoke with a vicious anger, as if she were already looking for someone to blame for her brother's death . . . But we don't know he's dead, Cordelia thought, trying desperately to cling to a shred of hope. We don't even know they were on that train . . . But the dread clung like a leaden net about her heart, and she knew that something appalling had happened. To Timothy. And, therefore, to Declan. And to Jensen.

The road was crowded now with people making their way to the scene of the disaster. Together, speaking only in hushed tones, they poured along the railroad line and over the bridge that led to the west of the frozen mass of Billinghursts Island, where so many people took picnics and played games in the summer. They tramped along the track, straining their eyes in their efforts to see where the accident had happened. And at last there was a cry from those in front and everyone lifted their heads and peered anxiously into the brilliant, snow-lit darkness.

'Mother of Christ,' Grainne said quietly, 'it's on fire.'

The glow could be seen clearly now, a blood-red stain on the dimpled snow. As they drew nearer Cordelia could see, in the midst of the flickering light, the mangled wreckage of the coaches: great struts of iron, black against the orange flames, rearing skywards; sheets of metal that had once been doors, twisted and melting in the intense heat; slabs of burning wood and upholstery that had once been seats, with people sitting on them.

And other things, things she hardly dared look at; things that lay like old rag dolls, their limbs scorched and deformed, their faces horrific with pain and fear, gone now beyond recovery.

'Stand back. This is no place for women,' a man said authoritatively, and Cordelia felt her anger rise and shook off his restraining hand.

'Let me alone! My brother may be in there – and in any case, they need help.' Quickly, she knelt by a figure that lay moving stiffly, moaning with pain. 'This man's burnt. Help me to lay him in the snow.'

'In the *snow*?' The man stared at her as if she were mad. 'You'll kill him –'

'He'll die if he's left like this,' she said crisply. 'The snow will cool his burns – don't you ever dip your finger in cold water if you scorch it? It will help him while we wait for medical help . . . Is there no doctor here?'

'There's two, but they're busy over the other side.' Still doubtful, the man helped Cordelia lift the burned passenger away from the train and into the snow. 'Guess we got to get him away from the thing, anyway . . . There's a fella here with a broken leg, I reckon – know anything about broken bones?'

'Not enough.' Cordelia knelt again, running her fingers lightly over the groaning body. 'Have you anything to bind him with? Quick, tear up these sheets,' she said, thrusting the sheets at the man. 'Help me bind his legs together. The good one will act as a splint. It will do for the moment . . .' The man stared at her again, but did as she bade, and they lifted their second patient and laid him beside the first. 'If we put them all close, the doctors can look at them when they come . . .' She lifted her head as a ragged cheer went up from the people who were milling about the scene, helping, shouting orders and all too often doing no more than get in each other's way. 'Oh, thank God, the fire brigade.'

'It won't do no good,' said somebody else, his face gruesomely raddled by the snarling flames. 'There ain't no one left alive in there. Can't be – stands to reason. Might as well let the whole thing burn itself out and attend to them that were thrown clear.'

Cordelia opened her mouth to contradict, then saw that he was right. The fire had taken too much of a hold and burned too fiercely for anyone left inside the coaches to have survived. But there were other coaches too, she saw now – coaches that were less badly damaged, where people might still be trapped, alive, and which could catch fire within the next few minutes if something were not done.

Tim could be in one of those coaches! And Jensen – and Grainne's brother, Declan – all of them together, trapped, injured, waiting for rescue and knowing only that their iron and steel prison was growing warmer every moment . . .

Sick with fear, Cordelia turned and ran for the line. She could see now, in the searing light of the fire, that there were two trains involved in the accident. One had run into the back of the other, which had presumably been standing or going slowly. The engine had ploughed into the last few coaches, scattering wreckage and bodies to either side in its ruthless progress, and as the resistance forced it to a halt its own front cars had piled into it, tipping towards the sky, splintering around it and almost burying it in their own destruction.

Tim and the others could have been in either of those trains, in any of those coaches. Could they possibly have lived? And if not, would they even be recognisable now? Or would they, like the glassmakers coming home for their summer holiday, end in a common grave, alongside all the others whose dearest relatives could not look on their mutilated faces and say who they were?

Cordelia faltered and buried her face in her hands, too sickened by the sights and sounds around her to go any further. But, after only a moment, she roused herself and lifted her eyes to the sky. Give me strength, she prayed, give me the strength to go on through this terrible night. For Tim's sake, for Jensen and for Declan O'Donnell – for all these poor, suffering people, give me strength . . .

How long it was that she toiled after that, she had no idea. With the fire almost out, people were being brought out of the damaged coaches and laid on the trampled snow, and with Grainne and many others, Cordelia worked against time to save them. Within minutes, they had formed a routine; each casualty was given a quick, comprehensive glance to see what the injuries were. Internal injuries were left for the doctors, burns and bleeding attended to at once. Bandages were produced – sheets and towels, torn into strips, shirts and shawls ripped and twisted to make bindings. Broken legs were splinted together, broken arms tied into roughly made slings. Some of the injuries were beyond the skills of the rescuers and they could do nothing but gently lay the sufferers down and wrap them in whatever they could find to keep them warm until sleighs and carts, drawn by steaming ponies, arrived to take them to the city.

'And if anyone thinks we don't need a hospital in Corning, let 'em deal with this lot,' Grainne muttered, appearing at Cordelia's elbow as they lifted a groaning bundle into one of the sleighs. 'Cordelia, half these poor souls are going to die before they even get to the city . . . And I haven't seen Declan or Tim, or Mr Novak, anywhere.'

'Then perhaps they weren't on either of the trains,' Cordelia said, her heart lifting. 'Or maybe they were taken off before we got here and are already in town . . .' She looked at Grainne and read the thought in her eyes. *Or maybe we've already seen them and didn't know it.*

But such a thought could not be acknowledged – not yet. And Cordelia turned away, unable to look at the fear in Grainne's face, and went back to work.

'Could you see after this little girl, miss? She's wanderin' about all alone – lost her mammy, I guess.' One of the men came towards her, holding a small, indescribably filthy child by the hand. 'She'll get hurt if she's left by herself here.'

Cordelia bent quickly and took the little girl by the shoulders. She was covered with dirt, her small face blackened by the fire, curls sooty and dishevelled. Her eyes wide and terrified, she stared at Cordelia and then stumbled into her arms and clung tightly, her face buried in Cordelia's shoulder.

'You poor little thing!' Cordelia hugged the slender, trembling body to her, marvelling that something so frail could have survived the holocaust without injury. And what of her parents – where were they? Wandering about the scene of the disaster, searching for their child? Injured and already on their way to the city . . . or dead, lying in the row of bodies that would never move again?

'It's all right,' she said gently. 'It's all over now. Nothing's going to hurt you.' She lifted her head to look around. The fire was out. Men were searching amongst the smouldering wreckage, but few people were being brought out now. And of those who were still to be found, most were being taken straight to the increasing number of dead.

She would have to look at those dead. She would have to go with Grainne and look at the burnt and damaged faces, the scorched and twisted bodies. She would have to look closely enough to know, to say with certainty that this one was or was not her brother; that this one was or was not the man who had held her in his arms and kissed her.

Away to the east, Cordelia saw a second red glow, a glow that spread across the sky and turned its darkness to a bruise of green and blue and apricot. For a moment, fear gripped her again; then, in vague astonishment, she realised that it was dawn. They had worked here all night, and now day was breaking to show the disaster in all its horror to a bleak, cold world.

And now Grainne was coming towards her, her face white under the blood and soot that smeared it. She came with a drooping stance, with shoulders that told their own story. And behind her walked with slow and dragging steps, a man who was tall and slender, with blackened face and bandaged head, and one arm tied roughly in a sling made from a woman's blouse.

Still clutching the child against her, Cordelia stood up. She stared unbelievingly at the man. Her eyes moved over him slowly, from the scorched hair, burnt close against his

298

head, to the long, tapering fingers that held the sling in place. She looked at the narrow waist, the slim legs; she watched him walk and knew that her bounding heart was right, and that at least one of their anxieties was at an end.

'*Tim!*' she whispered, and flew across the slush and mud towards him, only just preventing herself from hugging his bruised and shivering body against her, contenting herself instead with running her free hand over his face and laughing with sudden release.

But Tim looked grave, and Grainne's tears were falling fast. And Cordelia looked from one to the other and felt the lead settle once more in her heart.

'Grainne . . .?' she breathed, and knew the truth before the other girl spoke.

'Declan's dead,' Grainne said in a dull tone. 'He was killed at once. He's over there.'

Cordelia looked towards the row of dead, now being examined by people afraid of what they might see. Her throat ached and she reached out blindly, hardly knowing whether she needed to receive comfort or to give it. She found Tim's good arm and looked up into his face.

'And . . . Jensen?'

He shook his head wearily. 'I don't know, sis. He wasn't with us. He was a couple of coaches further back.' He looked with empty eyes at the wreckage, at the coaches that had risen up from the middle of the train as if they were trying to ride on the backs of their fellows. 'I haven't seen him since we left White Mills.'

'Jes' look at the state of you! All over dirt and soot and blood – my stars, I've never seen anythin' like it. And who's this poor scrap of a person, then?' Martha Robinson swooped out of the house and caught Cordelia and her burden in a warm hug. 'You come right indoors this minute, the pair of you, and I'll hev you bathed and fed before you can say knife. And then you can tell me jes' what happened out there.' She stopped as they went through the door and gave Cordelia a quick look. 'What about your brother, Cordelia? Is he all right?'

Cordelia nodded. Faced with the warmth and cleanliness of the house, with the thoughts of a hot bath and food inside her, she felt suddenly exhausted. The past hours were already taking on the quality of a nightmare, and she felt faint as she thought of the sights she had seen, the sounds she had heard and the things she had been compelled to do.

'Tim's all right. He's hurt his head and his arm but that's all. He's gone home with Grainne. Her brother – Declan –' her voice broke on a sob – 'he's dead, Martha. And Jensen –' Her throat seemed to close up and she shook her head dumbly.

'Was he killed too?' Martha asked quietly, and the tears fell from Cordelia's eyes and soaked the sooty curls of the child in her arms.

'I don't know. I think he must have been. We couldn't find him – we looked at . . . everyone. But there were some we didn't – couldn't –' She shook her head again and swayed.

Martha's arms were warm and strong as she led her into the big, comfortable living room. A fire was glowing in the hearth, but Cordelia turned her eyes away from it; she had seen enough flames for one night. She sank down into a big chair, her arms still holding the little girl close. She was as reluctant to let the small body go as the child seemed to be to part from her. And since there had been nobody to claim her, it had seemed only sensible for Cordelia to bring her here, where Martha would dispense warmth and food and motherly comfort, and where the little girl might gain courage to lift her eyes from Cordelia's shoulder at last and look

300

on a world more kindly than the one which had treated her so cruelly last night.

'And you mean to say she's said nothin'? Ain't told you her name, even? Poor little mite.' Martha prised the clutching fingers gently away from Cordelia's shoulder and began to unfasten the torn clothes. 'Why, she's terrified. And no wonder, after what she's been through. How old d'you reckon she is – about five or six?'

'I should think so.' Through a daze of weariness, Cordelia watched as Martha's maid brought in a large zinc tub of hot water and set it before the fire. Together, she and Martha lifted the little body in and gently washed away the blood and grime of the night's terrors. The child was unresisting now. Her eyes were wide and blue, a blue as bright as speedwell when the spring sun shines on its tiny flowers, and as blank. Her face was expressionless, as if she had wiped out all memory, and her small, slender body was shivering as if it would never be warm again.

'Poor little thing,' Martha said again, tenderly. 'She's too shocked to speak. But she'll be all right after a good sleep, I don't doubt – it's wonderful how children bounce back. And maybe her ma will come for her before too long . . .' Her voice faded as she looked up and caught Cordelia's eye. They both knew that it was all too likely that the little girl would never see her mother again. And the tears thickened again in Cordelia's throat.

A maid came in to tell Cordelia that there was a hot bath ready for her upstairs, and she rose stiffly to her feet, aware of her body now as a mass of aches and pains. She looked down at Martha, still kneeling at the zinc tub, sponging the child's body.

'Leave her with me,' Martha said. 'I'll take care of the little thing. You get yourself into that hot bath and then go straight to bed – warmth and rest, that's what you want.

And I'll bring you a cup of good hot chocolate before you go to sleep.' She gave Cordelia a sharp look and got up quickly, catching her as she swayed. 'Stars above, you're nearly out on your feet. Here, let me call Bob and he can help you up the stairs – and I'll bring this little one up directly, for she don't seem to want to let you out of her sight, and that's the truth.'

She laid the child in Cordelia's bed, the little girl's hair still damp from the thorough washing it had just been given, and then she undressed Cordelia as though she too were only five years old, and bathed her with the same gentle tenderness. Cordelia, in a daze of weariness and aware of a grief that hung over her like a dim, heavy shadow and would attack her with unbearable sharpness as soon as her fatigue allowed it, was as unresisting as the child. She barely noticed as Martha laid her at last in the big bed, where she turned at once and drew the small, warm body of the little girl into her arms; she hardly knew whether she sat up to drink the chocolate or not. And she had no idea, as she slept and woke and slept again, whether she was there for a day and a night or for longer; nor whether the horrific events of the night had been real, or no more than an appalling nightmare.

Timothy and Grainne moved slowly and painfully back along the track. They were not alone; again, a convoy of people was moving in the same direction, back towards the town. Most of them were townspeople who had hurried out to the scene as soon as news of the accident had reached them. Some were passengers, unhurt but shaken, a few of them resilient enough to have helped in the rescue but many too shocked and bewildered to have done much more than crumple into the snow and whimper. Some, like Timothy, were injured but still able to walk, albeit slowly and with difficulty.

'Ye should be going straight back to your own home, so ye

should,' Grainne said as they plodded along. 'You're tired out and hurt besides. That arm must be paining ye something shocking.'

'I'm all right. I want to see you home, Grainne, and do whatever I can.'

'And what could ye be doin', with one arm tucked up in a sling?'

'I can be with you,' he said quietly. 'Grainne, you know you need me. I can't leave you to go alone, and carry such news to your mother as well.' He looked down at her sad, dirt-streaked face. 'It's taken me months to find you, Grainne. Don't turn me away now.'

For a few moments, she was silent. Then she sighed and said, as if answering some unspoken question, 'Aye, I know. But it's all ye can do for the minute, Tim. With Declan killed an' all, I cannot be thinking of anything else just now. There's just too much trouble . . .'

'I know,' Tim said gently. 'And all I'm asking is that you let me share it. For as long as you need.'

The way back to town was long and cold, and more than one traveller collapsed in the snow before they reached the stores and houses that were just beginning to open to the new day. The sun that Cordelia had seen rising, throwing its flaming mantle across the sparkling snow, was now shining down on snow-crusted roofs and trees that were encased in glittering ice. The city was white under a blanket of softest swansdown; but as the sun swept its way across the high, pale sky a million tiny sparks flashed from each frozen surface, a dazzling scintillation almost too bright for the eyes to bear. And Corning was indeed a Crystal City.

But neither Tim nor Grainne could take any pleasure in the beauty of the scene, nor any delight in the merriment of the children who swooped down the hilly streets on sledges or skated on the icy stretches of the river. For them, the morning light was harsh, the dancing sunshine an offence. For them, the brightness was the brightness of death, slicing the frosty air with the sharp cruelty of a sword thrust, the clear notes of the clock chimes as heavy as a funeral knell.

Slowly, heavily, supporting each other they moved along Market Street. With the ceasing of the blizzard, life was beginning to return to normal; the worst of the snow had been cleared from the road and the electric trolley-cars were already running. Boys and young men were sweeping snow from the sidewalks and piling it in the gutters, and people were emerging from their homes to come and shop, replenishing larders that had been depleted during their siege. Storekeepers were opening their doors and placing stands outside, ready to resume the business that had been so poor during the past few days.

The few people who had not known before of the disaster were gathered together outside the stores, talking eagerly and staring at those who were clearly returning from the line. They watched as Grainne and Timothy came slowly along, clucking with sympathy, offering help and showering them with questions. What had happened, how had it come about, how many had been killed? Was it true that there were two hundred casualties, that everyone had been smashed to pieces, that there was not one body left whole . . .? Grainne turned her face away, sickened, and Timothy quickened his own painful steps, careless of the jarring on his arm, hurrying her past the knots of people.

'It's not far now,' he said encouragingly. 'Just over the bridge and we're almost there. Don't cry, Grainne, please don't cry. They're fools, all of them, and not worth taking notice of.'

'Oh, they don't mean any harm by it,' she said through her tears. 'I know that. It's just – I can't help thinking of our Declan. He never had any life, Tim. He worked hard ever since we came here, and never had anything till he fell in love with Carina, and even that had to be spoilt for him. And if 'tweren't for me father, he'd never have gone away, and never been on that train at all.'

'And if I hadn't been such a fool on the train out he wouldn't have been on it either,' Tim said grimly. 'We wouldn't have had to wait for Jensen to come with more money – we'd have been back a day earlier, and him safe in your house with your mother holding his hand . . . I'll always blame myself for that, Grainne. I'll never be able to make that up to you.'

'Well, maybe it was God's will after all,' she said sadly. 'Maybe there's nothing any of us can do, once He decides it's our time to go. But I wish I didn't have to tell me mother. I wish I didn't have to tell her that.'

They crossed the bridge. Below, the Chemung lay under a sheet of thick ice. Boys had already cleared away the snow, and it was alive with skaters, swooping like birds along the glassy surface. Their cries and laughter tinkled in the clear air. Grainne stopped for a moment and looked down.

'Declan had a pair of skates once,' she said. 'An old pair someone gave him. He used to come here every day when he'd finished working. I think it was the only fun he ever had.'

'Then he did at least have some fun,' Tim said softly. 'And he knew what it was to love someone. And he had you, and your mother and father, and the rest of your family. He had a lot, Grainne, when you think of it. A lot to be thankful for.'

She stared down in silence for a moment. The skaters slid by: a young man and woman, arms around each other's waists, skating as gracefully as dancers; a girl, giggling uncontrollably as she lurched along in the arms of her father; a couple of boys, agile as grasshoppers, sliding in and out of the crowds and causing mischief wherever they went. And a young man, tall and dark-haired, skating alone and bareheaded through the rest and away, away down the river until he disappeared from sight around a swooping curve.

Grainne's eyes watched him and to Tim it seemed that she was imagining that the young man was her brother, skating out of her life, and that she was wishing him farewell. And when she turned to Timothy again, her eyes were bright and wet and as blue as the flames of a salt-drenched log on a winter's fire.

'Let's go,' she said, and took his hand. 'I can't put it off any longer. I'll have to tell me mother.'

But when they reached the O'Donnell house at last, they found that there was no need to tell Mary O'Donnell anything. Her blood-soaked pillow told its own story, and the faces of her husband and children confirmed it. While they had all been out at the train crash the night before, she had had a final haemorrhage. Mary O'Donnell had died less than two hours after her son. And the only members of her family with her had been young Danny, and his wide-eyed, frightened sister Bridget.

'Thirty-five dead,' Bob said when Cordelia came down to breakfast next morning, ignoring Martha's anxious advice that she should stay in bed for one more day. 'And over forty injured. It was a bad business.'

'Terrible,' Martha said, pouring coffee. 'Terrible. And how's that poor child this mornin'?'

'Sleeping still,' Cordelia answered. 'Martha, tell me, have I slept a whole day and a night? I can't seem to get it straight in my head.'

'You have, and you ought to be in bed still, this very minute. You look as pale as whitewash, and that's the truth. And the little one will be lookin' for you as soon as she opens her eyes – wouldn't leave your side all day yesterday, not that she was in any better state to start gettin' up and gallivantin' about. She never spoke a word, not a single word. And her eyes – well, poor midgeon, 'tis no wonder, she must have seen some terrible things out there on the railroad.'

'There were terrible things to see.' Cordelia sat down and lifted the coffee to her lips. 'Oh, that's good.' Her dazed mind was beginning to clear. She thought of the darkness of the night, the white snow lit crimson by fire and blood. With a shock, she remembered Grainne, coming towards her across the mud and the slush, drooping with sorrow, to tell her that Declan was dead. And Tim – bandaged, his arm in a sling, telling her that he must take Grainne home, that she must go to Martha's with the child . . . 'Tim?' she asked in sudden panic that he might have had worse injuries and never told her. 'Have you seen him? Is he all right?'

Martha glanced at her husband. 'He came in yesterday for a few minutes, just to see how you were,' she said. 'And your cousin too, that Mr T'ittry. Don't you go worryin' yourself over Tim, child – he's mendin' fast. Got the bandage off his head already, 'tweren't no more than a graze, and the doctor says his arm will be as strong as ever in less than three months.'

'Three months! But what about his glass?'

'Just thank God he's alive,' Bob said, sounding unusually stern, 'and never mind his glass.' And Cordelia fell silent, blushing, knowing that she had spoken out of turn and ashamed of her reaction.

'Where is he now?' she asked humbly after a few moments, and Bob relented and gave her a comforting smile. Martha spoke quickly.

'Why, he's gone over to the O'Donnells, of course, where

he's been every moment since you all came back to town. Reckons they need him over there, and I guess he's right too, only it's my opinion it's that young Grainne he's hopin' needs him most. Did *you* know they'd met before, Cordelia?'

'No, apparently he saw her at the railway station when she went to see Declan off, but he never mentioned her to me.' She looked at them, a puzzled frown on her brow. 'Martha, is there something you're not telling me? You and Bob keep looking at each other – what is it?' A sudden fear gripped her heart and she half rose from her chair. 'It's Mary, isn't it? Mary O'Donnell. Is she – is she worse?'

Martha looked at Bob again and then got up and came round the table. She bent over Cordelia, surrounding her with her warmth and compassion, and Cordelia knew the truth. She looked up at the motherly face and her eyes filled with tears.

'Mary's dead, isn't she?'

'She is, child, and I guess it's a happy release for her. She weren't goin' to get better, you knew that yourself. And she never knew about her boy – she never knew Declan was killed in that terrible accident. She died before they ever got home to tell her. It's all over for them both, Cordelia, and we must just pray they're safe and happy with our Lord in Heaven, that's all we can do now.'

'Dead,' Cordelia said in a low, dry voice. 'Dead, and Declan killed on the railroad. He might just as well have stayed in White Mills, Martha. It was all for nothing. And Tim hurt, and Jensen . . .' She bent her head suddenly, unable to check the rush of tears that stormed out of her heart, and covered her face with her hands. Great sobs tore her body, wrenching savagely at her breast, driving the pain of grief and loss through her brain until she felt that she must collapse with the agony of it, collapse or die. She felt

Martha's arms around her, strong and firm, and she turned into the soft bosom and cried as she could not remember crying since she was a baby. And yet, if she had been asked exactly why she was crying, she would not have known how to answer. For Declan? For Mary? For her brother and his broken arm? Or for the man who had kissed her and then held her at arm's length – the man who had looked at her with a question in his dark blue eyes, an enigma she did not know how to solve, and then had left her with all her own questions unanswered?

She might even be weeping for her own father, dead for less than a year. Or her mother, whose reason had so very nearly left her as Cordelia feared now she might be losing her own.

'Hush, baby, hush,' Martha crooned. 'There now, cry all you want. It'll do you good . . . It's the shock, that's all . . . Ssh, ssh, Martha's here, Martha won't let anythin' else happen to you. You're safe now, and your brother's safe – just hold on to that, baby, just hold on to that.'

Gradually, Cordelia's sobs diminished. She felt the despair lighten a little as she heard Martha's words. The old woman was right. She was safe, and so was Tim. She must hold on to that. She must.

At last she lifted her head and groped in her pocket. Martha gave her a handkerchief and she smiled tremulously and blew her nose. She drew herself out of Martha's arms and sat up straight.

'I'm sorry, Martha. I don't know what came over me. I didn't mean to cry so.'

'Don't say a word about it, honey. I could see it had to come out. Like I said, it was just the shock. Now you hev a cup of coffee, it's good and hot still, and that'll make you feel better, and then my Bob'll go on over to the O'Donnells and bring your brother right back here. You need him with you, I know. Miss Grainne will jes' have to do without him a while, she's had him long enough when all's said and done.' She called out of the open door. 'Bob! Will you go over to Knoxville and bring young Tim back? His sister needs him.'

'Oh, no,' Cordelia said quickly. 'Please don't, if he wants to be with Grainne –'

'Family comes first,' Martha said firmly, and went out to see if Bob had heard her.

Cordelia leaned her elbows on the table and sipped at her coffee. The hot liquid scalded her mouth; its heat seemed to flow through her and revive her. She stared unseeingly at the table, haunted once again by visions of fire, of blackened wreckage silhouetted against an orange glow, of scorched bodies and imploring eyes.

She was barely conscious of the sound of the door opening; hardly felt the strong arms that came around her. Thinking that it must be her brother, she leaned into them, drawing hungrily from the warmth and strength of the body that was so close to hers. And then she sensed a difference – a leanness that was hard and whiplike, a muscular power that could come only with years, with a maturity that Tim had not yet attained.

Slowly, Cordelia turned. And looked up into a face she had thought never to see again. Into dark blue eyes, set against honey-gold skin; into a smile that was white and strong.

'Jensen!' she breathed, and slipped into a faint.

The faint lasted for only a few moments, and Cordelia opened her eyes to find herself lying on Martha's couch and still looking up into those eyes, still held in the same firm grasp. She lay for a moment dazed and uncertain, then lifted a tentative hand and touched the cheek that now she

310

saw was faintly bruised. She raised her eyes and saw a bandage round the corn-ripened hair, and a shudder shook her body.

'Jensen . . . is it really you?'

'It's really me,' he assured her, and she heard the familiar note of faint amusement in his voice.

'But . . . I thought you were dead. Your head . . .'

'I was thrown away from the train and knocked my head on a rock. Or so they tell me.' He touched the bandage ruefully. 'Should have been frozen to death out there in the snow, but they found me just in time – said I was as cold as a fish. But you don't get rid of Jensen Novak that easy – once they got me back to town and warmed up, I was as good as new, bar a bang on the skull, and that'll heal.' He looked gravely down at Cordelia. 'They tell me Declan O'Donnell was killed.'

Cordelia nodded.

'And Mary?'

'She died in the night. She never knew.'

He had to bend low to hear her whisper, and his cheek brushed hers, rough and unshaven. She closed her eyes, feeling the faintness waft over her once more, dizzy and disturbed.

'But Tim's all right.' He spoke it as a statement, but she knew it was a question and responded to the need in his voice. If Tim had been killed too, he would never forgive himself. He had blamed himself for not going to find Declan in the first place . . . Hastily, thrusting aside her own weakness, she sat up into his arms.

'Tim's all right. He has a broken arm, but it'll mend and the doctor says it will be as strong as ever. Perhaps even stronger . . . Jensen – there's something I need to ask you. Something you were going to tell me . . .' She could not remember what it was. The time before the accident seemed

311

to be no more than a memory of another life now; the fear and pain and violence of the past two days was still too vivid in her mind. Yet she knew that there was something important to be said between herself and Jensen, something that must not be left any longer. She looked up at him with imploring eyes, mutely begging him to end the questions between them.

'There is something I must tell you,' he said gently. 'But this isn't the time, Cordelia. You're exhausted and shocked still by what you saw and did out there . . . Yes, Martha and Bob have told me – I met Bob on the way in and they wouldn't let me see you before I knew.' He paused and held her close. 'I wish I'd known you were out there, Cordelia, I wish it had been you who found me and warmed me back to life. I can't believe that we were so close and never knew it. And when I think of you, amidst all that carnage, seeing the sights you must have seen, doing what you did . . . Cordelia, I can't begin to tell you how much I admire you for that – admire you and I—'

'Land's sakes,' said Martha's voice from the doorway. 'Is that poor child faintin' again? Why didn't you call me, Jensen? I'd hev had the smellin' salts in here in two shakes of a duck's tail, so I would.'

Cordelia felt Jensen's arms tighten momentarily and then fall away. He lifted himself away from her and rose to his feet.

'It's all right, Martha. She just felt a little dizzy, that's all, and no wonder after what she's been through. A sip more of your excellent coffee and she'll be herself again, I'm certain.' He brought Cordelia's cup to her and raised her against the cushions. 'Try this. It's cooler now.'

Cordelia drank obediently, her eyes on his. Frustration seethed in her breast. When were she and Jensen going to be left alone, so that they could talk at length and clear the air of questions and enigma? When was she ever going to know what was in his mind when he looked at her in that strange, disturbing way, when he kissed her and then withdrew?

The door opened behind him and the little girl who had wandered into Cordelia's arms and clung there, as if to a rock, appeared. She wore a long nightdress belonging to one of Martha's grandchildren. Her hair was long and as brightly golden as Jensen's, curling below her shoulders. Her eyes were a brilliant, dark blue.

Cordelia looked past Jensen's shoulder and smiled, and he turned to see who had come in.

There was a long moment of tense, electric silence. And then, with a tiny cry, the child flung herself into his arms and clamped her body to his. And Jensen wrapped himself about her and gripped her close, his head bent to hers, the gold hairs mingling. His shoulders trembled and Cordelia, staring in disbelief, let her coffee spill into her lap and didn't even notice it.

After a long time, Jensen lifted his head and turned. His face was wet with tears. He took one hand away from the small, shaking body and held it out to Cordelia in a curious gesture of supplication.

'This is what I've been trying to tell you,' he said in a husky voice. 'This is my daughter . . . Karin.'

Chapter Fourteen

The great red cones of Henzel's glasshouse were now almost a hundred years old. They had been begun before the nineteenth century was born and completed when it was barely able to toddle. Christina's own grandfather, old Roger Henzel, had built them when her father Joshua was a young man. She had listened many times as he described to her how the circular courses, red with the bricks made only a few miles away, had been laid one on top of the other, broad at the base and then slowly tapering to the open mouth at the top. She had shared with her father the excitement of his memory of the first day the furnace was lit inside – the pleasure of seeing the first curl of smoke emerge from the towering jaw, the suspense of waiting for the first pot of molten metal to come to temperature, the triumph of the blowing of the first piece of glass.

The vase blown that day was still in Henzel Court, standing alone on a small table in the library window. Christina saw it and touched it every day. But it was not the only historic piece of glass in the house, and it did not hold as many memories for her as the two later pieces that stood on the mantelpiece – the Chalice, blown by Joe and engraved by Jean-Paul; and the first piece of Black Cameo, a huge vase blown by her best gaffer, Ben Taylor, and carved with meticulous care and dazzling artistry by her son Paul.

Christina stood as she so often did, gazing at these two pieces of glass and wondering when – if ever – they would be joined by a third, by a piece equally magnificent, and equally individual, made by her grandson Timothy. What it would be like she had no idea. She knew only that Timothy, away in America, was discovering new and exciting ways of making glass – new colours, new styles, new forms. And she sighed a little, wishing sadly that he could have done these things in his home town, in the cones in which his family had worked for so long, and knowing that it was impossible. Paul's death, and Emily's breakdown, had made it impossible. And now that Emily was at last recovering, it was too late.

Christina's first anger at discovering what Timothy and Cordelia had done, had cooled now, but she still felt bitterly betrayed by the grandson in whom she had rested such hopes. The name of Henzel, which had always meant so much to her and which Timothy had inherited through her own son, seemed to have counted for little after all. The glasshouse, the towering red cones which had been her life, had been tossed aside. And although she understood that the twins had taken their step partly for Emily's own sake, she could not accept that they had been right to do so. They ought to have stayed. They ought to have shouldered their burden, whatever it was, and continued in the family tradition that had come down through the centuries, through old Roger, through her father Joshua, through herself. With Timothy at its head, Henzel Crystal could have continued to be great. Now . . .

But it was not in Christina's nature to be wistful for long over what might have been. Briskly, she turned away from the mantelpiece and stepped quickly out into the hall. The new maid came forward at once with her hat and jacket, and Christina put them on.

'Though it's almost too warm for a jacket this morning, Annie,' she remarked, looking out at the spring sunshine. 'You would hardly believe that April has only just begun, especially after such a winter as we have just had.'

'No, m'm,' Annie said demurely, and Christina sighed again. She still missed Rose with her haughty, disapproving ways – the old parlourmaid had been a part of her life since she was a child and had stubbornly refused to retire, hobbling up from the kitchen until she was barely able to walk and ruling the younger maids with a tongue as sharp as a shard of broken glass. She had died in her own chair by the kitchen fire one night, and the house had breathed a sigh of relief even while it mourned the old termagant. The stiffness that Rose had imposed was relaxed a little, though discipline was as tight as ever, and there was an easier, more friendly atmosphere throughout the kitchen and servants' hall. But little Annie's demure respect still grated on Christina, and she found herself more than once thinking nostalgically of Rose's asperity and of her expressive sniff.

Heavens, what was wrong with her this morning? Was this a sign of old age, this harking back to the past, to old ways and old customs? Perhaps it was the effect of Cordelia's recent letter, bringing back old memories. Who would have thought that Gabriel's children would turn up in America . . .? With an impatient shrug, Christina opened the door for herself, before Annie could reach it, and marched out into the sunshine that filtered down through the pall of smoke that hung permanently over the town. From the front steps, she looked across the garden, down to the tall wrought-iron gates, and beyond to the crowded roofs. The village of Wordsley, now so built up that its streets ran into those of neighbouring Amblecote and so into Stourbridge itself, lay at the foot of the hill. And its factory chimneys and smoking glasshouses were a constant, comforting reminder of the prosperity which had been brought – not just to Stourbridge, not just to Staffordshire, but to the whole of the Black Country.

'Grandmother! Are you going out?'

Christina turned with a quick smile. 'Indeed I am, Mark. Do you wish to accompany me?'

'If you're going to the cones,' he said, grinning. 'Not if you're going to the shops to pick over satins and silks and ribbons and things.'

'Mark!' she said, laughing. 'Have you ever known me do such a thing? Especially on such a morning as this.' She lifted her face to the sunshine. 'It reminds me of the days when I was a girl and my father used to take me to the glasshouse.'

'Girls didn't do that sort of thing then, did they?' He fell into step beside her and she looked sideways at the coltish grace of the tall body, so quickly filling out. In a year or two he would be the image of Joe as a young man . . . And will you break hearts as your grandfather so nearly broke mine? she wondered silently. And even after all these years, she could not quite repress a shiver at the thought of what her life might have been.

'Are you cold, Grandmother?' He was instantly all concern, his black curls falling over his broad forehead as he turned his head to look at her. 'Shall I go and fetch you a scarf, or a cape?'

'No, I'm not cold – just a goose walking over my grave.' And she shivered again, wishing she had not chosen that particular metaphor. So many graves – her father's, Jean-Paul's, Jeremy's, Maggie Haden's, Aunt Susan's . . . And now Paul's. 'Talk to me, Mark,' she commanded. 'Tell me something to make me laugh.'

He obeyed – for with Mark, laughter was never far away. And in that, he was different from his grandfather, for Joe had always displayed a brooding temper that had made her half fear him in those times when she had gone to see him in the glasshouse, the best gaffer in Henzel's employ, and the one with most influence over his mates.

Half afraid, half attracted – it had been impossible to oust him from her thoughts. And if she had been deliciously aware of his jealousy when she had brought Jean-Paul over from France, she had later had cause to fear that, too. And it had come near to destroying them all.

But despite all the memories that were crowding on her this day, she was laughing like a girl when she and Mark arrived at the double doors of the main cone, the one where Joe had worked and where Ben Taylor was now gaffer of the caster-hole chair, making the biggest and finest pieces of crystal that Henzel's produced. Today, he would be working on the punch bowls that were proving so popular now – huge half-domes of gleaming crystal, each with twelve small hooks around its rim for the cups to hang from. The bowls were heavy; their weight alone made the blowing and shaping a difficult task, but the graceful shape meant that only the most skilled gaffer could be trusted to make them. The bowls had been Joe's design, and although she knew her husband would never really like the engraving and the cutting that was carried out afterwards to make them suit public taste, Christina believed that they were the best example of his work ever made. Even now, at home, she possessed the bowl he had blown himself, the first of the line. Uncut and free of engraving, as he loved his crystal best.

Quietly, she and Mark stood near Ben's chair and watched as another great bowl was shaped. As always, the cone was dim, lit by a few gas-lamps at the sides but with most of its illumination coming from the furnace that rose in a massive dome in the centre of the floor, its pots open and glowing like the reddened jaws of some monstrous, roaring dragon. The sullen light fell on the bodies of the men as they worked, stripped to the waist in its heat, moving in the muscular ballet that had been part of Christina's

319

life ever since she was a child; thrusting long rods deep into the fiery mouths and withdrawing them tipped with shimmering golden bulbs which swelled and grew under the tender yet powerful breath of the blower; returning them again and again to the glory-hole for reheating as the glass slowly took shape and held it; sitting in the rough wooden chair that was every gaffer's pride, marvering the glass by rolling the iron back and forth, stroking and caressing it into shape with pattens and pucellas; finally slicing away the trembling edges to leave a rim that was clean and perfect, and then snapping it from the punty-iron to be taken to the *lehr* for its final annealing.

Always then, as the glass started on its journey down the cooling tunnel, the gaffer would rise from his chair and stretch the body that the muscular exercise of blowing and shaping inevitably made magnificent, as if he had been released from some deep physical tension. And Christina, too, sighed and felt the same peaceful release. It had been so when she was a young woman, and it was the same now.

'It's good to see you, Mrs Compson,' Ben said, coming towards them as they stood in the shadows. 'We don't see enough of you here these days – though I suppose that's to be expected. It's time you had a rest, you and Mr Compson.'

'And what of you, Ben? Don't you think you deserve a rest too?' He had been only eleven years old when she had first known him as a ragged urchin from the Lye Waste. 'You must be quite sixty,' she said thoughtfully.

Ben snorted. 'Years! What do they mean? I'm as fit as ever I was when I was a lanky boy, and as good a blower too. There's still none to touch me here, bar my Frank.'

Christina smiled. Like every other glassmaker, Ben was anxious to see that his skill was handed down through the generations. He would not give up his chair to any man other than his own son Frank, and he would expect it to go then to Frank's son, if he had one. As undoubtedly he would – glassmakers were a fecund race and made very sure that there was little room in the cones for any apprentice from outside their own tight circle. Ben, coming as a ragged urchin from the Lye with no glassmaking background, had been one of the rare exceptions – but Ben had possessed skills that they could respect, as well as being owed a debt that Christina felt she could never fully repay.

'How's Miss Emily now?' he asked abruptly. He had never accustomed himself to calling her Mrs Henzel, for there was a deep bond between Emily and Ben, and a friendship that went beyond the glasshouse. Until Paul's death, Emily had been a frequent visitor to Ben's little terraced house where she had spent a good deal of time talking with him and his wife Florrie. Florrie might have been the one to help her through her crisis, Christina had sometimes thought, but her own death, from a growth in her breast, had come only a few days before Paul's – a double shock for Emily, who had had no time to recover from the one before being hit by the second. And Ben, who might have reached through her grief, was wrapped in his own, for he had been as close to Paul as a brother and as deeply in love with his wife as when he had first known her as a girl.

But Ben had recovered without bitterness. He had not turned to his son, as Emily had done; he had simply put on his coat and gone back to work. Nevertheless, he rarely mentioned the names of either of the people who had been so important in his life, and Christina knew that the wound was still deep and raw.

'Emily's getting better now,' she said and turned to her grandson. 'She is, isn't she, Mark?'

'Yes.' He looked serious. He had suffered through this illness of his mother's, for she had shut him out during her concentration on Timothy, and he would have been lonely indeed without his grandmother's care. Only now was Emily beginning to take notice of him again, to see him as a son who was almost a man, a comfort to her in her continuing pain. But with him, she was not making the mistake she had made with Timothy. And he was safe from her jealous possessiveness, for he did not resemble Paul as Timothy did. He was too much like Joe – the father she had always loved, but loved with an awe that kept them slightly apart.

'She even asked after Timothy and Cordelia the other day,' Christina continued. 'And asked me to read Cordelia's letter aloud. It's strange – she couldn't bring herself to take it in her own hand and read it, but she was glad to hear me. And it's a step forward, for when they first went to America she wouldn't even allow their names to be mentioned. And when we first heard the news of the Thietrys, I was afraid she would relapse completely, it brought back so many memories.'

'Ah, she took the whole thing hard,' Ben said. 'I don't think any of us realised just how she depended on Paul. We all thought she was the strong one, but seems we were wrong there.'

'She needed him to give her strength to,' Christina said. 'Without him, there was nowhere for her to give it, so she turned to Timothy – and he didn't want it. That was Emily's tragedy.' She gazed across the cone, through the flickering shadows, the movements of the men. 'But I believe she's coming out of her unhappiness now. She's beginning to take an interest in her schools again, and in her other works. She's talking of going down to the Lye soon.'

'They'll be glad enough to see her down there. They think a lot of Miss Em.'

Christina smiled. 'And so they should – Emily's done a great deal for the Lye Waste.'

Ben's gatherer came to him with a fresh iron loaded with glowing metal, and he nodded and turned back to his work. Christina and Mark continued their progress round the cone, pausing at each chair for a word with the gaffer and his team. The air was filled with the roar of the furnace, the clang of iron as a man dropped a rod, the occasional sound of breaking glass as a man smashed a badly shaped or cracked wineglass or tumbler and tossed the shards to the floor to be swept up and used as cullet. Above them the walls of the cone, blackened by the soot of almost a century, sloped up to the disc of sky that was almost blotted out by the smoke that poured through it. In the deepest recesses of the cone, the pot-arches stood ready to heat fresh pots for when the old ones needed changing; and the long tunnel of the *lehr*, operated by a man who sat permanently at the far end and wound steadily on the handle, took the finished glass to cool and harden.

'Didn't you want to go with your great-uncle today?' Christina asked as they came out again through the double doors and into air that seemed cool and sharp after the heat inside.

Mark shook his head. 'He's gone to see the big railway sheds in Birmingham,' he said, and they both laughed. 'I quite enjoyed the first few trips, but now I feel I've seen enough railways to last me for the rest of my life. But Uncle Harry's never tired of them.'

'Well, he's spent a lifetime thinking about them and I suppose habit dies as hard with him as it does with me. I think about glass and he thinks about railways. And it's a long time since he's had the opportunity to look at our English railways – he finds them interesting after the great railroads he's been building across America.'

'It's strange, isn't it,' Mark mused, 'that he should retire to live in Corning, where glass is as important as it is here in

323

Stourbridge. As if glass is still in his blood and he can't quite rid himself of it.'

'Perhaps that's true. The love of glass has been in our family for generations, after all, ever since our forefathers came over from the Lorraine. And the area where Corning is – Steuben County, did Cordelia call it? – seems, from what she tells us, to be very like this part of England . . . The railway was important too, though. He spent a lot of time there when the Erie Railroad was being built and he says he just felt at home there and decided to settle. And Ruth, of course, is happy to be wherever Harry is.'

'Well, it was all very convenient for Tim and Cordelia – even if Uncle Harry and Aunt Ruth weren't there when they arrived!'

'Yes. And they seem to be happy enough. They're in good lodgings, Cordelia says, though I agree with Emily that they ought to have taken Harry's offer to move into the house . . . But she's an independent minx, as stubborn as I was at her age.' Christina smiled ruefully, thinking once again that Cordelia having inherited her own obstinacy, it was hardly to be expected that she would behave as her family wished. Then she frowned a little. 'I must admit I was anxious when we heard that Timothy had broken his arm, but it seems to be mending now and he's still working on his new glass, apparently. I should dearly like to see a piece.'

'Well, you will. They'll come back someday,' Mark said encouragingly, and Christina looked at him and smiled.

'Of course they will,' she said and took his arm. 'And very soon now, I'm sure. Take no notice of me, Mark – I'm in a strange, nostalgic mood this morning. Make me laugh again, and then we'll go and look round the other cones. We mustn't show favouritism!'

*   *   *

324

In the wake of Emily's steady improvement, there came a fresh worry to the Compson and Henzel household. Joe, over eighty and apparently as big and powerful as he had ever been, began to fail.

It was almost unnoticeable at first. A reluctance to get out of his chair, a slowness in his walk. An occasional absence of mind, when he would stare suddenly into a high corner of the room and then, after a moment or two, frown and rub his eyes and complain of an odd smell or a peculiar taste. He did not appear to hear what was said to him during these brief periods, but they were over so quickly that nobody took much notice. Only Christina, alive to every nuance of his behaviour, watched him with an anxiety she took care to conceal.

'Do you think you're wise to go to the glasshouse today?' she asked when she came upon him one morning, about to set out in his working clothes. 'It's so hot in the cone. I'm afraid you'll take a chill.'

'A chill?' His voice was as strong and as deep as ever. 'What nonsense are you talking now, woman? Why should I start to take chills now, after near seventy years of going in and out of glass cones?'

'Simply because you *have* been going in and out for so long. Joe, we have to face the fact that we're growing older. Do you really need to go on working? Can't you decide to rest?'

'I wouldn't know what to do with a rest, and neither would you, my love.' He stopped in the doorway, filling it with his bulk as he had always done, only the white hair, once as black as Mark's, betraying his age. 'Christina, I know what's in your mind,' he said gently. 'You're afraid I'll do too much – overstrain my heart as that fool of a doctor warned me I might. But as you say yourself, we're growing old, both of us. We can't have so very long to stay here, making a nuisance of ourselves to the younger folk. And if I've a mind to go with a blowing iron in my hand, I don't see that any of these modern young doctors with their newfangled notions has a right to stop me. And I don't believe you would wish them to,' he added, moving forward to take her in his arms.

'Oh, Joe.' She leaned against him, wondering a little that they could still, after so many years, find joy in the closeness of their bodies. Gone now were the days of their youth, when they had revelled in their tumultuous love-making, yet they could still find arousal in a kiss and satisfaction of a gentler kind. She felt the beat of his heart against her cheek and wondered if it were really weakening, as Dr Marsh had warned her. To her, it seemed as strong and as steady as ever.

'Go to the cone then,' she said with a smile. 'You can still blow as fine a piece of glass as any man there. Go and show them all how it's done, and bring me back a new frigger. It's a long time since you made me a glass toy, and I have a fancy for a – oh, for an animal of some kind. Or a bird. Remember the swan you made for me the day you blew the Chalice? He's still on my dressing-table.'

'I'll bring him a mate,' Joe said, and stepped out into the sunshine. 'With my apologies for making him wait so long.'

He strode away down the path and Christina watched. But, in spite of her words, there was an aching sorrow in her heart. For she knew that Joe was, in spite of all he said to the contrary, beginning to feel his years. And she knew that he had not enough patience to endure a helpless old age.

Chapter Fifteen

Spring came to Corning with a rush of melting snow and heavy rain. The Chemung flooded, as Jensen had said it would, and the water rose to the top of the river bank and spread in a great, shining sheet over the wide, flat valley floor. Cordelia, walking daily over the iron bridge, looked across the bleak waters which lay like hammered pewter over the tobacco fields and shivered, wondering if the weather would ever grow warm again. The hot, sultry days of last summer, when she and Tim had arrived in Corning, seemed very far away.

It seemed impossible that they could have been here for almost nine months. Their lives had settled down now into a routine, with Cordelia walking each morning to the little schoolhouse in Knoxville where the children came now with freshly washed faces and brushed hair, ready and eager to learn what she had to teach them. She knew them all now and understood the problems in each young life. Many came from poor families, their poverty stemming as often as not from too many children and not enough income; some were ill-used at home and found school a haven of peace and companionship. Others, like Danny, were tough and wary, needing especially careful guidance for they had run wild for too long to accept authority easily. But they all loved Cordelia, and in that small schoolhouse her word was law. And they had crept into her heart; she did not like to look ahead to the time when she would have to leave them.

Timothy, his arm now healed and strong again, went to the glass-house each day to work on the new styles he was evolving – so rapidly now that production could barely keep pace with him. The Opalene glass had been a great success and was now made regularly, both to order and for general sale. But to his and Jensen's annoyance, an imitation had already appeared on the market – a glass colourful enough at first glance to deceive those without a discriminating eye, or those who were unwilling to pay Jensen's prices, yet which was gaudy and crude, its iridescence harsh where Timothy's glass glowed softly, its shapes ugly and badly blown.

'It's bound to happen, I suppose,' Timothy said, looking with disgust at a vase Jensen had discovered in a shop in Elmira. 'People will always try to imitate anything new. But this has happened so quickly – it was on sale almost as soon as Opalene. And the name's similar too – Opalesce. Almost as if they knew.'

'I suppose we may have a cuckoo in our nest somewhere,' Jensen said thoughtfully. 'Someone who's not above selling a secret or two to a rival glasshouse. But I don't even know who's making this stuff, Tim – the store manager couldn't tell me. All he'd say was that they bought it off some huckster who came in with a job lot of goods – things he'd bought from different factories. It could have come from anywhere between here and New York.'

'Well, there's not much we can do about it now. Unless the man comes round again.'

'I don't suppose the manager would even recognise him.' Jensen gave the vase a contemptuous glance. 'It won't compete with us, anyway – or only on a small scale. Our steady customers wouldn't give it shelf room.'

Tim agreed. All the same, it was annoying to be copied. He hated the thought that this inferior glass might be mistaken for his. And he determined to keep his eyes and ears open in the glasshouse. He didn't want the same thing happening to the new glass he was working on – the glass Cordelia had named Damascene, with gold and silver inlaid between thin layers of finest crystal, so that it gleamed and shimmered like a precious silk. A few experimental pieces had already been made, and Cordelia owned a tiny vase, just large enough for a single flower. She kept it on her dressing table and looked at it each day, marvelling at the satin surface and the hidden gleams of precious metal, glittering as she turned it under the light.

'It isn't absolutely right yet,' Timothy told her. 'But once we've overcome these last few problems, I'll make the chalice for Grandmother. I think Damascene will look very well on that mantelpiece in Henzel Court, with Grandfather's Chalice and the Black Cameo. Three generations of glass . . . it's a great thought, Cordelia.'

'There were other generations before us,' Cordelia reminded him. 'Our family goes back three centuries or more, all glassmakers.'

'That's true. But for such a long time there were hardly any changes. And the excise on lead, that Grandmother and Grandfather still talk about, held up progress in crystal for a hundred years. Now we can go ahead and discover new techniques all the time. This is the most exciting period glassmaking has ever known, Cordelia – and this was the right place to come.' His eyes glowed. 'I could never have developed my glass in this way at home. I would never have been given a free hand at Henzel's as I have been here, thanks to Jensen.'

'He has been good to you, this man,' Pierre remarked. He and Ginette were living in the rented house on Cedar Street now, with Timothy and Cordelia. The furniture in the large front room had been changed so that Ginette could have her couch there during the day, and the family would gather around her in the evenings. A small room leading from it had become her bedroom, and Pierre slept in the room across the hall – previously the dining-room – so that he could be on hand should she need anything during the night. Meals were taken in the small breakfast-room off the kitchen, and so far everything had worked out well.

'Jensen? Oh yes,' Tim said carelessly. 'He was the only one to see what I could do when I first came to Corning. The others – good enough men, I like them pretty well – just didn't have the vision he has. Or the courage to try something new – take a risk or two.'

'And your new glass – Damascene,' Ginette said softly. 'It's going to be even better than Opalene?'

'It certainly is.' Tim's eyes glowed and he leaned forward. 'Nothing quite like it has ever been made before. There's been inlaying, of course – but never quite like this. It's going to take the glass world by storm – well, you've seen Cordelia's little vase. When it's perfected –'

'It will be beautiful. I should love a piece for myself,' Ginette murmured. Her enormous black eyes were fixed on Timothy's face and he coloured and grinned, brushing back his tousled hair.

'You shall have one. As soon as we're in production. The first piece of true Damascene made,' he promised recklessly, and Cordelia gave him a glance of surprise. Surely he would have wanted to give that to Grainne . . .? But perhaps he meant to make a piece for her himself, a tiny ornament for her to treasure as all the Henzel women treasured some small frigger – Christina's swan, the pony Ben had once given to Emily at a glassmaker's picnic. Her own little vase.

Ginette smiled like a cat, her lips curving gently. She lay in a froth of lace, her sable hair in loose waves to her shoulders. All Pierre's earnings at the glasshouse had so far gone to make Ginette more comfortable, more exotically beautiful. Her *peignoirs* were almost as elaborate as ball-gowns, and she was surrounded with satin cushions, frilled with lace so that she appeared to be almost immersed in foam, like a mermaid rising from the waves. Her skin was smoothed with creams and lotions, keeping her hands white and supple, her complexion as pale and soft as cream. There was always a bowl of fresh fruit at her side, a box of chocolates and candies and, even in winter, a vase of sweet-smelling flowers.

Perhaps it was not surprising that Timothy should be fascinated by Ginette and happy to spend evenings in her boudoir that he might otherwise have spent with the friends Cordelia disliked so much. But wouldn't it have been more natural for him to spend his spare time with Grainne? The two had seemed so close after the terrible railroad accident. And lately, Cordelia had noticed a fresh sadness in the Irish girl's eyes.

'I still go to see Grainne,' Tim said defensively as they walked through the city together, he on his way to the glass-house, she going to school. 'I went only yesterday. But I have to spend some time with Ginette too. She's our cousin and she must be lonely during the day, with only Bessie for company. I'm surprised you don't ask me to stay at home more, not less,' he added, changing his tone to one of attack. 'Or maybe you want them all to yourself.'

'Don't be silly, Tim,' Cordelia said sharply, but his words brought a flush to her cheeks. 'Of course I want us all to be together.' But the thought of being alone with Pierre made her heart kick uncomfortably. There was something in his dark eyes that made her look quickly away when she met his questioning glance, something in the tone of his voice . . . It was simply that they didn't know each other very well, she told herself irritably. Even if they were cousins of a sort, with some of the same blood in their veins, their backgrounds were so different, their lives so disparate, that it was bound to take time to adjust to living in the same house. And she had known so few men outside her own family . . . Few women, too, to meet in such close contact as she had now with Ginette, to share her life with so intimately.

It had been more difficult than she had expected, this living together. There had been so many adjustments to be made. Meal-times, for instance – Pierre and Ginette had been used to strange, erratic hours at the fairground, with friends coming into the wagon late at night to sit for hours talking, drinking and playing cards. Cordelia's regular hours seemed rigid and formal to them. And even though Cordelia's upbringing had been less repressive than for most girls of her age, she was disconcerted by her French cousins' casual way of life, with Pierre wandering in and out of Ginette's room half dressed and taking upon himself the tasks of washing and performing intimate tasks for his sister. And even though she scolded herself for being narrow-minded, and reminded herself that they had lived for years in a tiny wagon, with no one else to help Ginette, it still came as a small shock to hear soft laughter and deep murmurings coming from behind Ginette's closed door and to know that behind it Pierre was giving his sister a bath.

'She is accustomed to me now,' he would explain easily as he carried the zinc bath out of the room later. 'And although she's so small, she's surprisingly heavy. I would not wish you to damage yourself in any way, Cordelia.'

'No . . .' she said doubtfully. 'But perhaps Bessie –'

'Bessie? A maid?' He made an expressive sound. 'No, I think we will go on as we have always done. It is better for all.'

And Ginette seemed to agree. 'I should not eat so many chocolates,' she observed. 'Then I should not be so heavy,

332

and you could help me, *ma chère* Cordelia. As it is, I'm afraid I need the strength of a man. Timothy, perhaps –' her eyes laughed at Tim's fiery blush – 'or that so-handsome Mr Novak. I am sure he would be quite strong enough . . .'

Jensen. Cordelia, standing on the bridge, stared down into the grey water and wrapped her arms around her chilled body, thinking back as she did so often to the day after the railroad accident, when Jensen had come back almost from the dead – and claimed Karin as his daughter.

The scene came back to Cordelia as vividly as if it were happening again.

'Your *daughter*? But I don't understand, you've never mentioned a daughter – or a wife . . .' She had looked up at him, her eyes bewildered, and he met her glance above the curly head.

'I've been trying to tell you,' he said soberly. 'For a long time, I put it off.' He paused and rubbed a hand across his tired face. 'Cordelia, it's still too difficult to talk about now. We must have time alone. And I have so much to arrange.' He looked down at his daughter and Cordelia caught a strange expression on his face, a sadness that seemed out of place when he had only just found the daughter he must have believed dead. 'Can I leave Karin here until I've fixed up a nurse for her? I could take her to the new house – the housekeeper's there, getting everything ready – but I feel she'd be better with you. I'd like to know how she came to be here, but I just can't think . . . The fact that she *is* here, safe and well, is all that matters at the moment . . . Thank God you were there, Cordelia.' He lifted his eyes to hers and she saw the shadows in them, shadows of weariness and pain. 'I'll come to you this evening,' he said quietly. 'Tell Martha we need to be undisturbed, will you? And then I'll tell you everything.'

Cordelia nodded. She was still too exhausted, too over-whelmed herself to be able to take in everything that was happening. Mary and Declan dead – Tim injured – Jensen alive, when she had thought him lost – and now this child, the little girl who had slept wrapped in her own arms, proving to be his daughter. A daughter whose existence Cordelia had never even suspected.

Why could he not have told her? she asked herself over and over again during that long day. Why was he so afraid of the truth? Was he ashamed? And if he had a daughter . . . surely he must also have a wife?

Cordelia remembered the kisses he had given her, the way she had lain in his arms in the big chair, and her face burned. But there was no time to examine her feelings. There was Karin to think of – Karin, blonde and blue-eyed as her father, almost lost in the big armchair where he had placed her so gently before kissing her and telling her to wait for him to come back. She had still not spoken and her wide speedwell eyes watched Cordelia as if she were afraid to lose sight of her. Poor little mite, Cordelia thought com-passionately. Whatever your father has done, none of it is your fault. And you've been through so much in the past two days . . . Swiftly, she moved across the room and gathered the child into her arms. And as she felt the fragile body against her heart, and the two soft arms wind them-selves about her neck, she felt a great rush of tenderness, and knew that there was a bond forming between her and this small, quivering scrap of humanity that had nothing to do with any relationship between herself and Jensen; a bond that was stronger than either of them and that would never be broken.

She and Jensen had not had their promised talk that evening. There was still too much to think about. He had spent the day looking for a nursemaid for his daughter, and supervising the arrangements for moving into the new house on the hill. His housekeeper, having expected more time, was in a fluster and he was forced to delay the move for another week. Martha agreed readily that Karin should stay with her in the meantime; but when Cordelia proposed that she and Tim should move back to their own lodgings, the little girl clung to her and refused to let go, and she was forced to agree to stay with the Robinsons for as long as Karin was there.

'But we can't go to your new house with you,' she said. 'Your Daddy will be there, and Mrs Sankey, and another nice lady who will look after you. I have to go to my house and look after Tim.'

Karin's eyes were fixed on her imploringly, and Cordelia sighed. If only the child would speak! But she seemed unable to say a word, and it was impossible to divine what was going on in the small golden head.

'I suppose the shock will wear off eventually,' she said to Martha. 'The doctor can't find anything wrong with her – no injuries at all. She just seems to be frozen inside.'

'And I guess that's just exactly what it is,' Martha said. 'But it'll go. She's a bright little thing, you can tell that, and she'll jes' open up one day and surprise us all. I guess an experience like she had is too much for any kiddie to handle. She jes' needs lovin', and then she'll be all right.'

'If only we knew more. Jensen has told us nothing. We don't even know what's happened to her mother – is she alive or dead?' Cordelia felt a spark of anger bright and hard in her heart. 'He ought to have told us *something*, Martha.'

'Guess there ain't been a chance. And he's pretty rough himself still – you can see by his eyes. Jes' about out on his feet, he was when he came in last night. That was some crack he had on the head an' he ain't over it yet, not if I'm any judge. Goin' into old history won't help him any.'

'I suppose you're right. And I know he'll tell us eventually.' Karin was curled up on Cordelia's lap, fast asleep, and Cordelia stroked the soft curls. 'But she's such a dear little thing – and I *can't* understand why he never mentioned her before.'

'I allow, it's surprisin' nobody knew,' Martha agreed. 'But White Mills is a long way from here an' I guess there's only glass folks have any contact. And if he cared to keep it quiet, it'd be easy enough. It was long enough since he lived in Corning, after all.'

'Well, I suppose we'll find out in the end. And it really isn't any of our business, is it?' Cordelia looked up and found Martha watching her. 'It isn't,' she repeated, disconcerted by the expression on the older woman's face.

Martha looked at her with compassion, and Cordelia knew that her voice had given her away. There had been a world of loneliness in her tone, an echo of the sadness she couldn't help feeling. With the coming of Karin, Jensen seemed to have drawn further than ever away from her. The withdrawal she had sensed when he held her in his arms and then gently put her away from him was much more defined. And it was closely bound up with his daughter, sleeping now in her arms, her body as light as gossamer and her helpless dependence binding a mesh as fine as silk and as strong as steel about Cordelia's heart.

It was a week before Jensen was sufficiently organised to be able to take Karin home. Martha and Cordelia went with them, Martha agog to see over the new house and Cordelia with mixed feelings; remembering that October day when she had stood at the window of the master bedroom and Jensen had kissed her.

As the trap clattered up the icy roads, she stole a look at him. Staring straight ahead, wrapped in a heavy sheepskin coat, with his bare head glinting in the sunshine, he looked like one of his Viking forebears on his way to conquer a new land. There was a set to his lips, a firmness of purpose in his eyes, that told of inner strength, a steeliness that would never waver. It was both admirable and a little frightening, Cordelia thought. Once Jensen had set his mind on a course of action, nothing would swerve him from it. And woe betide anyone who tried.

The house stood back from the road, a wide lawn already sweeping down in front of it. At the back, the garden ran up into woods that were still deep in snow. But the trees were not dark and forbidding; their denseness had been carefully thinned with felling so that space and light streamed between them. They curved behind the house in a wide semi-circle, as if the forest itself had flung its arms around the building, holding it in a strong embrace. It looked already as if it had stood there for years, as if it had grown out of the ground.

'Why, it's a lovely house!' Martha exclaimed. 'It looks so right – see, Karin, this is your Daddy's house and this is where you're goin' to live. Ain't you a lucky girl?'

Karin clambered down from the trap into Cordelia's arms and stared across the lawn. Cordelia felt the small fingers digging into her flesh. She set the child down gently.

'Let's go inside.'

This was the moment she had half longed for, half dreaded. She had not been to the house since that day, so many weeks ago, before the railroad disaster. The work had been completed since then and Jensen's housekeeper, Mrs Sankey, had been busy setting all to rights. Until this moment, nobody had ever lived here; now it was about to become a home.

Jensen opened the door and they all stepped inside.

There was a momentary silence.

'My, oh *my*,' Martha said at last.

Jensen looked at Cordelia. She turned her head, letting her eyes move slowly round the square hall with its softly gleaming polished wood panelling, its rich drapes of figured crimson silk, its ornate mirrors and the thick, deep carpet which ran from the floor up the long, curving staircase. She looked at the pictures on the walls and at the ornaments on the tables and shelves – glass of all kinds, porcelain and a few Indian artefacts such as many American houses possessed to remind them of wild pioneering days only just gone by. She looked at the few photographs that were placed in silver frames on the top of a glass-fronted cabinet.

'You have made it into a home, Jensen,' she said softly.

He looked down at Karin, standing at Cordelia's knee, wide-eyed as a kitten. 'Do you like your new home, Karin?' he asked gently.

The golden head nodded slowly, but the clutching fingers did not let go of Cordelia's skirt. There's going to be trouble with her when I leave, Cordelia thought. She has become too dependent, too attached. 'May we see the rest of the house?' she asked, hoping that it would provide a distraction.

Jensen led them through the rooms, all as beautifully decorated and furnished as the hall. In the master bedroom, Cordelia felt her colour rise. The windows were draped now in the heavy, glowing velvet they had discussed, and a fire burned steadily in the grate. The big bed was made up and covered with a patchwork quilt that brought a touch of homespun lightness to the room, and there was a large jug of hothouse flowers placed in the window.

'Why, this is real lovely,' Martha declared. 'I'm goin' to go right home and tell Bob we've got to have a bedroom like this, even if we have to build a new house to go around it! I reckon any woman would be pleased to have a room as good as this one –' She broke off, her eyes on Cordelia's face. 'Why, I'm sorry, I know I'm speakin' out of turn, but you've got to admit, Cordelia, this is a real pretty room.'

'It is. It's lovely.' Her voice was toneless and she turned away, feeling suddenly oppressed by the rich comfort all around her. She would be almost glad to get back to the plain lodgings she shared with Timothy . . . 'May we see Karin's room?' she asked. 'I'm sure she must want to know where she's going to sleep.'

'Why, of course. And her new nursemaid ought to be there, too – I told her to have a little surprise ready.' Jensen led them quickly across the wide landing and opened a door. 'Mary Sue? Is everything ready?'

Cordelia heard a soft voice say something indistinguishable. She felt Karin's hand clutch suddenly tighter and gave the little fingers a reassuring squeeze. Together, they followed Jensen into the room.

It was a wide, airy room with large windows and walls papered in pale ivory that made it seem light and spacious. The furniture was light too, with cane and rattan chairs holding bright cushions that complemented the pale blue carpet and the flower-sprigged curtains. Before one of the windows, looking out over the town, a table was laid for tea, with sandwiches, fruit jellies and cakes. A bright fire burned on a wide hearth; and on the rug in front of it, kicking tiny paws into the air, rolled a very small tortoiseshell kitten.

'*Oh-h-h!*' Karin gasped, and let go of Cordelia's hand.

She fell on her knees beside the kitten, scooping it up into her arms, her face alive with tender joy. Cordelia watched, a lump in her throat. The speedwell eyes looked up at her, no longer blank but dancing with pleasure and excitement, and the pale face flushed like a rose with delight.

'A kitten!' Karin said, and her voice was like the tinkling of a tiny glass bell. 'I've always wanted a kitten. Daddy said I could when we came to Corning, but I thought he'd forgotten.' The words bubbled from her lips and it was as if she had never lost her voice, never suffered from any traumatic shock. 'Oh, Daddy, thank you, *thank* you!' And she scrambled to her feet, still holding the kitten, and rushed to embrace him.

Jensen dropped to his knees and took his daughter into his arms. His eyes met Cordelia's over her head and she saw that they were filled with tears. The ache in her throat grew and she longed to join them, to throw her own arms about them both, to be caught in that joyful embrace, but she could not. She felt a wave of loneliness.

'Ain't that just lovely,' Martha said, and blew her nose. 'And the little dear's speakin' again too – I knew she would, jes' as soon as she was happy again.'

There was a slight movement from the corner of the room, and Cordelia turned. Beside the tea table sat a girl of about her own age, small and plump with curly brown hair and a round, smiling face. She rose and held out her hand.

'I'm Mary Sue Beckwith. I've come to look after Karin.'

Cordelia took her hand. She looked at the warm brown eyes and then glanced around the comfortable nursery. She looked at Karin, released from her father's arms and playing with the kitten, her light voice tinkling like a brook running over sunwashed pebbles.

'I think she'll be very happy here,' she said, and felt a burden of worry lift from her shoulders, a burden that surprised her – she had not realised until that moment how much Karin already meant to her, how reluctant she had been to give her up. 'You'll look after her well, I know.'

But once again, as she took in the scene, she felt as if she were an outsider. And she was painfully aware of how little she knew, even now, about this daughter of Jensen's. Or, indeed, about any of his past life.

It was later that evening, as she and Jensen sat alone

before the parlour fire, that she learned at last the truth that Jensen had found so difficult to tell her.

Martha had gone home, agreeing that Cordelia should stay until after Karin was in bed, to make sure that the child settled in her new home. Mary Sue was upstairs in her own room, adjoining Karin's, and the housekeeper, Mrs Sankey, was in the large, comfortable kitchen quarters where she had her private sitting-room.

Except for the crackling of the log fire, the parlour was quiet. Through the window, Cordelia could see a deep azure sky, lit by a moon that was almost full and as pale as ice. It shed a cold light on the snow that still lay like a thick coverlet over the ground, and already the night's frost was glittering as it encased the branches of the trees.

Jensen paused at the window as he began to draw the curtains across. 'It seems a shame to shut it out. But it'll be warmer inside with the drapes across.' He turned and looked down at her, his eyes sombre. 'Can you stay a little longer, Cordelia? I think we should talk.'

She inclined her head. Her heart was beating fast, irregularly. 'Yes, I'll stay.' She watched him as he made sure that there were no draughts coming through the thick velvet curtains. He came to the fire, settled another log on the blaze, and dropped into the armchair opposite her. The flickering light played on his face, casting shadows across his eyes so that they were hidden from Cordelia's sight. She looked at him, trying to read his expression and finding it impossible.

'Please,' she said after a long time, 'tell me about Karin.'

He removed his gaze from the fire and turned his face towards her. The fine planes of his features were set in grave lines. His eyes searched hers and she looked back steadily.

'You have to tell me,' she said, and he nodded.

'I've known that for a long time, Cordelia. But like I

said, it wasn't easy to find the right time. There was always someone around, something needing to be done. Or maybe I'd find there were other things I wanted to say to you.' His eyes darkened. 'Things I didn't have the right to say . . . I know I should have told you before. It would have made things easier now, a whole sight easier. But – well, I guess there's a lot of coward in me when it comes to talking about myself.'

Cordelia leaned forward impulsively, reaching out a hand to him. 'But you don't have to be afraid of me, surely? I'm your friend –' She felt herself blush and was glad of the firelight colouring her face. 'Go on, Jensen.'

He stared into the fire, leaning his chin on one hand. For a brief space of time, he seemed to be seeking the right words, and then, at last, he began to speak.

'It goes back a long time, Cordelia. To when my mother and father and I went away from Corning to expand our business. We'd have expanded it here, but there were problems. We chose two sites – one in Findlay, Ohio, and the other at White Mills. There was a good glassmaking tradition already – Christian Dorflinger founded the White Mills Glass Works there in 1865 and it flourished. It's getting bigger all the time. Dorflinger's sons joined him in 1881, and I hear that his grandsons will be taken into partnership in a year or so. It's a good place for glassmaking and it seemed a good place for the Novaks.'

He sighed a little. 'We settled there. Findlay was never quite the same – it never became a home. But White Mills – well, it's not so very different from Corning. Hills, forests, valleys – the same kinds of trees, the river. And somehow, although we'd had a lot of sadness in Corning, we didn't want to move too far away from it. Maybe because Freya's buried here, maybe because it was the first American town to take us in. We always talked of it as home and meant to come back one day.

'Meanwhile, the business at White Mills expanded faster than we'd expected. And then, just as it started to be really successful, my father died. And my mother just never seemed to have the strength to move again. So I knew I'd have to wait.'

He turned his eyes on Cordelia, as if he were now coming to the most important part of his story. 'There were a great many pretty young women around that part of the world,' he said quietly. 'And I was a normal young man. I was lonely, too. I'd lost two of the people I loved most and I desperately needed comfort and love.'

'So you got married,' Cordelia said.

'I got married. She was one of the local beauties – hair like cloth of gold, eyes like a summer sky, a smile that could have warmed a stone statue into life. Yes, I loved her,' he said with sudden energy. 'I don't want you to think there was any other reason for our marriage. We were in love, and we were happy. We made a home together; we shared everything. And then our daughter was born – Karin – and everything changed.'

He stopped speaking. His face was hard with a pain he fought not to reveal. Cordelia watched his struggle and longed to hold out a hand to him, but she dared not. The battle was his and she knew instinctively that he must fight it alone.

'Amelia changed, after the birth,' he said in a low voice. 'She'd been so looking forward to our baby. She'd wanted a girl. She recovered quickly, physically – but she was never the same again.' He looked at Cordelia with tortured eyes. 'It was as if she hated our baby. She wanted nothing to do with her – she couldn't bear even the sight of her and I had to get a wet-nurse and put her and the baby right at the other end of the house, so that they couldn't even be heard. I tried, over and over again I tried to make her accept

Karin – but she would simply fly into a frenzy at the mere suggestion. I was at my wits' end. And then I realised that she hated *me* as well.' He paused for a moment. 'She had gone quite out of her head,' he said. 'She was quite mad.'

'Oh, *Jensen*,' Cordelia breathed, and reached out again for his hand.

He said in a dry voice, 'We had every doctor, every specialist we could think of, and nobody could do a thing for her. She would sit for hours in a deep depression – she wouldn't hear what you said, she didn't even seem to know where she was. Sometimes she would talk and even laugh, as if someone else were with her. Her looks went; her face was pale and flabby, her lovely hair thin and lifeless. I could hardly bear to look at her – but she was my wife and I loved her. I was sure that if we could only find the right doctor, get the right advice, she could be cured.' He rose and began to pace the room. 'I heard of a man in New York. I dared not take Amelia so far. I asked him to come to see her and he agreed. But he might as well not have bothered.' He stood quite still for a moment and Cordelia knew that he was staring into a haunted past. 'He told me quite clearly. Nobody will ever be able to help her. She'll be the same until the day she dies.'

'Jensen . . .' Swiftly, Cordelia rose and went to him. She stood in front of him, her hands on his arms, looking up into the tormented face. 'Jensen, how terrible.' She could find nothing else to say. The shock of the story he had just told her was ringing in her head and she could feel only an overwhelming sorrow that anyone should suffer such anguish.

'I had to get a nurse for her,' he went on tonelessly. 'My mother looked after Karin. But she was old and tired and she'd known too much hardship. She died when Karin was a year old and I had to find a nurse for her too. I stayed in

344

White Mills then, trying to live with it all – but it was impossible. There were too many reminders of the time before – when we'd been happy together. I knew I had to get away. And that was when I decided to come back to Corning.' He looked down into her face. 'I was making my first trip back when I met you and Timothy, and it was like being born again.'

'Jensen,' she whispered again, and laid her face against his chest.

After a few moments, she felt his hands on her shoulders, and then his fingers at her chin. He lifted her face and looked down at her, and his eyes were sombre.

'I've been in turmoil all these months,' he said quietly. 'Amelia is my wife still, in name – but she'll never be a true wife to me again. She barely knows that I exist. My love for her has turned to pity. I never thought to love a woman again, not as I loved her. I had made up my mind to spend the rest of my life alone. I took care not to seek out female society, in case I should be tempted. And it was easy enough; there was never a woman who could threaten my heart . . . until you came into my life.

'I could not stop thinking of you. Dreaming of you. All the time I was in Corning, I looked for you. I looked for you in the streets, I sought out places where you might be. Did you think it was coincidence when we met so often "by chance"? And when your brother needed help, I was happy to give it because it gave me good reason to be near you.' He smiled, and the smile lit his face for a moment and was gone again. 'I gained a double benefit there, for Tim's turned out to be everything you said he was – an artist, possibly a genius. But there have been times when I've wished I never travelled on the train that day, never met either of you. Because of you, my heart has been in chaos.' His eyes were as dark as a winter's sky. 'I would like, more than anything on this earth, to marry you,' he said, and his voice shook a little. 'And it will never be possible.'

The words fell like cold stones into the silence of the room. Cordelia felt their chill enter her heart and drag it low and heavy in her breast.

He moved away from her and sank into his chair, and Cordelia knelt beside him, trembling a little. The fact that Jensen had never even spoken of marriage to her, that she had never even considered the idea seemed irrelevant. Had she really never considered it? It seemed to her now that she had always felt their love to be her destiny. That was why she had felt so uneasy with him, almost hostile, in the early days of their acquaintanceship. That was why, when their friendship had begun to bloom, she had been unable to prevent an increasing closeness; why she had clung to him and let him kiss her, and responded to his kisses.

Why she had felt her heart breaking when she had thought him dead.

At last she spoke into the silence.

'Your wife . . . where is she now?'

He had been staring into the fire, his expression withdrawn, his eyes veiled as though he saw there the ghosts of a lost past. He turned his face towards her, gazing for a moment as if he had forgotten who she was, and then he sighed and answered.

'Here, of course – in her home.' At Cordelia's gasp, he added almost savagely, 'Where should she be? In some asylum somewhere? Have you any idea how they live, the poor creatures incarcerated there – yes, I've seen them. I admit I thought of it – I went to look at some. But I couldn't condemn my poor Amelia to that living death – I couldn't go on with my own life knowing that she was shut up in an institution, dirty and neglected, treated as nothing better than an animal. Even if she's my Amelia no longer,' he added in a low voice. 'Even if she has no consciousness at all.'

There was another silence. Then Cordelia asked, because she must know it all now, 'But where is she? I've seen no signs –'

'No, and you'll see none either.' He spoke as if he were half ashamed. 'You see, I still shut her away. She has her own quarters at the back of the house – her nurse to take care of her. She can walk in the woods on fine days, and she has her toys – toys Karin outgrew years ago. She's as happy as anyone could be in her pitiful circumstances. At least, I suppose her to be – who can know what goes on in her poor damaged mind? Who knows whether a smile means happiness or despair?'

Cordelia gazed at him, her heart filled with pity. To see a person who is loved and cherished, so terribly struck down, must be almost too tragic to endure. She wondered how he had managed all these years, with Karin to care for as well. But perhaps Karin had been his lifeline. For her, he had been forced to carry on.

Karin! she thought suddenly, with a tremor of fear. What of her, so sunny, so enchanting – so like her mother must have been? Was she, too, doomed, tainted with this dreadful sickness of the mind? But she dared not ask. She could only reach out with her heart, willing her eyes to convey all what she felt.

'No doctor can tell me what caused it,' he went on, 'or whether Karin will suffer in the same way. I just pray that she won't, and I am thankful for each day I have with her.' He thrust himself up from his chair. 'Well, now you know it all. You know why I could never tell you what was in my heart, why we can never let our friendship grow into anything more.'

'Yes . . .' She looked at him and said, 'May I see your wife, Jensen? Would – would it upset her?'

He stared at her. 'It wouldn't upset her, no – she'd have forgotten you in five minutes. But it might upset you, Cordelia. Amelia is not the pretty sight she was once.' He frowned. 'Why? Why should you want to see her?'

She shrugged helplessly. 'I don't know. I simply feel that if I do – well, I might be able to share it with you a little more. Can you understand that? If we're to be friends . . .' She looked up at him, not fully understanding her own reasons yet knowing that it was important for her to see Amelia – Jensen's wife. Karin's mother. 'Please.'

He hesitated for a moment, then shrugged in his turn. 'Very well. I don't see that it'll do her any harm. Though I still think . . . Are you quite sure, Cordelia?'

'Quite sure,' she said, and he looked at her again.

'Have you ever seen anyone sick in their mind before?'

'No. But my grandmother had a brother once – he was what they call a congenital idiot – and her father refused to have him put into an asylum. She's told me often about his nursery at the top of the house – the family used to go there whenever they could. It was a happy place. They were all sorry when he died.'

Jensen made a wry face. 'I don't think Amelia's room will ever be like that. But you can see for yourself – only don't say I didn't warn you.' He led her out of the room and along the passage to the back of the house, where Cordelia had supposed the kitchen and housekeeper's rooms to be. They were, but there was also a wing she had not seen from the road. It was closed off from the rest of the house, its communicating door locked. Jensen produced a key from his pocket.

'You're sure?' he said again, and she nodded. He unlocked the door.

Cordelia followed him into a second passage. There were three doors leading from it. Her heart beating quickly, she waited while he opened one, and then went slowly after him into the room.

It was large and sparsely furnished. There were few ornaments here, and none of glass, china or any other fragile substance. A fire, surrounded by a nursery guard, burned in the grate, with a big armchair on either side. In the middle of the room stood a large kitchen table. Working at it were two women; one in the plain dress of a servant, the other in a loose woollen gown.

The servant looked up in surprise and began to get to her feet, but Jensen motioned her to stay where she was.

'It's all right, Hester. Miss Henzel has just come to visit with Mrs Novak. Amelia –' his voice rose slightly – 'it's me, Jensen.'

The second woman looked round slowly and Cordelia felt a sharp pang of compassion.

Amelia Novak might once have been a beauty, but there was no sign of it now. The hair that Jensen had described as being like cloth of gold was now as coarse and dry as old hay, the delicate complexion rough and colourless. Her eyes – blue as a summer sky? – had lost their colour and were pale and blank. They rested on Jensen without recognition, without interest, and then moved slowly to Cordelia.

It was like looking at the empty sockets of a statue. Cordelia felt the ice of horror shiver across her skin. She stepped back.

Jensen took no notice. He moved forward, laid his hand on his wife's shoulder. 'Is she well today?' he asked the nurse, and the woman nodded.

'Much as usual, Mr Novak. We've been doing some painting, haven't we, Mrs Novak? Painting pretty pictures.' She indicated the sheet of paper lying on the table, and Cordelia saw that Amelia was using a child's paintbox, her brush stuck in a jar of water, the colours scribbled aimlessly across the page. 'Show Mr Novak your picture,' Hester went on in an encouraging tone. 'It's the best you've done – real pretty.'

As Jensen bent to admire the scrawl, Cordelia turned away. Her eyes were wet, her throat aching. What good had she done by coming here, by insisting on being shown this pathetic sight? She felt ashamed, as if she had pried into matters that did not concern her. Yet they did concern her – there could be no secrets now between herself and Jensen, no denying the feeling that existed between them. The love that was so hopeless.

She walked slowly back along the passage to the main part of the house and as she reached the hall, Jensen came up behind her.

'Don't go yet,' he said, and opened the parlour door.

While they were in Amelia's room, Mrs Sankey had been in to replenish the fire. It burned cheerfully in the hearth, an apparent denial of the tragedy that lived only a few steps away, and Cordelia sat down close to it, chilled through with the unhappiness she had seen and feeling that she would never be warm again.

Jensen stood just inside the door.

'Well, Cordelia,' he said quietly, 'you know it all now. I won't blame you if you never want to come here again.'

At once, she was on her feet. 'Not come any more! But why not?' She faltered, but the time for modesty was past. 'Jensen, you've told me Amelia is no longer any wife to you. You – you've told me you could love me – that you *do* love me.' She waited for him to deny it, but he said nothing, stared at her with eyes that burned like the coals Mrs Sankey had just put on the fire. 'And I love you, Jensen. I want to share your life – everything – the good things and the bad. Karin – and Amelia.' She paused, then added in a low voice: 'Have you the right to refuse me?'

'For God's sake,' he said, 'what are you suggesting?'

'What can I suggest?' she asked. 'I know we can never marry. But must we forsake our love – our chance of happiness together? Can't we take what there is? We'd be hurting no one,' she said pleadingly. 'Amelia would never even know. And Karin . . . Or do you think I'm unfit to be her stepmother?'

'Cordelia, you're more fit to be Karin's stepmother than any woman I've ever known. Watching you together – it's torn me to pieces that you can't be, that we can never be a real family.' He shook his head blindly. 'It's not possible! What you suggest – it would put us beyond the pale, don't you understand that? *Living in sin* . . . America may be freethinking and progressive, but we don't go that far. Even the suffragettes . . . No. It's madness even to think of it. We'd be cast out.'

Cordelia stepped closer. Her heart was hammering against her ribs. She looked up at him, not knowing how her green eyes shone, how the firelight glinted in her hair.

'Cast out!' she said scornfully. 'By whom? By the leaders of society? By all those who believe they know best, who have never understood about suffering and love, whose minds are so narrow that they would fit through the eye of a needle? I can tell you about convention! My grandmother bore an illegitimate child and brought him up to be one of the most respected glassmakers in the Black Country. Yes, my father – Tim's father. And my mother – she was a bastard, too, born in a mud hut to a woman who died in poverty and squalor. Yet our family has risen above all that. It can be done.' She touched his arm, her head flung back while pride and defiance blazed in her face. 'We could do it too, Jensen. We could live together here, you and I, and rise above it.' She paused and then added: 'Unless . . .

unless you don't really love me after all. Unless you feel nothing for me . . .'

He had begun to turn away, his eyes avoiding hers, but at those words he jerked round again and his face blazed.

'Cordelia, that's not fair. You know how I feel –'

'Do I?'

He looked at her. Agony and anger warred in his eyes, and she trembled.

'God, if you don't know by now, you never will.' With a sudden movement, he stepped forward and pulled her into his arms. Cordelia gasped, the breath forced out of her. Her heart kicked against her ribs. She felt his hand at her neck, moving with a trembling urgency over her cheek to her brow, and then he pulled her head back so that she looked up into his eyes. They were almost black, the pupils wide with only the narrowest of blue borders; she felt a surge of violent emotion and her lips parted.

'Jensen . . .'

Swiftly, he bent his head and his lips were firm on hers. Her eyes closed and her arms stole up around his neck. Her breasts tingled, hardening the nipples that were thrust against his chest. His mouth shaped hers with a smooth, warm strength that needed no force, and she felt her lips respond, moving under his and returning the kisses with tender passion.

'Jensen, I love you so much . . .'

'Cordelia . . .' he muttered, and it was as if her name were being ground from his soul. 'Cordelia . . . oh, my love, my love . . .'

His hand was on her breast now, firm yet gentle, caressing it with a touch that brought her almost to ecstasy. Instinctively, she let her head droop back, arching her back so that her breasts were thrust more invitingly into his searching palm. He tightened his hold about her waist and

352

her body pressed close against him. He lifted his head and looked down into her eyes and the hunger she saw in his face brought a tremor to her heart. She reached up and drew him down to her lips again, losing herself in the kiss, and closed her eyes as his mouth sought the hollow of her throat and his fingers left her breast to undo the tiny pearl buttons at her throat.

Cordelia's legs were trembling beneath her. She clung to his shoulders and felt her body quiver in his arms. She felt them tighten about her and then he lifted her and carried her swiftly to the sofa. He laid her gently on the cushions and then looked gravely into her eyes.

'Cordelia, do you understand what is happening?'

Her eyes half closed, she nodded and reached up to draw his head to her again.

'Please, Jensen . . . I want you so much.'

He stared at her. She saw his gaze on her hair, loosened by his seeking fingers and curling in soft bronze tendrils around her cheeks. She saw his eyes move down to the throat he had just exposed, the whiteness of her breasts. She felt his fingertips touch her breasts, and she shuddered with longing and her body twisted under his.

'Jensen . . .'

'No,' he muttered. 'No . . .' He kissed her again, with a new, desperate hunger. 'Cordelia, you're driving me wild . . .' His lips were hard, taking hers with small, fierce bites, moving over her face, her eyes, her hair, her ears. His hands were on her body, holding her up against him, and in the midst of a whirl of sensation Cordelia heard a soft moaning and realised that it was her own.

And then, as suddenly as he had caught her into his arms, he let her go, and turned away, his fingers running through his hair.

Cordelia lay dazed, her body still aching with the desire

he had awoken in her, her blood thundering in her ears. She stared up at him, bewildered, unable to understand.

'Jensen – what is it? What's wrong?'

'What's wrong?' he exclaimed. 'Cordelia, everything's wrong! Don't you see?' He stood up and moved away. 'This must stop now,' he said hoarsely. 'What you're asking – it's impossible. For Karin's sake, if for no other reason. The people here – they're not like your Black Country people. Back there, your family's known, established, it's been respected for generations. Here, we're still beginning. And I know what it can be like . . . Why do you think I left White Mills? Because people talked about Amelia, about her condition, about what might have caused it. They were blaming me . . . I didn't care for myself, but for Karin – can you imagine what malicious gossip like that can do to a child? And if we lived together, it would be the same here. No!' He turned back and she saw the pain in his face. 'Don't doubt my love, Cordelia. It's because I love you that I won't do this to you.'

Tears stood hot in her eyes, but she knew that he would not be persuaded. She sat up slowly, drawing her bodice together.

'What – what shall we do?'

'Nothing,' he said in a heavy tone. 'Nothing. Oh, we'll go on much as before, as far as other people are concerned. I'll work with Tim in the glasshouse – visit you occasionally. You can come here to see Karin – if you still want to. But we must never be alone together again. I can't be with you without wanting you, Cordelia, and that's the truth. And that's why I *won't* be alone with you – ever again.'

Cordelia stared at him. Slowly, she raised her fingers to her mouth and touched her swollen lips. They tingled as if they had been stung by bees, but it was a sting she would have welcomed again. Her breasts ached and there was a dull, throbbing pain somewhere below her stomach. And there was another sensation too, a slowly growing sensation that she recognised as an anger of her own.

'And do I have no say in this?' she demanded. 'Do I have no feelings to be taken into account? Jensen, I love you! I want to be with you – I want to live with you and Karin. Can't you see how right it would be, for us all? Jensen, please!' She rose quickly to her feet and pulled him round to face her. 'You're being a fool,' she declared passionately. 'You're throwing away something that's important to us all – you're throwing away our lives.'

He looked down at her and shook his head. For a moment, he laid his hand over hers as it lay on his sleeve, and then he gently removed it.

'Believe me, Cordelia, it's better this way. I've seen what it can do, to be cast out. I won't expose you to that, Cordelia. You deserve better of life.'

'I deserve no more and no less than any other woman,' she said quietly. 'But I love you, Jensen, and I'd willingly share with you anything that life might choose to send us. And if you can't accept what I offer –'

He shook his head, and turned away.

'– then there's nothing more I can do,' Cordelia said in a hopeless voice.

There was a moment's silence. The air was heavy with emotion that had been denied. The tension was like elastic, drawn out to its limits; at any moment, it could snap. Surely must snap. It needed only one small movement from either of them and they would be in each other's arms again. And this time there would be no pulling back.

She stood very still, hardly daring to breathe. If Jensen should touch her now . . .

He moved slightly. His eyes were on her face, dark and burning. She lifted her head slightly, let her lips part, turned her body towards him and raised her hands, palms up. She saw the light dawn slowly in his face.

And then the door opened and Karin ran in, holding her newest doll. The moment snapped, as Cordelia had known it must. And when Jensen looked at her again, she knew that the shutters had come down and closed her out for ever.

A cold wind blew thinly up the river and across the bridge, and Cordelia felt it touch her bones as chillingly as she had felt Jensen's rejection of her on that day a few weeks, an eternity, ago. She looked down at the grey cold water and thought that it was like her own life, flowing relentlessly away. She thought of her mother Emily, grieving over Paul. And of Christina, mourning her first lover.

Christina had not given way to grief. And Christina had always said how like herself Cordelia was.

It was time to go on. To cross the bridge and go forward with the rest of her life.

Chapter Sixteen

'You can't know,' Pierre said, 'how much it means to Ginette and me to be here.'

Cordelia turned and smiled at him. She was standing at the kitchen table, elbow deep in flour as she baked bread and cakes for the coming week, assisted by her maid Bessie. Really, she thought, she ought to have taken on an extra girl when Pierre and Ginette had moved in, but she and Tim had agreed that their cousins should pay as little as possible towards their keep, in order to save money for treatment for Ginette. And since Pierre would certainly have wanted to contribute to the wages for a new maid, Cordelia decided it was better simply to do the extra work herself. Anyway, she enjoyed cooking, and she enjoyed seeing Pierre eat the food she prepared.

'I'm so glad you decided to stay,' she said. 'We couldn't have forgiven ourselves if you'd gone on with the circus – such a hard life. And for poor Ginette – well, Tim and I are just thankful that we found you.' She looked for more eggs and found that the crock was empty. 'Bessie, run and get some more, will you? There's some money on the dresser.' She looked back at Pierre. 'I've written to tell them at Stourbridge, and I know they'll be as pleased as we are.'

'Well, perhaps,' Pierre said. 'But people do not always react in the way one expects. Don't be surprised if your family aren't overjoyed, Cordelia.'

She looked at him in surprise. 'Why on earth shouldn't they be?'

'Oh, I don't know.' He dipped his finger in a bowl of cake

mixture and licked it. 'Why do you bother to bake this when it's already delicious as it is? You know, I used to go into the kitchen at the château and do this. Our old cook would chase me away . . .' His eyes were dark. 'It seems so long ago.'

'It must seem like another world,' Cordelia said. She spooned the mixture into a pan and set it in the oven, then took a bowl of rising dough and began to knead it. 'Don't you ever want to go back?'

'To the château?' He shrugged. 'What would it be like there now? It isn't even in France any more.' He leaned across the table, his face close to hers. 'This is my home now, Cordelia – the first true home I have had since I was a child. And it's a home because you are in it.'

Cordelia stared at him. Her heart thumped a little. His dark brown eyes glowed and his full lips smiled.

'You are a true homemaker,' he said, and drew back. 'No man in his right mind would ever want to leave while you are in his house, Cordelia. It is a fortunate man who will be able to call you wife.'

Tell Jensen that, Cordelia thought and the bitter pain shot through her again. Since the day when she had taken Karin to her new home on the hill and learned the truth, she had hardly seen Jensen Novak. Saying that he wanted to continue the security that Cordelia had begun to impart to her, he had brought Karin to her school and the little girl had settled wonderfully, treated with tender awe by even the roughest boys in the class, but it was Mary Sue who brought her each day, and Jensen had stayed firmly out of Cordelia's way. And although she had yearned for a sight of him, though her body had ached for his touch, she had known that further contact could only make the pain worse.

Over and over again, she wished that she could leave Corning and go home to Stourbridge, to take up her old life and forget the sorrow in her heart. But there was too much now to tie her here. Tim, Karin, the school, and Pierre and Ginette. She couldn't leave, not yet.

Meanwhile, nobody must know of her unhappiness. And she kept her voice light and her eyes laughing, even when it hurt her most.

'Oh, I shan't marry,' she said, spooning cake mixture into small pans. 'I shall stay a spinster like my Aunt Sarah at home, and look after Tim as she looks after Uncle Roger.'

'And will Tim not marry either? What about the little Irish girl?'

Cordelia paused. 'Well, I suppose he probably will. They're very fond of each other.'

'And then?' Pierre said shrewdly. 'Will there be a home for Cordelia when Timothy has a wife?'

'Then I shall go home,' Cordelia said, and there was a desolation in her voice she could not hide. She looked down at her hands and saw them blur, and with a swift movement she turned away.

Pierre came round the table and caught her by the shoulders. He turned her to face him.

'You're unhappy, little cousin.' His finger touched her cheek. 'There are tears . . . Tell me, what is it? What's wrong?'

Cordelia shook her head. 'It's nothing. Just a little home-sickness, that's all. And wondering what the future will be . . . Nothing ever stays the same, does it? Nothing is for ever.'

'A few things are,' he said, and she looked at him, startled by the strange note in his voice. His eyes were dark, brooding under the heavy black brows. 'A few things never change. Things like love . . . and hate. They are always with us.'

'Hate?' Cordelia said. 'I don't believe I have ever hated anyone – not really. I don't know what it's like.'

'Then you are lucky,' he said, and his voice was sombre.

'Hate eats away at your soul. It consumes you – burns you up. It's the strongest emotion of all and once it has you by the throat it will not let you go.'

Cordelia shivered. She wanted to ask how he knew this, who it was he hated and why. But when she looked at his face, she knew she dared not. The smouldering expression was turned inwards, as though he saw pictures in his mind, pictures he would never describe. The war had come to his home . . . did he see the slaughter taking place before his father had sent him and his brothers and sisters away? Did he see his mother, dragged away by her own people to be executed for treason? Did he see the ship that had carried his family to their deaths, or the Americans who had thrust him aside as he begged in the gutter for the scraps that would keep him and his little sister alive? Did his hatred encompass all these . . . and were there yet more memories to torture him at night, to fuel the bitterness in his heart? Memories he never spoke of, never would reveal?

'Pierre, you must try not to hate,' she said, looking up into the dark face. 'You're right, it eats away at your soul. And all those things – they're over now. You have a different life. You don't hate America, do you?'

'Should I love it?' he asked cynically. 'I wasn't exactly welcomed here, was I? We would have been on that ship with the others, Ginette and I, sent to our deaths as our brothers and sister were. No, America never offered me a new life, Cordelia. I had to snatch it where I could. And the events that brought me here, they are in the past? No, Cordelia – they're here with me now. The past is never dead.'

Cordelia was silent. Only once before had she encountered such deep-rooted bitterness, and that was in her Uncle Roger, disfigured and deformed by an accident of his own making. In Roger's case, the anger had turned inwards, making him irascible and sour but never interfering with his desire to make money, to push Henzel's forward in the world of glass. In Pierre . . . Cordelia shivered. What was it she sensed about her cousin? What was the dark force that seemed to lurk behind those brooding eyes, the menace that Jensen had talked of and that she had recognised in that first strange meeting?

'You spoke of love too,' she said in a low voice. 'Do you believe in that? Do you believe that love can defeat hate?'

He looked at her, and she felt her heart move again.

'Perhaps it can,' he said slowly. 'But the love would need to be very strong, Cordelia. It would need to be very strong indeed . . .'

There was a new depth in his eyes now, a spark of warmth that lit them far, far inside. He held her look for a moment and Cordelia felt a trickle of sensation down her spine. She wanted to look away, but found her eyes irresistibly held by his. A tightening of the skin on the back of her neck told her that the hairs there were rising slowly, and she closed her eyes.

When she opened them again, Pierre had moved away and Bessie was coming back into the kitchen with a basket of eggs. And Cordelia, hiding her feelings as she had become so used to doing, went on with making her cakes.

Having two people living in the house who were really strangers, however much Cordelia might tell herself they were family, was not without its difficulties. Not least of them was the way Pierre would look at her with those dark, disturbing eyes and the expression that made her heart bump so uncomfortably. But there were other aspects, too.

Cordelia had been dismayed to find that she did not really take to Ginette. At first, she had refused to admit it, even to herself, and had spent a good deal of time in inventing reasons why Ginette should seem so different. The older woman was French, after all, though she had left her native land when hardly more than a baby, and she had had a difficult life. A dreadful childhood, living almost in the gutter until Pierre had managed to earn enough to find them a squalid little room. The circus, with all its wildness and rough company. And then, when she had begun to find happiness – for Pierre said Ginette had adored the beautiful ponies she rode so well – the accident which had left her crippled. Years of pain and immobility, an outlook which held no promise – it was no wonder that her sweet temper should sometimes fail her, a frown mar that beautiful face.

And she *was* beautiful. As dark as Pierre, her hair left loose to flow in rippling waves of jet across her pillow, her eyes glowing like brightly burning coals in a creamy-rose complexion, she was like a princess from a fairy tale, and Cordelia felt the tears fill her own eyes as she thought of Ginette standing proudly on the back of a galloping pony, her hair streaming in a shimmering banner behind her, her body glittering with sequins and silk. To think that such beauty was now confined to a couch! It was too cruel.

'Land's sakes, I never seen anythin' like her,' Martha confided to Cordelia after a visit one afternoon. 'She could knock that so-called America's Handsomest Woman into a cocked hat any day of the week! And ain't it jes' tragic, the way she is. A blessin' she's had that brother of hers to look after her all these years.'

'Yes, Pierre's been wonderful. He obviously worships the ground she –' Cordelia pulled herself up short. 'Well, you know what I mean. He adores her.'

'And I guess he's not the only one. Maybe she can't get about, but she sure knows how to draw the men to her.' Martha chuckled. 'My Bob hasn't been so fascinated since he saw John Comosh – you know John, runs the bookstore on Market Street? – do his triple somersault back in the seventies. He's the only man that ever did it regular, and my

Bob always admired him. But I reckon your cousin there's got the edge. He'd spend hours there, jes' lookin' at her, if I allowed him.'

Cordelia smiled a little sadly. It was ironic that Ginette should be compared, however remotely, with a circus acrobat, but she knew what Martha meant. Ginette did indeed exert a fascination over other people – and particularly over men. Even Timothy, absorbed as he was in his glass, was drawn to her side and spent his evenings sitting by her sofa telling her about his day, reading to her, listening to the soft voice with its mixture of American twang and the French intonation she still retained from having spoken French with Pierre since childhood, and watching the curving smile. He rarely came home without bringing some little gift – a fresh, glowing peach to match her complexion, a tiny glass plaything that shimmered as bright as her eyes, a piece of Damascene, nearing perfection at last.

'You're a poet as well as an artist in glass,' Ginette declared, and her soft, velvet eyes smiled into his. 'But you shouldn't be bringing such presents to me, Timothy. What of that little Irish girl who comes here sometimes – the one with the strange name? Don't you give her little gifts of glass and peaches?'

'Oh yes,' Tim said, flushing a little. 'But Grainne isn't like – I mean, she doesn't have to – she can –' Scarlet by now, he stopped and Ginette laughed the pretty, tinkling laugh that sounded most when she had a man by her side.

'You mean she's not confined to a sofa as I am – she can walk about and pick her own peaches. It's all right, Timothy – I'm quite accustomed to my disability. I should be – I've lived with it for ten years now. You needn't be afraid to mention it.' She leaned forward and touched his hand. 'And think how lucky I am – I have delightful visitors all day long. Your Mr Novak himself came today to see me.'

363

'Did he?' Timothy was startled and glanced involuntarily at his sister, who was busy at the table, painting some sketches she had made of the birds and spring flowers she had seen around Corning. But Cordelia gave no sign of having heard; she bent her head a little closer over her work and didn't even look up.

'He's a charming man,' Ginette observed. 'He stayed with me for – oh, an hour or more, drinking coffee and talking. Such a tragedy, his wife being an invalid. They have no real life together at all, I understand . . . He told me all about his little girl and she sounds *très adorable* – he promised to bring her the next time he comes. And I shall teach her to sew and do fine embroidery, for that's something dear Cordelia is not so fond of, I think!'

Tim grinned. 'No, Cordelia's never been too happy with a needle in her hand – couldn't sit still long enough and since neither Mother nor Grandmother liked sewing either, she never had to do much. They made you do buttonholes at school, though, didn't they, sis!'

Cordelia looked up and smiled. 'They did indeed. I had to be able to make a buttonhole in order to be admitted at all and I worked at it for a whole week, doing nothing else. In the end, I think I produced a buttonhole of such perfection that they expected me to be the star seamstress of the school – but I never could manage anything else. Still, if you need any buttonholes at any time . . .'

Ginette laughed. 'I shall certainly come to you. I must admit, I prefer to concentrate on finer sewing.' She lifted the delicate ruffles she was making for a new blouse. 'I used to make all my own costumes, you know.'

Her voice was wistful and Timothy felt a quick compassion for the beautiful girl, so cruelly injured. He imagined her on one of the dappled ponies at the circus, riding bareback as it cantered round the ring, rising to stand proudly on its back, her slender arms lifted high, the sequinned costume glittering on her body. The music playing as they went, the crowd clapping and shouting with delight – and then the fatal stumble, the pony's hooves slipping, the gasp of horror as it fell to its knees and the tiny, pink-clad figure flew over its head to land crumpled on the sawdust floor . . .

'I'm glad we found you,' he said impulsively, and reached out to take both her hands in his. 'You'll stay with us now, won't you? You won't go back to the circus.'

Across the room, he was conscious of Cordelia's head lifted again but he kept his eyes fixed on Ginette's smooth, oval face. He wanted suddenly to protect her, to keep her from any further harm, and he tightened his fingers around hers.

Ginette laughed, and glanced across the room to where Cordelia sat watching them.

'As to that, *cher* Timothy, we shall have to see. It depends on Pierre, doesn't it, and how he goes on in Mr Novak's glasshouse. I am like dear Cordelia, you see – I am dependent on my brother and where he goes, there go I.'

Cordelia rose abruptly from the table and gathered together the painting she had been making for her class. She came across the room, and Timothy saw to his surprise that she was trembling slightly.

'I think you have misunderstood, Ginette,' she said, and her voice was taut. 'I'm not at all dependent on Timothy. I came to Corning to be with him, it's true – but I don't have to stay here simply because he does. In fact, I've been thinking lately that it's more than time for me to go home. And if Timothy prefers to stay here . . . well, then I shall go alone.'

She looked down at them both for a moment, as if she were about to say something else. And then she folded her lips, in exactly the way in which Timothy had sometimes seen his grandmother fold hers, turned and left the room.

Timothy turned his head and met Ginette's eyes. They were soft and lustrous, the colour of pansies in a summer garden, and they seemed full of secrets.

'Did I say something to anger your sister?' she asked, and her brows lifted in amusement. 'Does it offend her to be thought dependent on a man? Perhaps she is one of the new feminists – an *emancipated* woman?'

'She's always been like that – an independent miss,' Timothy acknowledged. 'Our mother's the same – and our grandmother ran the family business when she was only twenty-one years old. No, I don't think she does like to be dependent on a man – or on anyone. That's why she runs that school of hers, though of course I could support her perfectly well.'

'Well, each to her own,' Ginette observed. 'Though for myself I am very happy to be dependent, and not only because of the way I am.' Her violet eyes met Tim's again and she smiled, her lips curving sensuously. 'And it does not have to be my brother,' she added in a murmur. 'After all, Pierre has cared for me for long enough. He needs his own life. And that's what meeting you and Cordelia has begun to give him.'

Timothy stared at her. His heart was beating rapidly and his hands were still in hers. He looked down at the slenderness of Ginette's fingers, entwined with his own, at the contrast between her frailty and his strength. He thought of the fragile body hidden beneath the lace flounces with which Ginette surrounded herself, of the bones no thicker than a bird's.

Ginette would always need care and protection. And who would give it, if Pierre were no longer there?

'I didn't mean to wait for ye,' Grainne said. 'I wouldn't do that, Tim – hang about to catch ye coming out of work. I was just passing.'

He looked down at her. She had been by the bridge as he left the glasshouse, a cotton shawl thrown round her shoulders, her dark curls blowing free in the light, warm breeze. But her eyes were sad and he found it difficult to meet them.

'I'm glad to see you,' he said, a little too heartily. 'I've been meaning to call – but we've been so busy at the glasshouse, you understand.'

'Oh, aye,' she said carelessly, 'and at home too, from what I hear.'

Timothy stopped. 'And just what do you hear?'

'Oh, not a lot. Cordelia's not one for gossip, ye know that. She's talked about your French cousins. Pierre and – Janet, is it? Doesn't sound very French to me –'

'It's Ginette. It's an abbreviation for Geneviève.'

'Oh, is that so? Well, I'm sure I'd abbreviate it, too, if 'twere my name.' Grainne spoke carelessly and her step was quick, her head held proudly as if none of this mattered in the slightest. But Tim, disturbed by her tone, glanced at her and saw the glint of tears on her lashes. He felt dismayed and then irritated. What on earth was there to cry for?

'Is everything all right at home?' he asked casually. 'Your father's got work again, and the boys, so Cordelia says. And Danny and Bridget are doing well at school.'

'Sure, everything's fine, why shouldn't it be? Considering it's only a few months since we lost me mother and brother.' Grainne stopped and bit her lip, then went on again. 'I'm sorry, Tim, I shouldn't have said that. Yes, everything's all right, thank ye.'

He walked silently beside her, cursing himself. Grainne was clearly upset and he was honest enough to admit that he knew why. His visits to the crowded rooms in Knoxville had grown fewer lately and it must be almost two weeks since he had been there. And, apart from one or two chance meetings, two weeks since he'd seen Grainne. Yet it was hardly any time since he had found it essential to catch at least a glimpse of her, or if that were impossible to walk past her house, whistling the tune they called their own, just in case she could hear . . . What had happened to him?

'And how is Miss T'ittry?' Grainne asked in the same careless tone. 'Keeping well, I hope? I daresay having her to live with ye makes a lot more work for ye all, and you're needed at home.'

Yes, needed to wind wool and laugh at little stories and bring peaches and glass ornaments and other playthings . . . Tim felt ashamed, but it was a sensation he disliked and he quickly converted it to a further annoyance. What business was it of Grainne's, after all, what he did with his time? He didn't belong to her, did he?

'Well, I have to help Cordelia quite a lot,' he said defensively. 'After all, she's out all day, and Ginette can't do anything. We only have one servant, you know.' He stopped but Grainne took him up at once.

'Oh yes, of course, I was forgetting you'd only one servant. It must be hard for ye, that.' He had never heard her voice so sarcastic – had never heard her sarcastic at all. He looked down in dismay at her bright, angry eyes and reddened cheeks. 'Well, hadn't ye better be getting off home, then?' she went on, still in that hard, angry voice. 'I shouldn't like Ginette to be worrying about ye.'

Tim stopped and caught at her arm, turning her to face him. Her eyes were glittering with tears and she held her head high so that they would not fall. He stared down at her, remembering the day when they had first met, how he had held her warm, quivering body in his arms; the day when he had come in out of the snow and found her desperate about her mother and brother. The early morning, with a rising sun flushing the newly fallen snow to apricot, when he had told her about Declan's death.

Since then, they had grown closer, yet there had been little said between them. It was as if their fate had been decided long ago, and there was no need for discussion now. As if their lives together would work out without effort.

But was that really possible? Could anyone's life be so easy? He looked down into the unhappy eyes and knew that he had been behaving like a child, expecting someone else to solve all his problems for him. Expecting to drift happily along, reaching out to pluck whatever fruit seemed most attractive, confident that the rest would be there, still ripe and ready, whenever he thought to take them from the branch.

It didn't work like that. And Grainne's sadness was the proof.

But was it so wrong to have given some time and attention to Ginette, whose own life had been so hard, who faced a lifetime's imprisonment on a couch, dependent on those around her?

'Grainne,' he began. 'You must understand –'

'Oh, I understand,' she broke in, tossing her head. 'I understand very well. She's beautiful, your cousin, Cordelia told me so. And Bridget, she's been there with Karin, she says she's like a lovely doll, all satins and lace. Different from a poor Irish girl with nothing but a few rags to her back and none of those expensive creams and lotions to keep her skin soft.' She held out her hands, rough and worn with scrubbing floors, preparing vegetables, washing clothes for a family of men who laboured at hard, dirty jobs. 'It's easy enough to understand,' she said bitterly.

'Grainne, you're not being fair.'

'No, I don't suppose I am. Is there any reason why I should be? I thought there was something between us, Tim – something good and worth working for.' She lifted her eyes, huge dark pools of pain. 'I'd have done anything for ye, Tim, anything. I'd have worked for ye. I'd have given ye my heart, my life. And I thought ye felt the same.'

He wanted to tell her that he did feel the same, that Ginette was nothing to him. But even as he looked down into the great dark eyes and saw the tears that were beginning to overflow, he remembered Ginette's eyes, like velvet pansies, smiling, cajoling, promising . . . His blood heated and his heart thumped. Ginette's spell was like the silken web of a spider, reaching out to him, meshing itself about him, drawing him back.

'Don't ye love me at all, Tim?' Grainne asked softly.

He felt helpless, trapped. And once again, he translated his emotions to anger. Why *should* he have to feel like this? He'd made no promises, taken no vows. Neither Grainne nor Ginette had any claim on him. Nor any right to waylay him like this, harangue him in the open street, embarrass him in front of anyone who might be passing . . .

He let his hand fall from Grainne's sleeve and his face darkened. He saw her flinch at his abrupt movement and his irritation increased.

'For God's sake, Grainne – leave me alone!' he said explosively. 'Can't a fellow even walk the streets without being accosted? Look, I've said I'll come to see you when I've got time and I will. But it's a busy time for us right now, we're busy on a new glass and I've got to get the production sorted out. I don't *have* that much time – ask Cordelia if you don't believe me. As for Ginette – well, if you can begrudge a girl who can't walk an hour or two of an evening, you're not the girl I thought you were. And now I'm sorry, Grainne, but I've got to go – there's someone I've got to see, and I'm late already.'

He turned and strode back across the bridge. He had successfully worked up his anger until he almost believed his own words. But as he swung through the town, almost walking in front of an electric tram as he hurried unseeingly across the street, he found that his anger was not quite enough to crush the knowledge that he had behaved badly; that Grainne deserved better treatment that this. And, most uncomfortable of all, that he had probably hurt her too deeply now for the wound ever to heal.

Cordelia climbed the stairs to her room and closed the door. She crossed to the window and sat down, staring through the leaves of the tall white birch that grew outside, her heart thudding uncomfortably.

Yet she could not define just what had upset her so much. Was it the way in which Ginette seemed able to attract every man to her side with such ease – Bob Robinson, Timothy, even Jensen who must have come while Cordelia was at school and hadn't even left her a message? Was it the way she seemed content to be so dependent and assumed that every woman, even Cordelia, must be equally content? Was it the almost excessive aura of femininity that she radiated, with her delicate complexion, her luxuriant black hair rippling loose to her shoulders, her fragility and her tinkling laughter?

Cordelia moved restlessly. Ginette, so frail and delicate, made her feel large and clumsy. Lying there on that sofa, covered with frills of silk and lace, she looked almost transparent, and Cordelia by contrast felt embarrassingly healthy. And Ginette did not even *look* older – it was as if the fall had arrested any sign of ageing. Pale though she was – as ivory pale as the cameo carvings Cordelia's father had once perfected – her skin had the bloom of a twenty-year-old's, and although she was almost frighteningly slender, the breasts revealed by the low, lacy necklines of her gowns still possessed the firm roundness of a girl's.

It might have been expected, Cordelia thought, that the hardships of Ginette's life would have left their mark – but even that she seemed to have escaped. Living rough on the streets of New York, making a childish home in the squalor of one small room, and later contact with all the rough elements of circus life, had done nothing to destroy her air of gentility, the natural pride that came from birth in a French château and a background that was, if not of the nobility itself, of a certain class. Much of the credit for that must, of course, go to Pierre, who had clearly looked after his small sister with a care beyond any that could normally be expected of a young boy. But perhaps it was natural for him to cherish her, since she was all he had.

No, there was nothing that Cordelia could find that could count as a rational objection to Ginette. So why should she be so disturbed?

It was something indefinable – something in the pansy-dark eyes, a narrowing when Ginette looked at Timothy or herself, as if there were some calculation going on in the brain that was so active in the helpless body. That very helplessness – Cordelia did not doubt its authenticity, but did Ginette make more use of it than was strictly necessary? Didn't she play on it, at least a little, when others were around her? Didn't she know quite well the effect she had – the protectiveness she aroused in men like Timothy – and didn't she perhaps exaggerate just a little, to enhance that effect?

Did she have the same effect on Jensen?

Impatiently, Cordelia jumped to her feet. She spread her paintings out on the table and stared at them. Tomorrow she would take them to school and pin them on the walls so that the children could learn the names of the wildlife that surrounded them, and of which they were so woefully ignorant. To most of them, all birds were sparrows, and flowers either yellow or blue. Cordelia intended to open their eyes to the beauty of the world, to compensate for some of its ugliness.

The 'whoomph' of a ruby-throated hummingbird as it darted at a flower, or the sunlight glow of a tree covered with golden blossom could lighten the day for someone whose own life was drab and cheerless, and who knew what these children might face as they grew older?

Of all the children in her school, Karin was the most sensitive to beauty and her presence in the classroom had already made a difference to the rough edges that Cordelia feared she would never be able to smooth away from some of her pupils. In spite of her confident words, she had been afraid, when Jensen had first agreed to let his daughter try the school in Knoxville, that they would not accept her. Deprived as so many of them were, even of adequate clothing, how would they view the little girl who came each morning dressed in prettily sprigged muslin, with a frilled and embroidered pinafore that was almost as fine as the dress it protected, her little bag packed with a luncheon of delicacies such as most of her schoolfellows saw only through shop windows?

Karin herself seemed quite unaware of any possible hostility. Ever since her arrival in Corning, she had been longing to go to Cordelia's school, and she had turned up on that first morning serenely confident of her welcome. In her white dress and pinafore, with her hair shimmering in the morning light, she had looked like a sunbeam floating through the door, and Cordelia, glancing anxiously around the room, saw the children stare, their mouths open at the sight.

'Good morning, Karin.' She held out her hand and smiled at Mary Sue, hovering behind her charge. 'Thank you, Mary Sue. Why don't you sit down by the door until you're sure Karin is settling down?' She watched as the child approached her desk and laid a hand on the small shoulder before turning back to the class. 'This is a new girl who has come to join us. Her name is Karin – Karin Novak.' She paused for a moment, her eyes moving slowly over the upturned faces. 'I know you are all going to welcome her. Now, who is going to offer to look after her for the first few days, until she knows where everything is?'

There was a silence as the children looked at each other. Then Danny, sitting in the front row, got to his feet.

'You were in that train crash,' he said bluntly to Karin. 'The one where my brother was killed.'

Cordelia froze. Nobody had ever spoken to Karin about the crash since those dreadful days when it had seemed that the shock had robbed her for ever of her speech. I ought to have warned Danny, she thought, but it was too late now. She looked down at Karin and tightened her hand on the child's shoulder.

'Reckon I ought to look after you, then,' Danny said and came up to the little platform where Cordelia's desk stood. He reached out a grubby hand. 'You can sit between me and my sister.'

Cordelia held her breath. Beside Karin's slight figure, Danny looked big and rough. Even Bridget, clean and tidy as Grainne could make her, was clearly from a different, and much poorer, background. Between them, Karin would look like a fragile blossom growing in a patch of sturdy weeds.

Karin looked at Danny. She looked at his stocky figure, planted with feet apart in front of her, at his shabby clothes and untidy hair. She looked at the streak of dirt that already adorned his cheek from the games he had played on the way to school, and she looked at the square hand he was holding out to her, laid her own small fingers in it and skipped down from the platform. He led her to the place beside him on the front bench, and she sat down between him and Bridget.

From that moment, Cordelia knew that it would be all right. Danny – the leader of the school – had accepted Karin and, equally important, she had accepted him. The rest of the school would follow suit.

And so it had proved. Karin's dainty clothes and manners were a source of interest and admiration to the other children and, far from rousing hostility, she seemed to inspire in them the kind of good manners that Cordelia had been trying to instil ever since the school had opened. Some of the words that Cordelia had tried so hard to eradicate from their vocabularies disappeared altogether, and she had told Ginette that Karin was proving to have a better influence on the children than she had ever been able to achieve.

'Well, it's because she is a real little lady and they see that,' Ginette replied. 'Not that you are not a lady, of course, dear Cordelia – but you are their *teacher*, you see – there is a difference.'

Cordelia laughed a little ruefully. 'All the same, I did think I was doing rather well with them. They behave well enough in class and do their lessons – but Karin's effect seems to last outside as well.'

'She is a delightful child,' Ginette said thoughtfully. 'It is so sad that she has, in effect, no mother. And poor Jensen, no wife. Does he not even have a mistress, do you know, Cordelia?'

'A mistress?' Cordelia was startled by Ginette's casual tone. Jensen with a mistress! But wasn't that exactly what she had suggested herself, wasn't that the proposition she had made to him? Only she had never thought of it in those terms . . . Her cheeks burned and she spoke shortly. 'I've no idea. I imagine he feels it is better not to.'

'Oh, but why? All men need a woman to love. It is nothing to be shocked about, Cordelia.' She examined Cordelia's face and smiled. 'You English! You are so strange about these things – we French know that it is simply a fact of life.' Her lips curved wider. Her eyes were dark; her pale skin gleamed in the afternoon sunlight that filtered through the curtains. She seemed to have forgotten that Cordelia was there. 'Yes,' she said softly, 'Jensen should have a mistress . . .'

And now, gazing down at the paintings that lay on her dressing-table, Cordelia thought again of Ginette's words and, with a swift, angry movement, swept up the paintings and thrust them into the small case she used for school. You're imagining it all, she told herself crossly. Ginette's bored, lying on that couch all day, and no wonder. You should be pitying her – helping her – instead of letting her words make you angry, jealous and unhappy. And all because you can't have what *you* want . . .

And what do you want? she asked herself then, sadly. To be here in Corning, married to Jensen, living in Hill House for the rest of your life? Or to be back in England, going to Cambridge as you'd planned, becoming a teacher and perhaps running your own school?

The career which she had once planned for herself seemed to have lost its brightness, its allure. And the future she longed for was out of her reach, forbidden by the man she loved so hopelessly.

She would have to turn her attention to something else. And as she moved again to the window and gazed down through the dancing leaves, she saw a figure come into view. A man, broad and powerful, whose walk was self-confident almost to the point of aggressiveness, whose dark hair fell over a lowering brow, whose eyes were dark and brooding and held secrets that made Cordelia's heart quiver.

Pierre. She stared down at him and felt that strange shaking inside that he always seemed to engender. Not love – it couldn't be love – but something else, something dark and frightening yet which drew her to him as if it answered some deep, unacknowledged need in her. As if she too had a dark side, a side that needed equal fulfilment . . .

Chapter Seventeen

'And this,' Timothy said, 'is where we're making the Damascene.'

He beckoned to Pierre to follow him to the men working around the Damascene pot. It looked no different from any other; the gaping jaw glowed with the eye-scorching heat of the molten glass inside, and the gatherer thrust his long iron rod into the depths and drew out a mass of golden metal in just the same way as the other gatherers, twisting it as he did so to keep it in place. But this glass was unlike that in any of the other pots; when cool, it would be the colour of ebony – as densely black as the glass Paul had used for his Black Cameo back in Stourbridge. It would be blown with care into the shapes Timothy had designed – even these different from the traditional round vases and decanters which were still being made at the other chairs – and layered with fine leaves of gold and silver which would glimmer softly through the outer coating of clear glass, giving the rich, silky texture of the damask fabric after which the glass was named.

Pierre had already seen some of the first pieces to be made, the experimental oval urn, the square vase, the tall, narrow twisted jar, and he watched with interest as the gaffer shaped the heavy goblet he was working on now.

'It calls for great skill, this glass,' he observed to Tim. 'You must have your best men working on this chair.'

'We certainly have some of the finest, but it's difficult to say who is the best man in this glasshouse,' Timothy answered. 'Jensen's managed to collect an excellent workforce. But the men on this chair are interested in experimental work, so they're ideal for anything new.' He nodded towards the gaffer, who had now finished the goblet and handed it to the taker-in, who was setting it carefully inside the *lehr*. 'Wal Dailey's been my right-hand man in every new glass I've attempted so far.'

'And you have tried many?'

'Oh yes – and not all of them successful, by any means!' Tim grinned. 'But when a glass does do well – as Opalene has, and as I believe Damascene will – well, it makes up for all the failures. Doesn't it, Wal?'

The big American glassblower nodded. He came closer to the two men, lifting his voice to be heard above the clatter of the glasshouse. 'Goin' to be a winner, this one, sure enough. Pricey, mind – you won't see Damascene on any ordinary table. But for those that can afford it – well, I guess there won't be many fine houses without at least one piece. And those smart glasshouses up in Brooklyn, well, I reckon they're goin' to be eatin' their hearts out when they see Damascene in the stores, and wishin' they'd thought of doin' it too.'

Tim laughed. 'Let's hope so! And let's hope we can get it perfected before any other manufacturers hear of it and start working on their own – I'd hate to be pipped at the post. That's why we've kept it all pretty secret,' he added, turning to Pierre. 'The workers are all under contract not to mention it to anyone outside the glasshouse and the actual inlaying process is only known to a few of us – it isn't like the old types of inlays which have been done for a while. So you'll understand if I don't tell you any more.' Jensen would be quite annoyed enough to think that Pierre had seen as much as this – he was still not fully reconciled to having the French glassblower working in his factory and even though Timothy shrugged his doubts away, dismissing them as prejudice, he knew that the final decision as to who worked in his factory must lie with Jensen himself. But Pierre was a cousin, he thought rebelliously, almost a Henzel. Why shouldn't he see what Timothy was working on?

'Oh, sure.' Pierre gave the gaffer and his team of men a friendly nod and followed Tim as he moved away. 'I can see you have very loyal employees,' he remarked. 'Don't you ever fear that one of them might be tempted, perhaps, to sell some of your secrets?'

Tim shrugged. 'It's always a risk, with any new manufacturing process. And we did have that problem with Opalene – we still don't know how that process leaked out. But two or three men have left since then, and since we've had no more trouble, we assumed it was one of them. Anyway, we feel pretty confident. Jensen's a good boss. And anyone who betrayed us wouldn't be likely to be trusted by anyone else – it'd be a very short-sighted thing to do. No, I think we're safe enough.'

He looked at the man beside him. Pierre was a few inches shorter than Timothy, but the breadth of his shoulders and his muscular sturdiness gave him a look of tough vigour that Timothy envied. And that wasn't all that the younger man admired: Pierre, older by nearly twenty years, had lived mainly by his wits, making his way through a world that had given him nothing, forced to fight for everything he wanted, from the scraps of food that had kept him and Ginette alive when they were children to the precarious life they had shared with the circus. Timothy felt his own life to be sharply contrasted – sheltered by a loving family, given everything he needed, educated, allowed to work at the art he loved . . . until those last few months, when his mother's illness had caused him to leave home. And even now, squarely on his feet again with the excitements of working with Jensen Novak, able to experiment as he pleased and with an expanding market greedy for new ideas.

I've had everything handed to me on a plate, Timothy thought, and Pierre, whose own inheritance should have been so similar, has nothing. Cordelia's right – we ought to do everything we can for him and Ginette. Especially as we're related.

'How would you like to work with me on Damascene?' he asked abruptly, and wondered immediately what Jensen might say to this idea. To hell with Jensen! Damascene was *his* glass – he would say who worked on it with him. He looked at Pierre again and saw the dark eyes staring at him with some disbelief.

'Work with you on Damascene? But there is Jensen to think of – what would he say to this? He doesn't like me, Timothy.'

'Oh, rubbish!' Tim said, uncomfortably aware that this was true.

'You know it isn't rubbish.' Pierre gave him a keen look. 'Why have you suddenly asked me this, Tim? I'm pretty sure you hadn't thought of it when we came in here. What made you offer me such a chance?'

Timothy looked at him helplessly. Clearly, Pierre wasn't going to be fobbed off with any evasions; he was too intelligent not to guess the truth, so he might as well be told it. 'All right, then, you can have it straight. I guess it's because I reckon you ought to have a chance. And maybe because I feel it's my family ought to give it to you. And it's also –' he laid heavy emphasis on his words – 'because I think you can do the job. You're a good glassmaker, Pierre. I've watched you with it – you've got a feeling for the stuff. And I wouldn't suggest you coming in on Damascene if I didn't think that, however much you might deserve it.'

Pierre studied him for a few moments, then nodded as if satisfied. There was a small smile hovering at the corner of his mouth but his face was otherwise grave as he held his hand out towards Timothy.

'Thank you, Tim. I appreciate that. I'll work with you on Damascene and on any other glass you make. I only hope that Jensen will agree with what you've done.'

'Oh, he'll agree,' Tim said with a lightness he didn't wholly feel. He shook Pierre's hand and grinned broadly. 'Here's to a successful partnership, Pierre. Let's get home and tell the girls – I reckon they'll be as pleased as we are over this.'

'Yes,' Pierre said, and his smile widened a little. 'I believe they will.'

'Jensen was here? This afternoon?'

Cordelia stood in the middle of the parlour and stared at Ginette, who was looking especially lovely today, the shell-pink ruffles of her gown clustered almost up to her ears while still plunging to a deep V between her soft white breasts. She raised a slender hand to touch the black curls that tumbled artlessly over her brow and her dark eyes gleamed at Cordelia.

'Yes, wasn't it kind of him? He called in just to see how I was – as if it could be important to him, and he so busy all the time. But he spared me over an hour. We had coffee and some of those delicious buns you were making yesterday.'

'I'm glad there was something to offer him.' Cordelia spoke with an asperity she immediately regretted. Why shouldn't Jensen visit Ginette, after all, and why shouldn't he be offered refreshment? She turned away quickly, not wanting Ginette to see the vexation in her face, and added carelessly, 'He often does call in, of course, but he usually comes when I'm home from school.'

'Really? Bessie seemed quite surprised to see him – I rather gathered it was several weeks since he'd last been here. I guess he'd forgotten you'd be out.' Ginette smiled, and Cordelia knew that neither of them believed her statement.

'He's good company, sure enough – kept me laughing all the time he was here. And what an attractive man!'

'Yes, I suppose he is.' Cordelia picked up Ginette's embroidery. Remarkably little appeared to have been done to it today. 'Ours is really more of a business relationship, of course, with he and Tim working together.'

'Oh, I realise that. Though his little girl's fond of you, isn't she? You see quite a lot of her. I guess that's a great help to him, to have you go up to the house and give the nursemaid some time off. Especially as you know Karin so well, teaching her in school.'

Cordelia, feeling reduced in one swoop to the status of substitute nanny and schoolteacher, dropped the embroidery. Scarcely knowing whether she were annoyed with herself or with Ginette, she turned restlessly away and stared out of the window. Why had Jensen come to see Ginette? It wasn't necessary for him to make such courtesy calls – Ginette was nothing to him, and he'd made it clear enough that he didn't like Pierre and hadn't wanted to employ him. And it wasn't even the first time he'd called when Cordelia was out – he had been twice last week at least, and Ginette had taken particular care to tell her each time. It was almost as if she knew how Cordelia felt about him, and delighted in making her misery worse.

But that was nonsense! Ginette could have no idea – nobody had. Even Martha, whose greatest pleasure was in matchmaking, had forgotten any ideas she might have once entertained about Cordelia and Jensen. And even if Cordelia didn't always feel in tune with Ginette, she had no reason to believe the Frenchwoman was spiteful.

You're being mean and petty, she told herself. Ginette can't even walk across the room, and you begrudge her a little company. Just because it's the company you desire most in the world and can't have . . . Does that mean

382

nobody must have it? She shook her head angrily and brushed away the tears that blurred her vision.

Ginette was watching her. She spoke with sympathy in her voice.

'You're tired, Cordelia. Sit down and let me call Bessie to make you some of the tea you like so much. You work too hard in that horrid little school.'

'It isn't horrid,' Cordelia protested automatically, but she sat down and smiled with a touch of ruefulness. 'But it's certainly hard work at times, teaching a class of children from five years old to eleven. Perhaps I am a little tired. And I'd love some tea and one of those buns – if you and Jensen haven't eaten them all.'

As she drank her tea, she responded to Ginette's chatter with only part of her attention. Nodding and smiling, needing to interject only occasionally with a 'Really?', and 'Imagine that!', or a 'Yes, I'm sure', she was able to let her mind wander. Inevitably, it wandered straight back to the subject that, try as she might to eliminate it, still occupied her thoughts whenever she was unwary enough to allow them to meander in this way – to Jensen Novak, and the question of why he had come to see Ginette, not once, but several times.

Cordelia nibbled the bun she had made and looked reflectively at the Frenchwoman, wondering yet again how she had managed to retain so much of her personality despite the strange life she had led. Looking at Ginette now, it would have been easy to suppose that she had only recently arrived from Paris, bringing all the latest fashions with her. Her manners too were exactly what one would expect in a woman accustomed to holding court in the most exclusive *salons*. Her voice, her accent, her pretty gestures, all were those of the stylish Parisienne. Yet Ginette had left France before she was five years old and had lived in poverty on the streets of Manhattan and Brooklyn before joining the motley company of a circus.

'You have not heard a word I have said,' Ginette accused Cordelia suddenly. 'Here have I been telling you all about the comical Martha and what she says about the fashionable restaurant in Elmira – what is its name, now, Peers, Pearsons –'

'Pierce's,' Cordelia supplied, and Ginette nodded energetically.

'That's right, Pierce's – and how good she says it is, with such sumptuous food that I shall *insist* that Timothy takes us all there one evening – anyway, here I am telling you all this and you do not listen. Not to one word!' The full red lips pouted and then relaxed into the smile that was so charming, and Ginette reached over and touched Cordelia's hand. 'So what are you thinking about that is so much more interesting than my chatter?'

Cordelia smiled. 'You may be disappointed! I was thinking about you, as it happens. Wondering how you come to be as you are, after the life you've had. No one would believe that you and Pierre had had such a hard time – you could have spent your life in a château and I just wondered how you managed it. To be so stylish and – and everything,' she finished lamely.

Ginette gave a little trill of laughter. 'That! But it is quite simple, my dear Cordelia. You see, Pierre has never allowed me to forget who I am – a Frenchwoman and a Thietry. He is proud of that, you understand. He remembers those days when our family counted for something in the district. Ever since I can remember, he has told me about them, over and over again, describing our mother and father, the other members of our family – *Tante* Cécile, *Oncle* Marc, René and Véronique and the others – until I am not sure whether I really remember them or simply have the pictures he has put into my mind. And it doesn't really matter – the important thing is that I do have those pictures. They are a part of me, just as they are a part of Pierre.' She stopped and gave Cordelia a doubtful glance. 'Do you understand me? It must be difficult, when you've always known your home and family – when you don't have to cling to a few shreds of memory.'

'I think I understand,' Cordelia said. She felt ashamed that she had thought uncharitably of her cousin. 'Please go on.'

'Well, then, that is one thing. Also, there is the fact that when we came here Pierre could speak only a little English and I none at all – I could barely speak my own language, I was so young. And he was determined that I should learn that first. That was easy enough – once he had found a room for us to live in, I saw only him and he spoke nothing but French to me. It wasn't until I was quite a lot older – oh, six or seven years old, that I began to learn English from other children. By then, Pierre was working in the glass factory and I was going to school. But we always spoke French at home together, and we lived as much as possible in the French way.'

'I suppose he hoped to go back some day,' Cordelia observed. 'I wonder why he never did.'

'Oh, he dreamed of it often. But so many changes have been made – our family broken up, our brothers and my twin sister dead, the Lorraine no longer even in France – what would be the point? And then the circus – there are many foreigners in a circus, Cordelia. We found other French people there, we made a little group together. And after my accident – well, I had little to do, but Pierre never failed to bring me the latest fashion magazines, especially those which had to do with French fashion, and so I kept in touch. And as you know, I have never quite lost my accent.'

'You haven't lost it at all,' said Tim's voice from the doorway. 'And it's charming.'

Cordelia turned quickly in her chair. 'Tim! Pierre – how long have you been there?'

'Only a few minutes.' The two men came in, smiling broadly, and Tim lifted Ginette's hand and kissed it. 'And we've got good news for you.'

'Good news? What?' Cordelia, watching, saw Ginette keep his hand in hers and smile up into his eyes. She felt a twinge of unease. Timothy was another who seemed to be enslaved by the Frenchwoman. But she was ten years older than he – and what about Grainne?

'Pierre's going to work with me on Damascene. What d'you think of that? He did a lot of work on new glass processes in the Brooklyn place, apparently –' Tim was talking to Cordelia now – ' and he's already had one or two good ideas. I reckon we'll be able to overcome all the problems between us.'

'On Damascene?' Cordelia stared at him. Ginette was already exclaiming with pleasure, congratulating her brother. 'But what does Jensen say about it? You have discussed it with him, haven't you?'

'Well – not yet.' Timothy looked first abashed, then rebellious. 'Well, why should I anyway? Damascene is *my* glass and it's up to me who I discuss it with. And if I think Pierre could help –'

'Yes, of course. It has to be your decision. All the same – I think you'll have to be very tactful about telling Jensen. It *is* his factory, after all . . .' She looked past her brother at Pierre, standing between her and the window, his bulk throwing a shadow across the room.

His back was to the light and she could not see his expression as he returned her gaze. But after a few seconds, he turned away and looked down again at his sister. And a look passed between them that Cordelia could not begin to analyse. A look of shared emotion, of understanding, almost of complicity. As if they communicated on some deep level that needed no words; deeper than the normal level of communication between brother and sister.

A little shiver ran across her body. And then Pierre moved and the sunlight flooded into the room once more. He looked at her with a smile in his eyes and the shiver disappeared. She lifted her head and felt the warmth of his dark brown gaze.

With a distinct effort, she thrust the thought of Jensen from her mind and smiled up at her French cousin.

'I'm very pleased,' she said. 'It's time Henzels and Thietrys worked together again.'

'On Damascene? You're letting him work on Damascene?'

Jensen and Tim faced each other in Jensen's office. Outside, there was a clatter and a cheer as someone dropped an iron, smashing the almost completed glass still attached to it. Jensen muttered impatiently and strode across the room to slam the door shut. He turned back to Timothy, his face set in angry lines.

'Don't you think you should have consulted me first? This does happen to be my factory.'

'And Damascene is my glass. I say who's to work with me on it –'

'Out of the present workforce, yes.'

'Pierre *is* part of the present workforce. You agreed to his employment yourself –'

'Under protest, Tim, under protest.' Jensen swung away and stalked across to the window. He stood staring out at the long buildings of the glasshouse, the tall chimneys pouring out the smoke that hung above the town on days like this, when there was little wind and the heat created its own heavy haze. Next week, the factory would close for the hottest weeks of summer and he had been thinking of taking Karin away for a holiday – the idea of getting away from Corning, away from the disturbing influence of the Henzel twins and their French cousins had been more and more attractive just lately. But now . . . He swung back again and glared accusingly at Timothy.

'I suppose you'll be wanting to keep on working during the vacation? You and the Frenchman?'

Tim blinked. 'Yes, I imagine so. We can do quite a lot of experimental work with just the small furnace going. There's always someone willing to come in for extra pay.'

'Oh, always,' Jensen agreed bitterly. 'Look, Tim, you seem to have arranged all this anyway and there's not much I can do about it now. But I tell you, I don't like it. I don't like that cousin of yours – I don't trust him. And if anything happens – well, I'll hold you responsible, you understand that?'

'What should happen?' Timothy asked. Jensen didn't answer, and after a moment he shrugged. 'All right – I'm responsible. But I think you're being unreasonable about this, Jensen –'

'And that's just where you're wrong – I'm being a darned sight *too* reasonable. Most men would tell you to get the hell out of it, your cousin and you both. Look, I don't *have* to give you the run of my glasshouse for your experiments, I don't have to let you have a free hand with my employees and my materials. I never had to take you on in the first place. And I don't have to let you take advantage of me now.' Jensen's eyes blazed into Tim's astonished face. 'So just remember that, will you? *I'm* the one who calls the shots around here, understand? So just you watch that Frenchman and like I said before, if anything happens, *you're* responsible.'

Tim's face was white. He stared at the angry blue eyes, and his jaw tightened. He raised a hand and ran his fingers through his hair and felt them shake.

'All right,' he said, 'if that's how you want it. I thought we were friends, Jensen. I thought we trusted each other. But from now on, I'll check everything out with you. You won't accuse me of taking advantage again. *Okay?*'

He wheeled and jerked open the door. Jensen moved and lifted a hand, but Timothy ignored him. He swung through the door and slammed it shut behind him. In one of the brief silences that fell now and then, his footsteps could be heard stamping away through the glasshouse. Then the clatter broke out once more.

Jensen stared at the door, still shivering on its hinges, his hand still half raised as if to call the younger man back. Then he dropped his arm and sighed. He turned back to the window and stared down once again at the long, sooty rooftops and the wooded hills beyond.

Henzels! Since those two had come to Corning he'd never had a moment's peace. And now it was worse than ever.

He had a sudden longing for the day when Cordelia had come to his house before it was completed and they had stood in his half-finished bedroom together. He had allowed himself to dream then, just for a while – to dream of bringing her there as his bride, taking her in his arms in the sure, safe knowledge that the rest of their lives lay before them, rich with loving.

Even as he dreamt it, he had known it could never be. And now he hardly dared see Cordelia for the yearning in his heart. He knew that it would have been better for them both if he could have broken all the ties between them. But that was impossible. There was Timothy, and the glass. And now there were the Thietrys.

* * *

'So, let us see what Corning has to offer in the way of entertainment,' Pierre said as he and Timothy left the glasshouse.

It was a hot evening. The air was thick with the sultry haze of approaching thunder, although as yet the sky was still cloudless. There was no breeze to freshen the heavy atmosphere and the smoke from the tall chimney stacks muffled the town in an acrid blanket. The Monkey Run was no more than a trickle running down the hill to the Chemung, whose waters wound sluggishly through the valley leaving banks of large white pebbles exposed on either side.

'We have lived quietly here so far,' Pierre continued as he and Timothy crossed the bridge into Corning. 'But there must be something to do in the evenings, even when the circus isn't here. Tell me how you amuse yourself, you and your friends.'

Tim hesitated. It seemed a long time since he had joined up with the friends he had made when he first came to Corning – Andrew, Frank and the rest of them. He remembered the evenings they had spent together last summer – could it really be a year ago? – evenings in the billiard saloons and at cockfights. Was that the kind of thing Pierre meant? It would surely seem very tame to a man who had spent years travelling with a circus.

'Cockfighting?' Pierre said. 'But there's nothing I enjoy more! Well –' he gave Timothy a sly glance – 'let us say there is very little. Is there a main on this evening?'

'There's almost always something on. Look, I've a friend in the bank – he'll know.' Timothy led the way along Market Street, past the clock on its tall tower, and into the corner building where Andrew Hyde worked. Inside, there was a chatter of typewriters, most of them operated by young women who sat in rows at the back of the big hall.

The tellers were all men and Andrew Hyde climbed off his high stool to come to the counter. He grinned at Timothy.

'Hi. I thought you'd forgotten us.' His dark eyes moved to Pierre with curiosity. 'Friend of yours?'

'He's a relative – a sort of cousin.' Tim introduced them. 'Pierre works with me in the glasshouse, but he wants some entertainment – we wondered if there was a main on tonight anywhere.'

Andrew wrinkled his nose. 'Nothing much. Lowell's away, getting more stock, and Palmer hasn't any birds worth taking out of the bag. Moran's aren't bad, but with nothing worth fighting against it's poor sport.' His eyes brightened suddenly. 'There's a dogfight though, out towards Painted Post.'

'A dogfight?' Tim drew back a little. There had been plenty of dogfights in the year he had been in Corning, but he'd always managed to avoid them. Fighting cocks, he could just stomach – but dogs, animals that many people kept as pets and friends, set to fight and tear each other to pieces, were something else. He glanced at Pierre and saw a light in the Frenchman's eyes.

'A dogfight? Now that's even better. And where is this painted post? Is it easy to find?'

Andrew laughed. 'It's the next town from Corning. I guess it's called that because of that old monument the Iroquois left there – it's gone now, but they say it was covered with pictures of bodies, a lot of them without heads. Pretty gruesome! There's a kind of a weathervane now, of an old Indian chief dressed in feathers and such. Anyway, you don't have to look for that. The dogfight'll be this side of the town.'

'Will you be going?' Pierre asked eagerly. 'It's a long time since I saw a good dogfight.'

'Sure, I don't mind going,' Andrew said easily. 'And I bet Tim'll be glad to come along.' He gave Timothy a mischievous glance. 'We've never managed to get him to a dogfight,' he confided. 'Seen him look a bit sick after one or two of the mains, so this'll do him good. Make a man of him, yeah?'

'Oh, it will do that,' Pierre agreed with a slow smile. 'Yes, it will certainly do that.'

It seemed that the whole male population of Painted Post and Corning combined must have decided to go to the dog-fight that evening.

Timothy, still wishing that he could find some excuse not to attend, climbed down from the cab that Pierre and Andrew had hired and looked around him. The field was crowded. They would never get near enough to see any-thing, he thought hopefully, and was just about to suggest that they return and have a game of billiards instead, when he saw that there were several 'pits', each with a small knot of men gathered around it. The apparently formless, mill-ing crowd was broken up into a number of groups, each watching a separate fight.

'That'll be the best one, over there!' Andrew shouted above the noise. 'Jack Dooley – he breeds some real scorchers. Come on!'

Pierre looked round at Timothy, his eyes gleaming. His face was darker than ever tonight, suffused with excite-ment, his eyes reddened in the sultry glow of the torches that were placed around the pits, even though darkness had not yet fallen. Around them sounded the shouts of men placing bets, and Timothy could already hear the whining of the dogs. He felt sweat break out on his forehead and knew that he didn't want to be here. But Pierre was urging him on and, just as he had been unable to break away from his friends at the cockfights, so he was unable now to stand free of Pierre.

'Come on, Timothy,' Pierre said, and his mouth quirked almost as if in challenge. 'Let us introduce you to the gentlemanly sport of dogfighting.'

The pit was actually a ring, its low wall formed of stones and sacks. Inside, it was scattered with fresh sawdust from the timber yard. There seemed to be very little difference between this and a cockfight; the setters were already in position, their dogs muzzled and held tightly apart, while around them the punters were placing their final bets.

'That's Dooley,' Andrew said, indicating a short, wiry-looking man with black hair streaked across a balding skull. 'See that terrier – he's a real killer. I've seen him fight before.'

Timothy looked at the dog Dooley was holding. He was a blunt-nosed, surly-looking beast with long scars running down his face and a torn ear. His lips were drawn back in a snarl as he glared at his opponent and Timothy could see that he was already straining to be free. My God, he thought, what do they do to these animals to make them hate each other so? He thought of his Aunt Sarah's dog at home, who would roll over at a word, and sit up to beg for titbits. And Martha Robinson's two Pekinese, who would sometimes scrap wildly for no apparent reason, only to be found minutes later curled up together in blissful contentment.

Dooley's terrier looked as if he had never known bliss in his life. And neither did the dog he was about to fight, a burly, growling bruiser of an animal who looked ready to bite off the hand of his owner himself, should he be so unwary as to let him get near enough. What joy was there in owning dogs like these, in driving them to such snapping, angry loathing of everything that lived?

'My money's on Dooley's brute,' Andrew said in a judicious tone. 'What d'you think, Pierre?'

'I'm not so sure. The other one looks fierce enough . . . Perhaps I will wait and see which comes best out of this fight. Do they fight again tonight?'

'If they can stand,' Andrew said with a grin. 'Or if they live . . . No, they don't usually fight twice in a night. Now's your only chance, if you fancy either of them.'

'Well, then, I will back the other and we shall see who's right.' Pierre looked at Timothy. 'And you?'

Tim shook his head. He was feeling slightly sick. He wanted to get out of here, to leave the whole crowd behind, to get back to the cool comfort of Cordelia's parlour or the shabby homeliness of Grainne's house. But he was held by the awareness that both Andrew and Pierre were waiting for him to do just that; by the feeling that if he did, it would confirm something about himself in their minds, something he didn't want confirmed.

'I won't back anything this time,' he said, stammering slightly. 'I'll wait – wait and see.'

Andrew smiled slightly but said nothing. He went off to place his bet and Pierre fixed his dark eyes on Timothy's face.

'It is nothing, this,' he said, waving his hand at the crowd, the pit, the snarling, snapping dogs. 'It is just part of being a man, you know? There are other parts too, that you might find more enjoyable.'

Timothy reddened. 'I'm not a child, Pierre,' he said sharply. 'I do know what life is about.'

'Oh, I am sure . . . but we all have much to learn, you will agree. And to learn a little, we have to experience a lot.' He gave Timothy a sudden grin that gave him, in the flare of the torches, a satyr-like look. 'Perhaps later on we'll experience something different, yes?'

Timothy remembered the cockfights he had attended with the others, how they had so often ended with a search for excitement of a different kind. As if the brutality of the fight woke dark desires that lay dormant at all other times, but demanded satisfaction. It was a satisfaction that had left him feeling soiled and ashamed, and it was that as much as a distaste for watching two birds reduce each other to a pile of blood-soaked feathers that had finally caused him to stop going.

And this, he knew, was going to be worse, much worse. He looked at the dogs, slavering now in their dreadful eagerness to get at each other, and he listened to the animal noises of the crowd, and he felt the familiar, sickening excitement rise in his own breast. And he knew that it was only his own weakness that kept him there, between Andrew and Pierre, watching. He knew that real courage lay in simply walking away; and he could not do it.

Afterwards, he could never believe that it had been so quick. It seemed at the time to go on almost eternally – the growing murmurs of anticipation from the crowd, the snarling of the dogs as they were finally let loose, jaws agape after their confinement in the steel-banded muzzles, the roar that went up at the first sight of blood. Tim watched, unable to look away, as the two terriers went straight for each other's throats, twisting and snapping as they tried simultaneously to evade the other's teeth while getting their own buried in an exposed neck. Within seconds, blood was staining the fresh sawdust of the pit; the torn ear of Dooley's dog was ripped away completely and tossed to the side of the ring, where an onlooker quickly snatched it up as a souvenir. The air was filled with the yelps and growls of the two protagonists, with the howling of a crowd who seemed themselves to be reduced to brutes, with the smell of fresh blood and of human excitement.

Timothy stood rigid. His own blood thundered in his ears. He was sick and dizzy. He could not bear to watch what was happening in the pit, yet he could not look away. He felt condemned to watch every last writhing tussle, every kick, every bite. And as Dooley's terrier finally staggered under the last vicious snap of his opponent's jaws and collapsed under a fountain of blood that sprayed from his throat to reach even the men who crouched yelling around the low stone wall, he felt his gorge rise and turned away, blindly seeking a way out, his need to stay with Pierre and Andrew forgotten, desperate to escape the horror of the scene that excited every man about him to a fervour that was both nauseating and terrifying.

He found his way to the edge of the field and knelt in the brown, trodden grass, retching painfully. He no longer cared what Pierre thought of him. He looked up at the sky, cleared of smoke now, a few stars pricking its pale evening twilight. A fresh wave of sickness rolled over him and he groaned and retched again. When it was over, he lay down in a shivering huddle, thankful for the creeping darkness.

He could still hear the shouts of the men at the pits. Presumably Pierre and Andrew were still among them, still assessing the straining dogs as they were held up to each other, taunted and excited to make them fight more viciously. Presumably they were still discussing which was the better choice to back, which was likely to survive.

Timothy didn't care any more. He got up slowly and stumbled across the tussocky grass. He looked for a cab and felt in his pockets for some money for the fare.

His pockets were empty. At some point during the evening, someone had stolen everything that was in them. He would either have to wait for Pierre and Andrew, or walk back to Corning.

A howl of delight went up from the field and he knew that another dog had given up the struggle. He turned away, and began the long walk home.

The memory of Pierre's face, dark with excitement, his

eyes glittering with anticipation, his lips wet as if he too were slavering with the desire to savage an opponent, returned to haunt him as he walked slowly along the road. And he thought uncomfortably of Cordelia, who had seemed several times lately as if she might be growing fond of their French cousin.

He had been pleased to think that there might be a closeness between them, that it might develop into something deeper. Cordelia and Pierre . . . there was a good deal to be said for it. The completion of a circle, the satisfactory ending to a story. But now . . .

He walked along the dusty road, between the high, wooded hills towards Corning. And tried to forget what he had seen looking out of Pierre's eyes.

Chapter Eighteen

In England that summer, they were talking of trouble in South Africa and it seemed that Britain would go to war against the Boers. The century was drawing to a close and surely the life of old Queen Victoria must close with it? There was an air of excitement, a wondering anticipation at what a new era might bring. With telephones that enabled people to talk to each other over long distances, motor-cars that made travel faster than ever before, and now even talk of flying, who knew what the twentieth century might bring? Writers like Jules Verne and H G Wells tried to imagine, and to communicate their ideas through their stories, but the idea of travelling through space to the planets remained no more than an amusing entertainment for most people.

Harry Henzel, returning to Stourbridge with Ruth after their travels through Europe, was more inclined to take them seriously.

'Flight's bound to come,' he declared, reminding Christina of the day – could it really be over fifty years ago? – when he had told her of his own ambitions to work on railways, his young face alight with enthusiasm as he declared that they were the transport of the future and would revolutionise the country. As indeed they had, she admitted, thinking of the first time she had sent a consignment of Henzel Crystal by rail to London. She had been the first local glassmaker to make full use of the new transport, and it had given her an edge over her competitors – the edge she never stopped seeking, always striving to keep one step ahead of them and usually succeeding.

Now, however, she looked at her brother with amusement, still seeing the boyishness behind the grey beard and white hair, the spark of excitement that some new development in engineering had always been able to bring to the bright blue eyes.

'Flight? Are you sure? But the pictures I've seen of the craft men are making – they look so flimsy. They can't even support a human body – how could they ever be put to any real use?'

'You're just looking at the beginning,' he said doggedly. 'Flight hasn't even reached its infancy yet – it hasn't been born. But it will be. Within – well, let's say within five years – someone will make a machine fly. And once they've discovered the secret, there's no reason why they won't be able to build bigger and better flying machines. Machines that can carry men all over the world, flying faster than any ship can sail. Wait and see!'

'And I suppose,' Joe said from the chair where he spent much of his time now, 'you'll tell us next they'll be flying to the Moon. Like people keep writing about in stories. Lot of nonsense!'

'Well, so it may be, but there could be a grain of truth in it,' Harry said. 'Once we can fly – why shouldn't we go out into space? To the Moon – even to Mars and the other planets. The stars themselves! There'll be no stopping man once he has wings.' His eyes sparkled and Christina was reminded again of the small boy, building dams in the stream, constructing mills, drawing railways and engines, talking with awe of his idol, Brunel.

'Well, I reckon we're going to have to wait a long time before we see that,' Joe grunted. 'Longer'n I've got, anyway.' He lifted himself slowly from his chair and reached for his stick. 'Do something useful with that new-fangled contraption you've got outside the door. Drive me down to the cone. There's something I want to check up on.'

Harry glanced at Christina doubtfully but, although her eyes were anxious as she watched Joe's slow progress across the room, she gave no sign. He got to his feet and went to open the door for his brother-in-law, and Christina turned to the woman who had once been her maid and had become her dearest friend even before marriage had related them.

'You can see that Joe is failing,' she said quietly, and Ruth's soft eyes were filled with tears as she nodded. 'He grows slower every day and complains of a pain in his back, under his left shoulder. It frightens me.'

'I've noticed how short of breath he is at times,' Ruth said sadly. 'Yet you still allow him to go to the glasshouse. And the atmosphere alone –'

'It's his life. How can I confine him here, like a prisoner? As long as he is still able, I shall allow – no, *encourage* – him to go. You see, I understand him. I know what he would like.' Christina's voice faltered a little. 'He would like to die in the cone, with a blowing iron in his hands. And I should like it for him.' She looked down suddenly, staring at her small hands, no longer the smooth hands of a young girl but wrinkled now with age. 'So each time he goes to the glasshouse, I know that he may not return alive.'

Ruth sat silent, shocked by Christina's calm acceptance yet understanding it. She had known her brother for too long, even though they had been parted for many years, to think that he would want to die peacefully in bed. No, as Christina said, the glasshouse was his life, always had been. It was there that he would wish to die, amongst the men he knew and understood, doing the work he had excelled in for so many years. And she understood, too, why Christina accompanied him to the cones so often. She wanted to be there when it finally happened.

'I almost wish we were not returning to America at all,' she said quietly. 'Now that we've made this long journey and seen all the things we've wanted to see, I believe I could settle again in Stourbridge, with you and Joe. But Harry wants to go back, I know. He's lived too long in America to accept the English way of life again. It's too slow for him, too cramped.' She smiled. 'He's still as full of life as ever, still eager for new things, especially when they are to do with engines. That's why he does so well in America – they're as keen as he is. In England, people are slower to accept change.'

'That's true – I remember the difficulties I had with the glassmakers whenever I wanted to try something new. And that's why Timothy is doing well there, too – because he had the same difficulties here. I know that now. He was right to go, even though it hurt us so much at the time. And I believe it was, after all, the saving of Emily's reason – while Tim was here, she would never have accepted Paul's death. All the same . . .' Christina looked wistful. 'I wonder if he will ever come back, he and Cordelia. They've been there over a year now and I'm afraid . . . I wonder sometimes if we'll ever see them again.'

'Emily is completely recovered now, isn't she? She seems well and happy, as strong as ever.'

'Oh yes, she's quite better. Out campaigning somewhere now, I've no doubt! This issue of votes for women is beginning to take up all her time – she says it's at the core of every other issue, that nothing else can be achieved without it and until women have the vote, nothing else is worth fighting for. Whether she's right or not, I don't know – I've always managed to achieve whatever I set out to do, even though I encountered a great deal of opposition from men. But I do see that many women have quite dreadful problems.'

402

'And quite dreadful husbands,' Ruth observed. 'We've been lucky, Christina.'

'Yes.' But as Christina looked thoughtfully at her friend's serene face, it struck her that they had had two very different marriages. Ruth was the conventional wife, meek, submissive, content to follow her husband wherever he might decree they should go. She hadn't wanted to go America all those years ago, but she had packed up her home and gone, happy so long as she was with Harry.

She had accepted his decisions without question, and she had been fortunate in that he loved her as much as she loved him, that he was kind and caring. Not all wives, however submissive, were as blessed.

For Christina, marriage had been quite different. Christina would never have submitted to her husband's decrees. Independent and self-willed from childhood, she had always been determined to go her own way. And although she had married a man as strong-minded as she was herself, a marriage which most people had thought doomed from the beginning – for wasn't Joe Compson nothing more than a common workman in her own glass-house, skilled at blowing though he might be? – she had, almost without knowing it, chosen one of the few men who would treat her as an equal, simply because, to him, that was exactly what he was.

Their marriage had been stormy enough at times. But they had never tried to dominate each other, and their quarrels had soon been resolved, with a passion that made them almost worthwhile.

The thought that it might soon all be over, that Joe's slowness, the aches he complained of, the moments of forgetfulness he suffered, were signs that couldn't be ignored, brought her a deep sadness. But Christina had never yet refused to face reality; and she faced it now with the same defiant courage that she had faced every other crisis in her life.

'I think,' Pierre remarked as he and Cordelia strolled along the woodland paths on the hill above Corning, 'that it must have been Destiny that brought us both here.'

She looked up at him. He looked like a gipsy today, a red scarf knotted carelessly round his neck, his black hair flying wild in the breeze. His eyes were intense, snapping with energy, and his teeth flashed white in his dark face as he smiled down at her.

Cordelia felt the familiar quickening of her heartbeat, the tingle over her skin. All through the summer, she had been aware of a growing tension in the relationship between herself and this strange French cousin. Now, with the cooling autumn weather turning the leaves to a blaze of glory around their heads, she sensed that they were reaching a turning-point. She was half excited, half afraid; she wanted both to draw back and to go on.

'Destiny?' she said, trying to keep her voice light. 'How do you mean?'

Pierre stopped and turned to her. He took both her hands in his and gazed down into her face, his eyes steady, his smile gone to leave a gravity that startled her. She felt a tremor deep inside and wanted to pull her hands away, but did not dare. There was a sense of hidden power about Pierre, a hint of danger, that both frightened and attracted her.

'Why else should we both come to Corning?' he asked in a low voice. 'Why else should you and Tim have come to the circus that night and seen me working? Why else should I have recognised him immediately, seen the likeness between him and your father and known he must be a Henzel?'

'Coincidences do happen –' Cordelia began, but he

shook his head and his fingers tightened almost cruelly on hers.

'It was Destiny. We were meant to find each other, Cordelia.' He drew her closer. 'Don't pretend that you don't know it's true.'

Cordelia shook her head. She felt weak, almost dizzy. Pierre's gaze held hers and she could not look away; she was aware only of the glowing bronze of the leaves above them, blazing like the jaws of an open furnace, and of Pierre's intense face, his black eyes smouldering into hers.

'Cordelia,' he murmured, 'don't you think it is time we both stopped pretending? Don't we know each other well enough, after all these months, to be honest?'

He drew her hands up against his chest and held them there. She could feel the steady beating of his heart, the rise and fall of his powerful lungs. He pressed her palms against him and she felt the warmth of his body through the jacket he wore. The muscles of his chest were hard under her trembling fingers.

'Pierre . . .'

He looked at her for a moment longer, and his eyes softened. He released her hands from the iron grip he had taken on them, keeping his fingers loosely entwined with hers as he let them fall back to her sides. His mouth relaxed into a smile.

'I'm sorry, Cordelia. I'm frightening you, I think. I didn't mean to do that. Let's walk a little further and find somewhere to sit down for a while, and then I'll tell you just what I mean.'

Still trembling a little, Cordelia allowed him to lead her on through the wood. There were several paths here, cleared by animals and widened by hunters, used often by strollers who liked to walk in the shade of the trees on hot summer days, or through drifts of snow in the winter.

Cordelia had been here with Timothy during their first winter, when they had walked briskly in the biting cold air, marvelling at bare branches that glittered with ice, or trees that stood like giant ostrich feathers, coated with frozen snow.

She had been here with Jensen, too. They had wandered these paths just as she and Pierre were doing now; they had picked sprays of copper-coloured leaves to take home, had gathered nuts to roast on the fire, had once built a snowman for Karin's delight. But those days were past; she rarely saw Jensen now, though Ginette had told her he was as frequent a visitor as ever in the afternoons.

Once again, Cordelia was thankful that the summer was over. She had still not become accustomed to the heat that Corning could suffer during the months of July and August, and longed for coolness. Jensen had installed electric fans in his house and she wished they could have them in the house she and Timothy still rented, but the landlord was reluctant to incur the expense. Even opening the windows didn't help, since the air outside was as hot as – or even hotter than – that indoors. The only coolness to be found was up in the woods, and the climb up the hill to reach them was almost too much on a hot day.

She had also been suffering again from homesickness, longing desperately for the dust and smoke of Stourbridge, the bustle of the streets and the noise of the factories. She read the letters that came from home over and over again, devouring every scrap of news. Mother was better now, campaigning again and involving herself deeply in the 'Votes for Women' issue. Grandmother was as active as ever, her letters long and filled with news about the glasshouse, about Ben Taylor and his son Frank, about the new glass Webbs were making and the new electric tramway that had been opened between Stourbridge and Dudley. An art school had been opened in Wordsley, with Frederick Carder as its chief instructor in glass-making. Carder had won gold medals with his glass and had become prominent in Stourbridge, Christina wrote, and Cordelia sensed that she was wishing that it could have been Timothy who was there, making a name for himself. When would they return and take up their inheritance in England? Why were they staying so long in this small American town?

But Timothy was not yet ready to leave. He was still working on Damascene, bringing it to the perfection he demanded of all his glass, and he was developing other ideas too. And Cordelia doubted now if he would ever be ready. She was beginning to believe that Tim, like Harry, had found fulfilment with the American way of life. England would cramp him now.

And herself? Would she go home if Timothy decided to stay? Would the homesickness she so often felt be strong enough to tear her away from the life she had built up here? Or was she also too tightly bound now to this fascinating and vibrant country, and the people in it?

Pierre led her without speaking along the broad path, spread now with a sunburnt carpet of tawny leaves, dappled with sunlight to shades of cinnamon and gold. His hand still clasped hers, loosely enough for her to withdraw if she wished; but she found that she didn't want to leave the warmth of the large, strong fingers that interlaced so closely and comfortingly with her own. It was easier, with Pierre's hand palm to palm with hers, to shut out those memories of other days spent wandering in these woods, with a man who was tall and lean, with hair the colour of sunlight and eyes that glinted as blue as the summer sky. It was easier, when Pierre looked at her and her heart thudded with an excitement that was at least partly fear, to forget those other moments when another man had held her in his arms and kissed her with tenderness and love . . .

'Here,' Pierre said, and indicated a fallen log, as broad as a sofa, lying beside the path on a carpet of thick green moss. 'Let's sit down for a few moments, Cordelia.'

Still uncertain, she sat on the log, spreading her skirt carefully around her. Pierre sat down beside her. He took her hand in his and looked earnestly into her eyes.

'I know I frightened you just now,' he said again. 'It wasn't intentional – but I wonder, Cordelia, if you have any idea what it means to be a man? Subject to such passions – a prey to such desires. Do women ever feel the same intensity of emotion, I wonder? Can they – can you – ever understand what drives a man to such despair that he could willingly kill himself, knowing that he can never have what he so ardently desires?'

Cordelia blinked. Pierre's voice was low and impassioned, almost like that of an actor in the plays she had seen in the Corning Opera House. He spoke rapidly, as if he had rehearsed his speech many times. Yet she could not look into those burning eyes and doubt his sincerity. She did not know what to say.

'Cordelia, don't you know what I am trying to tell you? Don't you understand even now what is in my heart? For over four months now we've lived in the same house, meeting each day, eating our meals at the same table. Can you look into my eyes this afternoon and say that you don't understand – that you don't feel it, too?' He lifted her chin with his fingertips, so that she was forced to meet his gaze. 'Can you?' he repeated softly.

'Pierre . . .'

'Tell me you understand,' he insisted, still in that low, fervent tone. 'Tell me, Cordelia.'

His hands gripped hers again, tightly, and she felt once more the quick spasm of fear. Her fingers twisted in his and instantly he loosened his grasp, smiling ruefully. 'There, I'm doing it again – going too fast, frightening you. But I can't help myself, Cordelia. Ever since that first evening when I saw you there in the darkness of the circus ground, watching me . . . I've wanted to say to you all that is in my heart. Can you blame me that the waiting has been too much for me?'

Cordelia swallowed. Her heart seemed to be leaping in her throat. She tried to speak but found no words. Pierre was gazing at her with an intensity she found herself unable to meet. She looked away, at the branches that dipped around them, at the coppery leaves around their feet, at the hands that still imprisoned her own.

Pierre waited. She knew she must speak. At last, she found her voice, though it was little more than a breath as she began to answer him.

'Pierre . . . you ask me to say that I understand, but I don't think I can. I don't know what – what you're saying. I don't even know how *I* feel – how can I tell what your feelings might be? I'm afraid I –' she faltered and added at last in a voice so low she could scarcely hear it herself – 'I *am* afraid.'

She heard Pierre sigh and whisper something in French. Then he dropped her hands and laid large, gentle palms on her shoulders. As she looked up at him, he drew her into his arms, as tenderly as if she had been a delicate child, and with one hand pressed her head softly against his shoulder.

'My poor Cordelia! What am I doing to you? Why, you're trembling, just like a frightened bird. And it is all my fault – so clumsy, so selfish, thinking only of myself.' He lifted her face and looked down into it, his eyes now soft and melting, as brown and warm as the shifting leaves that still clung to the trees around them. 'But you have no need to fear me,' he said softly. 'I am Pierre, your cousin, who loves you.'

Cordelia's lips parted a little. She could feel the strength of his sturdy body, the breadth of his chest, the thick sinews of his arms. In his arms, she felt fragile, dependent. With one movement, he could snap her in two. Or, if he chose, handle her as tenderly as he handled the brittle glass from which he could fashion such delicate shapes.

'Yes,' he said quietly. 'Your cousin, who loves you. But not simply as a cousin. You know that, Cordelia, don't you? They say a woman always does. And you must have known for a long time now what is my feeling for you – how deep, how true. You know that you have my heart.'

She shook her head helplessly. 'I didn't – I couldn't – how could I even dream of such a thing –'

'I think you have dreamed of very little else,' he murmured, his hand against her cheek keeping her face turned up to him. '*Chérie*, I've seen it in your eyes – the knowledge that you have in your heart, yet try so hard not to believe. Why don't you want to believe it, Cordelia? Why do you deny what is happening between us?'

She began to shake her head again, but before she could utter a sound he had bent his head to hers and laid his mouth over her parted lips. She felt her heart leap, and tried instinctively to twist her head aside, but Pierre's hand was firm on her cheek and his other arm was close around her shoulders, holding her against him. His mouth was warm against her lips, parting them and shaping them with gentle insistence, and after a moment Cordelia felt the longing that had been a part of her for so long crystallise into a hard, leaping desire. Her body relaxed in Pierre's arms and she felt the tightening of his arms as he gathered her more closely against him and his kiss deepened. Cordelia felt her hands creep up his chest, her arms wind themselves about his neck. It was as if her body had taken control, as if reason had no part in this, thinking no place. Only the senses were involved now, only touch and pressure were important, and the closeness of one human body to another.

Pierre explored her mouth with lips and tongue and teeth, letting his tongue caress hers with a rhythmic sensuousness that had her weak and gasping. His fingers were in her hair now, loosening the pins that held it swept up, his palm cupping her slender neck. She felt the bronze cloud descend to her shoulders and put up her hand, half laughing, half dismayed.

'Pierre, what are you doing? I can't go home like this.'

'You can't go home at all yet,' he murmured, and set his lips on hers again. Cordelia let her mouth respond, softening under his, returning his kiss. His hand was on her breast, tightening on the fullness, and even through the clothes she wore, Cordelia could feel the pressure of his fingers, the excitement of his touch.

She strained against him, knowing that this was what she had wanted for so long. Ever since the first time Jensen had kissed her, her body had clamoured for the release of turbulent emotions and desires that she had barely recognised. Night after night she had lain in bed, tortured by a need for something she could not name, knowing only that to think of Jensen could bring release for a while, only to be followed by an increase in the torment. She had recalled his kisses over and over again, reliving each one, holding on to the sensation that they still produced in her. And she had been left with an increased yearning, a growingly desperate longing, until she wished that she had never met him.

And then Pierre had come. Pierre, with the dark eyes and the smouldering glance that had seemed to promise something, yet had made her feel strangely afraid. As if he knew some dark secret; as if he wielded some black and terrifying power.

But afraid though she had been, Cordelia had been drawn to him, fascinated as a rabbit is fascinated by a snake or a stoat. And his magnetism had overridden her fear, so that it was now as often Pierre that she thought of in bed as it was Jensen. And it was Pierre who haunted her dreams with his dark satyr's face and his brooding eyes.

He withdrew from her a little and looked down again, his eyes searching hers. A little shyly, she returned his gaze and saw his lips curve in a smile.

'My little one. It is as if you had been waiting for me.'

'Perhaps I have,' she whispered, and laid her head against his breast.

'And isn't that exactly what I said just now? It is Destiny which has brought us together, Cordelia – it must be. Why else should we both travel half-way across the world to this little town? Why else should we meet? Our families have been bound together for generations – your grandmother and grandfather were Henzel and Thietry, your father and mother the same. There is something, some force that decrees that we should be together – we can't deny it, Cordelia. Why should we try?'

Shaken by his passion, she looked up at him again. He was staring into the trees, his eyes blazing with a force of emotion that shook her to the heart. She quivered against him, and felt his arms respond, holding her more closely. For a moment, she felt imprisoned and moved uneasily in his grasp, and again Pierre's arms tightened.

'Pierre – please. I can hardly breathe.'

He looked down at her, almost as if startled to find her there, as if his thoughts had been far away. Then he smiled and relaxed.

'My poor Cordelia. What a brute I am, to crush you so. But you will forgive me, I know – it is simply because I can scarcely believe that we're here together like this. I've dreamed so often of holding you in my arms . . . I never believed it would really come true.' He stroked back her flowing hair and she felt the strength in his hand as it touched her neck. 'You'll be mine, won't you, my little one?' he murmured. 'You *are* mine . . .'

Cordelia stirred again. Something in Pierre's throbbing tone disturbed her, yet she could not deny the excitement that still tingled in her blood, making her turn her face to his again, lips parted for his kiss. As his hand moved over her body, she twisted against him, longing to feel his fingers on her breast, and when he caressed her she quivered sharply and moaned. For a moment, his hand tightened, almost convulsively, and she gasped with sudden pain; yet when he released her she felt a sense of loss.

'Pierre . . .'

Gently, he put her away from him. He was smiling oddly as he looked down at her imploring face, and his fingers touched her cheek almost in admonition.

'No, my sweet. That is enough. We must keep control of our senses – delightful though it would be to give way to them. I am older than you, I know how these things can be. One loses all sanity . . . But our time will come. I promise you that.'

He raised her to her feet. The afternoon sun had sunk low in the sky and a blue twilight crept through the trees. Soon it would be dark; already the woodland animals, the racoons and the foxes, were stirring in the undergrowth, while the birds were beginning to roost above. A russet leaf drifted down and landed at Cordelia's feet. Pierre bent and picked it up.

'I would give you jewels if I had them,' he said, offering it to her. 'But since I have not, here's a jewel of the forest to remind you that you have my heart. And –' he bent again – 'another for me, to remind me of the colour of your hair. Leave it loose like that, Cordelia. It's a cloud of glory around your head.'

Silently, she took the leaf and tucked its stalk through the buttonhole of her jacket. She could find no words to thank him. Her eyes brimmed and she slipped her hand into his, comforted by its warm strength.

As they walked slowly down the hill and back to the twinkling lights of Corning, she allowed herself one fleeting thought of Jensen. She tightened her clasp on Pierre's hand and, when they stopped at the edge of the wood for one last kiss, she invested it with all the frustrated passion that her heart contained.

It was not to be supposed that their new relationship should go unnoticed.

Ginette's sharp eyes saw it at once. She took one look at them as they came home from that Saturday afternoon walk, and a curious smile curved her lips before she gave Pierre a quick, almost questioning glance. Cordelia felt her colour rise and turned away hastily, murmuring something about tea, and Tim glanced up from the *Corning Daily Journal*.

'What's up, sis? You look a bit queer.'

She gave him a swift, furious flash of her eyes. Really – did Tim have to be so obtuse? Couldn't he see she didn't want to explain anything right now? She sometimes wondered whether being her twin meant anything at all to him these days – he seemed to have no more understanding of her than any other brother might. Perhaps the bond between them was something they were growing out of. If that were so, it would mean she was free – free to go back to England if she wanted to. Free to leave Corning, and Jensen Novak, and to take up her own life once again.

She turned and met Pierre's dark, brooding gaze, and remembrance jerked back. Pierre! How could she have forgotten, even for that brief second, what had happened up in the forest – the kisses they had exchanged, the vows . . . She frowned. *Had* they actually exchanged vows? She felt

414

vaguely conscious of a promise of some kind being assumed. But nothing had been definitely said. And, glancing at Tim again, she knew that until it had been, she wanted no one to know. It was still too new, too delicate; a secret between her and Pierre.

She ignored Timothy's tactless question and went to stir the fire. The evenings were chilly now and Ginette felt the cold, even swathed as she was in coverlets of soft, fine wool. As Cordelia stared at the coals, Pierre lit one of the lamps and she was reminded suddenly of twilit evenings back home in Henzel Court, with the velvet curtains drawn to make a rich glow of colour over the windows, and the room lit by leaping flames.

'They'll be having muffins for tea now,' she said, half to herself. 'The man will have come round the streets, ringing his bell, and the maid will have run out to buy a plateful. Grandmother will toast them at the fire, she always does, and Mark will butter them for her. And Grandfather will eat far too many and then complain of indigestion, and Mother will scold him for bringing it on himself. And they'll wonder what we're doing here and if we're thinking of them.' She brushed away a tear and added firmly, 'And of course, I know they won't be doing any of those things at this very minute, because the time's different – they'll have done them already, hours ago. And muffins are different in England from the ones we have here. But we could still make toast.' She looked round at the little group. 'I'd like to make toast this evening,' she said, and could not restrain the longing in her tone.

Later, as they sat amongst the crumbs and finished the tea that even Ginette had consented to drink, Pierre announced that he intended to go away.

Cordelia turned in quick consternation. 'Go away? But where? Why?'

'Only for a few days,' he reassured her, and she glanced at the other two, wondering if they had noticed her reaction. Tim, still licking butter from his fingers, looked mildly surprised by Pierre's announcement but Ginette was smiling her strange, curving smile, as if she had known already what he was going to say.

Yet he had said nothing to Cordelia, and she felt a tiny pang of hurt which she quickly thrust away.

'Where are you going?' she asked again.

'New York. You know we lived there for some time, and we made friends there. One of them – an old man now – has sent for me to go and see him. He's dying and knows it, and he wants to say goodbye.' Pierre smiled sadly. 'I can't refuse him that. I shall only be away for a few days – three or four, at the most.' He gave her an apologetic glance. 'I shall have to ask you to take care of Ginette for me. And Tim – it means taking time off from the glasshouse, but you will manage without me, I know. I am no more than a very small cog in the machine, after all.'

'A useful one, though,' Tim said. 'But now that Damascene has been perfected and we haven't started work on the new glass, it's not a bad time to be away.' He turned to Cordelia, his eyes alight. 'We're going to make Grandmother's Chalice next week. Everything's ready, I've done the design and Dailey's had a couple of practice blowings. It's going to be a fine piece.'

'That's wonderful,' she said warmly. 'And, Tim, it would be a fine opportunity for something I've wanted to do for some time – bring my children along to watch something really special being blown. Could I do that? Dailey wouldn't mind, would he?'

'Well, I guess not,' Tim said, slightly taken aback. 'The whole school, d'you mean? How many are there – forty, fifty?'

416

'About forty,' she answered, laughing a little. 'And there's no need to look so scared! They'll behave themselves – why, a good many of them have fathers and brothers already working in the glasshouse, so they won't get up to any mischief. And if they do, I shan't allow them to come to the Hallowe'en party we're having at the end of the week.'

Ginette lifted herself a little on her sofa. 'Do let them go, Tim. And I shall come as well, if someone will carry me. I've never seen a piece of glass being blown, and to watch a piece so *exceptionelle* – it will be a special treat for me too.'

Tim looked at Ginette and coloured a little.

'Well, of course, if you would really like to. But it's not very pleasant in the glasshouse – it's dirty and noisy and –'

'I shall enjoy it,' she said positively, and Pierre smiled, a glint in his eyes as he looked at her.

'So that is settled,' he said. 'I shall go to New York and you will all watch the blowing of this special chalice. And at the end of the week, a Hallowe'en party will be held at the school. It seems we are all to be busy. And at the end of it all – who knows what might have happened to us all?'

He laughed. But Cordelia, watching their faces as the other two joined in, felt a cold trickle of fear. It was as if Pierre's words had been some kind of incantation – a calling on some strange, dark power that could intercede in all their lives. What *would* have happened to them all by the end of the week? What could?

She shook herself angrily. You're getting superstitious, she thought. Nothing will happen. Nothing at all.

Chapter Nineteen

The fine autumn weather began to change on the day that Pierre left to go to New York. Low, heavy-bellied clouds rolled across the sky, bringing with them a dull menace that seemed to creep into every corner of the town. Even Market Street, with its electric tramway and bright lights, seemed deserted and people looked up anxiously at the sky and talked of the disastrous floods of other years.

'But we won't get that old river floodin' up again like it used to,' Martha Robinson prophesied confidently. 'Why, since they finished the dikes a couple of years back, we ain't had no trouble at all. Even the Monkey Run's no more'n a trickle these days.'

'Well, it's been uncommon dry lately,' Bob agreed doubtfully. 'But I dunno – seems to me they're a whole lot too pleased with themselves over those new dikes. I reckon they could give way if we had a real downpour.'

'You!' Martha said, giving him a little push. 'You're always ready to look on the black side. Now, you jes' take those dogs out for their walk, Bob Robinson, and stop lookin' for excuses to stay indoors – a little drop of rain won't melt any of us away.'

'I'd better go now, too,' Cordelia said, putting on her coat. 'I'll walk along with you, Bob. I've got a lot to do to prepare for the party.'

'Hallowe'en!' Martha said. 'Reckon all the kids are gettin' some excited, aren't they? Witches' hats and broomsticks and all that – they love it. And the pumpkin lanterns – hope you've got the pumpkins ready, Cordelia.'

Cordelia smiled. She had bought two immense pumpkins for the party, and for the next week the children would be busily occupied in making witches' hats and cloaks from black paper, and sticking shiny silver stars all over them. The classroom was taking on a sinister atmosphere, with string cobwebs festooning the corners and black cats leering from every wall. Cordelia wasn't at all sure that she liked this festival – it seemed to highlight all the grimmer aspects of superstition. But perhaps it was healthier than having the children huddle in corners, frightening themselves and each other with dark tales, and she was careful to take every opportunity of explaining that ghosts were mere figments of the imagination, and that witches were a thing of the past.

A few raindrops were beginning to fall as she walked along with Bob, and they both looked up at the sky.

'It certainly looks threatening,' Cordelia said with a shiver. 'And it's colder, too. Winter's beginning, Bob.'

'Sure is. Your second winter here. Heard any news of when Harry and Ruth might be comin' home?'

Cordelia felt a quick glow of pleasure. 'Yes – we had a letter this morning. They're hoping to sail in a week or two – they could be home by the end of November. Oh, it will be good to see them.'

'Good for us too,' he said. 'Seems a long time since they went away. Don't reckon they ever intended it to be so long to start with, but I guess they thought it'd be their last big trip and better make the most of it.'

'Yes. And with Grandfather getting old, I think they've been reluctant to leave.' Cordelia's face clouded a little. 'He doesn't seem to be at all well. I wish we could go home – but Tim is so busy, and since Uncle Harry and Aunt Ruth are just about to come back, it seems only sensible to wait a few more weeks, at least.' And there was

Pierre, too. Did she want to marry him? She was still haunted by thoughts of Jensen, of his tall figure, his corn-gold hair, his flashing smile. Of the way he had looked when he told her about his wife, about Karin. And the pain of that sent her swinging away like a pendulum, swinging towards Pierre.

If she married Pierre, she would have to stay in America. Or – perhaps – go to France. Unless he were to agree to go with her to England.

Well, there was little use in speculating. Pierre would be back from New York by the end of the week, and she could talk to him then. And perhaps her confusion would be at an end; she could look at him and see the truth, understand at last the dark desires that heated her blood and brought restlessness to her nights, and know whether they were indeed the desires of love.

The children were in a fever of excitement. All morning, they had been asking questions about the glassworks and the new Chalice, until at last Cordelia had been forced to abandon normal lessons and give them one on glassmaking instead. Since this involved drawings on the blackboard of the old cones still in use in England, the furnaces inside with the men working around them and a good many contributions from some of the children themselves, whose own fathers were glassmakers, the lesson lasted longer than she had intended and it was well past their usual lunch hour when the door opened and she glanced up to see Jensen standing there, watching her with a strange expression on his face. She felt her cheeks grow suddenly warm.

'Jensen! I didn't expect to see you.' She glanced swiftly at Karin, who was half on her feet, eyes alight at the unexpected treat of seeing her father in school. 'Sit down, please, Karin. We haven't had prayers yet.' What on earth was he doing here?

He came inside, his eyes on her burning face. 'I thought you might need some help shepherding this crowd over to the factory. How are you, Cordelia?'

'I'm well enough, thank you.' Her voice was stiff and she turned away, collecting up the chalk she had been using for her drawings. 'All right, children, you may stand for prayers and then eat your lunches at your desks. It's still raining outside, so I hope you've all brought coats and hats for the walk to the glasshouse.'

The children stood up and folded their hands. Cordelia nodded at Danny, whose turn it was to say the prayer for breaking up after morning school, and then watched as they sat down again and began to take out their small lunch pails, diminutive replicas of the growlers their fathers took to work. Those who went home for lunch scampered out of the door, with instructions from Cordelia to make sure they were back in good time, or they'd be left behind. For a few more minutes, she busied herself in wiping the blackboard clean and writing up some notes for tomorrow's lessons. At last, able to think of nothing further to do, she turned reluctantly back to Jensen, who was just setting his daughter back on her feet after the kiss she had claimed from him.

'I'm afraid you're rather early. As you see, our lessons went on a little longer than usual and the children haven't had lunch yet. In any case, I'm sure I can manage – we quite often go out on nature walks, as I'm sure Karin will have told you.' Her voice was polite but trembling, and she knew she was speaking too quickly. But it was so long since she had been as close as this to Jensen, and her heart was thudding rapidly. Almost against her will, she raised her eyes to his, unaware of the shimmering green depths that so clearly revealed her confusion.

'It's all right, Cordelia. I'm happy to wait.' He watched her curiously and then touched her arm. 'Come outside and talk to me for a little. It isn't raining now.' Karin was back in her seat, unpacking the lunch that Mary Sue had given her that morning and swapping it cheerfully for Danny's more robust hunk of bread and cheese.

'Do they always do that?' Jensen enquired.

'As often as not. I hope you don't mind – Karin does seem to enjoy Danny's doorsteps, and I don't believe she suffers from it. And he thinks himself nothing short of a prince, dining on the delicacies from Hill House.'

'He's a pleasant enough lad. He's been up to Hill House with his sister – Bridget, is it? – a few times. Your friend Grainne's doing a good job with them. Tim seems fond of her – any chance of a wedding there, d'you think?'

Cordelia followed him out to the steps. The clouds had broken, letting a little sunlight filter through. It glittered on the raindrops that hung from the trees and she caught flashes of diamond-bright colour, as if the hedges were decked with jewels.

'I hope so,' she said. 'Grainne's a lovely girl and suits Tim very well. But since Ginette came –'

'You think he's interested in Ginette?' he asked sharply, and she remembered his own afternoon visits to the Frenchwoman.

'I think most men are interested in Ginette, don't you?' she replied evenly. 'And Ginette enjoys their interest. After all, why not? She isn't likely ever to have anything more.'

'That isn't worthy of you,' Jensen said after a pause.

'Perhaps not. And perhaps I'm wrong – perhaps one day some man will feel more than a mere interest in her.' She looked up at him. Her momentary confusion had left her and she felt a cool anger with this man, who had played with her heart and then left her to find her own way. 'Perhaps you might do so yourself.'

'I?'

'Why not? You visit her often – you must have some reason. And you always make sure that I'm out of the house when you come.'

'You know why that is,' he said quietly, his eyes on the low white picket fence that surrounded the playground. 'I can't risk our being together too much.'

'I might ask why you're here now, then,' Cordelia retorted. 'Although I suppose forty children might conceivably be considered an adequate chaperone.'

Jensen sighed. 'Cordelia, let's leave this. I didn't come to discuss Ginette, or even you and me. I came –' he hesitated, his eyes on her face, and then went on, 'I'm sorry if you don't like this, but I have to say it. I came because of you and Pierre Thietry.'

Cordelia's head snapped back. She stared at him with eyes that suddenly blazed. 'Me and Pierre? What do you mean?'

His expression hardened. 'Don't pretend with me, Cordelia. I happened to be looking out of my bedroom window last Saturday afternoon, just before it got dark, and I saw the pair of you coming down the path from the woods. You looked half dazed, and he looked darned pleased with himself. It didn't take much imagination to figure out what had been going on and –'

'Going on?' Cordelia interrupted. 'And just what do you mean by that? What exactly do you think had been "going on"?'

'Look, your hair was down all over your shoulders and he looked like the cat that had the cream. If he hadn't been kissing you, I'm a monkey's uncle –'

'And suppose he had?' Cordelia broke in again. 'Is it any of your business, Jensen? Do you have any right to say whom I should or shouldn't kiss?'

He stared at her, his jaw tight. His dark blue eyes flickered for a moment and she had the impression that he was holding himself under control with difficulty. When he spoke again, his voice was taut, biting off the words.

'Don't speak to me like that, Cordelia. It's crude and unnecessary. I just don't want to see you make a fool of yourself with that – that charlatan –'

'I'd like to remind you that Pierre is my cousin –'

'Very distantly –'

'– and I take strong exception to your calling him a –'

'Charlatan. Well, you would, wouldn't you. No one likes to have their taste in either cousins or lovers called into dispute. But that's what he is, Cordelia, I'm telling you, and if you let him make love to you you're courting trouble.' He moved closer, laying his hand on her arm. 'Listen, I'm serious about this. That man is *trouble*. I've known it ever since he first came here. And I've a feeling you know it too, only you won't admit it. You're not in love with him, Cordelia. All right, maybe he excites you, but that's not love. That's something else.' He stopped and looked deep into her eyes and she stared back at him, unable to wrench her gaze away even though she knew that he was looking directly into her heart. 'You don't love Pierre Thietry,' he said quietly. 'You're afraid of him.'

Cordelia drew in her breath. Her blood thundered in her ears; she felt a wave of dizziness. Then she tore her arm away from Jensen's hand and backed towards the door. Her face was as white as marble, her green eyes brilliant against the pallor, and her hair blazed around her head like a nimbus of curling bronze.

'Go away, Jensen,' she hissed. 'Go away and leave me alone. How dare you talk to me about Pierre, when you visit his sister at least once a week? Well, for your information, let me tell you this – I intend to *marry* Pierre Thietry. And I won't be inviting you to the wedding!'

His face as white as hers, he said almost inaudibly, 'If you did, I wouldn't come.' He turned away, then paused for one final searing glance. 'Very well, Cordelia. I'll leave you to organise your own life. Starting with bringing forty children to my glasshouse and keeping them all under control there.' He glanced up at the sky. The brief flash of sunlight had gone and the clouds were massing even more heavily than before. 'Just don't drown 'em in the river, that's all.'

He stalked out of the playground and along the road, and Cordelia watched him, the tears forming a hard, iron lump in her aching throat. Oh Jensen, Jensen, she thought despairingly, you know it's you I should be marrying . . . But Jensen was out of reach, and Pierre wanted her. And once married, surely, surely she would be immune – safe from this incessant yearning . . .

The children who lived near enough to the school to go home for lunch were beginning to return. Inside the classroom, she could hear the voices of those who had finished their own meal and were growing impatient for the afternoon's excitement to begin. With a sigh, she turned and went inside.

Getting forty children into line and walking them along the road was one thing. Organising them in the noisy environment of the glasshouse was another.

Cordelia had frequently, through the summer, taken them for walks to introduce them to the birds and flowers which she had drawn and painted for them. They walked dutifully two by two through the pouring rain, the bigger children looking after the smaller ones, Danny – as always – aggressively protective of Karin, although as unanimously elected queen of the school she scarcely needed his protection. Cordelia, bringing up the rear, remembered the early problems she had encountered with them, and felt proud of her charges. If she accomplished nothing else, she thought, she would always be remembered by these children as they made their own way through life. Perhaps that would be enough.

But she knew that there ought to be more than this for her. And the old restlessness came back as she thought of the new term starting now in the English universities, of young women going to Girton and Newnham, their heads ready to be filled with ideas. What could a woman not do who had enjoyed such an experience! And what chance did she have now of ever reaching her own true potential?

Her thoughts were abruptly interrupted as the long line of children reached the glasshouse that stood on the bank above the river. It was raining again and Cordelia looked down at the water, flowing strongly below. No wonder Jensen had warned her not to drown any of them! The floods were already spreading over the flat plain and it would be easy for a daring child, venturing too close, to get swept away. Thank goodness the glasshouse was built on higher ground, she thought, and most of Knoxville as well. She turned to usher them into the long building with its row of tall chimneys pouring out their thick, yellow smoke.

'Now, you must all behave very well in here – no running or shouting, or you'll have to come straight out again. Walk only where the men say you can walk, and once you are by the chair where the glassblower is going to make the Chalice, stand perfectly still and don't make a sound. Do you understand that?'

'Yes, miss,' the children responded, and straggled in, eyes and mouths wide open as they stared about them. None of them had been inside the factory before; Jensen was firm about not allowing children in and it was Timothy who had persuaded him that Cordelia's schoolchildren would benefit from seeing the new glass made. She looked at them now and smiled at their awed expressions, remembering her feelings on her own first visit to the Henzel glasshouse. There was no cone here, no sooty, tapering brick walls, but surely the atmosphere of a glasshouse must be the same anywhere? – that impression of entering the gates of Hades, filled with dark shadows, the jaws of the great domed furnace gaping redly, casting a deep, smouldering glow over the muscular bodies of the men who toiled around it, their gathering irons gleaming like blood-tipped spears in the flickering light. And the noise – the clatter of an iron dropped to the floor, the shouts for ale from a thirsty blower, the ring of metal against metal and the splintering sound of an ill-shaped glass, smashed to the floor to be swept up for use as cullet; and, over and under and through it all, the steady roar of the furnace, keeping the pots full of molten mixture at a temperature whose heat was barely imaginable.

Timothy was waiting for them inside the door. He looked at their dripping figures and showed them a corner where they could leave the assortment of coats and sacks which had protected them on the walk, and then he led them in file through the glasshouse.

'This is the *lehr*,' Cordelia said as they came to the end of the long cooling tunnel. 'See, these are new pieces of glass, gradually cooled so that they don't crack – remember how I explained it to you this morning? These women are inspecting the glass to see that there are no flaws.'

'What do they do if it's cracked or anything?' one of the children asked.

'Well, it depends how bad the flaw is. A cracked piece would be broken and used as cullet – melted down again in the pots. But if it were just a tiny bubble of air, the glass would be sold as second-grade, and it would be cheaper than the really perfect piece.'

'Well, I'd buy that then,' the boy commented. 'Who cares about an old bubble?'

Cordelia smiled. 'Quite a lot of people do. But you're right – a glass is just as good to drink from, even if it does have bubbles in.'

'I like bubbles,' one of the smaller children remarked. 'I had a drink once with bubbles in and they made my tongue go fizzy.'

One or two of the children began to drift away, fascinated by the great dome of the furnace which towered at the far end of the building. Hastily, Cordelia called them back. 'We're going to look at the cutters and engravers first. See how the glasses are marked, so that the cutters know just where to place the glass against the wheel. It looks easy, doesn't it, but it takes a long time to learn just how to hold it and how deeply to allow the edge to cut. And the engravers have an even more difficult job. Some of them have no pattern to follow at all – they engrave the picture or pattern straight from a drawing on a sheet of paper. You find it difficult to copy drawings on your slates, don't you? Imagine how hard it must be for them to do it on glass.' Keeping their interest, she took them slowly through the long building, explaining each stage of the glassmaking process as she went. The children listened, asking questions now and then, and Cordelia answered them all, pleased by this proof that they were genuinely interested. This was the best part of teaching – the rapport between teacher and pupils as they explored a subject together – and it could be as satisfying between herself and these children from a background of poverty and hardship as between any university lecturer and his highly educated audience. Perhaps even more so, she thought, looking at the eager faces and bright eyes that she had grown to know so well during the past year.

It was then, as she gathered them together and gave them

her final instructions before approaching the Damascene chair, that she noticed an addition to her class. Jensen Novak stood on the fringe of the group, his eyes meeting hers over the heads of the taller boys.

Cordelia stared at him silently. Of course, she should have known he would be here to see the new Chalice blown. But how long had he been following her through the glasshouse?

'You explain it all very well,' he said, as unsmiling as she. 'You obviously know all about the process.'

'I should, considering I've been in and out of a glass-house ever since I can remember, and considering that it's my own brother who created Damascene.'

'Of course. But not everyone who knows can teach.' He fell into step beside her as she shepherded the children over to the rail which had been set up so that they would not get too near the working area, and Cordelia saw that Grainne was there too, come to see Timothy's new achievement take shape.

The Irish girl looked pale and tired, as if she wasn't sleeping well. Her dark eyes were huge, shadowed as if she had rubbed her fingers in soot and then against weary eyelids. She was watching Timothy with a strange, intent hunger that she was clearly doing her best to conceal, and Cordelia felt her heart twist. It was as if Grainne's hunger mirrored her own, as if Timothy was as much out of her reach as Jensen was out of Cordelia's. And she felt a deep, aching pity for both Grainne and herself; for all women who lost their hearts in hopeless love.

But as soon as the thought formed, she struck it from her mind. All those hopes and desires must be forgotten now. She had Pierre. Deliberately, she conjured up a picture of his face, deliberately she recalled his kisses and felt the quick thud of her heart.

'Dailey's just about to begin the Chalice,' Tim's voice said in her ear. 'We've used some of this metal already, made a couple of small things – friggers, just to test it – and it's exactly as we want it. The gold and silver inlays will be applied after blowing, of course, and then the clear coating – we'll show the children all that too. Now – watch . . .'

The chatter of the children's voices ceased as the gatherer went to the pot and thrust in his iron. Cordelia watched, feeling the familiar excitement grip her heart. No one who loved glass could ever fail to be thrilled by this moment, when the almost white-hot metal was drawn from the simmering pot, like toffee on a stick, and carried glowing through the air to be handed to the blower. No one could turn away from the sight of this transformation of burnished incandescence to a swelling bulb of shimmering transparency, shaped first by the breath of one man's lungs down a slender pipe, and then by the expert caress of battledore and pucellas as the iron was rolled gently and constantly across the wide arms of the chair where the gaffer himself sat like a king on his throne.

And this afternoon, Wal Dailey was king in Jensen Novak's glasshouse. Watched by a class of forty children, by Timothy Henzel who had developed the new glass, by Jensen Novak himself and by Cordelia, he took the iron from the gatherer and began to blow.

The secret of good blowing lay, Cordelia knew, in the control a glassblower could exercise over his own lungs. Developed by years of blowing, they were invariably in superb condition and a master glassblower could thrust their power forth with the glory of a trumpeter sounding a victory, or restrain it to a whisper; first forcing his breath into the boiling mass so that it expanded like a bubble of soap blown by a child on a doorstep, then gentling it into exquisite shape.

Cordelia thought of the first Chalice, blown by her grandfather Joe and standing now on the mantelpiece in the library of Henzel Court. She had heard of the day when that had been blown, a day when the whole family had gone to the cone to watch the emergence of the first piece of Henzel Crystal, made to the recipe which was to bring fame. It had been a day of triumph for Christina, setting the seal she needed on her management of the family business and establishing her in the regard of those who made and bought glass all over the country. Cordelia had seen the daguerreotype which had been taken that day – a faded, sepia picture in which Christina could still be recognised as a young, slender girl, and Joe as a brawny young glass-blower, stiff and awkward in his Sunday suit.

Was today to be as historic in her own and Timothy's lives? Would this Chalice, forming now as she watched, stand on the same mantelpiece, to be handed down through the generations and handled with pride by their grandchildren?

She felt the warmth of Jensen's body close by her side and glanced up involuntarily to meet his eyes. For a moment there was perfect understanding between them, and her heart was pierced by a regret more sharp than any she had yet known. She saw the same answering look in his eyes, and her lips parted. His own lips moved; she knew he was about to speak, and her breath caught in her throat.

But whatever he had been about to say was drowned in a sudden commotion at the door.

Wal Dailey did not look round. He finished his shaping of the Chalice, cooling now to a dense black that sparkled with the iridescence that Timothy had worked so hard to achieve, snapped it from the punty-iron and handed it to the taker-in. The next stage was out of his hands. Cordelia saw her twin step forward, as intent on his work as the glassblower and totally unaware of any disturbance.

But Jensen's head snapped up at the first sound, a deep frown narrowing his eyes as he stared towards the glasshouse door. Cordelia, turning, saw a small knot of men, strangers to her, who seemed to be forcing their way in against a little crowd of Jensen's workmen. A sudden fear caught at her breast and she glanced round quickly, tightening her hand on Karin's.

Grainne was at her side as Jensen, muttering something under his breath, strode across the glass-littered floor.

'What's happening? Who are they?'

'I don't know.' Cordelia raised her voice, commanding the children to stand still. 'There's nothing to stare at – it's probably somebody making a mistake. Now see what Mr Henzel is going to do with the Chalice –'

But the children had lost interest in the glass. And it was clear that whatever was happening, it was no simple mistake. The men were advancing on the Damascene chair now, their faces set and determined, and Jensen was coming with them, looking angrier than Cordelia had ever known him. She trembled a little and drew Karin even closer. What could be happening?

'I tell you, it's the truth,' Jensen was saying as they came within earshot. 'Developed by my own man – yes, Henzel. He's dealing with it now, you can ask him as soon as he's through. What you're alleging is a lot of nonsense – a complete fabrication. The man's a genius, I tell you, why would he want to –'

The leader of the group of strangers was a tall man, dressed in city clothes and with a face that looked as if it had been carved from stone. He stopped close to Cordelia and stared with hard eyes at the men who stood around Wal Dailey's chair. He looked at Tim and at the Chalice that was just being placed carefully in the *lehr*.

'Can't say nothing about that,' he said at last, and even his voice sounded as if it came from stone. 'Ain't none of my business, what the truth is. That's for the judge to decide. I'm here to serve you, Jensen Novak, with a subpoena to answer a Bill of Complaints from Miller Furnaces, Brooklyn, that you have used their patented formula to produce this so-called Damascene glass of yours. Do you deny that you are making a glass known as Damascene?'

'Of course I don't!' Jensen said impatiently. 'But –'

'And do you deny that it is identical in composition to the glass known as Sharlene, made by Miller Furnaces?'

'I've never even seen Sharlene, nor heard the name until this afternoon. But I'll eat my own cullet if it's the same! Tim Henzel's been working on this formula for months. He couldn't possibly have –'

'Like I said, that's not my business.' The man handed Jensen a roll of paper. 'There's your subpoena, Mr Novak. It's been given to you in the presence of witnesses.' He glanced around, apparently noticing the open-mouthed children for the first time, acknowledging them with the barest flicker of his stony eyes, and then turned away. 'I'll bid you good day.'

Jensen stood rock-still. He stared at the roll of papers in his hands, and then looked up again, his mouth opening angrily to speak. But the city man and his followers were already on their way out of the glasshouse.

'Well, I'll be damned!' Jensen exploded, and Tim, satisfied at last that the Chalice was safely on its way, came over and stared at him in bewilderment.

'What in God's name was all that about?'

'You may well ask,' Jensen said grimly. 'We've been served with a subpoena, Tim. Some tinpot little glasshouse in Brooklyn says we've stolen their formula. They're taking us to court, and until the case is heard we won't be able to make any more Damascene.' He looked at the men, gathered round in consternation, at the dismayed faces of Grainne and Cordelia, at the frightened expressions of the children. 'And if they win their case – which I can't see they've a cat in hell's chance of doing, but then I'd never have expected anyone even to *bring* such a crazy action in the first place – then we'll never make it at all. Damascene, as far as Novak Crystal goes, could be a complete non-starter.'

There was a deathly silence. He looked down again at the papers, and when he next raised his eyes he was staring straight at Cordelia.

'We know who's doing this, don't we?' he said quietly. 'Didn't I tell you he was trouble? Pierre Thietry. *He* worked in Brooklyn and he's been in New York this very week, hasn't he? He's been working on Damascene – nothing would be easier than for him to take that formula and show them how it's done. And I'd take bets that he was the one who let out the Opalene process – this factory's the same one that's producing that cheap imitation, I'd stake my last dollar on that.' He slammed the papers against the steel rail, and Cordelia flinched. '*Now* perhaps you'll believe me!' he said savagely, and wheeled away from them.

He strode away, past the chairs, past the cutters and engravers, past the women who inspected and packed the finished glass and out of the far door. And Cordelia, watching him go, felt ice form around her heart.

Could he be right? Could Pierre really have done this? And if so – why? What could he possibly hope to achieve?

'I don't believe it,' she said quietly. And then, a little louder: 'I *won't* believe it . . .'

It was the most dismal week Cordelia could ever remember.

Each day, the rain continued, falling steadily to fill the river which overflowed and swept across the flat fields on either side and even reached into some of the lower-lying streets of Knoxville. People looked at it and shook their heads and talked of the floods of previous years, but the new dikes still held firm and it was generally felt that there was no danger of any serious flooding.

But it wasn't simply the weather that depressed her. There had still been no word from Pierre and even Ginette could not – or would not – say where he had gone. 'A friend,' she answered, shrugging her pretty shoulders whenever anyone questioned her. 'That is all I know. Pierre had many friends in New York – in Manhattan, yes, and in Brooklyn. Of course he did. We lived there a long time and people were kind to us. But I was only a child, I didn't know their names. And as for where he worked – that I have forgotten long ago.' And she would smile the curving smile that had captivated so many men and play with the kitten nestling on her couch.

'She knows,' Jensen said over and over again, striding frustratedly up and down the kitchen where he and Tim spent their evenings in fruitless discussion. 'I'll swear she knows. But she's not going to give him away, and until he returns or we can prove –'

'Prove what?' Cordelia was still striving to keep her faith in Pierre. 'You've already made up your mind, Jensen. As far as you're concerned, Pierre's guilty – and if you were given proof that he's not, you simply wouldn't believe it. You don't *want* to believe it. Why, he would never have gone off and left Ginette here alone, if he'd been working against us.'

Jensen glared at her. 'And you don't want to believe he is. You're a bad case of misplaced loyalty, you've totally lost any sense of rational judgement. Can't you see the facts? They're plain enough, for God's sake.' He began to tick off the points on his fingers. 'One. Pierre insinuates himself into my factory, using his relationship with Tim as a lever. Two. Tim feels he's had a raw deal and tries to make

436

it up to him by offering him the chance to work on Damascene, without consulting me – no doubt because he knew that if he did I'd refuse point blank. Three. *In the very week* that we make the first piece of Damascene, Pierre lights off for New York, to some mythical friend even his sister hasn't heard of. Four – we get a subpoena just as the Damascene is being made. From a factory in Brooklyn, where Pierre himself almost certainly –'

'You've no *proof* of that!'

'– almost certainly once worked,' Jensen finished. 'All right, so it could be all one giant coincidence. But can you really believe it is, Cordelia? Can *you*, Tim? As for Ginette –' he lowered his voice, aware of Ginette's presence only a room or two away –' that lady might be unable to walk but she can take care of herself, never fear. And they're in this together.' His eyes were on Cordelia, his next words for her. 'Why d'you think I've been visiting her, afternoons? I've been trying to get to the bottom of what it is I find so sneaky about those two – why I find them both such a threat.' He turned back to Tim. 'Well?'

Timothy looked miserable. He remembered Pierre's apparent diffidence at Tim's suggestion that he should join in the production of Damascene. Surely that indicated his innocence? And his eagerness to make himself agreeable to both himself and Cordelia. Cordelia's own growing fondness for him, and his open admiration of her.

Why should he want to destroy all that?

But there were other memories too. Pierre at the dog-fight, his eyes gleaming with pleasure as he watched two animals reduce each other to a bloody pulp. The cruelty Tim had caught in his face and had, with discomfort, tried to forget. His own sense of unease, hastily dismissed, when he had thought of his sister and the Frenchman together.

Was it too late to face the knowledge that he had buried

for so long, that there were depths to Pierre's nature that Tim had never cared to explore? Was it too late to admit that Jensen might have been right from the beginning – that there was something sinister about the Frenchman, something that did mean trouble, and trouble of a nature none of them had foreseen?

Timothy looked at his sister, sitting at the kitchen table, her face pale and unhappy, clearly torn between the two men who had made a battlefield of her heart. He looked at Jensen, tall and blond, raging around the room as his Viking ancestors might have done centuries before. And he knew that he could not deny the truth.

His eyes on Cordelia, he shook his head slowly, sorrowfully.

'No, Jensen,' he said quietly, 'I don't believe it was a coincidence. I agree with you. Pierre must be guilty.'

Chapter Twenty

The rain was incessant. It hammered on the roofs and ran down the roads like a river. It wrenched the last of the gold and russet leaves from the trees and flung them to lie in a treacherous sludge on the sidewalks. It turned the minor roads into a quagmire, and Cordelia found it impossible to keep the schoolroom free from mud. She began to develop an almost superstitious feeling about it; as long as it kept on raining, nothing would come right. Only when the sun shone again would Pierre return and everything be explained.

But by Tuesday, the day of Hallowe'en, Pierre had still not appeared, and with the clouds still lowering over the city, Cordelia was finding it more and more difficult to maintain her confidence in him.

'I *know* he didn't do it,' she said repeatedly, but her voice carried less conviction each time. He had been absent for a week now, without a word. Surely he would have written to her? She could not understand his silence, and she found it impossible to settle to any task. She could not look at Tim without reproach, neither could she sit with Ginette and endure her insinuating smiles. Like Jensen, she was sure that Ginette knew more about Pierre's absence than she would say, and her silence seemed designed to aggravate an already tense situation.

Cordelia's only comfort was in her school where, for a few hours each day, she could forget her worries in the strenuous, sometimes frustrating but often rewarding task of imparting her own pleasure in learning. And with the

Hallowe'en party taking up their thoughts, she found the children more exacting than ever, and was glad of it. She spent her evenings in her room, making new decorations for the schoolroom, or in the kitchen with Bessie, baking flap-jacks, spiced buns and other goodies, and endeavoured to eliminate the problems of the glasshouse from her mind.

She could not succeed entirely, though. And at night, exhausted though she was when she finally went to bed, she would lie staring into the darkness and try without success to thrust from her mind the faces of the two men who had, it seemed, brought her nothing but turmoil in the months since she had known them: the strong planes of Jensen Novak's lean Scandinavian features, and the smouldering Gallic darkness of her distant cousin Pierre. Together, they would loom into her dreams, constantly shifting, first one, then the other, as if engaged in incessant battle for posses-sion of both her bewildered mind and her torn and aching heart.

On Tuesday morning, she rose early, her head aching and her eyes heavy. Her sleep had been filled with disturbing dreams – dreams of the rail crash, with Karin stumbling about in the snow and Jensen feared dead; dreams of Jensen's wife Amelia, blank-eyed and lost in her own con-fused world; dreams of the forest above the town, where she ran through trees that spread angry branches across the path to trap and entangle her; dreams of the glasshouse filled with leering, leaping demons who brandished spears that dripped with blood and turned to her with faces that resembled Pierre's in horrible travesty . . . Each time she jerked awake, she fell again into heavy slumber and was disturbed yet again, by nightmares more horrifying than ever, until when morning came she was thankful to get out of bed and creep down to the silent kitchen and make her-self a pot of strong tea to clear the muzziness from her head.

There would be no time today, at least, to worry about Pierre. The party that afternoon would mean a great deal of work, and Cordelia threw herself into it, sorting the children into groups and enlisting Danny's help to command them like a general. The desks and benches were rearranged to form long tables around the room, with a space cleared in the middle for games. Martha, who had insisted in helping and done a good deal of the baking, spent the morning going back and forth with trays of cookies and a large iced cake, baked by Bessie, with a paper witch and four black cats perched on the top. Fresh lemonade came in in large jugs, and one of the local farmers sent a boy with a box of apples. Bowls of nuts were placed at intervals along the tables and in the middle and at each end were the grinning faces of pumpkin lanterns.

By the time the afternoon light began to fade, everything was ready. The children, flushed and excited, sat on the floor and Cordelia announced that the feast would begin.

'Apple-bobbing first,' she said, and Martha and Danny entered bearing large bowls which they proceeded to fill with water. They tipped the apples in and the children lined up to take turns in trying to catch them with their teeth. A good deal of splashing and choking resulted from this, but at last each child had managed to secure an apple and the bowls were carried out again, to be replaced by mounds of nuts and raisins for snapdragon. Karin proved herself an easy winner here, her fingers darting nimbly in and out to acquire a vast pile of fruit which she shared with the more timid Bridget.

'Now we've got a visitor,' Cordelia announced, and the door opened to admit a strange, stooping figure, swathed in a dark cloak which was drawn up over the head, with one hand resting on a gnarled stick as it fumbled its way across the room in the dim glow cast by the pumpkin lanterns.

The children gasped and some of the smaller ones screamed and were quickly hushed by their neighbours. The figure came slowly across the room, stopping beside Cordelia, and sank into the chair she had placed ready.

'I am the Spirit of Hallowe'en,' it intoned in a voice remarkably like Bob Robinson's. 'An' I'm here to tell you a few stories. So jes' you sit and listen, for I won't be tellin' 'em twice and anyone that so much as twitches an eyebrow while I'm talkin' will be changed into – into –' the children held their breath – 'into *black beetles*!' he finished fiercely, and there were further gasps and screams. 'So jes' mind what I say, now.'

Cordelia smiled and sat back in her own chair to listen. Bob's fund of stories was apparently endless; some chilling, some funny, they were lapped up by the children who hung on his every word. The only problem would be to stop him. But she could rely on Martha, who had slipped into the classroom behind him, to decide when the children had had enough and when Bob should be brought to a halt, and before any of them had begun to show signs of restlessness the lamps were lit and the ghostly atmosphere dispelled as the children were called to the tables, where they fell upon the delicacies as if they had not seen food for a week.

'And I don't reckon most of 'em sees this kind of tucker once in a blue moon,' Bob remarked, watching them. 'This was a good idea of yours, Cordelia. First party most of 'em's ever been to, if I'm not mistaken.'

'But not the last,' Cordelia said firmly. 'They need some fun in their lives, these little ones.' She glanced up as the rain sounded louder than ever on the roof. 'Goodness, is it never going to stop? I don't believe we've had a moment without rain for a week now.'

Bob looked up with some anxiety. 'Sure sounds a lot worse. I reckon you ought to get these kids home, Cordelia.

It's getting dark out there, and some of the places round Knoxville are pretty low-lying.'

She gave him a quick glance. 'You don't think there's any danger, do you? The dikes –'

'The dikes ain't perfect, not by a long chalk,' he said. 'Look, they've mostly finished eatin' now – not that there's much left to eat. Get 'em into their coats and send 'em home.' He went to the door and peered out into the streaming darkness. 'I don't like it,' he said, coming back, his usually cheerful face tight with worry. 'It's raining pitchforks out there now. Reminds me of the storm in '95. Get those kids ready right away. I'll start running 'em back in the trap. We can't send 'em out by theirselves in this weather.'

Quickly, Cordelia began to do as he had directed. With Martha's help, she marshalled the children into order and began to sort out their coats. Those that lived furthest away were bundled into the trap with Bob, and he set off, his pony's hooves splashing through the water. Martha took those that lived nearest, making sure that there was someone in each house to look after them. With the noise of the rain louder than ever, Cordelia was left alone at last with only Karin, Danny and Bridget.

'Will anyone be at home yet?' she asked, but Danny shook his head.

'Dad's working late all this week and Grainne's had to go over to our auntie's in Corning. We'll be all right – I'll look after Bridget.'

Cordelia looked uncertainly at him. Danny was a sensible boy, but he was barely ten years old. And the O'Donnell house was low, not far from the river. She turned as Bob came in, water pouring from his coat.

'I think we'd better take Danny and Bridget back with us – there's no one at home and I can't leave them on their

443

own. No, Danny, not this time – I know you're perfectly capable but a flood's different.' She had never been in such a situation before, and could barely imagine the devastation if the river did indeed break through the dikes, but she knew that it would be terrifying and dangerous. She shook her head firmly as he protested again. 'You're coming back with me. You can help look after the girls.'

Outside, it was even worse than she had thought. The rain was now an almost impenetrable curtain of water that dropped from the sky with relentless ferocity. Although not yet sundown, the light was fading and the glimmer from Bob's lantern showed the water lying across the road like a sheet of black steel, pricked by a million invisible spears. Cordelia looked down and realised that it was already several inches deep and beginning to lap over the bottom of the three steps that led to the schoolroom door.

She looked at Bob with fear in her eyes.

'It's flooding already!'

He shook his head. 'Don't think so. That's just the rain, comin' down too fast to run away. But I don't reckon there's any time to lose. Let's go.'

Martha had returned with the trap, and Cordelia bundled the children into it. Casting a frightened look at the water, she scrambled up and huddled on the seat, her arm around Bridget's shoulders. Karin pressed against her other side and even Danny looked wide-eyed. Bob jumped up into the driver's seat and flicked the reins.

It was difficult to see now just where the road was. The water lay across the sidewalks, bubbling here and there where a drain was too full to accept any more, running down from banks and forming deep pools where the road dipped into a hollow. The pony staggered, the trap heavy and hard to drag through the flood, and after a few minutes Bob shook his head and turned.

'You'll have to take the reins, Martha – poor old Joey can't manage this. I'll get down and go to his head, encourage him a bit.'

With his load lightened, the pony made better headway, but progress was still slow and Cordelia took her arm from Bridget's shoulder.

'Danny, come and sit here. Keep tight hold of the girls, you understand? I'm going to get out and walk with Bob.'

Martha turned at once. 'Cordelia, you can't do that. If the dikes go –'

'If the dikes go, none of us will have much say in what happens,' Cordelia said, trying to keep her voice from shaking. 'We're never going to get across the bridge at this rate, Martha – the poor pony's got all he can do to stay on his feet.' She scrambled down and found herself almost knee-deep in cold water. Her skirts, already soaked, dragged heavily and she pulled them up, gathering them into a sodden mass which almost filled her arms. 'Heavens, I can't manage with these!' she exclaimed and found the waist fastenings of her skirt.

'Cordelia!' Martha exclaimed, scandalised, as Cordelia dropped her skirt and stepped out of it to stand in her petticoats. Then she laughed. 'Well, I guess no one's goin' to be lookin' at you on a night like this. But it's a shame to lose that good skirt.'

'It'd be a bigger shame if we didn't get home at all,' Cordelia retorted and waded through the water to join Bob. To her relief, the pony was able to make better progress now and they forged steadily through the encroaching water. It was easier to see now through the shifting twilight, and the bridge was just visible, a hard black line against the bruised sky.

As they came nearer to it, Cordelia could see that the river was within inches of the tops of the dikes. She stared at

445

it with fear. It was impossible to believe that these man-made banks would hold back the tremendous weight of water that boiled against them as the river, fed by streams that came down from the hills all along the valley, swelled and surged and rampaged its way down a bed that had become too shallow, too confining. She saw the bridge shudder and realised that the passage of water underneath it was almost blocked by debris swept down from above – trees, their branches splayed against the stanchions, their roots torn from the ground and upended like grotesque hands clawing at the sky, the wreckage of a shed built too near the banks and dragged from its foundations, the bodies of cattle that had been left too long on the low grazing meadows.

She looked at Bob and saw his face, grim in the flickering light of his lantern.

'We'd better get across here quick,' he said, urging the pony forward again. 'That bridge ain't goin' to last much longer.'

Cordelia looked down into the swirling blackness and shuddered. Suppose the bridge gave way as they crossed it? But there was no time to draw back. The debris had formed a thick dam and the water was already piling into a threatening mass on the upstream side. The bridge groaned and creaked with a pressure that increased with every second. If the bridge gave way, the dikes would never withstand the sudden rush of thousands of tons of water, trees and other detritus; they would crumble and be swept away with the bridge itself, a thundering accumulation to bring destruction to anything that lay in its implacable path.

'Bob. We can't cross that!' Martha cried from the trap. 'It's goin' to go at any moment –'

'And if it does, we'll go with it anyway,' he retorted. 'That water's goin' to flood this part of Knoxville and take

everythin' in its way – includin' us. We've *got* to cross.
And there ain't no time to hang about.' He tugged at the
frightened pony's head and spoke soothingly to it, urging it
to set its hooves on the bridge. 'Come on, boy, come on.
Ain't nothin' to be afeared of. It's just that little old bridge
you've been across more times'n you've had hot dinners
. . . Come on, now, that's it. Little bit more. Soon be in
your stable again, eatin' hot mash . . . That's it. That's
right. That's my brave boy, come on now, come on.'

Cordelia laid her hand on the side of the trap. She was
soaked through, her petticoats clinging to her legs, but she
hardly noticed the cold as she struggled through the driving
rain. Her hair was loose and streaming round her head; it
fell across her face and she pushed it back with one hand,
peering anxiously ahead. The bridge seemed endless; she
could feel it, groaning and shifting under her feet. Martha
was right, it wasn't going to hold. Nothing could withstand
the weight of water that was pounding against it now. They
would all be swept away, drowned in the cold, black waters
that threatened the whole city . . . The bridge swayed suddenly and she stifled a scream, hearing Martha and the
children cry out close beside her. Her hand tightened on
the trap and she braced herself for the final collapse of the
bridge; but, miraculously, it held. She could hear Martha
praying aloud and her heart echoed with a fervent amen.
Ahead, Bob was still encouraging the terrified pony. They
moved forward slowly, inch by inch, and Cordelia could
feel the bridge moving under her feet, swaying, jerking,
lurching as the dammed-up water thrust and boiled around
it. How far was it now to the safety of the far bank? How
far had they gone? It could have been a yard, it could have
been twenty; she had no idea, and there were no lights to
guide her. The world had shrunk to this tiny space, a narrow,
trembling bridge across an angry river.

They were not going to make it. With a sudden deadly certainty, she knew that this was the end.

She never knew whether there were tears on her face then, streaming down with the rain that had soaked her through. She never knew whether she had been weeping for herself, for the children, for Bob and Martha or for all those others she would never see again – Jensen, Tim, Pierre, her mother and grandparents at home. Each face passed before her eyes as she bade them all a silent farewell. And as she did so, she plodded on through the water, almost ankle deep even on the bridge; not because she hoped now that they would ever reach safety but because there was nothing else to do; because even in this last extremity, her spirit would not allow her simply to stop and wait for death.

When the swaying ceased, when the frightening lurching of the bridge stopped and the surface under her feet changed, Cordelia did not even notice it. Still doggedly trudging forward, she was startled when Bob let out a cheer and Martha gave a thankful cry. She lifted her head and stared around her and then saw, just behind them, the silhouette of the bridge, outlined momentarily against the racing sky. She could see the mass of torn and broken flotsam, piled high against the bridge now; the water on the upstream side was considerably higher than that below and battered angrily at the stanchions, seeking a way through. Cordelia stared at it and shuddered. Had they really come across that creaking, lurching, almost derelict-looking structure?

'No time to stop now,' Bob shouted as he urged the pony on again. 'We ain't out of this wood yet – we've got to get to high ground. Reckon all Market Street's goin' to be under when that lot gives way. It could even get up into First and Second Street, like it did in '95.' He staggered on, almost dragging the pony along by its harness, and Cordelia lent her own weight to the trap, thrusting at it with her shoulder and both hands. 'I'm goin' to make for the hill,' she heard Bob shout. 'We'll take these youngsters up to Jensen's place. They'll be safe there.'

Cordelia imagined the waters rushing through the centre of the town, flooding even up to the street where she and Timothy lived. For the first time, she thought of her brother – where was he in this dreadful emergency? On a normal day at this time, he would still be at the glasshouse – was he there now? Had he and Jensen sent their workers home early when the threat of flooding was first realised – had they gone themselves? At once, she knew that they would not have left. The glasshouse itself was on low ground near the river, on the Knoxville side. They would have stayed there, to rescue as much as possible of the glass that was stored on the ground floor, even in the deep basement. Her heart shook as she thought of them in the basement when the dikes finally gave way. They would have no chance . . .

And hard on the heels of that thought came another. A picture of Ginette, alone in the house on the corner of Pine and Second Streets. Helpless on her bed in the ground-floor parlour when the waters came swirling down the street.

They crossed Market Street. It was almost deserted, the shops closed and shuttered; only a few scurrying figures were to be seen, anxiously bent on saving their own families and possessions. Erie Street was the same, a sinister emptiness. The railroad station was empty, a train standing as if waiting for passengers, but the driver and engineer had disappeared and there was nobody to sell tickets.

As they approached Second Street, Cordelia let go of the trap and caught up with Bob. 'I'm going to the house. Ginette's there all alone – I can't leave her.'

He turned and stared at her. 'Ginette! Land's sakes if I hadn't forgotten all about her. Look, I'll take her in the trap –'

449

'No. The pony must be exhausted, he'll never make it up that hill. You're all going to have to walk the last bit, it's so steep. Ginette could never manage.' She spoke quickly, breathlessly, knowing that time was growing dangerously short. 'I'll get her upstairs – we'll be all right there. You and Martha see to the children.'

Bob shook his head, his face desperate with anxiety. 'I dunno, Cordelia. I don't like leavin' you all alone –'

'*Please*, Bob.' She pushed his shoulder, urging him to move on. 'Get the children to safety. Get up to Jensen's house. We'll be all right, I promise. The water won't get above the ground floor.' She wished she could be certain of that. Just what had happened during earlier floods? How bad had they been – and was there any reason why this one shouldn't be even worse? But Bob, after an obvious battle with himself, nodded at last and turned away. The trap moved slowly away, up the first slope of the hill, and Cordelia watched it with fear in her heart.

She stood there for only a few seconds before turning and making her way as quickly as possible to the house. It was Bessie's afternoon off, she remembered, and Ginette would have been alone for hours. And although she probably had no idea what it was like out here, she must be aware that the storm had worsened. Had she heard the stories of the floods that had so often and disastrously beset Corning? It was impossible that she had not.

Cordelia came within sight of the front parlour window and saw to her relief that a light burned behind it. The curtains had been drawn – was Bessie at home after all, then? – and it looked welcoming and friendly. Almost, she thought as she fumbled with the door, as if once inside there would be safety and the threat from the river would cease to exist.

The door would not open. She jerked and twisted at the

handle, suddenly panic-stricken, as if the floods were at that very moment on her heels. All the terror of the past hour, held in check as they struggled through the water-logged streets and across the swaying bridge, surged through her heart and she began to sob, pulling desperately at the handle, convinced suddenly that she was doomed to die here on her own doorstep.

The lock released at last. She stumbled into the hall, half falling, and slammed the door behind her. She leaned against it in the sudden calm, breathing heavily, and caught sight of herself in the hall mirror.

She had never seen herself look so dishevelled. Her hair was tangled and matted around her dirt-streaked face, her jacket torn, her petticoats almost ripped away. Water streamed down her body, forming a filthy puddle on the floor, and her eyes were wild.

She lifted a shaking hand to her brow and then opened the parlour door.

Pierre was kneeling beside Ginette's couch. His head was bent over her breasts which spilled naked from a tumble of lace. As Cordelia stood, shaken and uncomprehending at the door, they both looked round and saw her.

Ginette's smile curved in a way that Cordelia recognised, sickeningly, as being wholly evil. And Pierre, taking in Cordelia's bedraggled appearance, rose slowly to his feet, a curious expression on his face; an expression that brought fear of a different kind into Cordelia's thumping heart.

The first intimation Timothy had of the danger threatening the city was when Jensen burst into his office late in the afternoon and commanded him abruptly to stop whatever he was doing and get down to the basement right away.

'Hey, steady on,' Tim protested. 'I'm just putting the final touches to the Chalice. Look – what d'you think?' He

451

held up the large goblet in both hands, turning it under the light so that the gold shimmered against its black, iridescent background. 'I think that's just the most beautiful piece of glass I've ever made,' he said quietly. 'And if any judge believes that one-horse bunch of cullet-grabbers in Brooklyn could have made Damascene before we did, well, I reckon we'll see pigs flying overhead any day now.' He gazed again at the heavy glass and there was a deep, quiet pride in his eyes and in his voice. 'I think Grandmother's going to be very pleased when she sees this,' he said.

'Yes, I daresay, but never mind it now.' Jensen spoke quickly, barely glancing at the piece of glass that had cost them so much time and anxiety in its making and now stood perfect on Timothy's workbench. 'Listen, Tim, there's bad news. The river's too high – there was a guy in here just now who's been up in the hills and he says it's real bad up there. The Monkey Run's liable to flood down through the city, and the Chemung's rising every minute. He doesn't think the dikes will take it.'

Timothy stared at him. 'You mean they could burst?'

'That's it – and if they go, heaven help us all. Now you know our position here – the glasshouse itself is virtually a part of the dike, and the basement's way below water level – it seeps with water as it is –'

'But we've got a lot of stock down there!'

'That's just what I'm saying,' Jensen said grimly. 'I'm getting all the men down there to shift it. If that water breaks through we stand to lose a hell of a lot of stock – it'd ruin us. We've got to get it out.' He turned back to the door. 'There's no time to lose, Tim, and we need every hand in the place.'

Tim pushed back his stool. 'I'm right behind you, Jensen.' He picked up the Chalice and stood irresolute for a moment, weighing it in his hand. Then he reached up to a glass cabinet high on the wall and pulled open the doors. Quickly, he lifted out the glass already in there and thrust the Chalice inside. He closed the doors on it and fastened them securely.

'I hope to God you'll be safe enough there,' he muttered. But the water surely wouldn't come this high – that was if it flooded at all? Jensen and his informant could be wrong. After all the flooding Corning had suffered in the past, the dikes must have been built to withstand weather that was at least as severe as any that had been experienced before. Surely they would hold.

The other workers did not seem to share his optimism. As Tim ran down the stairs to the basement, they were forming a long chain from the long underground room to the blowing room itself, passing glass to each other so quickly that there seemed more danger of it being dropped than smashed by floodwaters. But they were all accustomed to handling glass and few pieces slipped from their agile fingers. As Tim joined the end of the queue, the man ahead of him pointed to a pile of cases and jerked his head.

'Wineglasses. We'd better get 'em out of the way.' He lifted one in his arms and set off for the upper rooms.

Tim bent to follow his example, but before he could move Jensen was at his elbow, his lean face haggard with worry. He turned and caught one of the other workmen by the arm, ordering him curtly to help move the cases, and then drew Timothy aside.

'We'll have to get them out of here, Tim. I've been down to the dikes and had a look. The railroad bridge looks bad, and the other one's not much better. There's stuff being washed downstream and it's making a dam. There's a head of water behind it nearly two feet high. If that dam goes we'll be flooded in here – and if the water reaches the furnaces and puts the fires out, we'll have an explosion on our hands.'

'An explosion!' Tim stared at him and Jensen shook his arm impatiently.

'Think, man! All that molten glass inside the pots – if the water reaches that it'll go in all directions. We're heading for a major disaster here either way. We've got to get everyone out!'

'But the glass –' Tim looked down the stone steps with all the agony of a man whose whole life had been built around the art he loved. Jensen shook him again.

'The people are what matter most. I'd rather the whole factory went, and all the glass in it, than one man lost his life trying to save it all.' He raised his voice and called down the stairway. 'Stop work now, all of you. I want you to leave whatever you're doing and go to your homes. Your families need you.' He watched as they stared up at him and began to protest. 'Bring up whatever you have in your hands now, and then go,' he repeated, and the men began to move, still almost reluctant, as if they scarcely believed what their employer was telling them. 'You don't know what it's like out there,' he said urgently, and as they saw his face they began at last to hurry.

'Right,' Jensen said as he and Timothy watched the last man leave. 'Now let's make a tour – see there's no one left.' He led the way briskly through the blowing room, the cutting and engraving shops, the packing area and up into the offices above. Up here, there were only skylights and the hammering of the rain on the roof was the only sign of the weather outside. Apart from that sound, the whole place was eerily silent; there was no one there.

'Wait a minute, though!' Tim stopped suddenly. 'I can hear someone singing.'

'*Singing?*' Jensen stared at him in disbelief, then lifted his eyebrows. 'By all that's crazy, so can I!' He wrenched open the nearest door. 'What in Hell's name? What are *you* doing?'

Tim peered past him. A small man was inside the office, sweeping the floor with a huge broom and singing cheerfully. He looked round, startled, as the two men burst in, and then grinned.

'Well, hi there, Mr Novak. And Mr Henzel. Say, ain't that rain somethin'? Ain't heard it like that since '95, when the old dikes went – guess there must be a tidy flow goin' down river now.'

'There is,' Jensen said grimly. 'And it'll be through the town soon, if I know anything about it. What are you *doing*, for God's sake? Want to make sure the floors are clean before we're all swept to kingdom come?'

The janitor laughed. 'Well, it's not a bad thing at that. At least I'd be able to face my Maker with a clean conscience – clean floors, too!' He chuckled again. 'But what brings you up here at this time, Mr Novak? Anythin' I can do to help?'

'Yes, there is. You can put down that broom and get out of here. No, I'm *not* giving you the sack,' he added as the little man's face fell. 'I just want you to get home while you still can. Don't you realise, the whole town's liable to flood at any minute. The dikes aren't going to hold.'

The janitor stared at him. 'Not going to hold? But Mr Novak –'

'Don't argue,' Jensen said, and turned to the door.

At that moment the lights went out. The little office was plunged into darkness.

'My God,' Jensen said very quietly. 'That's the power gone. The dikes have burst.'

The three men stood silent in the darkened room. They could still hear the drumming of the rain on the skylight and the roof. And then they heard a new sound.

It was a dull roar. It seemed to come from somewhere a long way below their feet. It grew louder, and they felt the floor tremble beneath them. There was a crash, as if a huge

455

mass of glass had just been flung to the ground; another; and then another. Tim felt the agony tear at his breast, knowing that that was just what was happening. All the glass still down in the basement; probably, too, the glass in the blowing room, the cutting and engraving areas, the packing department. And the special experimental and display glass in his office and in Jensen's. The Chalice . . . He felt the building shake under the onslaught and instinctively reached out, half expecting the floor to give way. He felt Jensen close beside him and heard the intake of breath.

'I've got to see what's happening,' Jensen said quickly. 'We can get out on to the roof at the end of this corridor. Come – and keep close together.' He grabbed for Timothy's arm and gripped it tightly. 'Get hold of – what's your name?'

'Harris, sir.' The janitor's voice sounded less cheerful now; it quavered and when Timothy found his hand it was cold and sweaty. 'Are we goin' to die, Mr Novak?'

'Not if I have any say in the matter,' Jensen retorted, sounding as if he intended to have a good deal of say. 'But I've got to see – there's a door just along here. Let's pray it's not locked. Here.' He stopped and fumbled for a moment. 'Thank God.'

Cold air and driving rain rushed in and soaked them within minutes. But none of them were concerned with cold or wet now; they stepped out on to the flat roof and stared about them.

It was still just light enough to see. They looked down at the river and saw a vast tidal wave thundering through the valley, spreading evil tentacles through the streets. Both bridges had gone; there was only a twisted mass of iron to mark where they had been. Carts, trees, coal cars from the railroad bridge, even the roofs and walls of wooden buildings torn from their foundations, were washed past, collecting more debris as they went. On the far bank, in Corning itself, they could see that the water was rapidly filling Market Street, its powerful current sweeping away anything that had been left outside, tearing down lampposts and trees, ripping awnings from the shop windows. It was as if one of the great lakes had suddenly burst its banks and spilled into the little town, and Timothy, watching with sickness in his heart, knew that there was no defence against so terrible an onslaught.

'Cordelia,' he said, and felt Jensen shiver beside him.

'Where will she be? Will she have had the sense to get home? It was that damfool party this afternoon – surely she'll have realised –'

'Why should she?' Timothy strained his eyes through the fading light towards Knoxville, even though he knew that the school wasn't visible from here. 'We've never known anything like this before. God, if anything's happened to her . . .'

'It won't. It can't. It mustn't.' Jensen made for the door back into the building. 'Let's see how deep it is – maybe we can get to the school, make sure –'

'You'll never do it! It'd be suicide –' Tim followed him and Harris scuttled after them, bewildered and frightened, determined not to be left behind. Feeling their way through the darkness, they scrambled down the stairs. The water was almost waist deep and rising. Jensen waded through it to his office, where the door stood open; he floundered inside and Timothy heard him fumbling. 'There's a lantern on the shelf here – ah, thank God, and some matches as well.' There was the sound of a striking match and Timothy saw the flicker of a tiny flame. In a moment, the lantern was lit and they stared at each other across the swirling water.

'You can't go out,' Timothy said. 'It must be six or eight feet deep. Jensen, it's madness . . .'

457

'It's Cordelia,' Jensen said, and his face was bone-white in the guttering light of the lantern. 'If she's still there, I can't not know, Tim. I can't let her go like that . . .'

He waded back to the door. And as they stood there together in the passage, they heard a fresh roar of water. The crash of glass sounded in their ears again as the flood reached a new height. And they looked towards the end of the corridor and saw a wall of water rushing towards them; a wall that reached to the ceiling and moved with dreadful and inexorable speed.

Chapter Twenty-One

'Pierre . . .' Cordelia said faintly. 'Ginette! What . . .?'

'You should not have come back just now,' Pierre said softly, and Cordelia shivered with more than the cold of icy water and shock. She saw his eyes travel slowly over her face, down her wet, half-naked body. They darkened and his full lips parted slightly; his tongue flicked over them like a snake's.

'Pierre . . . Don't look at me like that. What is it? What's wrong?' She glanced desperately at Ginette, and saw with horror that her pansy eyes were as lascivious as her brother's. What had been happening between the two of them? What was happening now?

Pierre stepped forward and took her arm.

'Cordelia! My little one, what has happened to you? Has there been an accident – has someone attacked you? Come – you must get out of those wet clothes at once.' The smooth tones, so nearly concerned for her, were almost the most sinister sound she had ever heard. 'Cordelia, let me help you.'

'Yes,' Ginette said from the couch, 'let him help you. Pierre is very good at undressing a woman, Cordelia . . . and much else besides. You will be surprised.'

Cordelia flung her a bewildered glance and backed away as Pierre came nearer. Revulsion crawled across her skin and she tried to brush his hand away from her arm. But he only laughed, his lips drawn back over teeth that were like a dog's, and tightened his fingers on her trembling flesh.

'I think this is a good time, don't you?' he said to his sister. 'I think our moment has come.'

'Do it now,' she answered, and her eyes gleamed. 'Do it here. I want to see . . .'.

Cordelia looked from one to the other. Her bewilderment turned to fear, her fear to terror. With a quick movement, she twisted away from Pierre and ran to the door. She was out into the hall before he caught her, and she turned to face him like a creature at bay.

'Pierre, you don't understand. We're in danger, the whole city is in danger of flooding. They're expecting the dikes to go at any minute. I've just come across the bridge – I've seen it. And if – when – they do go, the water will reach us here. I came back to help Ginette – we must get her upstairs, into safety.'

He was coming closer, still with that frightening, animal distortion in his face. Cordelia searched desperately for escape. She found her feet on the bottom stair, retreated upwards, knowing that there could be no escape for her there, but frantic to get away from the clutching hands. Pierre's face was dark as he caught her and jerked her into his arms; she smelled the heat of his body, the sweat, and a strange, primitive smell that increased her terror even further. As she stared into the hot eyes, he lifted her bodily. Cordelia struggled, but her arms were crushed against his chest, her legs locked by an iron arm and her desperate wriggling only served to make Pierre tighten his fingers cruelly on her wet flesh.

'Let me go!' she panted. 'Pierre, have you gone mad? There's danger outside, I tell you – the whole city will be flooded and nobody knows how deep it will come. Ginette –'

'Do you really expect me to believe such a tale?' He stared down at her, his eyes burning. 'A flood! You are hysterical, all of you. A little rain and you expect disaster – well, you have never seen true disaster, and maybe it will do you good to know what it is like. Meanwhile –'

'Pierre, *please*.' They were at the door of her room now and his fingers were on the handle. 'You must bring Ginette upstairs. Pierre, I'm telling you the truth, please believe me.'

But he was not listening. He carried her across the room and threw her on the bed, then quickly lit the lamp. She lay on her back, her jacket wrenched half off her shoulders by his roughness, her blouse torn, the remnants of her petticoats shredded almost to nothing, staring up at him with dazed, terrified eyes.

He looked down at her and his eyes filled with contempt. 'Truth! What do you Henzels know about truth? You and your precious brother, you're nothing but the children of a bastard, the grandchildren of a whore! Yes, I know all about you and your so-respectable grandmother – my father made sure I knew. He told me everything – how she seduced Jean-Paul Thietry and persuaded him to break his betrothal, and how he would have done so, and brought shame on his own family, if he had not died before he could return to France. *That* is where your father came from – an illicit, immoral union between a scheming woman and a lonely man, far from home. And what was *he* – your father? A twig from the same branch – a womaniser who took nis pleasure where he could find it, without regard. Véronique, an innocent child – I remember her, she was like a fairy, she brought light and laughter to the château, everyone was happy when she was about. And my own mother, Annette.' His voice deepened, became hoarse and rough. 'Yes, he made love to my own mother, when he was a guest in my father's house. You would not have known that, would you? You would not wish to believe it – that your father, the artist, the *genius*, should seduce the wife of the man whose inheritance he planned to steal as well. He wanted it all, your father, and he took it. He left my father

461

nothing – no wife, no château, no livelihood. Nothing.'

'I don't believe it,' Cordelia whispered. 'It's not true. None of it's true.'

But when she looked into Pierre's dark, tormented eyes, she knew that it was, though in his mind it had become distorted. Her father had lain with Pierre's mother; and he had inherited what was left of the château.

'It wasn't like that –' she began, but he gave a harsh crack of laughter.

'Not like that? Then how was it, my little one who was not even there, who knew nothing of it until a moment ago? *I* was there,' he said, thumping himself on the chest. 'I, Pierre. I was only a child then, a child of eight, nine, ten years old – for yes, it went on for a long time, all the time that your father spent in France – but a child sees many things he may not understand at the time. It was only later – years later, that I began to piece the story together. What I had seen and heard for myself – their little glances, the way their hands would touch when they thought no one would see, the walks they took in the woods when they did not know a small boy was in a tree, watching and listening. Yes, there were many things I saw and heard and did not understand then. But now –' his eyes glittered and he began, slowly, to unfasten the buttons of his trousers '– now I understand them very well indeed.'

Cordelia's eyes followed the movement of his fingers. 'Pierre, what has happened to you? You said you loved me –' Her words were lost as he gave a bark of mirthless laughter. 'Pierre,' she said in a low urgent tone, 'don't do this. Don't take your revenge on me for something that happened thirty years ago. Think, Pierre –'

'Think?' he exclaimed. 'You tell me to *think*? When I have done little else but think of it for thirty years? Can't you imagine what it did to me, even when I didn't understand? I saw enough to know that my father was being humiliated. I saw the change in him, in my mother, whenever Paul Henzel came to the château. And that last night – the night before we heard the news of the war, when they all left to run back to Paris – I heard the screams, the shouting. I saw his face next day, scratched from brow to jaw, and I knew it was no bramble that had done that, but my mother's nails. And when it was all over and my father was about to send us to America, he made me swear vengeance. He told me that all our troubles, all our humiliation, had been caused by Paul Henzel and he made me vow that one day, somehow, I would find revenge. And when I saw you and your brother at the circus, I knew that my chance had come at last.'

He paused. Cordelia stared at him and knew that this, at last, was the truth. This was why Pierre had stayed in Corning, this was why he had courted her. Jensen had been right, and she had scorned his warnings. And Timothy . . .

'So they were right,' she said bitterly, thinking of the way she had defended Pierre over Damascene. 'You did take the secret of Timothy's glass to that man in Brooklyn, and agree to swear that he had made it first.'

'Of course. It fell into my lap like a ripe plum. And your brother – so young and naive, so easy to fool, it was almost a shame . . . Until he so kindly offered me a job. A *job*!' He spat the word out as if it were an obscenity. 'And then gave me the *opportunity* to work on his beloved Damascene – as if I were likely to be deceived. He didn't need my help! He was simply offering charity – so pleasantly, so patronisingly, when what he should have been doing was give me back my rights. *My* château, *my* business in Paris, that he inherited – it should all have been mine. And he offers me a *job*.' He looked at Cordelia again and smiled, and his smile was more terrifying than his frown. 'Well, I have ruined him now. His reputation will be nothing. And now I will complete the task I set myself. I have destroyed Paul Henzel's son and I shall take his daughter, as he took my mother.'

He moved slowly towards her, his eyes gleaming. Cordelia moved quickly, slithering up the bed and against the wall in a frantic effort to escape, but there was nowhere to go. Acutely aware of her half-naked state, she saw Pierre lunge towards her and she warded him off with the only weapons she had – her nails, held out towards him like claws, ready to scratch down his face. But already Pierre was on her, his hands gripping her wrists so that she was helpless, her arms held high above her head. His body covered hers, a crushing weight, hard and unyielding; his face was close to hers, laughing, vicious, cruel.

Cordelia turned her head aside, sickened by the thought of his mouth on hers, and Pierre shifted both her wrists into the grip of one hand, his fingers curling easily around the slender bones. With his free hand, he jerked her face roughly so that she was forced to look up at him, and then he assaulted her mouth with his, forcing her lips apart, thrusting his tongue deeply inside, bruising her with his teeth.

Cordelia bit him, hard. He jerked back and slapped her head. Her ear sang and the room whirled. He laid his mouth on hers again and she suffered the assault, too dazed to retaliate, and felt his hand on her breast, squeezing, pinching, kneading, and then between her legs, forcing her thighs apart.

Cordelia's head cleared and she began to struggle again. Let Pierre ravish her – she would die first! She heard him curse, felt his hand strike her again, and again, but she refused to give in. Her own hands were free of his gripping fingers and she pulled violently at his hair, clawed his face, jabbed her fingers at his eyes. With her legs, she kicked, using knees as well as feet, and she heard Pierre swear angrily in both French and English. She bit, scratched and twisted like a wildcat; but in the end, it was no use. He had her helpless again, her wrists manacled once more by one vice-like hand, and although there was blood on his face and bruises already round his eyes, his strength was too great for her to resist any longer and she lay panting, exhausted, knowing that he had defeated her.

Ginette lay on her couch in the room below. Outside, she could hear the wind raging round the house, the battering of heavy rain against the windows. Inside, all was still. Her kitten crept from its cushion and jumped up on to her lap, and she stroked it with long, sensuous fingers, holding it against her so that she could feel the softness of its fur against her cheek.

Upstairs, she could hear faint sounds. Bumping. A faint cry. Cordelia was not giving in so easily, but Pierre would enjoy that. And afterwards he would tell Ginette all about it.

She smiled her slow, curving smile and buried her face in the purring bundle of fur.

Slowly she became aware of the noise outside.

At first, she thought it was the wind, rising to even greater strength. Then that it must be rain, harder than she had ever heard it. But rain never roared like that, never thundered like an army coming down the street. It was the sound of water, of giant cataracts, of a river thundering through a gorge . . .

Of flood.

Ginette's breath caught in her throat. She tried to scream, but her voice had left her. She clutched at the kitten, which mewed in protest, and her eyes went to the door, left ajar as Pierre had rushed out in pursuit of Cordelia.

465

The thunder drew nearer. It filled her ears, made screaming futile. She lay helpless, unable to move, staring out into the hall. Her body trembled and the couch itself shook . . . though whether it was from the force of her own panic or from the thrust of the water as it hit the front door and knocked it from its hinges, she was never to know.

With an explosion that shook the house, a wall of water burst in through the narrow space, filling the hall before it thrust into each room. Ginette saw it as a great black wave, poised above her, hanging for an eternal moment before it fell to swamp everything in the room: the chairs, the table, the couch, herself. She felt it crash against her, a blow that knocked her from her bed, tore the lace from her throat, forced the breath from her body. She gasped, choked, struggled for breath, but the water was all around her now, filling her eyes, her ears, her nose and mouth. It was in her throat, in her lungs, searing her breast; she felt her chest must explode, burst with the pressure building up inside it, a pressure that was killing her. The engulfing darkness was all around her. Then it turned red, blood-red, and she knew that it was too late.

The kitten died before Ginette; strangled by the terror in her fingers.

Cordelia lay helpless under Pierre's heavy body, knowing that this was the end for her. Knowing that this was what he had intended from the very beginning: her humiliation, in revenge for his father's. She stared up at him, hating the dark eyes that looked down so triumphantly into hers, and then turned her head aside, wanting only to have it over with, wanting only to blot the next few minutes from her consciousness.

But even as Pierre moved for his final assault, she heard the roar of water and the crash of splintering wood as the flood broke into the rooms below.

Pierre stopped. 'What in the name of God was that?'

'I told you,' Cordelia said in a flat, exhausted voice. 'The dikes have broken. The town is flooding.'

He tore himself away from her. '*Mon Dieu!* Ginette – my Ginette –' He was searching blindly for his clothes, dragging on trousers and shirt, pulling a belt round his waist. 'Don't just lie there, you little slut! She could be drowning –'

'I told you that, too.' She turned her face aside and weak tears slipped from her eyes.

'*Get some clothes on, or I'll kill you!*' he snarled, and Cordelia, seeing the look in his eyes, scrambled from the bed. Shaking, she found a skirt and jacket, and dragged them around her. By the time she had thrust her feet into a pair of boots, Pierre was at the door, the lamp in his hand. Down below, they could hear the slurp of water, the sound of furniture as it crashed and floated against the walls. From Ginette there was no sound, and Cordelia felt a sudden stab of fear. Her own ordeal already thrust to the back of her mind, she followed Pierre down the stairs, and stopped in dismay.

The flood must have come down the street in one great wave. It had burst open the front door and surged into all the rooms. It reached half way up the stairs, a swirling black sink on which floated chairs, stools, ornaments. A photograph of her mother swept by, face up, and was carried into the kitchen where she could hear the stove hissing and the back door groaning under the pressure. A cushion – surely one of Ginette's, frilled with lace that splayed around it on the surface of the water – bobbed past, and a newspaper, grey and sodden, wrapped itself around the banister.

Pierre thrust the lamp into her hand and flung himself down through the eddying water. It was shoulder-deep as he plunged towards the parlour. He disappeared through the door and Cordelia heard him, splashing amongst the furniture, smashing at the water with furious hands, desperately calling his sister's name. There was a note in his voice Cordelia had never heard before, an agony that tore at her heart. And when he came slowly back through the door, she saw that his face was contorted with anguish, and she felt her heart contract.

He carried Ginette in his arms, bearing her slight body as tenderly as if she were a baby. She hung there, legs and head dangling, hair drifting on the currents that surged around them, and Cordelia knew that it was too late.

He bent his head over his sister's body and Cordelia, watching in silent horror, saw the tears drop to Ginette's wet, white face. She shook her head in pity, and lifted a hand towards him.

Pierre's lips lifted in a snarl. His face twisted. He turned away from Cordelia, towards the door, and she cried out in consternation.

'No! Pierre, you can't go out there. You'll never survive – the water's getting deeper. Pierre, please –'

He turned once more and she felt the hatred scathe her mind, an almost physical assault more searing, more violent than the one he had committed on her body. She looked into his eyes, saw the passion in his face, the tenderness in his hands as he held his sister close against his heart, and knew the truth at last.

'Do you think I *want* to survive without her?' he demanded harshly. He stood for a moment on the threshold, looking out into the street that had become a raging torrent. And then he was gone, and Cordelia stood on the stairs in darkness, with nothing but the boiling surge of the water to accompany her dread.

Shuddering, she felt her way up the stairs and back into her bedroom. The water was rising steadily and had almost reached the landing. She could feel the house rock on its foundations, moving sickeningly from side to side, tilting like a ship about to capsize. The water poured across the room. By the light of her lamp, Cordelia could see that it was almost two feet deep under the window, while by the door it was no more than a few inches. She scrambled up on to the bed and stared at it. There was a heavy thump against the side of the house as if something large had collided with it, and she wrapped her arms around her body and bent her head, wondering what was happening outside.

Where was Timothy now, and Jensen? The glasshouse was even lower, closer to the river – were they still there, trapped or perhaps, like Ginette, drowned? And the Robinsons and the children, had they reached the high ground in safety? And Grainne – where was she? Would any of them come through this nightmare alive?

Oh, where are you all? she asked silently. And knew that she might, indeed, never see any of them again.

Timothy had been right. There was no way out of the glasshouse now, at least until daylight. Jensen raged around the office like a caged lion, thumping his fist against the wall, stopping to stare out of the window into the impenetrable darkness, listening in despair to the wind and the rain, to the surge of water below, to the shattering sound of millions of fragments of glass being washed against the walls.

The three men had only just escaped the wall of water that had thundered through the narrow corridor towards them. At the first sight, Jensen had grabbed Harris and Timothy and jerked them bodily towards the stairs that led up to the next floor. He thrust the little janitor ahead and almost kicked Timothy up after him, feeling the water catch at his ankles as he leapt in their wake. By the time he had scrambled up four or five steps, the water was around his waist, tugging at him with a strength that almost dragged him under again. It swept him off his feet, lifted him high and he felt a body fall past him. He plunged beneath the surface, groping frantically, and came up at last with his hands around Harris's neck. The water lifted them again and he scrabbled at the walls, then found a step under his feet once more. Tim's hand was on his collar, hauling him higher; together, they dragged Harris up with them and fell in a heap on the landing. The lantern had disappeared, torn from Jensen's hand by the rushing water, and they clutched at each other in the darkness to keep contact.

'It doesn't seem to be getting this far,' Timothy said cautiously. 'But I can't see anything now. Are you all right, Jensen?'

'Let's get out of this before we start wondering if we're still alive,' Jensen growled. 'That flood's only just broken through – there's a hell of a lot more to come. We must get to the top floor – give me a hand with this man, he's a damned sight heavier than he looks, and he seems to be unconscious.'

They reached the top floor breathless, still uncertain as to just how high the flood had risen. Surely it wouldn't completely engulf the glasshouse? But neither of them could suppress a fear that it might. The new dikes and the bridges, with their dam of debris, had brought the swelling river to a greater height than had ever been known before.

'Well, this is as far as we can go,' Jensen said at last as they pushed open the door of the office where they had first found Harris. 'Lay him down here. There should be a lamp somewhere . . .' He groped on the shelves around the walls for the lamp that each office possessed in case of a power failure; the lighting plant which the glassworks, like most of Corning's industries, had run for several years now, was still liable to occasional failure and the old lamps had been kept for emergency use. 'Here it is. And some matches, thank God. At least we'll be able to see what's happening in here. But first we'd better do what we can for this poor fellow.'

They both knelt over the slumped figure of Harris and Jensen laid his hand on the man's shoulder and turned him over. His face was pale in the guttering light, but he was breathing with quick, irregular gasps as if half choking, and Jensen quickly rolled him on to his stomach and began to press with both hands between his shoulder-blades. After a few minutes, Harris choked and gasped; water ran out of his mouth and nose, and Jensen pressed again, rhythmically squeezing the man's body so that his lungs were forced into action. Harris groaned and vomited. Jensen lifted him away and looked intently into his face. The eyelids fluttered and the janitor looked up at him, dazed and bewildered.

'Say, what's goin' on? I feel like I've been run over by a wagon. Where am I?' He frowned. 'Mr Novak? What . . .?'

'It's all right, Harris. We're in the glasshouse. There's been a flood, remember? You slipped in the water.'

Harris stared at him and Jensen saw the memory stir in his eyes. 'Gee, that's right. We were down on the first floor and all this water –' He glanced around wildly. 'Look, is it going to get in here? Because if it is, I don't want to be around –'

'None of us does,' Jensen said grimly. 'But it's all right, Harris, I think we're safe here. We're back up on the top floor. Now look, Mr Henzel and I want to go out on the roof and have a look, see if we can tell what's going on. You stay here, right? Don't try to move yet, just get used to breathing again. We'll have to take the lamp with us, but we'll get another one from somewhere.'

He straightened up and glanced at Timothy, who took the lamp from the table. Together they went out of the door, leaving the office in darkness. They made their way along the corridor to the door which led out on to the roof, and pulled it open.

The wind seemed to have died down, but the rain was still falling steadily. They looked around them and could see nothing. Corning was in darkness. And all that could be heard was the rushing of water, as the Chemung, now a mighty torrent, surged through the streets, taking with it anything that stood in its way: carts left standing outside shops and houses were swept away, trees and lampposts were wrenched from the ground, stables shattered and their terrified occupants drowned, houses torn from their foundations. And Tim and Jensen stood on the roof of the glasshouse and knew themselves to be impotent. Like the rest of the inhabitants of Corning, trapped and helpless inside their houses, they could do nothing. Until morning came, they could not even see the extent of the damage.

They knew only that dawn must bring a sight that would ravage their hearts. And they could only wait.

Morning came at last, creeping with dull grey shame across the drowned city of Corning. From the roof of the glasshouse, Jensen, Tim and Harris watched in stricken silence.

The water was brown and thick, a liquid mud that still roared through the town like a hundred rivers, swirling along the streets, meeting at intersections, thundering through the stores and houses. The current was at its strongest where the original river-bed lay deep beneath the torrent but even in the centre of the town, a quarter of a mile away, it could be seen flowing swiftly, bringing with it an ever-increasing cargo of flotsam – trees, the wreckage of smashed wooden buildings, dead horses and cattle, fences, carts and a mass of other debris too badly damaged even to be identified.

'My God,' Jensen said quietly, staring out across the surging waters, 'it's covered just about everything.'

'How far up the town d'you think it's reached?' Tim

472

asked, and they strained their eyes through the dim light, both thinking of the house on the corner of Pine and Second Streets, Cordelia in both their minds.

'I can't tell yet,' Jensen said at last. 'We may be able to see when it gets a bit lighter. Tim, if anything's happened to Cordelia . . .'

Tim nodded and turned away, his eyes searching now the low-lying streets of Knoxville. Had Grainne and the rest of the O'Donnells survived the terrible night?

As the light grew stronger, they could see that many houses had been ripped away from their foundations and were lying overturned against each other, those that might have withstood the waters smashed to a tangle of splinters by the force of their neighbours' falling.

'Look,' Jensen said suddenly. 'There are people up there – above the floodline. You can see them standing there.'

Tim followed his pointing finger and saw the knots of people on the slopes above the water. Some were standing still, staring, others were moving about, probably organising help. 'They'll need boats to get people out,' he said. 'How many boats d'you reckon there are in Corning?'

Jensen shrugged. 'Who knows? I guess there are some moored down by the river, but they could be all under water themselves now, or swept away. A few people up on the hill have got boats to use in the summer on Keuka Lake, but I don't know if they'll have brought them back to Corning for the winter.' He paused, then added quietly, 'The water's up above Second, Tim.'

'I know.' Timothy stared at the scene which was becoming clearer and more horrifying every minute. 'But they'll be all right, Jensen. It's not above the first floor. Cordelia will be all right – and she'll have got Ginette upstairs somehow.'

'I hope you're right,' Jensen said soberly, and stared

across at the tumbled buildings, the weltering debris, the devastation that one night had brought to the city he had begun to call home. Where was Cordelia now? And his daughter, little Karin? 'I hope to God you're right.'

As dawn sidled into the house on Second Street, Cordelia straightened her stiff limbs and climbed down from her bed to splash through the thick, muddy water to the tilted window.

Outside, she could see the dark water still sweeping through the street, carrying with it the mass of rubbish that it had gathered on its way. In the next house, her neighbours were also at their window, staring out at the chaos, and she could see other people at windows up and down the street, all white with shock as they gazed in numbed silence at the ruin of their town. Several houses had been overturned and the occupants of three of them had managed to climb out on to the roofs or walls that still showed above the water. The other two were deserted.

Nobody said much at first. They just looked at the devastation and then at each other. Then they began to call in hoarse, shaken voices – how are you over there? How about your grandma, is she all right? What about the little 'uns? Of the homes nearest to Cordelia, everyone was accounted for except for a brother, never returned from work, and an old man who had been out at one of the saloons when the disaster struck. Maybe they were safe somewhere else in the town . . . Cordelia told of Ginette's drowning and how Pierre had rushed out into the storm, crazy with grief, and disappeared. She didn't mention what had happened between herself and Pierre – indeed, she discovered that until that moment she had almost forgotten it. And her account was received in sombre silence.

'Well,' the man leaning out of the nearest window said at

last, 'I guess there ain't nothin' we can do just now. Jest have to wait, I reckon, till the water starts to go down or someone comes by with an ark. Hope it ain't too long, that's all – missed my supper last night, with all the to-do, and I'm gettin' mighty hungry now.'

They stayed at their windows, talking and staring. Nobody wanted to go inside; the feeling of companionship, even with a person who was unreachable across a chasm filled with streaming water, was a comfort nobody wanted to give up. Cordelia, almost knee-deep in water, dragged a chair across to the window and squatted in it. She had found some dry clothes in her cupboard and put them on. It was bone-chillingly cold and she realised that it was the first of November. Winter was beginning and for the citizens of Corning it must prove to be a winter of misery and discomfort as their lives returned slowly to normal.

But could any town survive such a catastrophe as this? she wondered, staring out at the flooded street. Would it ever recover from the ravages of this night?

The boats began to come soon after nine that morning. But rescue was slow; as long as the current flowed so strongly, many of the lower streets were unnavigable, and when the waters started to recede soon after ten, a new hazard appeared as the suction tore at trees, fences and even houses that had already been weakened by the force of the flood. The boats proceeded cautiously; already one had been swept away and flung against the side of a porch and its owner badly hurt. Nobody could be helped if the boats themselves ran into danger.

But at last Cordelia was lifted from her window and taken shivering with cold and reaction to the refugee centre which had been set up in the Free Academy, up on the hill. Here, above the water-line, people had been coming since early morning with blankets, dry clothes and food. The kitchens were filled with cheerful women making soup and brewing coffee, and the classrooms were strewn with families, some of them only just reunited, already reliving their experiences of the night and wondering what would happen next.

Cordelia accepted a mug of coffee and a dry, warm blanket. She clutched it around herself and wandered about. Was Jensen here, or Tim? Had the Robinsons managed to get up to Hill House? When she had left them, she had thought them safe; now she wasn't so sure.

'The Monkey Run backed up and flooded down the hill,' a man told her as she drank the scalding coffee and felt warmth return at last to her shivering limbs. 'Came down like Niagara. And when it met the river, coming up from the town, well, they say it was like the sea off Cape Horn. Never been nothing like it before in Corning, I know that. Been better if they hadn't ever built those new dikes. At least we had floods we could handle before – but this shambles . . .' He shook his head and moved on, leaving Cordelia feeling sick and dazed. The Monkey Run – she had forgotten the dangers presented by that usually innocuously trickling stream. She thought of Bob, leading the pony up Chestnut Street, so close to the Run. Had he managed to get up before it broke its banks?

But there was no time to think. With new arrivals being brought in at every minute, nobody could sit around and brood. All those who were able to help were needed, and Cordelia soon found herself working with the rest – handing coffee and soup to those who were hungry, wrapping blankets from the apparently endless supply around those who were cold and wet. There were a good many children, distressed and sobbing, separated from their families. Remembering the night of the railroad disaster, she gathered them together and kept them amused with stories and songs. They stared at her, wide-eyed and blank-faced at first, then slowly began to respond. She saw the life return to their white faces, thanked God that they had been saved and at the same moment prayed that their families were safe also.

She had no conception of how the hours were going by. And she was astonished when she glanced from a window to see that it was already growing dark again.

She stood quite still. Was the day really almost over? If Jensen and Timothy were alive, they would have been here by now, she thought with painful recognition. They would have searched each rescue centre until they found her. It would surely not have taken them as long as this to come to the Free Academy.

She turned away from the faces of the children and looked again out of the window. And there she saw a figure coming slowly across the big playground. The figure of a woman, bent and sorrowful; a woman she knew.

Martha Robinson came into the big hall where Cordelia was waiting, and walked straight into her arms. She was weeping uncontrollably, but whether from relief or distress it was impossible to tell. Cordelia held her in her arms and waited, knowing in her heart what Martha had come to say.

'They said I might find you here,' she gulped at last. 'Cordelia, I've been jest about everywhere, lookin', searchin' – but it ain't no good. They're gone, all of them – drowned. We ain't never goin' to see their little faces again.'

'All of them?' Cordelia said, and felt the ice grip her heart. 'Bob and the children – Danny and Bridget and Karin? Is that what you're trying to tell me, Martha?'

The American woman lifted her face. It was sodden with tears, distorted and ugly with grief. Cordelia felt the tears hot in her own eyes. Those poor, poor children, torn away in the darkness, dying in a maelstrom of whirling water, choking away the lives they had barely begun to live . . . 'Tell me what happened,' she said urgently. 'Tell me, Martha, please.'

Martha sniffed. She wiped her face with a scrap of rag that was already filthy with mud and tears, and said through her sobs, 'We was gettin' along nicely – I thought we were all safe, though the pony was jes' startin' to struggle and Bob said we ought to get out and walk, otherwise he'd never make it. I got down and I was jes' gettin' the little ones down when the water hit us. It was the Monkey Run. It was like an avalanche, Cordelia, all rocks and bits of tree and bushes and wood and stuff, all mixed up with the water. I never even heard 'em cry out. The pony went too . . . I hung on to somethin', a bit of wood or such, I don't know, and then I was washed up against a house and someone was leanin' down out of an upstairs window and haulin' me inside. I been there ever since, till a boat come along 'bout an hour ago and took us all out. We went to a rescue place and I had a cup of coffee, but I couldn't stop there. I had to come and look for the rest of you.' She buried her head against Cordelia's shoulder and broke into fresh tears. 'Those poor, poor little children,' she sobbed. 'And Bob, my Bob – how'm I ever goin' to manage without him?'

Cordelia held her close. She could not speak. The vision of the three children was vivid in her mind. It would stay with her, she knew, for the rest of her life.

Chapter Twenty-Two

With more and more people arriving at the school every minute, there was no time for grief.

Cordelia and Martha, after those first heartbroken moments, turned back to their work. They took in toddlers who were pale and trembling, crying for their mothers, older children who tried hard to put a brave face on their fear, young women distraught as they sought their babies, and old people who were shaking and bewildered. People were coming in from all over Corning; families split up because they hadn't seen or heard the warning signs, because men were at work, children at school, mothers out shopping, visiting or in their own jobs in factories and stores. Rescuers, some of them from miles away who had come as word spread of the disaster, had been busy all day in the few boats they could find, rowing back and forth, searching for those still trapped in their houses, bringing them to the rescue centres set up all over the still-dry parts of the city. And, occasionally, bringing back the bodies of those who had not survived, and laying them on the floor of one of the churches where a priest kept watch and prayed for them and their families.

'We shall have to go,' Cordelia said to Martha when they heard of this. 'We shall have to go and see . . .' She could not finish, did not need to. Martha's reddened eyes filled with the tears that had barely ceased to flow all evening. She looked exhausted, almost at the end of her endurance, and Cordelia knew that she could not take much more.

'It's time you rested,' she said gently. 'Take a blanket

and go and lie down for a while. I'll go to the church. There's no need for us both . . . not yet.' She swallowed the pain, knowing that to go alone to the church where the dead were being laid out in a tragic row would be almost more than she could bear. But she had to bear it, just as so many people had been compelled to bear the pain of seeing their loved ones die. And she had to bear it for Martha too, for one night at least.

The older woman looked as if she might protest, but her weariness was too great. She bowed her head and Cordelia touched her gently on the shoulder.

'I'll come back as soon as I can,' she promised huskily, and turned away.

It was dark when she left the Academy, but the rain had stopped at last and a few stars spangled the apologetic sky. The road here was already beginning to dry; the floods had receded down the hill, though Cordelia could still see the glimmer of water down in the centre of the town. The aftermath could already be seen in a dereliction of fallen trees, torn-up hedges and fences, smashed carts and wagons, and roofless sheds that filled some of the streets below the highest water line. Cordelia looked down through the growing darkness at the tumbled mess, and shivered. The smell of mud, sewage and decay wafted up the hill; already there was a threat of disease and she wondered how many more would die before Corning was a smiling, prosperous town again.

The church was about three streets away. She came to the door and hesitated.

There were people inside, people going in and coming out. Lamps shone at the door; there was the soft, solemn sound of an organ playing. It could have been any Sunday evening, with worshippers arriving for the last service of the day. But those who were going in had dread in their faces, and those that emerged had features distorted with grief or furrowed with a strange mixture of hope and despair. They passed Cordelia without seeing her, entirely absorbed in their own pain, and she shrank at the thought of adding such anguish to that already in her heart.

A tall young priest came down the steps. He paused beside her and looked down into her face.

'Are you looking for someone?'

She nodded. 'My brother. My – his employer. And a friend and three children. Do you know –'

He sighed and shrugged. 'We have a number of bodies of people who haven't yet been identified. There are men, women and children amongst them. Are you alone? Would you like me to come with you?'

Cordelia looked at him. His face was pale and tired, grave with the horrors he had seen, but there was a strength and calmness that reached out to her. He touched her arm with his hand, and she closed her eyes and swayed a little.

'Please,' she whispered, and he turned to lead her into the church.

Inside, it was cold and dim, lit by only a few lamps which were set around the space at the back of the pews. The bodies lay in a row, as she had pictured them, each one covered by a blanket. The young priest looked at her.

'Are you ready?'

Cordelia nodded. He went slowly along the row, lifting the blanket from each still face, and she followed slowly, her eyes wet with pity as she looked down at them, her heart aching. But she saw no one she recognised, and when there were only two left she raised her eyes and looked at him, mutely pleading with him not to lift the last blankets, for she was tasting now the hope and the despair that had been in the faces of those who had come out of the church, and she did not think she could bear it.

'You have to see,' he said, and Cordelia knew that he understood. 'I'm afraid you must look.'

'I know,' she said quietly, and clasped her hands tightly in front of her. Would it be Jensen? Timothy? Or Bob? In that moment, she hardly knew which she dreaded most. Could some horrific coincidence have brought two of them to lie beside each other in death? Who had survived that terrible night – was she to go through this ordeal again and again until all were accounted for?

There was a sound behind her as someone else came into the church, but Cordelia did not turn. Lift it, she begged the priest silently, lift the blanket and let us know the worst. She heard a low exclamation, saw him hesitate and look past her; unable to tolerate any more suspense, she stepped forward as if to lift the covering herself and expose the dead face that lay beneath it.

But before she could do so, a pair of strong hands gripped her from behind. She gasped and cried out as she was turned around and found herself staring up into a lean face, haggard as an old man's, etched with lines that only despair could have drawn there; into a pair of eyes that burned like hollows of dark blue fire and gazed down with a devouring hunger, searching her face as if they could never have enough; into a mouth that moved silently, shaping her name with incredulous disbelief.

'*Jensen*,' she whispered, and felt her legs give way beneath her.

He caught her against him, holding her close against the mud that was drying on his torn jacket, and Cordelia let go all the tears that had been growing all day in her breast. Her mind was whirling, but there were no coherent thoughts, no questions, nothing but a giddy vortex of emotion – the pain of the last day and night, the fear, the dread, the certainty of her loss. All had to be wept out before she could begin to

482

grasp the new situation – that he was alive and here, close in her arms, that for them at least there was still hope, still a life to be lived.

She looked up at him at last, meeting the sober joy of his gaze, and knew that even if he could never be hers, she could be content knowing that he was at least still alive. And that she would never again turn to another man as she had so nearly, so disastrously, turned to Pierre.

'Thank God you're safe,' she whispered. 'I came to look for you, and Tim . . .' She thought of Bob and the children, of what she must tell him, and her voice failed.

Jensen held her closer. 'Tim's all right, Cordelia. We escaped from the glasshouse together. We were trapped there all night –'

'Tim? Tim's here too? Oh –' as he moved forward from the shadows and elbowed Jensen aside to wrap his own arms about her – 'oh, thank God, thank God! I thought I was never going to see you again. Oh, *Tim* . . .' Her tears began to flow again and she wiped them away with her sleeve. 'I'm sorry, I don't seem to be able to stop.'

They held her between them, the two men she loved best in the world, and for a few moments she knew a contentment so deep that it seemed nothing could mar it. And then the young priest, who had retreated to the shadows when Jensen had appeared, stepped forward again and coughed.

'I'm sorry to intrude, folks, but are you looking for anyone else?' He looked apologetically at Cordelia. 'You said you were looking for three men, I believe. Do you still want to see . . .?'

'Oh.' Cordelia stared at him and felt shame wash over her. How could she have forgotten the others – Bob and the three children? She turned slowly to Jensen, wondering how she could break the news of his daughter's disappearance. He had already been through all this once, on the night of the rail crash. How could he endure such pain again?

'Bob Robinson and the children are missing,' she said quietly. 'They were going up to your house when the Monkey Run broke its banks. Martha was just handing them out of the trap – the pony couldn't pull it any more – and they were all washed away. Martha was saved, but the others –' Her voice broke and she turned away, shaking her head.

Jensen stared at her. He looked at the row of covered bodies on the floor.

'And these –'

'None of them, so far,' she said in a low voice. 'There were just two left when you came in.' She turned back to the priest. 'Let us see, please,' she said in a small, clear voice, and the young man slowly pulled back the first blanket.

Cordelia drew close to Jensen and raised her hand to her mouth. She stared down and felt a fresh stab of pain. She thought of Martha, cheerfully ordering her mild and amiable husband about, treating him like one of her children and depending on him so much more than she knew.

Bob Robinson lay on the floor of the church. His face was almost unmarked. He looked as if he had just fallen quietly asleep.

Beside him lay Amelia Novak.

The children were found, miraculously safe and well, in a house on Cedar Street. The first wave of water, which had carried Bob away with it and swept him into a pile of debris where he had been discovered next morning, had been gentler with Danny and the two girls. It had carried them, still in the trap and clinging to each other with desperation, to the porch of a house where an elderly woman had been crouching at her window. The rising water brought them within reach; she reached out and dragged them in, and there they had stayed, huddled close on her bed. By morning they were all exhausted and had fallen asleep like puppies, hearing nothing of the rescuers who rowed and paddled by outside, and when they woke it was dark again and nobody was near.

'Danny looked after us,' Karin said when she was at last safe in her father's arms once more. 'I would have floated away in the water if he hadn't kept hold of me. And while we were waiting for the boat, he told us stories and poems, the ones we learnt at school. And he found dry blankets and clothes for us to put on. Bridget was scared, but I wasn't because Danny was there and I knew it would be all right.'

Jensen looked at the boy, now devouring a large bowl of stew, and reached out a hand to squeeze his shoulder. Cordelia said softly, 'He's always looked after Karin. He thinks the world of her.' And they both smiled as a dark blush coloured Danny's face and he pulled himself away from Jensen's hand.

As the floods slowly receded, families were being reunited all over the city. Stories were being told everywhere of heroism and courage, of lives saved and others tragically lost. In the end it was found that thirty people had died and for the first week or two there was a constant sad procession of funeral cortèges through the mud-slicked streets.

Amelia Novak's story was pieced together, partly from what little her nurse and Mrs Sankey knew, partly from guesswork. For some weeks now, she had been prone to wandering, slipping out of her room and even away from the house on several occasions. Twice she had been found as far into the city as Second Street, and once had managed to reach the river where she had been found on the bridge, staring fascinated into the swiftly running water. When discovered, she had returned meekly, as gentle as a bewildered child; but it had been necessary to keep the doors locked all the time and her nurse kept a careful watch on her at night, when she was most liable to try to slip out.

'She seemed to want to get to the glasshouse,' Jensen said soberly. 'Perhaps some buried memory trying to stir . . . who knows? Yet when I saw her, she seemed to have forgotten who I was or that we ever had a life together. And we dared not let her wander, she has – had – no idea of danger. That day we found her on the bridge, I thought she was going to drown herself.'

And now she had indeed drowned, swept away by the flood on her last bewildered bid to escape. Cordelia saw the thought mirrored in his face. She touched his cheek with tentative fingers, and he looked at her, bringing his gaze back from some unseen landscape, and smiled sadly.

'It's over now for Amelia,' he said quietly. 'And the future . . . it can be ours now, if you want it to be.'

His eyes were questioning, as if he were in doubt. And Cordelia gave a little sigh and let her heart show in her eyes. She drew his head down to hers and laid her cheek against his.

Grainne, who had been in Corning with her aunt when the water roared through the streets, was found on the roof of the house with her relative, the two of them clinging to the chimney. Timothy, searching frantically, was in the boat which found her and as he brought her down he held her close, feeling her soft, dark hair against his face. 'Don't ever frighten me like that again,' he said as if the flood were all her fault. 'I couldn't bear it.'

Grainne laughed a little, sounding nearer to tears than to mirth. 'And d'ye think I enjoyed it? We weren't having a picnic up there, ye know.'

'Nobody's been having a picnic,' he said soberly. 'Oh, Grainne, I've been such a fool . . . Doing such stupid things. Cockfights – dogs – and all because I was afraid to admit I really hated it all. Because I thought the other fellows would think me less of a man – as if it mattered what they thought!'

'You're man enough, Tim,' she said softly. ' And anyone who can do what ye can do – bring beauty into the world the way ye can – doesn't have to prove anything, anything at all.'

'I don't know what got into me,' he said honestly. 'And – about Ginette –'

'It doesn't matter, Tim,' she said, and laid her fingers on his lips.

'I love you, Grainne. And you will marry me, won't you?'

'If we ever get away from this house that's about to tip into the water, yes! Tim, can we not talk about this later –' She laughed into his eyes, but he saw she was shivering and exhausted and drew her down on to the seat, cursing himself again for a selfish, inconsiderate fool. Her aunt was already there, upright on the thwart, glaring at the murky floodwaters as if daring them to rise again. Tim gave Grainne another glance. His face was sober.

'Ginette's dead now, Grainne. She was drowned when the water came into the house. Cordelia and Pierre were there . . . they couldn't reach her in time.'

'And Pierre?' She already knew that Cordelia and the children were safe.

'He disappeared. Cordelia said he just ran out, holding Ginette's body in his arms. Nobody's seen either of them since.'

They were found a week later, washed up amongst a tangle of trees three miles down the valley. Ginette was still held fast in Pierre's arms, and his face was twisted with the despairing agony of a man who had witnessed the death of the one person who mattered to him in the entire world. They were buried together, the last of a long succession of sad funerals which took place in Corning then. And as Cordelia and Timothy turned away from the churchyard, they felt that they had seen the end of an era.

'There are no Thietrys left now,' Cordelia said later, to Jensen. 'Pierre and Ginette were the last. And all so quickly – in only thirty years.' She looked up at him. 'Was it really our fault? Was Pierre right – that the Henzels always bring tragedy? Our grandfather, killed – the things that happened in France when Father was there – and now Pierre and Ginette. Do you believe that, Jensen?'

Jensen held her in his arms and touched her cheek with one tender fingertip. His voice was serious as he answered her. 'No, I don't believe that. I believe people bring their own luck, good or bad. We're what we make of ourselves, Cordelia, and we can blame nobody but ourselves if things turn out badly. We all have our chances.' He got up and went to the window, staring down over the wrecked city, the streets still thick with stinking mud, the battered houses with soaked furniture left outside to dry while the floors and walls were scrubbed clean of clinging filth. 'I had the best chance I've ever had when I came back here,' he said. 'And it's my place now. I shan't leave it, Cordelia. This is where I shall stay.' He came back to her and sat down again, his eyes dark and serious as he searched her face. 'You do know that, don't you?'

'I know. It's my place, too – even though I've thought at times that I would never learn to love it.' She smiled. 'Somehow, it's wound itself round my heart without my even noticing! But when I saw it that first morning after the flood – oh, Jensen, everything looked so *sad* – like a mother who's lost all her children. I couldn't bear it. I just wanted to help put everything right again. We will do it, won't we? Corning will live again?'

'It will.' He bent his head and covered her lips with his. 'And we shall live with it. You and I – and Karin.' His lips moved over hers and she lifted her face gladly, discarding for ever that dark side of her that had responded for a while to Pierre's satanic passion.

Once again, she remembered the night of the flood and Pierre's attack on her. He had planned that all along, she realised; every move, every tiny step in his courtship had been designed to bring about her eventual humiliation, all the more shocking because he had set out to win her trust. And afterwards, bruised, aching, sickened by his assault, she had believed that she would never again want any man to touch her. She had feared that Pierre's brutality had destroyed both her feeling for Jensen and her response to him.

But the events which had so quickly followed had driven it from her mind. And when she thought of it again, it seemed to be no more than a nightmare, just one more part of that terrifying night, and she knew that like the rest it could be put behind her.

She thought of Stourbridge, of her ambitions, of the grand college for girls that she had hoped to run one day. She thought of Corning and her little school, the barefoot children who came to learn from her. And she knew that her life here, bringing learning and beauty and appreciation into these children's minds, was just as worthwhile as the one she had planned back in England, teaching the daughters of prosperous businessmen. A child was a child wherever you were. And, as she had told Jensen a few moments ago, Corning was her place, too. She would never leave it now.

Chapter Twenty-Three

News of the disaster in Corning reached Stourbridge to find Christina sitting beside the great bed she had shared with Joe for over fifty years, waiting for him to die.

He had not been granted his wish to die in the glasshouse with a blowing iron in his hand. But he had come near to it, for he had collapsed there while instructing one of the youngest gaffers in the cone and had been only semiconscious ever since. Now, two days later, he was sinking fast and the family, gathered round in the room that looked out over Wordsley, knew that he could not live for many more hours.

Christina sat close beside him, his big, still powerful hand clasped in both her own. As she gazed down at his face, her eyes tracing the lines she had come to know and love so well, she remembered another grey November day, back in her girlhood, when she had sat here in just the same way; holding the hand of a man who was all her world, watching as he, too, slipped away into the darkness of eternal night. She had cried out in denial then, angry and afraid, refusing to let her father go; now, although pain filled her heart and brought tears crowding to her throat, she would not defy the forces of nature. She had seen too much death, known too much suffering, to try so futile a task.

On the other side of the bed, keeping watch with her, sat Ruth and Harry. Occasionally, they would glance up towards her and their eyes meet across the bed, Ruth's as softly brown as a deer's, Harry's still as bright a blue as when they had all been young. Christina saw her own sadness reflected there, and felt thankful that Ruth had at least had these last few months with her brother. After a lifetime spent largely apart, they had needed to learn each other's ways again, and their shared memories of a childhood spent in one of the backstreets of Wordsley, in a glassmaker's terraced house with only two rooms upstairs and two down, had brought them close and given Joe a good deal of pleasure as he became less able to go to the cones.

The bedroom door opened and Emily came in, carrying a newspaper. Christina looked at her with trepidation, seeing a fear in her eyes that had not been there earlier, a new pallor to her skin. She had regained her health completely now, but would her grief over her father's death disturb her balance again? Christina removed one of her hands from Joe's and lifted it towards her stepdaughter.

'Come and sit by me for a while, Emily. He's sleeping just now.' As Emily came closer, her anxiety increased. Christina took her hand and held it tightly. 'Emily, what is it? My dear, you mustn't grieve too much. I don't think he is suffering at all – just slipping away from us . . . And he's over eighty. We wouldn't wish any better for him than that.'

'No.' Emily's eyes filled with tears but the fear did not leave them. As if with an effort, she said, 'Do you think he'll wake again? I – I just wish I could tell him all the things I should have said. I wish I could tell him how I love him – how I've always loved him. I never did. I never thought he'd care.'

'Never thought he'd care!' Christina looked at her in amazement. 'But, Emily, he thought the world of you.'

'Did he?' The question was wistful. 'I was never really sure. When I was a child – I always felt there was something not quite right between us. I always knew he preferred Sarah. And when Paul and I found out the truth about ourselves – I used to wonder if he blamed me. If he hated me because of it.'

Christina shook her head. 'It wasn't like that.' She looked at Emily and knew that in this moment only truth would suffice. 'Your father did have difficulties, it's true. It took him a long time to be able to – to accept you, I suppose. But it wasn't you who were the problem. It was his own feelings about you – about the way you were born.' She took a breath. Such things were not openly spoken of, but Christina had never been afraid of the truth, even though its effects were sometimes unexpected. 'You see, your mother wanted very badly to marry him, and she took steps to become pregnant deliberately. But before she could tell him her condition, he had ended their relationship. And afterwards it became impossible. He knew nothing of it until just before you were born, when it was too late for either of them, and then Maggie simply disappeared. It wasn't until much later that she came to ask for help, and by then your father and I were married.'

'And you took me in,' Emily said.

'Not at once. Not until she had died. And then you were two years old. It wasn't easy for your father,' Christina said, gripping Emily's hand with one of her own while she still held Joe's with the other. 'Every time he looked at you, he was reminded of her. He felt guilty and ashamed. It was that feeling that came between you and him. But he never blamed or hated you. And he always cared.'

'Yes,' Emily said. 'Thank you.' But her voice was abstracted as if she had barely heard what Christina had been saying. She sat for a while without speaking, and Christina watched her, wondering what was in her mind. And then she turned her dark eyes on her stepmother and the terror was there again, naked and shocking, and Christina knew suddenly that it was not for Joe at all; there was something else. Gripped herself now by apprehension, she opened her mouth, but before she could speak, Emily said in a trembling voice, 'I have some news. From Corning.' She glanced across at Ruth and Harry. 'It's in today's newspaper. There's been a flood.'

'A flood!' Harry exclaimed. 'But they built new dikes!'

'It mentions them here.' Her hand shaking, she passed the newspaper across to him and Harry fumbled for his spectacles and began to read the tiny print. Ruth, leaning over his shoulder, drew in her breath.

'What is it?' Christina asked urgently. 'What's happened?'

Harry read on to the end of the column. Then he laid the paper on his knee and looked across the bed, his face grave.

'Apparently, the new dikes gave way after a heavy storm, and the water rushed through the town. More than twenty people were killed and some are still missing. No names are given.'

Christina was half on her feet. 'The twins –'

'We'll have to wait,' Harry said. 'According to this report, there's very little communication between Corning and the outside world. The city is still cut off. Help is pouring in from other districts, but no more will be known until they can begin to return to normal.'

'And when will that be?'

He shrugged. 'Who can say? I've seen floods in Corning – there's been hardly a year without one – but I've never known anything like this one appears to be. God knows when they'll get everything straight again . . . if ever they do.' He looked again at the newspaper. 'It talks here of widespread devastation. Ruth, I guess we ought to go back. They need help out there.'

Christina stared at him. He was a Stourbridge man, born and bred; yet in this extremity, it was in Corning that his

494

allegiance lay, in a small American town that she had never seen, lying now under a sea of mud, destroyed perhaps for ever. Corning was where he belonged.

And Timothy? Cordelia? Did they too feel this same allegiance? Had the Crystal City twined itself around their hearts, so that they, too, would want to stay and help rebuild it – presuming they were still alive?

She looked down at her husband's face and in that moment detected a tiny change. In the fingers still clasped in hers, there was a minute cooling. And even as she caught the hand against her breast and bent to lay her cheek against his, Joe opened his dark eyes and looked straight at her.

'Petticoat government,' he said clearly, and smiled. 'It's been a good life, my love.'

He closed his eyes again and his breath cooled on her cheek. And Christina, letting her tears flow on to his face for the last time, echoed his words in her heart.

The news that Timothy and Cordelia were safe reached Stourbridge on the day that Joe Compson took his final journey to the churchyard. And there, on the hill where she had stood on the day of her father's funeral and sworn never to be defeated, Christina stood outside the yellow-brick church and looked down over the streets of Wordsley.

There had been many changes since that day. Over half a century had passed by; there had been other occasions to come to this church. Other funerals. Jean-Paul's, on an afternoon that was offensively warm and sunny, when she had followed his coffin to the grave and stayed there afterwards, alone, and Joe Compson had come to her and been sent cruelly away. Paul's, when Emily's stony silence had ended and she had displayed the first of the heart-wrenching attacks of grief that had threatened to destroy her mind. Jeremy's and Stephen's, held on the same day while Roger hovered between life and death. All those lay here, together with her Aunt Susan and the uncles who had tried so hard to overcome her determination to keep her glasshouse – Harold, Samuel, Reuben. And, not far away, the glassmakers whose lives had been so tightly bound up with theirs – Joe's parents, old Will Compson and his wife Sal. And other Henzel glassmakers – Jem Husselbee, George Scrivens and many, many more.

There had been happy occasions here too – the christenings of her own children and and grandchildren, the marriages of Harry and Ruth, Emily and Paul. But how many more would there be, for Henzels? America had claimed her brother and his wife, and now it seemed that Cordelia and Timothy would never come home. Since the day of Joe's death, there had been no further news from Corning and all attempts to discover what had happened had failed. Telegrams went unanswered, letters took too painfully long. There was no communication yet with the drowned city, and English newspapers had moved on to other excitements. The Boer War, only a month old, was of more vital interest than a flood in some small American town that most people had never heard of.

Christina stared down at the streets, almost obscured now by the thick pall of smoke that mingled with the winter twilight. Was this to be the end of the Henzel saga? Would the cones continue to flourish under some other hand? Her son Mark stood at her side, tall as Joe had once been, promising to fill out soon into a replica of his grandfather. Would he be the man to take Henzel Crystal into the twentieth century?

I'm tired, she thought as the family mourners went back to Henzel Court for the meal that had been prepared for them. I'm tired of it all – Stourbridge, the cones, glass itself. I've done enough. I've given enough.

She left the gathering and went into the library where the Compson Chalice stood gleaming on the mantelpiece. She lifted it down and gazed at it again, as she had gazed at it so many times over the years. The shape that Joe had designed and blown for her; the engraving that Jean-Paul had made. The picture, still sharp and delicate as if it had come fresh from his long, sensitive fingers, of Wordsley as it had been then, the Henzel cones with their plumes of smoke towering over the crowded streets. The entwined initials C and J which he had intended as Christina and Jean-Paul, but which had come later to mean Christina and Joe.

She was holding it still when the door opened and Mark came in with the telegram, Emily close behind him, and Harry and Ruth smiling at the door. She was holding it when she knew that Cordelia and Timothy were alive after all, and that Cordelia was going to be married.

She was holding it when she looked up, her eyes once more alive, ablaze with the tiger's shine that Joe had loved to see.

'We shall go to America,' she said, and sounded once more like the young Christina, refusing to admit defeat. 'We shall go to the wedding. Wire back to them, Mark, and tell them. They're not to get married without us!'

Christmas came bright and cold, with a fall of snow that smoothed a clean white coverlet over those parts of Corning which still bore witness to the ravages of the flood. And with it came the family from Stourbridge. They found a town that was, as Jensen declared, pulling itself up by its own bootstraps.

Since the beginning of November, when the waters had finally returned to their rightful place, the whole town had concentrated on clearing up the chaos that had been left. It had been a long, difficult and laborious task.

The sun, as if ashamed of its long absence, had shone throughout the first few weeks. There was little heat in it now, but it helped to dry out the furniture, the carpets and curtains which were strewn outside the houses while cleaning went on inside – cleaning that involved pumping out basements still filled with thick brown water, carrying out bucket after bucket of evil-smelling mud which dried to a thick, fine dust that blew into everything; even stripping homes of ruined floorboards and rotting wallpaper. Gradually, large, pathetic heaps of possessions appeared at the roadsides, many of them destroyed beyond recovery. Large carts came round the streets to carry them away and people stood with tears in their eyes, watching as the accumulation of memories was borne away for ever.

'We've got to get as much done before the winter sets in as we possibly can,' Jensen said. 'And that means the glass-house as much as people's homes – they're going to need work as well as places to live. Thank God for all the folk who've come in from other places to help – without them, I don't think we'd get through the winter at all.'

They all knew that this was true. People had come from as far afield as Rochester, a hundred miles away, to help Corning and the rest of the valley to get back on its feet. They brought tents, set up makeshift huts or lodged in the schools and churches as they worked, and they went round the streets, helping wherever they saw the need, bringing hope and cheer to hearts that had been broken by the storm. If asked who they were, they simply gave their first names, too busy for real introductions, and when the work was done they moved on, to the next house, the next street.

There was, as Jensen had said, as much to do in the factories as in the homes and the stores. Nevertheless, it was with real reluctance that he and Timothy went back to the glasshouse for the first time and surveyed the destruction

498

there. And as they moved slowly through the corridors, carpeted with the same reeking mud that had been left like a calling-card over the whole city, they wondered bleakly if anything could ever be salvaged from so complete an inundation.

'Every piece of glass must be smashed to smithereens,' Tim said, and thought sadly of the Chalice, so carefully placed in its cupboard in his workroom only moments before the danger had been recognised. 'We'll have to start all over again.' He stared across the blowing room, chaotic under a tumble of chairs and benches, tools and irons thrusting from the mire like accusing fingers, the furnace cold and silent with pots that oozed slime from mouths that should have been red and blazing. 'At least it didn't explode, as we were afraid it would. But the whole place will have to be stripped out and rebuilt, Jensen. It's going to take months.'

'So the sooner we start, the sooner we'll have work to offer again.' Jensen's voice was grim. 'Everyone else is in the same position, Tim. We've all got to turn to and work together.' He thought for a moment. 'The best thing to do is work shifts, just as if it were normal. Get some notices done, asking the men to come back as and when they can, and work regular hours helping to clear up. We'll pay them the same rates as they normally earn. They'll come – they're going to need that money. And if there are any cases of real hardship – more than the rest are suffering, I mean – we'll make extra payments.' He looked at Tim. 'Glassmakers have always stood together,' he said quietly. 'We stand together now.'

And as she stood at Jensen's side on that Christmas morning, radiant in her white wedding-dress, Cordelia looked out from the church door and smiled at the crowd who had collected to wish them well. Martha, still grieving for Bob but giving all her time and energy to help those who had lost their own homes and families; Grainne, soon to marry Timothy; the glassmakers who had worked so hard, were working still, to bring Novak Crystal back into full production.

The children of her school were there too, waving and laughing, and around her skirts were the three who meant most to her, Danny, Bridget and Karin. On her other side stood Tim, her twin, the reason she had come to Corning in the first place, the reason – at first – that she had stayed here.

Her eyes moved on to the rest of her family – her uncle and aunt, back at last, her mother, as straight and commanding as ever she had been, and her grandmother, tiny and indomitable, who had demanded to come to America to see Cordelia married and refused to take no for an answer.

'As soon as your cable came, telling us you were safe and that you were going to be married, she said she was coming to the wedding,' Ruth had told Cordelia on the day they had arrived. 'The doctor didn't want to allow it – he said that after the shock of Joe's death, she should just stay quietly at home. He told her she was too old to travel so far – but you know your grandmother. She has never taken any notice of advice if it doesn't happen to suit her.' Ruth smiled. 'And I believe she was right – to have stayed in Stourbridge, without Joe, would have slowly killed her. There's nothing there for her now, with him gone. Nothing.'

'Not even the glasshouse?' Cordelia asked. 'She used to love it so much – she was always in and out of the cones. It was her life.'

'Joe was her life. The glass never took more than second place, though we never knew it.' Ruth looked sad for a moment, then added with a smile, 'But they knew it,

Cordelia. I believe they always knew it.'

The news of her grandfather's death, coming so soon after the great flood, had brought a fresh sadness into Cordelia's life. But there could be no lasting regrets on this day, so bright and full of new hope. And as the family returned to Hill House for the Christmas dinner which was also their wedding breakfast, she caught her grandmother's eye and smiled, feeling closer than ever before to the old lady who was so much like herself. And afterwards, when they gathered in the big parlour to exchange presents, she was not surprised when Christina rose and took her place by the leaping flames of the log fire, commanding attention as she had done all through her life.

'I won't talk for long,' she said, smiling round at the assembled group. 'I simply want to wish Cordelia and Jensen all the happiness we know they deserve. I'm glad we came to see them married, and I think he will make my granddaughter a fine husband.' She paused. 'There's been a great deal of trouble in Corning,' she went on quietly. 'The flood has brought destruction and sadness to so many. Lives and homes have been lost, businesses brought to ruin. Jensen's own glasshouse suffered more than most, yet he has kept on all his employees, paid them to bring the foundry back to a working condition – a task that's still going on – and kept his trust with the men who work with him. That is something I appreciate, something that's in the finest tradition of glassmaking. From the forest glassmakers of France, of whom poor Pierre Thietry was perhaps the last survivor, to the modern glasshouses of America, we have always kept that sense of family which is one of the most important aspects of our trade. I am very happy to think that Cordelia and Timothy are both to continue to be involved in such a fine business, in such a wonderful and lasting art.'

She paused for a moment, looking at the faces that watched her. The familiar ones of her own family; the strangers who were rapidly becoming friends. What she had to say next was a strange mixture of pain and comfort; a goodbye to an era that had just passed, a welcome to the new.

'I want to make an offer to you, Jensen,' she said, speaking directly to the man who had just taken her granddaughter as his wife. 'You have built up your own business, with glasshouses here and in other places. And you have taken my grandson Timothy as your partner, and my granddaughter Cordelia as your wife. Now I want you to take something more from the Henzels. I want you to take some of our money, too.' Her green eyes held all the old, sparkling enjoyment of her youth, when she had declared she would make Henzel Crystal the finest in the world. 'Let us become partners,' she said. 'Henzel and Novak. Let us go forward together into the new century and show *everyone* what can be done in the world of glass.'

She sat down, feeling suddenly exhausted, and looked around. Their faces were stunned, astonished; they looked at each other and then at Christina. Jensen opened his mouth to speak, but she waved her hand.

'Think about it. You don't have to answer now. And it's Christmas – we don't want to talk business any more.' She reached down beside her chair and brought out a box. 'Now – I have a present for you.'

'And I,' Timothy said, coming forward before she could hand it over, 'have a present for *you*. And I insist that you open it first.' He grinned, looking suddenly boyish. 'I've waited a long time for this moment, Grandmother – don't make me wait any longer!'

Christina took the box and unwrapped it. She lifted the lid and peeped inside and then, with an expression of wonder on her face, lifted out the glass that lay inside.

It was the Chalice. It gleamed, black and iridescent. Beneath its smooth, polished surface, there was a pattern in gold leaf, flecked with silver. In the dancing firelight, it glittered like a precious stone.

'It's beautiful,' Christina said, and her voice was awed.

'It's my Damascene,' Timothy said, and he couldn't quite keep the pride from his voice. 'We thought it must have been destroyed in the flood, but it was safe after all in its cupboard – under water, covered with slime and mud, but undamaged. I made it for you, Grandmother, to show what I can do.'

'And it proves everything I ever said about you,' Christina said quietly. 'You are the most gifted Henzel yet.' She kissed him and passed the Chalice to Emily. 'See what your son can do.'

The glass was passed from hand to hand, everyone exclaiming at its beauty, and Cordelia looked at her twin and felt her pride in him grow and swell. She knew that whatever glass he might make in the future, Damascene would always hold a special place in his heart, as it would in hers. It would always bring back this year to their memories – the year when so much had happened to them both, the year they had discovered themselves.

She felt a chill of sorrow then for Pierre, who had harboured his resentment for so long and failed at last to gain vengeance for the wrongs he believed had been done to his family. Pierre, who could himself have been a fine glassmaker, but had lost his way. Even the firm in Brooklyn had admitted that they had never made Damascene or anything like it. Jensen had been advised that he could have sued them, but he shrugged; let's forget it. There were more important things to concern themselves with and he wanted to forget Pierre.

'And now,' Christina said, the Damascene placed safely on a shelf, 'let me give you your gift.'

She handed the box to Cordelia, and Cordelia weighed it in her hands. Slowly, she unwrapped it. Like her grandmother, she lifted the lid; and gave a cry of unbelieving delight.

The glass that she lifted out was familiar to all those who had come from Stourbridge. It had stood for over fifty years on the mantelpiece at Henzel Court. It had been blown by Joe Compson and engraved by Jean-Paul Thietry.

'As soon as I knew you were marrying Jensen,' Christina said, 'I knew I must bring it to you. You see; your initials are already on it.'

Cordelia passed her fingertips slowly, tenderly, over the shining glass. Her heart was full of tears. She turned to her husband and held it out for him to see.

'The Compson Chalice,' she said softly. 'You see? C and J.'

Christina and Jean-Paul.

Christina and Joe.

Cordelia and Jensen.